WHAT LIES
BURIED

Margaret Kirk is a Highland Scot and a graduate of Glasgow University. She is the winner of the *Good Housekeeping* Novel Competition 2016, and *Shadow Man* was her debut novel.

To find out more, follow Margaret on Twitter
or visit her website.

🐦 @HighlandWriter
🌐 margaretmortonkirk.wordpress.com

Also by Margaret Kirk
Shadow Man

WHAT LIES BURIED

Margaret Kirk

ORION

First published in Great Britain in 2019 by Orion Fiction,
an imprint of The Orion Publishing Group Ltd
Carmelite House, 50 Victoria Embankment
London EC4Y 0DZ

An Hachette UK Company

1 3 5 7 9 10 8 6 4 2

A CIP catalogue record for this book is
available from the British Library.

ISBN (Trade Paperback) 9781409188650

Typeset by Input Data Services Ltd, Somerset

Printed and bound by Clays Ltd, Elcograf S.p.A

MIX
Paper from
responsible sources
FSC® C104740

www.orionbooks.co.uk

To Martin, Nicola and Roy
And to the wise women, witches and warriors. All of you.

I

Farr View Heights construction site, outside Inverness

Eight a.m. on a grey May Wednesday. The chill of last night's rain still hanging in the air above a city that's only half awake. Lorries whining their way up Slackbuie Hill, laden with aggregate and drainage pipes, towards the final phase of Farr View Heights: 'Thane Construction's exclusive new development of twenty-three executive homes', according to the brochure pinned to the noticeboard in Archie Paul's Portakabin office.

Archie shifts a little closer to the two-bar electric heater by his desk, wincing as the movement sets off the ache in his hip. Exclusive – aye, well, a price tag of half a million on the smallest plot is pretty much guaranteed to keep the riff-raff out, he supposes. Himself included. But price tags like that mean folk have expectations – private this, bespoke that. They sure as hell don't want to hear about delays or hold-ups with their posh new dream homes . . . but unless a miracle happens to get the groundworks back on schedule, that's exactly what's going to happen.

He looks at his watch, pushes back his chair and crosses to the door. Time to get down to the site and do the morning headcount – midweek, with their weekend partying out of their system, most of them will have turned up ready for a hard day's graft. At least, he bloody well hopes so. Gordon Tait, the development manager, is coming over for another site visit this morning. And 'a few words' with the squad, apparently. Archie's only glanced at the email Tait sent him last night, but he's guessing 'well done' or 'keep up the good work' aren't the words Tait has in mind.

He opens the door and sees Jason McIntyre belting up the track towards him, hi-vis jacket billowing out behind him like a bairn playing at superheroes. *Jason bloody McIntyre.* Archie's acid indigestion pushes a twist of bile up into his throat. Jason is six skinny feet of acned attitude, with the get-up-and-go of a doorknob. Whatever's got him moving this fast, Archie's damn sure it's nothing—

'Boss!' Jason skids to a gangly, wheezing halt in front of the Portakabin. 'We found . . . We were setting up the next line for the JCB, and Callum says what's that, and I looked over, and it was just lying there! Swear to God. And Ed says to come and get you, so—'

'Christ, Jason, calm down, will you?' Archie holds up his hand to stem the flow of words. 'It can't be that bloody bad.'

Only Archie's not too sure about that, not really. Jason's an eejit, and a lazy one at that. The only thing he's any good at is messing about, and if he wasn't the boss's nephew, he'd have been on his way long ago, with a boot up his arse. But one look at the boy's face is enough to tell Archie he's not messing about, not this time. Whatever Jason's turned up, it's stripped all the colour from his cheeks, his freckles standing out like a join-the-dots page from a kid's puzzle book. What could the boy have seen to make him look like that?

Images of rusting wartime munitions and unexploded bombs roll into Archie's head. Hadn't there been a farmer out at Rose-isle not that long ago who'd turned up a bit more than he was expecting when laying out a new boundary to one of his fields?

But there's no point spooking the lad any worse than he is already. 'Show me what you've found.'

Before Archie's finished speaking, Jason's off again, haring down the dirt track like a collie after a sheep.

It's not far, but by the time Archie's reached the men grouped round the silent JCB, the arthritis in his hip is singing and he's badly out of breath.

'Right then.' He walks up the ramp, squints down at the gleaming white objects the JCB has uncovered.

'They're bones, aren't they?' Jason's perched on the edge of the trench, fidgeting like a toddler with a wet nappy. 'I said they were bones!'

'Aye, they're bones all right,' Archie tells him. 'But don't go calling CSI just yet, eh? All this was farmland for years – and see that line of stone over there? I'll bet that was a byre. This'll be the remains of a beast, that's all. Nothing to get excited about.'

At least, he hopes not. But Archie's a bit of a history nerd, on the quiet. He catches up with *Timewatch* whenever he gets the chance, keeps his Historic Scotland membership up to date. And the more he looks at those bones, the more they seem . . . well, *placed*.

He stares down at the shallow, indented mound below him and wonders if it might have been better if they'd found an unexploded bomb after all.

'What if it's not, though?' An edge of excitement creeping into the boy's voice as he moves closer to the excavation. 'What if it's, like, an old . . . *tomb*, or something? With a body?'

Archie shakes his head. 'Up here? Been watching too many horror films, son. Now, come on—'

'Show me.' Edin, the new guy from the Forres site, walks over and peers into the trench. Archie rolls his eyes. Christ, is everyone up for a skive today? Edin's one of the new Scots Nicola Sturgeon's always on about, Forres by way of Albania

3

or something, and Archie doesn't know much about him. But he's got a good head on his shoulders and he knows when to let something go. Usually.

Archie gives him a weary look. 'Away and don't be daft. There's nothing to see—'

'Is not animal.' Edin shakes his head and straightens up, frowning. 'Bone is maybe femur, I think. Too long for cow, and—'

Skittering sounds, over where Jason's standing, like the first patter of rain against glass. Archie knows what's coming, of course he does, he's been working on sites like this half his life. Only he knows it half a second too late to do anything about it. He turns on his dodgy hip to see the boy up on tiptoe, right on the edge of the trench. For a moment, Jason looks like he's going to be okay. Then the skittering intensifies. Jason's feet slide forward, his arms pinwheel and he's gone, disappeared from sight. There's a high-pitched yell, and a thump. Then nothing.

'Jason!' Archie's stomach gives a quick, unhappy lurch. He takes a cautious step closer to the edge and peers down, but there's no sign of the boy. Jesus Christ, if he's hurt himself . . . 'Jason, are you all—'

'I go down.' Edin unzips his jacket. 'Boss, you can call doctor? We—'

Scrabbling sounds below them, then Jason reappears. Unharmed by the looks of it, and covered in mud from head to foot, like a swamp creature from a bad *Doctor Who* episode. Two watery blue eyes blinking out of a face caked in . . . aye, well, normally they'd all be killing themselves laughing at the sight of Jason looking as though he's taken a bath in the brown stuff. But no one's laughing now. The laughter's dead in their throats, the silence eerie, as though the whole world has stopped to look at what's sitting on a shelf of mud and stone, exposed by

4

the fault line in the trench Jason's fall has uncovered.

'Is not animal.'

Fuck's sake. Archie's never claimed to be a genius, but you don't need to have a brain the size of the big specky guy on *Pointless* to work that one out. 'I can see—'

'What's going on here?'

Footsteps behind them on the ramp. Archie turns to see Tait picking his way up the slope towards them, his wee pinched face pulled in on itself as though he's tasted something bitter. The kind of face his mother would have called 'sleekit', Archie always thinks. With his fussy little hands held out in front of him for balance and his nose pinky-red from the cold, Tait looks like a rat in a suit. And a bad-tempered rat, at that.

And coming up behind Tait . . . Ah, Christ. Since when does the CEO of Thane Construction drop in for unannounced site visits, for God's sake? And Archie had thought the day couldn't get any worse. He licks his dry lips, starts to say something, but Jason gets there before him.

'It's a skull.'

Tait takes a step backwards, glances at Thane. Who ignores him and addresses Jason.

'Where did it come from?'

Jason grabs the hand Edin offers him, heaves himself out of the trench. He gives a half-hearted wave behind him. 'Down there. But . . . but maybe it's not real. Maybe it's like a toy or something.'

Tait gives a nervous nod. 'More than likely, aye. Some joker got it off eBay, stuck it down there to give the boy a wee turn.' He glances at Archie. 'No need to be bothering our pals down at the Council about this, eh? Just some eejit having a laugh.'

Tait's words fall into the silence and crawl off to die. And, in spite of himself, Archie almost feels sorry for the man. Hadn't he been thinking pretty much the same thing himself? Yes, of course you're meant to report finding something like this. But the Highlands are full of old bones – the whole country's built on the graves of Picts and Celts and Vikings, generation upon generation of them. If every project stopped to call in the Council's history boys when they turned up a couple of old bones, the whole building industry would grind to a halt and they'd be knee-deep in archaeologists. And no one knows about this except the four of them, standing by the trench. A couple of passes with the JCB, a tiny deviation from the original line planned for the drainage pipes and the thing's covered over again, no one any the wiser. Only this . . .

Archie stares down at the skull. Tries one final time to tell himself he's wrong, there's no way he can be seeing what he thinks he's seeing. And shakes his head. 'Not the Council, no. We need to call the cops.'

'Why?'

Archie opens his mouth to say something, but Ed from Forres by way of Albania gets there first. He walks over to the edge of the trench. Squats down and points at the neat, semi-circular hole above one empty eye socket.

'Because of that.'

2

'It's definitely a bullet hole?' DS Iain 'Fergie' Ferguson squints down at the skull, now safely behind the ring of incident tape cordoning off the trench. 'I mean, it couldn't be damage from an old plough or something?'

The lead CSI eases herself up the series of slatted approach path steps, her pregnancy bump straining against the white Teletubby suit. She shakes her head. 'Classic circular entry point to the parietal, corresponding larger and more irregular exit through the occipital. I did two tours of Afghanistan, DS Ferguson, I know what gunshot trauma looks like. I just wasn't expecting to see it on a building site in Inverness.'

'You and me both.' Fergie takes another look at the skull. 'So, what can you tell me?'

'At this stage? Not that much. Almost certainly male, probably not recent – but the excavators have been all over this place for months, so whether we'll be able to properly isolate the soil layers . . .' She shrugs. 'The Fiscal's had a quick look, confirmed she's happy for us to call in CAHID.'

Fergie nods. The Centre for Anatomy & Human Identification at Dundee boasts a team of world-renowned forensic anthropologists – and if the occasional dog-walker phones

North Div's Control Room in a panic because wee Pepper's found a funny-looking bone, an emailed photo is usually enough for CAHID to confirm the mutt's found nothing more interesting than a dead sheep. Usually. But a skull with a bullet hole through its forehead—

'Mr Thane, you can't go in there! Stop!'

Footsteps behind him. Two sets, fast. Fergie turns to see a bulky man in a dark overcoat striding towards him, like a funeral director on steroids, followed by a young uniform PC.

'That's far enough.' Fergie reaches the foot of the slope before the man can get any closer and holds up his hand. 'This area's closed to the public right now, so I need you to—'

'I know the site's closed off – I put the call in to you myself, over three hours ago. And from what I can see, all you've done is put up a bit of tape and a bloody tent! You do know there's a hundred thousand pounds' worth of plant standing idle over there?'

An Inverness accent, buried under layers of acquired Edinburgh poshness. Fancy tailoring doing its best with a build like one of those American fridges Zofia's got her eye on. And the twitching, let-me-get-back-to-making-money attitude Fergie's seen a hundred times before. Mainly on guys like this with shedloads of the stuff.

Fergie flashes his ID, gives Fraser Thane his version of a sympathetic nod.

'Aye, it's a fair-size site, right enough. But as soon as the CSI team's finished—'

'How long's that going to take?'

'Oh, a wee while yet, I'm thinking. But any background you can give us on the location might speed things up a bit.' Fergie waves the uniform over. 'So we'll press on here while PC Duncan gets the details from you back at the site office.'

'Oh, for God's sake. Look, we found some bones.' Thane

moves closer, close enough for Fergie to smell the mint and alcohol mix of his breath. 'Mouldy old bones with a hole in them, that's all – but you lot are all over my site like flies on a midden. If I were you, I'd stop wasting my time here and get on with finding that wee girl that's gone missing. What is it now, a week? And you still haven't got a bloody scooby.'

'We've got teams working round the clock—'

'You haven't found her, have you? I'd tell them to get their finger out, if I were you. Before it's too late.'

Thane stamps off down the slope, and Fergie nods at the PC. 'Get after him – and make sure you take a full statement. Full as you can make it. And when you're finished, tell him to take a taxi to his next destination. From the state of his breath, Mr Thane's had a glass of wine or two with his lunch and I'll lay odds he's only borderline fit to drive.'

'Nice man.' The CSI pushes back her hood, glances at Fergie. 'So, *is* there any news? About Erin? I know, you can't say anything. I just . . . How many days is it now?'

'Five.'

Five days. Five days since ten-year-old Erin MacKenzie disappeared – vanished in the space of twenty minutes from a friend's birthday party in a quiet Inverness street. Fergie's walked that street half a dozen times since Erin was reported missing, along with half of Burnett Road's CID and most of the uniforms. And, knowing his boss, Fergie's betting Lukas Mahler will have done it as many times again, turning the thing over and over in his head. Trying to put the shape of it together. Trying, like the rest of them, to work out why they're still no further forward.

'Christ, those poor parents.' The CSI touches her bump, lightly, protectively. 'Do you think . . . after a week, surely—'

Fergie cuts her off before she can finish. 'It's not a week,' he tells her. 'Not yet.'

3

Day 7

Friday, 27 May 2016

Burnett Road Police Station, Inverness

Lukas Mahler knows it's going to be bad before he enters the room.

Forget the crush of journalists, shoehorned into the too-small space everyone's been moved to because of a last-minute cock-up with the conference room's electrics. Forget there's only one way in, so that Erin's parents, Krysia and Grant Mac-Kenzie, are forced to file past the sea of smartphones primed to catch each nuance of their misery. Forget even that DI Andy Black, who Mahler knows should be following up his side of their joint investigation, is lurking in the doorway like a surly, leather-jacketed bouncer.

What Mahler can't forget is the last time he was in this room, breaking the news to Kevin Ramsay's partner that the enquiry into his death was being wound down. Eighteen months after Ramsay's murder in a hit-and-run with all the hallmarks of a gangland killing, Gemma Fraser had looked Mahler in the eye, had listened to his assurances that the case would remain open, that he'd review it regularly. And she'd told him exactly what she thought those assurances were worth.

Now the MacKenzies are here, listening as Mahler reads out the opening statement. Grant MacKenzie's large, awkward hands are clutching a water glass, turning it this way and that, while his gaunt-faced wife sits statue-still. And the look in her eyes . . . Mahler's seen that look too many times, on too many faces. In too many rooms like this.

He glances round the room. Most of the journalists present have covered the story before, but he notices a couple of new faces listening intently as he gives a short recap of the day Erin disappeared.

'At 2.30 in the afternoon on Friday, the twentieth of May, Erin MacKenzie was dropped off by her mother at a friend's birthday party.'

He hits a key on his laptop, brings up Erin's school photo on the video screen.

'At 4.15 p.m., the girls settled down to watch a DVD. We've been told Erin went upstairs to the bathroom around 5.45, and this is the last reported sighting we have of her. At 6.05 p.m., pizzas were delivered to the house and Erin's absence was discovered. I'm now going to play a brief video reconstruction of Erin arriving at her friend's house in Columba Gardens.'

A collective hush in the room, the clicking smartphones briefly silenced as everyone absorbs the reality of why they're here; Erin MacKenzie, this solemn-faced child with pale butterscotch hair and wide brown eyes looking out from under a blunt fringe, hasn't been seen for seven days.

By the time the video ends, Krysia's hands are covering her face and Grant MacKenzie is shuddering by her side. Mahler catches the family liaison's eye, nods. Time to bring this to a close.

'Columba Gardens is close to the local primary school and a popular shortcut for dog-walkers. It's also only a ten-minute walk away from one of the main routes into the city. It's a busy road, particularly between five and six in the evening, and we're anxious to talk to anyone who might have seen or spoken to Erin around those times. If you think—'

'She needs to come home.' Grant MacKenzie lifts his head, looks round at the room. 'Whoever's got my wee girl, she needs to come home now. Please. We can't . . .'

Erin's school photo is the thing that breaks him, Mahler thinks afterwards. MacKenzie's eyes lock on the image on the screen and his voice gives way, crumbling into inarticulate sounds of grief as the cameras go to town.

And in the midst of everything, movement by the doorway. A uniform PC says something to Andy Black, passes him a note. As heads start to turn, meerkat-like, to see what's happening, Black looks up at Mahler, gives him a 'carry on' gesture. And disappears through the door with the young PC in tow.

As the heads turn back to him and a buzz of chatter rises, Mahler briefly considers letting the usual short Q&A go ahead. But the MacKenzies have nothing left to give today. Facing the cameras has drained them, plundered the last of their mental strength. And he suspects it would be pointless, anyway. With Andy Black's sudden exit, the journalists' focus has shifted from the parents; there's a bonfire of speculation blazing behind their eyes, and Mahler's got no intention of fuelling it further.

He nods at the press liaison officer to let her know he's winding up the session and closes his file.

'Erin MacKenzie has been away from her family and friends for seven days,' he finishes. 'It's our job to bring her back safe to those who love and miss her – and, with your help, we'll do everything we can to make that happen. Thank you.'

A moment's silence, then the expected volley of questions erupts. Mahler leaves the media team to fend them off while he and the FLO steer the parents back to the room they'd met in earlier.

Grant MacKenzie lets himself be led to a chair and sits down meekly, but they're barely in the door before his wife grabs Mahler's arm.

'There is news? The other detective – he left so quick, maybe he has found her?'

'I don't think so. I'm sorry.' Whatever update the PC had given Black, it was nothing good, he's sure of that. 'But today's appeal—'

'Is a waste of time!' Krysia MacKenzie looks at her husband, slumped across the row of institutional green seating, and shakes her head. 'I can go back to them, tell them more about Erin—'

'Not today.' Not until he's had a chance to talk to Andy Black, find out what's going on. 'I'm sorry, this can't have been easy for you. But appeals like these do bring results – and as soon as there are any developments, I'll come and let you know myself. I promise.'

'Developments?' She spits the word back at him like a curse. 'After one week, you think developments is enough? You bring my daughter home, Inspector – this is only promise we want from you!'

'I'll do everything I can.'

Not enough, he knows that, but it's the only promise he can give. He leaves Dawn, the FLO, to organise transport home for the MacKenzies and goes to find out what was important enough to make Andy Black walk out halfway through a press conference.

It doesn't take Mahler long to track him down. Black's voice reaches him before he's halfway up the stairs; the decibel level coming from the CCTV viewing room hasn't reached peak volume yet, but Black's definitely working up to it.

Mahler pushes open the door to see him chugging a can of Red Bull and jabbing at the monitor in front of 'Skivey' Pete Noble.

'Everything okay here?'

'Just great.' Black throws him a razor-blade smile. 'Made a real breakthrough, haven't we, Pete?'

A rising tide of pink creeps up Pete's neck. 'I said I didn't have the chance—'

'Come on now, don't be shy. Let's show DI Mahler what you pulled me out of a bloody media appeal to look at!'

'Sir.' Pete hits a key and the screen fills with a grid of black-and-white CCTV images. 'So, this is what I started with.'

Mahler takes a closer look at the central image. 'These aren't from the school?'

'No, the CCTV footage there didn't pick up anything,' Pete tells him. 'But you were right, the church did have a single fixed camera at the rear of the building. Ancient system, still using videotapes, if you can believe it, but I found something that looked interesting.'

'Go on.'

'At six-thirty, a van pulls up. The angle wouldn't let me see the reg, but the way it was parked . . .'

Pete enlarges a grainy shot of a light-coloured transit, parked by a group of scrubby bushes. The driver's door opens and a bulky, tracksuit-clad figure emerges. Male, Mahler thinks, judging by its approximate dimensions, and oddly furtive in its movements. Keeping his head down, tracksuit man looks round about him several times, as though making sure he's unobserved. After a moment or two, apparently satisfied, he goes to the rear of the van, opens the door and takes out a holdall . . . and the image dissolves into swirling electronic snow.

'I know it wasn't much to go on.' Pete looks up at Mahler. 'But I saw the holdall, and I thought—'

'Yes.' No need to put the thought into words, not here. On day seven of a missing child enquiry, there's not an officer in the station who wouldn't have seen that holdall, put it together with the man's furtive behaviour and jumped to the same chilling conclusion. 'Go on.'

'I didn't want to waste any time, so I called DI Black out to take a look. But then I realised the fault was only on that one section.' Pete hits another key and the next image appears.

'Ah.' Mahler winces as the man's tracksuit comes off to reveal a large, T-shirt-clad belly and a pair of running shorts. He stuffs the tracksuit into the holdall, puts it back in the boot and puffs his way through a series of stretching exercises before setting off down the path to the woods. At the far edge of the car park, he turns and glances behind him. And Mahler finally realises who the man reminds him of.

He takes a closer look. 'Hold on, isn't he—'

'That fat lad in Traffic who's doing the Loch Ness Marathon, aye.' Black leans forward, aims another finger-jab at the display. 'Going to stick my neck out and say he's maybe not our guy, eh? And our wee IT genius here dragged me out of a press appeal for that!'

A shamefaced nod from Pete. 'Got it wrong, boss,' he tells Mahler. 'Sorry. It's just . . . if it had been—'

'Understood.' Mahler inventories the litter of coffee cups and biscuit wrappers on the desk, surveys Pete's unshaven, fatigue-pouched face. 'We'll take a look at the site, check his movements against our timeline anyway, just to dot all the i's. Then we move on – once you've had a break, preferably. Go on, take ten minutes to get some fresh air.'

'Boss.' Pete snatches his jacket from the back of his chair and heads for the door.

Andy Black watches him leave and turns to glare at Mahler.

'Fuck's sake. Guy's a waste of desk space – sitting on his arse in here while the rest of us do the donkey work. How long are you going to let him get away with it?'

Pot, kettle. Though Mahler has to admit Black's been a lot more hands-on recently since losing the talented Karen Gilchrist to Police Scotland's shiny new Crime Campus at Gartcosh.

He's certainly been putting in the hours on this case, but so have they all. Including Pete.

'He made a mistake, Andy.' Out of tiredness. Out of frustration. Out of the need for some sort of breakthrough, even if it's the sort none of them want to think about. 'And after a chat with our marathon-running colleague, we can move on.'

Black gives him a disgusted look. 'That the best you can come up with? We've had uniforms crawling over all the back gardens in the road, volunteers tramping all over the woods, and we've got nothing. A big fat bloody zero.' He opens the file on Pete's desk, leafs through it. 'Jeez-oh. There's a sodding Facebook group now, "A Candle for Erin" or something. Bunch of tossers – if they want to do something, why not join a bloody search team?'

'They may have done that too. And sometimes these groups can throw up something we might otherwise miss.'

'Maybe.' Black scrubs at the stubble on his chin. 'But after a week . . . The DCI said you were on the Natalie Harper case when you were with the Met.'

'Only at a very junior level.' For which he remains cravenly, enduringly grateful. Ten years ago, the schoolgirl's abduction and brutal death had seared itself across the public consciousness . . . and faded slowly, year by year, as such things always do. But not for her family. Not for the detectives who'd sat for hours, listening to her killer's gleeful confession, detail by stomach-churning detail. 'That's not a name we want to call up, Andy. Trust me.'

'It's what our journo friends downstairs are doing, pal. In between calling us a bunch of eejits who can't do our fucking jobs. Natalie Harper was missing fifteen days, wasn't she? And we're already on day seven.'

Yes. Everyone knows how long eight-year-old Natalie was missing for, and where and how she was found. And that kind of thinking will break the team, shatter the tough, professional casing they're all clinging onto right now.

'Abductions don't happen in a vacuum, you know that – there's evidence out there somewhere. And we will find it. Find her.'

'Jesus Christ. Spare me the sodding pep talk, eh? You know as well as I do what we're looking for after a week.' Black crushes the empty drinks can he's holding, lobs it at the bin. 'Got some calls to make. I'll send Pete back up and tell him to get his skivey arse in gear.'

Mahler watches him go. And hopes Pete Noble has had the sense to get out of the building for his coffee instead of raiding the MIT room stash.

Mahler picks up his file, heads back downstairs to get an update from the MacKenzies' FLO. He's just reached the half-landing when a shout from above stops him in his tracks.

'Lukas, wait!'

He turns to see June Wallace coming down the stairs towards him. The DCI's been putting in the same hours as the MIT since Erin MacKenzie's disappearance, and Mahler suspects it's taking its toll; there's more grey showing in her blonde hair and her eyes are pouched with fatigue. 'Ma'am, if it's about the appeal—'

June shakes her head. 'Fill me in at the 4 p.m. debrief. There's something—' she breaks off as a door opens somewhere above them, followed by a tramping of booted feet towards the stair-well. 'Sod it. Fine, we'll go to your office.'

'Ma'am.' Mahler goes on ahead, starts shifting some of the box files lurking on the spare chair in the corner for her, but June holds up her hand.

'Never mind them, this won't take long. So, those remains found out at Slackbuie. Fergie still overseeing that?'

Whatever Mahler had been expecting, that wasn't it. 'He's

got it in hand, yes. The remains are unlikely to be recent, so—'

'It'll be a cold case. Yes, I know. Still, it's been a few days now, hasn't it?' An odd, uncomfortable expression on her face. 'So the Chief wants a senior officer to go over and take a look.'

'And do what, exactly? In case he hasn't noticed, we're a little busy right now—'

'You think I don't bloody know that? Christ!'

Mahler starts to say something, but June shakes her head.

'This isn't up for discussion. Look, it's Slackbuie, not the back of beyond – it'll take half an hour, tops. Make reassuring noises at Fraser Thane about getting his site back, tell Fergie to wrap things up over there and get his arse back to base smart-ish. Got it?'

'Ma'am.'

The words Mahler aims at his office door once June's left are not ones he uses often. Fraser Thane is one of the city's movers and shakers, a local boy who'd moved away and built a con-struction business in Scotland's central belt, before expanding his empire northwards. The sort of man who moves in similar circles to the Chief. Or at least, ones the Chief would *like* to move in. Someone worth chivvying along a probable cold case for? Mahler's pretty sure he knows the answer to that.

It *is* a cold case, though. And June's right, Fergie is needed back at Burnett Road. Mahler messages Fergie to let him know he's on his way and sets off for Thane's construction site.

4

By the time Mahler gets over to Slackbuie, the weather has turned. The morning brightness has gone, replaced by steel and graphite clouds, and the rain the forecasters promised wouldn't arrive until evening is already battering against the windscreen.

When he pulls in to the rough parking area at the base of the hill, Fergie's disreputable Audi is there, looking like a dustbin on wheels next to a sleek blue Mercedes. Further up, he spots the forensics van and taped-off approach path leading to the white CSI tent.

He takes a sealed pack of overshoes and suit from the bag in his boot, and sets off up the hill.

'Good timing, boss.' Fergie meets him by the tape, introduces the CAHID scientists, Drs Li and Falconer. 'Dr Li here's got a theory about who our mannie might turn out to be.'

'Already? I'm impressed.'

'Lauren, please.' A round-faced woman with scarlet hair and a Kiwi twang overlaying traces of a local accent, she gives Mahler a rueful smile. 'Slight exaggeration there, I'm afraid. But thanks to my history nerd friend and colleague here' – she grins up at the tall, broad-shouldered man by her side – 'we can make a reasonable guess at *what* he was. Craig?'

'Certainly can. Follow me?' Falconer leads Mahler and Fergie to what looks remarkably like a scene from an archaeological dig inside the tent. In the centre, surrounded by coloured marker flags, a near-complete set of skeletal remains are lying in a foetal position. The feet are still encased in the remnants of boots, and there's a dull metal band looped around one of the wrists.

'Wearing a watch but no wedding ring. Footwear old-fashioned in design but manufactured using at least some synthetic material. Any thoughts on how long he's been here?' Mahler moves to the edge of the trench to take a closer look, but Falconer holds up his hand in warning.

'Careful!' He points to a mound of tumbled earth and stones near where Fergie's standing. 'We were working there half an hour ago when it simply gave way. The guy who found our friend here . . . well, he's lucky the bones he broke weren't his own. If he'd landed a foot or so to the right, for example, things might have been different.'

'True.' At first, Mahler assumed the body had been buried in a hastily dug grave, but the size of the excavated area makes that unlikely. And the bones are surrounded by a bizarre collection of household objects – rusting springs, a broken mirror in a rotted wooden frame, even a trio of balding, splay-limbed dolls. 'I take it you've seen something like this before?'

'Not with a body in situ, no. But this didn't start out as a grave, you see. What we're looking at here—'

'Fuck.' Fergie's face is tight with anger. 'It's a midden pit, isn't it? They killed the guy and tossed him in a midden.'

Falconer gives a surprised nod. 'Spot on, Sergeant. You a bit of an armchair archaeologist on the quiet?'

'Just a country boy. My grandparents had a farm near Inver-urie – no bin lorries, no weekly collections, not then, so they just dug out a midden pit. Everything that wouldn't burn or couldn't be reused, they just tipped into it. Then, when it was full, they just took a tractor and filled it in.' Fergie glances at Mahler. 'Common practice in those days, boss.'

'I see.' Which could help to narrow down a time period for the disposal of the body. He turns to Falconer. 'You said you'd found something to help identify our victim?'

'If these are what I think they are, yes.' Falconer indicates two small, roughly circular objects joined by a length of cord, lying inside the ribcage. 'I'm pretty sure what we're looking at here is a set of British army identity discs from World War Two. They're not in the best condition, but if Lauren can work her magic on them back at the lab, we should be able to tell you a little more about our mystery man. Of course, that will leave you with another little puzzle to solve . . . well, two, actually.' He looks across at his colleague. 'Lauren?'

Dr Li nods. She touches the screen of her iPad and an image flashes up. 'The murder weapon. At least, we're going with that for now as the most likely scenario – obviously, you'll want to run specialised ballistic tests, but it was lying a few feet away from the body and it's consistent with the trauma to the skull.'

'I see. But if you have a likely murder weapon and a potential means of identification—'

'What's our problem?' Falconer's grin has a hint of the showman about it as Dr Li scrolls through to the next image. 'Those aren't the only dog tags we've found. And this second set? Pretty sure they're not British.'

'Then what—'

The Imperial March from Star Wars suddenly blares from the depths of Falconer's protective suit. He fishes out the mobile, mouths a name at Dr Li and ducks outside.

'Craig's partner,' she tells Mahler. 'She's near her due date and it's her first, so Craig's heading home to Dundee tonight.'

'I thought you'd be here for at least another twenty-four hours?'

She shakes her head. 'Now we've assessed what's here, it doesn't need both of us. Craig can start setting things up in the lab, and I'm happy to carry on alone – plus, it gives me a good excuse to have a catch-up with an old friend. She's been teaching at uni in San Diego for years, but her family's been through hell recently, so Anna's come home . . . sorry, are you all right?'

Anna. Anna Murray, back in Inverness.

Blood, thrumming in his ears. A tightness in his chest. Dr Li's smile fading as the sudden silence grows. 'Inspector?'

The tent flap opens. Falconer returns, waving his mobile at Dr Li, chattering about scans and follow-up appointments. And the pressure at the base of Mahler's skull, the migraine that's been stalking him for days, flares into a sudden pull of agony.

Not now. *Not now.*

He makes his way outside, dry-swallows a couple of pills and turns at the sound of the tent flap opening behind him.

'Going to be about two weeks for the full report, Dr Li reckons.' Fergie strips off his protective suit, runs a tissue over his sweating forehead. 'Our mannie there's not classed as urgent. We could push the identification faster, though. Dr Falconer says—'

'It's a cold case, Fergie.' Seventy years cold, if the CAHID team have called it right, and knowing their level of expertise, Mahler's got no reason to doubt them. 'We've got no distraught relatives demanding answers, no press pushing for updates and an irate businessman who wants his site back as of yesterday.'

'Thane can bloody well wait.' Fergie aims a glare at the Mercedes parked by the site entrance. 'That guy in the tent was probably listed missing, boss. That means there's a family somewhere he never came back to. You saying they don't matter, just because it happened a while ago? He was a soldier, that guy. Served in the war, and saw some things, I'll bet – awful things, probably. And he was tossed in a fucking *midden*. Like a pile of stinking rubbish.'

'I'm sorry.' Speaking slowly, carefully, because the migraine is biting hard now, fighting against the meds he's swallowed and doing its best to turn his brain to mush. 'But there's a child out there who might – note, *might* – still be alive. And that's where our resources need to go right now. All of them. Understood?'

'Boss.' Fergie glances at him, clears his throat. 'I've had a wee tidy-up in the Audi, if you're not up to driving back.'

'I'm fine.' Not true, not by a long way. But nor is he sufficiently tired of life to risk the passenger seat of Fergie's scrofulous plague pit. 'Thank you.'

'Uh-huh.' Another throat-clear. 'So, Anna Murray's home now. Bit of a surprise, eh? You went to her dad's funeral last year, didn't you?'

'I owed her that.'

An apology, Mahler had told himself. An act of contrition for the clues he'd missed two years ago when hunting her sister's killer. The mistakes he'd made that had allowed the man to kill again and put Anna in the kind of danger he still can't forgive himself for.

Watching her leave to return to San Diego was the price he'd paid for those mistakes. And if he'd still had hopes of something more between them, that possibility had ended when Anna had seen him standing at the graveside . . . and looked right through him, as though he wasn't there.

His mobile bleeps, reminding him he's only got an hour before the next briefing meeting with the DCI. Seconds later, a text from Andy Black arrives with a similar message – shorter, and composed almost entirely of four-letter words. 'I need to get back to Burnett Road. Get Dr Li to keep you—'

'Oh, Christ, that's all we need.' Fergie points at the posse of outside broadcast vans lumbering into the rough gravel car park at the foot of the hill. 'What's that lot doing back here? There's nothing for them to see.'

Mahler shakes his head. Day seven of a missing child enquiry, with no leads, no updates worth reporting and the press gets word of a detective inspector visiting the site of a CAHID investigation. Not hard to work out what they'd do next. Not hard to work out where the tip-off might have originated, either. If someone had a vested interest in hastening the scientists' departure, that is.

'Get Dr Li or Dr Falconer to throw our friends something, if they're willing,' he tells Fergie. 'Plenty of historical detail to occupy their minds, get their imaginations going. And be sure to let Mr Thane know they've had to take time away from their work to do it.'

Vigil for Erin – Facebook Public Group
Pinned Post

We've set up this group to show our support for the family of Erin MacKenzie. Erin went missing on her way home from a birthday party in Columba Gardens on Friday, 20 May 2016. We can't believe a wee girl could just disappear into thin air like that. Sadly, there are evil folk everywhere these days. Erin, you're in our prayers, sweetheart. We're lighting a candle for you on here and we'll never stop looking for you! Stay strong wee one.

Friday, 27 May, 10.35

Dylan Main posted a comment:
Kids don't just vanish, everyone knows that. What are the cops doing, for fuck's sake? They couldn't find there arses with a kennel full of guide dogs.

Janey Mack replied:
It's horrible to think of what might have happened to that wee girl. You only have to switch on your telly to see all the awful things going on in the world.

Tam Bell added a comment:
There's enough folk out there looking. How can they not have found anything? Something not right there.

Dylan Main replied to **Tam Bell's** comment:
Something on Moray Firth Radio just now about the searches being scaled down. What's that about, are the cops not getting enough tea breaks or something?

Tam Bell replied:
They know more than they're saying, stands to reason.

Janey Mack:
What are you saying?

Dylan Main:
It's obvious, isn't it? Come on, we've all seen stuff like this, like you said. And nine times out of ten, who's got something to do with it? Someone close to the family, that's who.

Janey Mack:
That's a horrible thing to say!

Tam Bell:
He's right though. Remember what happened to that lassie in London, Natalie something? And what about Shannon Matthews? The mother was in on that all along.

Admin:
Tam, Dylan, please read the pinned post. I know you're new to the group, but we're all here to support Erin's family and we don't allow comments like that. Put yourself in the parents' place and think how you'd feel if you saw that written about you! None of us know what's really going on, so please be more respectful in future.

Tam Bell:
'None of us know what's going on'. Maybe watch the TV appeal tonight and see what you think then, eh? #crocodiletears #dont-workonme #askthefamily

5

June Wallace has moved offices. *Been* moved, Mahler suspects, to be within instant summoning distance of the Chief Super, whose attitude to his DCI's independent tendencies has all the flexibility of a Stalinist-era Soviet bureaucrat. When Mahler goes upstairs with Andy Black to brief her with the latest on Erin MacKenzie, the fading ghost of an expensive cologne hangs in the air, hinting at a recent visit from Hunt. And from the drained look on June's face, he hadn't come to see how well she'd settled in.

'Andy, Lukas.' She closes the file on her desk, gives them a weary nod. 'Come in. And give me some good news, for God's sake.'

Which means she's got some of the other kind for them, Mahler suspects. He and Black bring her up to date on a list of negatives: no positive sightings from the hundreds of phone calls, no forensics from the scene or the army of volunteer searchers combing the surrounding woods. By the end of their reports, June's shaking her head.

'Not good enough. I've just had the Chief in here, and neither he nor the ACC are happy bunnies right now. What about the father – we still okay with him after today?'

Mahler glances at Black. In the video room, they'd gone through all the footage from the media appeal, focusing on the parents' reactions. Neither had shown any of the usual 'tells' a body language expert might seize on: no restless hands or feet, no crossed defensive arms to indicate deception. Which could mean everything or nothing, of course. Natalie Harper's killer had lounged in his chair throughout sixteen hours of police interviews, sipping tea and smiling like a game-show host.

'MacKenzie's breakdown seemed genuine,' he tells June. 'And both parents' statements are consistent. Their recorded movements on the day check out, and they've allowed us full access to the house from day one. Nothing to raise any red flags in the extended family either so far.'

'But?'

'Dawn phoned me thirty minutes ago with an update. The MacKenzies are making noises about needing their own space for a while – and she thinks they've been talking to one of the nationals on the quiet.'

Black makes a disgusted noise. 'For God's sake. Thought she was meant to be keeping an eye on them?'

'She's a family liaison officer, not a bloody jailer.' June scrubs a hand across her forehead. 'But we need to keep her in there. Lukas, we'll give them all the space they need tonight, but first thing tomorrow, go and talk to the MacKenzies, get them back on board. Andy, I need you out with the search teams. We've got another day or two at most before we'll have to stand them down, so—'

Black stares at her. 'We can't do that! If we widened the search area—'

'We've done that. Twice. And not found a damn thing.' Her mouth twists in a sour smile. 'Don't worry, I'll be the one taking the flak at the next press briefing – the Chief wants senior officers to be "highly visible" from now on, so I'll be breathing down your necks even more than usual until that wee lassie's found.' She pushes the file on her desk to one side. 'One way or another.'

And there it is. The one possibility no one's given voice to. At least, not in public.

Mahler turns to leave with Andy Black, but June waves at him to stay. 'Talk to me about Slackbuie. CAHID's winding things up there now, yes?'

'Very close to it, ma'am.' He updates her on the scientists' findings. 'The team will take the remains back to Dundee, so Mr Thane won't be inconvenienced any longer by our unfortunate murder victim.'

The look June gives him is distinctly Arctic in temperature. 'That's right, he won't – and we may not like it, but we will suck it up, Lukas. Because the Chief's getting it in the neck about Erin MacKenzie on a daily basis right now. He doesn't need any more from a jumped-up wee brickie with a bit of cash and plenty of pals in the media. Got it?'

'Perfectly.' And whatever grief Chae Hunt's been receiving, Mahler knows he won't have had any qualms about passing it on. 'I hadn't realised Thane was quite so well-connected.'

'This is Inverness, Lukas – scratch the surface and everyone's bloody connected. Something to bear in mind, maybe, for the future.'

'Ma'am?'

'Never mind.' An odd, sideways glance at him. 'You and Andy are handling things well, by the way. Joint lead cases are always tricky, but with something this big—'

'It makes operational sense, ma'am. Utilises our resources more efficiently.'

'Maybe tell that to your face, son. Because it's not looking very convinced right now.'

He starts to say something, but June shakes her head.

'I'd quit while you're ahead, if I were you. Go on, go and talk to the MacKenzies. And take Fergie with you – let them see we're throwing every ounce of manpower we can at this. And Lukas?'

'Ma'am?'

'Tell Pete not to take his eye off the ball again, or he'll find himself chapping on doors and taking witness statements, instead of sitting in a cosy wee viewing room watching the world go by.'

6

Day 8

Saturday, 28 May

Summer, of a kind, has arrived – by stealth, as it so often does in the Highlands. A pale uncertain sun is breaking through the early cloud, bringing a promise of warmth to the unfolding day. By the time Mahler's finishing his morning run through the Ness Islands, there are wader-clad fishermen dotted along the river, casting in graceful arcs into the silver-painted water.

Working through his cool-down routine, he takes a moment to watch them. Even now, three years after his return to the Highlands, his birthplace can still surprise him with images like these. Since the millennium, Inverness has technically been a city, but even with the advent of the new university, he suspects its small-town feel will linger for a good few years yet.

Mahler had planned to take Fergie with him to visit the Mac-Kenzies, but there's no sign of his DS's dustbin-on-wheels Audi in the car park at Burnett Road. When he gets to his office, there's a grubby Post-it on the door in Fergie's unmistakeable handwriting.

'Called out to a suspected arson incident down the Longman,' Donna Henderson calls out from behind a stack of files. 'Think that's what it says, anyway.'

Mahler picks up the scrawled note. Experiments with turning

it this way and that before nodding. 'Either that, or he's incinerating a lawnmower. But let's go with your reading of it for now. Why did it need a DS to attend, though? Surely someone else . . .' He looks round at the near-deserted MIT room and answers his own question.

Andy Black will have taken June Wallace's comments about visibility to heart and scooped up as many warm bodies as possible for the last two days of the search. But more than a week after Erin went missing, the chances of finding anything have to be vanishingly small. Anything good, that is.

'Never mind.' He glances at the tower of report files, shakes his head. 'Leave those for Big Gary when he gets in and come over to the MacKenzies' with me. I need to have a word before our journalist friends talk them into something they'll regret.'

The MacKenzies live on one of Inverness's newer housing developments on the western edges of the city – 'a unique design for contemporary living', according to the hoardings flanking the approach road. Mahler's undecided about the contemporary living part, but after DC Henderson's manoeuvred the pool car out of yet another dead end, he's ready to concede the site's bizarre layout gives it a certain uniqueness. Like a previously unknown circle of hell, perhaps.

'Ach, bugger it.' Donna reverses out and pulls up short of the junction to consult the Satnav again. 'Sorry, boss. But this thing's pretty useless, with all these new roads here. Affric Crescent, Affric Drive . . . they only allowed to use one bloody street name or something?'

By the time they pull up outside the MacKenzies', Mahler's running fifteen minutes late. For once, the usual posse of journalists camped outside the house is nowhere in sight. Moved on, he suspects, at least some of them; after a week with no developments, there are newer stories to be chased now. Other families' misery to be fed on.

'Thought Dawn's supposed to be here?' Donna rings the bell, steps back as it sets off a frenzied barking somewhere nearby. 'Can't see her car—'

The door opens a couple of inches and a gaunt face peers through the gap before it's closed again.

Donna bends to call through the letter box. 'Krysia—'

'Wait.' Rattling sounds as the security chain's undone and Krysia MacKenzie reappears. She's barefoot, a fluffy dressing gown hanging off her thin frame, and her face is set in tight, exhausted lines.

She glances at them – past them, Mahler amends – as though she's expecting someone else, and ushers them inside.

She leads them through to an open-plan living area. It's larger than he'd expected, show-home immaculate, but the air has a stale feel to it and the curtains are drawn against the light.

'The press?'

Krysia gives him a weary nod. 'All the time, at first. Now maybe not so many, but . . .' she gestures at the twin couches flanking a low pale oak table. 'Please. I have coffee, if you want. Or—'

'Why don't I do that?' Donna goes over to the kitchen area, starts filling the kettle at the sink. 'Should I make one for Dawn and Mr MacKenzie?'

'Grant's just gone out with the dog. And Dawn isn't coming today. Maybe not for a while.'

Mahler glances at Donna as she returns with a tray of mugs. The MacKenzies aren't suspected of any involvement in their daughter's disappearance, and they're free to choose whether to engage with Family Liaison or not . . . at least, that's the theory. But with no leads to speak of, Mahler's team can't afford to lose the sort of input Dawn can provide.

33

He leans over to pass Krysia a mug. 'That's one of the things we wanted to talk to you about. Dawn's here to help you—'

Her mouth twists in a bitter half-smile. 'Sure. This is why she watches us, like we are the criminals here. She says it's a bad idea to speak to journalists. Why? If they say they will pay some money, maybe someone will tell them what they know. And you have nothing, do you? After one week, still nothing. So what would you do, Inspector? If your child had been taken?'

'If I were in your position? Yes, I might be tempted to do what you're considering,' Mahler admits. 'But I'd talk it through with someone like Dawn first . . . and I'd never choose to cut myself off from her support. Because when the journalists are demanding 24-hour access and a piece of your soul, Dawn will have your back. Always.'

Silence, then a nod. 'Okay, we talk to her. For now.' Krysia pulls a tissue from her pocket, scrubs it over her eyes. 'But you don't know how it is for us, Inspector. How we try to live every day without going mad.'

'You're right, I don't. I'm sorry.' He glances at Donna, who picks up her cue.

'Krysia, I know we've talked about this before. But we need to be absolutely certain about this – are you sure Erin didn't seem upset or worried about anything in the days before she went missing? Nothing that might have made her, well—'

'You ask me this again?' Krysia glares at Donna. 'Why? I told you, Erin is . . . is always happy. Always.'

Donna nods. 'The thing is, Krysia, we've been talking to Erin's teacher. And Miss Benjamin said Erin had become a little . . . quiet in class recently. A bit withdrawn – in fact, she was going to mention it at the next parent-teacher meeting. You're quite sure there wasn't anything bothering her? Her school-work, maybe, or something else?'

'Bothering?' Krysia shakes her head. 'No, nothing. Oh, some

of the girls in her class, they weren't always so nice to her, you know? Because she always tries so hard. But this was a small thing only.'

Donna glances at Mahler, leans forward. 'Which girls, Krysia? Did Erin mention any names?'

A shrug. 'Jasmine, I think. Morgan, maybe. But this is how girls are these days, isn't it? Friends, then falling out, then friends again. When Erin got that invitation from Livvy, she was so excited. Smiling all day long.' She swallows, looks down at her hands. 'She was happy. I know she was.'

'I understand. But the thing is—'

'You think she ran away?' Krysia lifts her head, looks at Mahler. 'No. Someone took Erin – some bad man, some *evil* man. You know this, don't you?'

'Krysia, we can't—'

'You do, I see it in your face. So go and find her, Inspector. Go and find my daughter.'

Nothing he can say to that, no assurance he can give her apart from a promise to do everything he can. And of course, it's not enough.

Krysia shows them out in silence, sliding the door chain back into place as soon as it shuts behind them.

'She didn't say any of that the last time we spoke to her.' Donna glances behind her at the house as they walk back to the car. 'Why didn't she tell us Erin was getting grief from those lassies at school?'

Mahler shakes his head. 'I'm constantly surprised how little family members know about each other's day-to-day experience. Even the most caring ones. That said, it does paint the party in a slightly different light, doesn't it? If—'

Donna's mobile buzzes. She answers, her deepening frown telling Mahler there's nothing good about whatever news she's hearing.

'Thanks, Gary.' She ends the call, turns to Mahler. 'Update on Liam Buchan, Mandy McIver's partner.'

'The oil-rig worker? Go on.'

'Gary's been going through some of the background stuff on everyone at Livvy McIver's party,' she tells him. 'Mandy McIver told us her man was away on the rigs all that week, right?'

Mahler nods. 'Due back on the Sunday, yes.'

'Aye, that's right.' Donna's face is grim. 'Only he wasn't. He's just been promoted, which means his shift pattern's changed – he gets three weeks off and two on, instead of the usual two on, two off. So, either Buchan was here and she's lying about it, or he was off somewhere else without her knowledge. Either way, someone's telling us porkies, boss. Wonder why they'd do that, eh?'

'Good question. Let's go and see if we can get as good an answer, shall we?'

Westerwood Heights is on the other side of Inverness, a small development of twenty or so houses on the eastern fringes of the city, which, Mahler concedes, probably deserves its exclusive label. No identikit little boxes here, crammed into the smallest available space; these houses are built on spacious, individually designed plots, with sweeping drives and landscaped gardens offering unrestricted views across the firth to the Black Isle. Unrestricted for the moment, at least.

A little further along from the Heights, where the city inches out along the coast towards the planned new town at Torna-grain, there's more construction work in progress. And with the current demand for housing around the city, he can't imagine the developers leaving the surrounding fields untouched for much longer. The fringes of woodland are slowly disappearing, giving the new developments an oddly exposed feel.

'How the other half lives, eh?' Donna pulls up outside No. 20. 'Just as flash inside, too – Big Gary's eyes were out on stalks when we came over last time. No wonder Erin was chuffed to get an invite out here.'

Mahler looks up at the McIvers' house. Set on a slight incline, its high cathedral windows looking towards the Black Isle, it's blandly aspirational, the sort of property that belongs in the pages of a lifestyle magazine. Only the beaten-up Clio at the top of the drive looks out of place amongst the neighbouring houses' Range Rovers and BMWs. As out of place, Mahler suspects, as Grant MacKenzie must have felt dropping his daughter off at Livvy McIver's party. 'You think so? I suppose that rather depends.'

'What on?'

'On what lay behind it. Come on, let's have another word with the McIvers.'

Unsurprisingly, the faux-Georgian entrance isn't equipped with anything as mundane as a bell. With a disbelieving eye-roll, Donna raps the cast-iron door knocker a couple of times. When there's no response, she walks over and peers in one of the windows.

'Anything?' Mahler asks.

She shakes her head. 'Got to be someone in, though. We could try round the back? This gate's open—'

'Can I help you?'

The voice is coming from directly above him. Mahler steps off the porch, looks up at the grey-haired woman glaring down at him from an upstairs window. He introduces himself and Donna and asks the woman if the McIvers are at home.

'Sorry, pal, I'm just the cleaner.' She holds up a duster and can of polish, as though she suspects he might not take her at her word. 'Mandy and Livvy are away for the holiday weekend – girls' shopping trip to Edinburgh or something.'

'Any idea where they're staying?' Donna asks, but the woman shakes her head.

'Somewhere posh, knowing her. They'll be back on Monday morning, though. I can leave a note to say you came round, if you want—'

'That's OK,' Mahler tells her. 'Did Liam go with them, do you know?'

The woman gives a snort of laughter. 'Depends if he's back in the good books this week or not – that pair are like something out of *EastEnders* when they get going.' She looks at him and her grin disappears. 'You'll not let on I said that, right? Got a hell of a temper on her, that one.'

Mahler assures her she has nothing to worry about. He thanks her for her time and puts a card through the letter box asking Mandy McIver to get in touch urgently.

'Buchan's got a place in Burghead,' Donna tells him as they walk back down the drive. 'I'll get onto Elgin police to check it out. And I'll keep trying both his and Mandy's mobiles.'

'Do that. When you get back to Burnett Road, talk to his employers again, see if they have any alternative contact details for him. And see if Mandy was particularly friendly with any of the girls' mothers who came to the party – she may have mentioned this trip to them.'

Donna looks at him. 'You're not coming back to the shop, boss?'

Mahler shakes his head. 'Not right away. There's somewhere I need to call at first.'

7

Not for the first time, the weather's early promise has proved false. The unconvincing sun is fading, the warmth slowly leaching from the day as Donna drops him at the gates of Tomnahurich Cemetery.

'The Hill of the Fairies' his mother had called the high green mound in front of him, telling him tales of mortal fiddlers buried there, in thrall to fairy queens. In fact, the Gaelic means nothing more fanciful than hill of the yew trees. But thanks to a seventeenth-century mystic called the Brahan Seer, Tomnahurich's reputation as a place of legend has endured for centuries.

It isn't hard to see why; just a few metres beyond the gate, Mahler can hardly hear the traffic on the busy main road outside. Even the never-ending roadworks by Bught Park sound oddly muted. It's colder, too, the last of the sun's warmth dying as he makes his way amongst the lichen-covered headstones towards his destination.

The grave he's come to visit lies near the foot of the hill, in the newer part of the cemetery. The layout here always strikes him as oddly haphazard; small groups of headstones, half-obscured by dense rhododendron bushes, cluster at the end of maze-like paths.

A year since his last visit, Mahler sets off in one direction and decides he's taken a wrong turning. He looks round, starts to retrace his steps . . . and something dances on the edges of his vision, something pale and quick and flickering that paints the back of his neck with momentary ice.

It's moving along the winding path, dipping in and out of sight between the clustered bushes. Moving towards him in the heavy, soundless air, flashes of light and dark and scarlet. In spite of himself, he takes a half step backwards as the shape drifts closer . . . and Anna Murray, wrapped in a pale coat and flowing ruby scarf, walks out of the greying light towards him.

Outwardly, she's hardly changed. A little smarter, more consciously put-together, perhaps, as a result of the documentaries she's presented for the History Channel. And there's a new assurance about her, a resilience Mahler hasn't seen before. The past two years have marked her, traced new lines at the corners of her eyes. But the haunted look she'd carried for so long has gone.

He watches her face change when she catches sight of him, watches her expression cycle through shock and confusion before settling into a mask of calm. Only her hands are restless; thin, nervous fingers winding and unwinding the folds of her scarf as she looks at him.

'It was you, then, last year.' She nods at the flowers he'd picked up from the market on the way. 'I wondered, when there was no card.'

'I didn't want to intrude.' And what could he possibly have written in a card to excuse the way he'd failed her? If the words exist, Mahler can't imagine what they are. 'If you want me to go—'

'No, that's not . . .' a shrug. 'It was good of you to come. To remember.'

'At your father's funeral—'

'I blanked you. I know. It was just . . . seeing you there brought everything back into focus, I suppose. Not that it had ever gone away.'

'Anna, I'm sorry.'

A sigh. And then a nod. 'I know.' She produces an empty water bottle from her coat pocket, holds it out to him. 'Swap. I'll sort the flowers if you get water from the tap over there.'

He hands over the roses and retraces his steps to the standpipe by the fork in the path. By the time he returns, she's arranged the flowers in the vase and is brushing stray leaves from the base of the headstone. The rising wind is plucking at her hair, tangling its sleek glossiness and blowing it across the sharp contours of her cheeks, her jawline. Every one of which he could trace from memory for as long, he suspects, as his mind is capable of such things. And perhaps beyond that.

'Thanks.' She adds the water to the vase and stands up, shaking off the leaves still clinging to her coat. 'And thanks for . . . for not forgetting her. Most of her so-called friends have, you know. As soon as the trial was over, it was like she'd been air-brushed out of their lives.' Her mouth twists in a bitter half-smile. 'So much for all the public grief-fests, huh? And my mother's friends haven't been much better. After Dad died, I hoped they might . . . I don't know, rally round. But it's as though they think what happened might be catching.'

'I'm sorry.' But it's a reaction he's familiar with. The shadow of violent death has a half-life that spreads far beyond the act itself. 'Is that why you decided to come back? For your mother?'

'Partly. Though there were things I needed to . . . to reassess anyway. I'd started looking for a new job, so when one came through at UHI it felt like the right thing to do, I suppose.'

Not an easy choice to make, though. Or an easy transition. He'd learned that himself three years ago when his mother's deteriorating health had forced his return to Inverness. 'This is a permanent move, then? Are you managing to re-acclimatise?'

'Right now let's call it a work in progress.' A faint relaxing of the tension in her face. 'How's Grace?'

'She's doing well. Enjoying life again, I think.' For once, it's no more than the truth; following a change in medication and a move to a new flat, his mother's bad days are becoming less frequent. Her mental health is still fragile, but she too has started calling herself a work in progress. Mahler's opting to take that as a positive.

'I'm glad. For you both.' She looks away, makes a show of glancing at her watch. 'Actually, I'm supposed to be meeting Mam soon, so—'

'Can I offer you a lift? I'm going that way.' Remembering too late that he doesn't have his car, and calling himself fifty kinds of idiot. He could call a taxi, maybe . . . but Anna's shaking her head.

'I'm taking her for lunch at Eden Court. But thanks.'

'Then I won't hold you up. But I wondered . . . if you were free for coffee later, I know a couple of decent places—'

'I can't.'

'It's coffee, Anna. Just coffee.' His voice giving the lie to his words. He moves towards her, but she holds up a hand as though to ward him off.

'Lukas, don't. Please – look, I appreciated your support during the trial. I truly did. But I need to move on, somehow. And coming home is going to be tough enough, without . . . without other complications.' A momentary flush of pink on her cheeks. 'Because whatever possibilities we might have had, seeing you again is like . . . like I'm back there again. And I can't deal with that right now. I'm sorry.'

She turns and walks away. He watches until her pale coat and flash of scarlet scarf disappears beyond the trees. It's only then he realises the buzzing sound he's hearing is coming from his mobile.

When he hits 'accept', Fergie sounds out of breath, and there's a wail of sirens in the background. 'Boss, you still at Tomnahurich?'

'Leaving now.' He walks back towards the main entrance, picking up his pace. 'What's happened?'

'Attempted abduction of a wee girl near the Bught Drive flats. Guy in a hoodie seen taking off on foot towards the football pitches, something wrong with his leg. Got a few minutes on you, but if you're fast—'

'On it.' Before Fergie finishes speaking, Mahler breaks into a run. The flats are almost opposite the cemetery gates, and if the man's injured in some way. . . 'Check the ice-rink CCTV and get a car down Ness Walk. I'll meet you there.'

He runs across Glenurquhart Road, a chorus of horns sounding in his wake, and past the caravan park on Bught Drive. Scanning the dense bushes as he goes, in case the man's been smart enough to go to ground – though an abduction attempt in such a public place hardly argues for smart. Why here, why now?

Mahler reaches the fork in the road, and realises the abductor might just have chosen the perfect place to make a getaway. It's Bank Holiday weekend and Bught Park is heaving. To his right, a junior football match is in full swing, complete with yelling parents and excitable dogs. On the left, an open-air fitness class is warming up. Directly in front of him, an extended crocodile of tracksuited runners is making its way along the path that leads to the river. And nothing and no one looks remotely out of place.

He needs to make a decision. Which way? On pure instinct, he opts for the river path. Cursing, his leather-soled shoes losing purchase on the still-damp leaves, Mahler zigzags between the

runners, darting glances left and right. Looking for the conspic-
uous, the not quite right – looking for something to tell him
he's made the right choice. Knowing his chances of finding the
man are slipping away with every passing second. If he can't
pick up the trail before the first of the Ness Islands bridges—

Out of nowhere, a blur of barking chestnut fur launches itself
at his chest, winding him. His foot slips in a pile of leaves and
he goes down hard, jarring the base of his spine. Teeth bared,
the dog gives him an appraising look and plants its paws on his
shoulders, pinning him to the ground.

'Oh my god – bad girl, Bracken! No!'

Running footsteps. The dog's owner, brandishing a lead,
grabs the animal by the collar and hauls it off him. Between
breathless apologies, the red-faced woman assures him that
Bracken didn't mean him any harm. Not really.

'It's just men in suits, I'm afraid. Especially tall ones. She's a
rescue dog, you see, and—'

'Don't worry about it.' Mahler gets to his feet, musters a
smile. Thinks about offering the animal a conciliatory pat. And
thinks again as the hound growls, deep in its throat, before it's
dragged off by its still-apologising owner.

He's dusting himself down as the car arrives and three hefty
uniforms pile out. Mahler sends one after the dog-walker in
case Bracken's dislike of tall men extends to tracksuited child
abductors, and the others in opposite directions along the bank.
Too late to pick up the man now, he knows that. But there's
a slim chance someone might have seen something, and right
now he'll take any sort of chance he's offered.

A wheezing noise behind him, like the sound of a hundred
cats in torment. Mahler turns as Fergie's Audi shudders to a halt
by the verge.

Fergie clambers out, jogs over to him. 'No luck, then? Aye,
well, it was a long shot, I suppose.' He looks round at the scene.

'Weird place to pick, though, eh? The guy has to know we're scouring the town for him. Why risk grabbing a bairn here, with so many potential witnesses around? Not very smart of him, is it?'

'On the face of it, no.' But there's something about the whole incident that's nagging at Mahler. 'Who's with the girl? We're going to need a better description to stand any chance of tracking him down.'

'Donna and that new lassie, Nazreen. I was going to go over there myself to see how they're doing, if you want to come?'

Mahler does. Oh, he should leave Fergie to it, he knows that. This sort of nuts-and-bolts investigative work doesn't need a DI to handle it, and his desk at Burnett Road is disappearing into a paperwork sinkhole, where, he's convinced, half the admin in the division comes to die. There are reports to be gone through, actions to be signed off, overtime figures to be scrutinised before June Wallace and the Chief set eyes on them . . . urgent, all of them. Allegedly.

But he's been ordered to be more visible, hasn't he? And ploughing through the bureaucratic mountain awaiting him at Burnett Road will give him too much time to think. Too much time to replay the sight of Anna Murray walking away from him again. Too much time to wonder if there's anything he could have said or done to make her change her mind.

'I was first on the scene. Maybe something they mention might ring a bell.' He sets off for the Audi, pauses as a thought strikes him. 'How did you know I'd be at Tomnahurich?'

Fergie gives him a reproachful look. 'I know I'm not what you'd call technological, but I can just about work the calendar on my smartphone. Man, I can't believe it's two years since Morven Murray was killed.' A sideways glance. 'Was Anna there today?'

'Yes. I spoke to her. Briefly.'

'Right.' Another glance. 'She doing okay? After the trial and everything. Because—'

'She's doing fine.' Mahler quickens his pace. 'And moving on. Anna told me she's moving on.'

Vigil for Erin – Facebook Public Group
Dylan Main shared a link to the group: Vigil for Erin
28 mins

Highlands & Islands Police Division
Saturday 28 May at 15.45

Police Scotland is appealing for information following an incident in Inverness in which a man approached two young girls. The incident took place on Saturday, 28 May 2016 at around 11.30 a.m. in the area of Glenurquhart Road and Bught Drive.

The male is described as between 40 and 50 years of age and dark-haired. He was wearing a hooded top and jogging bottoms and may have had a beard. When approached by a passer-by, he ran off in the direction of the Bught Park pitches.

Detective Inspector Andy Black, who is leading enquiries, said police were looking at CCTV footage, and added: 'We are appealing for anyone who was in the area at the time to contact us if they think they have information which may help in identifying this male.

Anyone with information about this incident should call police on 101 or Crimestoppers on 0800 555 111.'

---

308 Shares

Tam Bell 4hrs:
A hoodie and joggers and maybe a beard? FFS. That's half the guys in The Keg any night of the week.

Janey Mack 7hrs:
Hope they find him soon. We all need to be watching out for the wee ones at the moment.

Dylan Main replied:

Cops know where the pedos live. They need to knock on a few doors, get them down to Burnett Road and have a wee word with them there. See how brave they are then.

Tam Bell replied:

No point moaning at the cops, they can't be everywhere. Inverness folk aren't the same these days. People used to know who their neighbours were, who to keep an eye on. Who to look out for. Too busy watching *Big Brother* or shite like that to bother about what's on their own doorstep.

Izzy MacLeod:

What about the other wee girls at the party? They're all in shock right now, and my Morgan's having nightmares about it. The police need to get their act together – if something else happens, it'll be down to them.

8

Day 9

Sunday, 29 May

Another child's photo on another whiteboard. Another name in stark black sharpie as Mahler arrives for the morning briefing. And Andy Black looming over DC Nazreen Khan, his mouth practically in her ear as she adds a final line of intel to the display.

'Everything okay, Andy?'

The faintest flush on Black's face as he turns round, enough to tell Mahler he'd thought no one else was around. 'Checking things over, that's all. Trying to rescue something from that pig's ear of an operation yesterday. How the fuck did the guy manage to get clean away from you?'

'He'd run before I got the call. Short of hopping in the Tardis, my options were a little limited. And the description we had—'

'What bloody description?' Black glances behind Mahler, raising his voice as people start to arrive, the scent of takeaway coffee and Gow's breakfast rolls slowly filling the air. 'We need to be stepping this up a gear, not sitting back hoping the guy's going to fall into our laps. Yes, thanks, DC Khan. I'll take over now.'

Playing to the gallery? Mahler looks round, catches the glint of buttons on a dress uniform and realises they've got company. Chief Superintendent-level company, no less – Chae Hunt, at

49

Burnett Road just after seven on a Sunday morning. In full formal, his carefully wrinkle-free features looking as though he's just been ironed. Mahler starts to wonder what's behind it, decides he doesn't actually care and turns back to Black.

'Let's work with what we've got, shall we?' Mahler turns to the board, indicates the solemn-faced girl peering out at them from behind her glasses. 'Celeste Taylor, ten years old. Fond of animals and swimming. Heading home from the Aquadome yesterday morning when she heard what she thought was a cat somewhere in the bushes. Worried it had been injured, she went over to find the animal. And her would-be-abductor was waiting for her. He tried to grab her arm and drag her off. If her younger brother hadn't appeared at that point . . .' Mahler shakes his head. No need to spell out the possible consequences if the boy had appeared a few minutes later. 'Celeste and her brother did their best to give us a description, but as you've no doubt been made aware through the wonders of social media, it's not exactly detailed. Fortunately, we now have a possible new sighting of our man around the time in question.'

It's not much to go on, just a couple out walking who'd seen a man in a tracksuit disappearing into some bushes by the Archive Centre. Assuming he was answering an urgent call of nature, they'd continued on their way and thought nothing further of it. Until they'd arrived home to see Fergie and an unhappy media liaison officer fielding questions on the six o'clock news.

Their call to the incident line had yielded a couple more details: glasses, a dark blue or black top, the wife had thought. But they were both absolutely sure the man they'd seen had nothing wrong with his leg.

'Glasses but no beard. And no limp.' Black settles his rear further back on the desk he's perched on, the furniture emitting a faint groan of protest. 'Sounds just like our guy, eh? Apart from a couple of wee points, that is.'

'It's not ideal, agreed. But the Archive Centre's got reasonably decent CCTV, so we'll see what turns up there.'

'A car, sir.' Nazreen sticks up her hand. 'He must have had some sort of vehicle nearby, mustn't he, if he was going to grab Celeste? A van, probably, or an SUV with heavily tinted windows. Couldn't we check the footage for those kinds of vehicles driving off after the attempt to snatch her? He'd have wanted to get out of there ASAP.'

Fergie shakes his head. 'Driving off from where, though – near the flats, or near the river? And which direction?'

'Also, he may not have driven off immediately,' Mahler points out. 'The smart option would have been to wait until the coast was clear.' On the other hand, if the man had left soon after the couple had seen him . . . 'It's worth looking at, though. We'll start with the vehicles parked by the flats and work out from there, then try to correlate with what we know was parked near Columba Gardens around the time Erin was abducted. Good spot, Nazreen.'

'You're definitely linking this to the Erin MacKenzie case, DI Mahler?' Chae Hunt's face is set in impassive lines, but the ice in his voice is enough to send the room's temperature plummeting. 'Because without clear-cut evidence backing it up, I'd prefer not to hear terms like "serial abductor" and "stalking children" bandied about during a media update.'

So that explains this morning's royal visit. Mahler shakes his head. The interviewer had been borderline aggressive, and, on top form, Fergie could have demolished her in thirty seconds. But he's not on top form; after nine days of minimal sleep and relentless pressure, none of them are. Even Chae Hunt has to realise that.

'Not terms used by DS Ferguson at any point, sir,' Mahler tells him. 'And we certainly won't be making any assumptions. But given the discrepancies that have come to light regarding the whereabouts of Mandy McIver's partner when Erin went missing, we're now following that up as a matter of urgency. And we'll be asking Mr Buchan for a satisfactory account of his movements on all the relevant dates.'

Mahler finishes up and hands over to Black to report on the progress of the search operations. Now in their final day, the teams have moved to a patch of overgrown waste ground near the planned extension road to the new bridge over the Ness. It's so far from the McIvers' house that Mahler feels a tinge of sympathy for Andy Black, trying to weave a report out of nothing while Chae Hunt looms in the doorway, the light reflecting off his gleaming buttons.

Mahler's preparing to close the briefing and hand over to Fergie to give out the daily task allocations when Hunt holds his hand up and strides across to the whiteboards.

'DIs Black and Mahler, a moment please, before you finish.' Hunt looks round the room. 'I know you're all keen to get out there and I don't propose to keep you too long, but I wanted to make everyone aware of a couple of organisational changes I'll be making to the investigating teams. DCI Wallace will continue to supervise the day-to-day running of the investigation, but as of now I will also be assuming a hands-on role. In particular, I will be consulted in advance regarding all media briefings and appearances connected with this case.'

'Sir, if this is about yesterday evening's media briefing, DS Ferguson had authority from me to proceed.'

'Despite my instructions that senior officers – senior officers, DI Mahler – take every opportunity to be more visible.' The hint of a frown touches Hunt's forehead as he looks Fergie up and down. 'Which is why that authority will come from me for the remainder of this operation. Are we clear? Then I'll let you get on. DI Black, a word.'

The silence holds until Hunt has left, Andy Black lumbering

in his wake. As the murmuring starts, Fergie glances at Mahler, but he shakes his head; if people are looking to him for answers, he has none to give them. Yet. But he knows exactly where to get some.

He leaves Fergie to give out the daily actions and goes to find June Wallace.

If moving the DCI closer to Chae Hunt's office was intended to make her more accessible to Hunt and less accessible to everyone else, it seems to be having an effect. For as long as Mahler's known her, June Wallace has had a genuine 'open door' office policy. But there's no answer to his first knock, and only a grunted query in response to his second. When he pushes the door open a cautious couple of inches, she's at her desk, glaring down at her laptop as though she's hoping it might burst into flames.

'Ma'am, a word?'

'Wait.' A burst of typing, then she shakes her head. 'Not a good time, Lukas. I've got a partnership meeting in half an hour and—'

'Five minutes, ma'am.'

More typing. 'Aye, right. Ach, bugger it!' She hits a couple of keys, looks up at him. Sighs. 'Fine. Get in here and close the door. Let me guess, the Chief's spoken to you and now your nose is out of joint. Right?'

'He spoke to the entire MIT at the morning briefing. Apparently we're no longer trusted to deliver a ten-minute media update without his say-so.'

'Ach, spare me the petted lip.' June waves at the chair by her desk. 'Sit. Have you seen the video clip? Fergie gave an update on the biggest case we're dealing with right now – Fergie, a bloody DS! He looked like an unmade bed and he let that wee lassie tie him in knots. Why the hell didn't you do it yourself?'

Mahler shakes his head. A quick bright wave of anger rises up, overriding the voice telling him June's right; half right, at least. He should have taken it off Fergie's shoulders, should have stood there with the cameras and mics thrust in his face, fielding the scores of questions he doesn't have answers for. But his instincts are telling him there's something else going on here, something that's got nothing to do with Fergie's dress sense or his capability. And the wary, closed-down look on June's face is seconding that.

'I didn't do it because you were jumping up and down for a progress report to feed Hunt. Because the authorised overspend on overtime this month is already blown, so we're relying on exhausted officers who haven't seen their beds for days not messing up, and we both know that's not sustainable for much longer. Because Fergie is an experienced officer who's more than capable of delivering a short media update and you know it.'

'Finished?'

He shrugs. 'Also, last time I did one you said I looked like Benedict Cumberbatch's evil twin. On an off day.'

'Aye, well.' One corner of her mouth lifts in weary amusement. 'More like Tom Hiddleston in those daft *Thor* films, to be fair. Nice suit, though.'

'I don't recall Fergie's . . . unique . . . dress sense being an issue before. And the Chief doesn't usually get so hands-on with an ongoing investigation.' Not until it's close to a satisfactory resolution, at least. In Mahler's experience, Hunt's more than happy to be in the public eye at that point. 'Ma'am, I have to ask – has something happened?'

June takes off her glasses, rubs the red horseshoe-shaped mark they've left on her nose. Without the shielding lenses, her eyes are laced with more lines than he remembers, the darkness under them showing her own tally of long, thankless hours at her desk.

'Last summer on the A9 is what happened, son. Two folk left dead in a car for three days – three bloody days! – before they were found. Remember that?'

He's hardly likely to forget it. Along with every officer in the force, he'd watched the unfolding story of a catastrophically misdirected RTC report with growing disbelief and horror. Whether the recently centralised call-handling system or simple human error had been to blame, the result had appalled everyone. And gifted Police Scotland's detractors another massive stick to beat it with.

'Of course I do,' Mahler tells her. 'But I don't see—'

'Don't you? Something like that's got consequences, and so it damn well should have. But it sets other things in motion.'

'Ma'am?'

'Stuff, Lukas. Let's just call it stuff. It's all happening down the road at Tulliallan, where the high heid yins hang out – stuff at shiny-button, dress-uniform level, you might say. Trust me, the Chief Super's got the world on his back right now. So a big case like this, where half the country's watching what we're up to, that's going to get his extra-special attention. And any suggestion of a serial child abductor running around Inverness is the last thing he wants to see on the ten o'clock news. Any clearer?'

'Not particularly, Ma'am.'

She gives a grim smile. 'Good enough. Keep it like that and you're not likely to get caught in the crossfire. Now bugger off, you've had your five minutes. And Lukas?'

'Ma'am?'

'Tell Fergie to get himself a decent jacket, for pity's sake.'

9

When Mahler gets back to the incident room, the teams have dispersed and there's no sign of Andy Black or the Chief. As he does most days, Mahler opts to take that as a positive.

He opens his laptop, runs down the list of actions while he's waiting for his emails to load. Donna and Gary are tracking down Mandy McIver's partner, the elusive Liam Buchan. Fergie's back at the suspected arson on the Longman industrial estate, handing it off to CID. And Pete's ploughing through the CCTV footage from yesterday; Fergie's media slot might have been a little rough round the edges, but it's generated a steady stream of calls about the attempted abduction of Celeste Taylor. Some useful calls, too, amongst the usual wind-up merchants and attention-seekers, many of them about the man spotted by the couple on Ness Walk.

No mention of a bad leg, though. Had the limp simply been an act, or could they be looking for more than one person? But there's something messy about the attempt on Celeste Taylor, something that doesn't fit with the coldly efficient way Erin MacKenzie had been taken.

Mahler stares at the faces on the whiteboards, tries to make the pieces come together in his mind. Tries to tell himself that

Erin's still alive, that the thumping sound he can hear in his head isn't the sound of her fading heartbeats as her time runs out . . .

'Pressure getting to you? Maybe you'd be better letting me take the lead for a while, let you concentrate on that big case you've got going on up at Slackbuie. Seventy-year-old bones, wasn't it? Sounds right up your street.'

Mahler turns to see Andy Black glowering at him from the doorway, his bulk sucking up the available light like a leather-clad black hole.

'Trust me, I'm enjoying the current arrangements as much as you are.' Not for the first time, Mahler contemplates the joys of an alternative universe in which Black's two-year-old dream of giving up policing to run a bar in Florida had actually come to pass. 'But fun though our little chats are, I'm a bit busy right now. So if you don't mind . . .' He indicates the endless scroll of emails filling his screen with red flags and exclamation marks. And frowns as a name he hasn't heard in years leaps off the page at him.

A growl from the doorway. 'Cheeky git. You think—'

'Shut up.' An ice pick of pain, tapping at the base of his skull as he skims the email. 'Come and look at this.'

Black walks over, leans on the desk to squint at the laptop. And lets out a low whistle. 'Fuck's sake. That's Bradley, isn't it? The posh-boy paedo who got caught with his fingers in the till. Don't tell me that bastard's out already?'

'He only got six years in the end. And without the fraud charges, I doubt he'd even have got that – so yes, he is. Which is not good news for us.' Mahler waits for Black to finish reading up. On a case Mahler's done his best to forget about.

Max Bradley had been a junior consultant at a health trust covering some of London's most deprived inner-city areas. He'd also been the founder of an online group sharing what the

57

sentencing judge had called 'truly vile images' of abused children under the guise of being a charitable organisation. It was only a chance investigation into the so-called charity's accounts that had uncovered its true purpose. And had led to one of the city's biggest child-abuse scandals in years.

When the case came to trial, Bradley's legal team had cited his previous good character and pointed to the recent death of his father. They'd painted an image of a distraught man experiencing a mental collapse, barely responsible for his own actions. Charged on multiple counts, he hadn't managed to avoid a custodial sentence. But to anyone who'd seen those images, a tariff of six years . . .

'He's been out for a whole bloody month, then. Bastard.' Black scowls at the face smirking at them from the screen. 'But what's it got to do with us? You're not with the Met now.'

'I have friends there. Who thought we should see this.' Mahler scrolls further down the email. 'Last week, on an unannounced visit to his notified address, the Public Protection Team found him gone. No answer from his mobile, he was absent on a follow-up visit on Thursday . . . and, as of two months ago, his mother's been living less than an hour's drive from here.'

'Jesus bloody Christ.' Black scrawls down the address, straightens up. 'Right. I'll take Naz with me – let's see what paedo boy's mammy has to say for herself when we turn up on her door, eh?'

Mahler's on his feet, already reaching for his mobile and keys. But with Fergie still dealing with the arson attack and Donna doing follow-ups, if he insists on going with Black, Pete Noble will be the highest-ranking officer left in the MIT. Mahler tries to envisage a scenario short of alien invasion in which he successfully defends that decision to the DCI. And fails. He nods, sits down again at his laptop.

'Sending you through the email now. Keep me updated.'

Bradley's mugshot is still on the screen as the door slams behind Black. An unremarkable face, Mahler realises. Attractive, even, in an amiable, unthreatening kind of way. A million miles from the shifty characters beloved of all the stranger-danger posters in schools and doctors' waiting rooms up and down the country.

Mahler's only seen Bradley in the flesh a couple of times; the first was when he'd been brought into Charing Cross nick when Mahler was on his way out. He'd looked bewildered then, the image of an innocent man caught in a nightmare not of his own making.

The second time, at the conclusion of Bradley's trial, had been a little different. As the evidence against him had mounted, Bradley had struggled to maintain his façade of confused innocence. But for a fragment of a second, as the verdict was delivered, the mask had slipped. Mahler had caught his eye across the court, caught the smirk as he'd collapsed in the dock, arms covering his face in apparent despair.

Predictably, the media had branded him as evil. But Mahler, whose acquaintance with all forms of evil has been more intimate than most, suspects the answer is simpler and more disturbing. What he'd seen in Bradley's face that day hadn't been the presence of active evil, it had been an absence. An emptiness of any emotion other than a faint, detached amusement.

And Erin MacKenzie's been missing for nine days . . . at the thought of her in Bradley's hands, the twist of pain sitting at the base of his skull gives another vicious pull.

He opens his desk drawer, reaching for his meds, when he hears the swing doors at the end of the corridor slam against the wall. By the time the running footsteps reach the incident room, Mahler's on his feet, shoving his mobile in his pocket and pulling on his jacket.

Pete Noble appears in the doorway, pink-cheeked and

breathless. Judging by the look on his face, he hasn't come with any sort of good news.

'Sir, it's Ewan MacRae, the guy leading the search teams. Fergie's on his way over now, but I thought you'd want to be there too. They . . . they've found something.'

The searchers, a mix of volunteers and uniformed officers, had started in the fields backing onto the McIvers' house. Now, on the ninth day of Erin's disappearance, only two full teams were still on site, working their way through dense woodland near yet another new housing development on the outskirts of the city.

Fergie's standing by his decrepit Audi, talking on his mobile, when Mahler pulls up. He raises a hand in acknowledgement, ending the call with a terse, 'Aye, fine,' as Mahler gets out and walks over.

'Problem?'

'You mean another one?' Fergie gives a grim nod. 'Aye, maybe. That suspected arson down the Longman? If I said the place had just had a massive refit for a new tenant, bankrolled by our old pal, semi-retired toe-rag Cazza MacKay—'

'I'd say fill me in back at the shop. Right now, we've got other priorities.' Mahler spots a police Land Rover halfway up the slope and a burly uniformed figure standing next to it. 'Let's see what MacRae's got for us.'

Not a body, thank God; there's no duty doctor in attendance and no one from the fiscal's office that Mahler can see. But no good news either; as they trudge up the debris-strewn approach path, MacRae brings them up to speed.

Knowing it was their last day, the teams had volunteered to stay past their allotted finishing times. But the rain which started as a barely-there drizzle had turned into a series of downpours. In the end, they'd been forced to give up. The final team was heading back to the marshalling point when one of the volunteers, a local doctor, had spotted something lying in a puddle of water at the foot of a muddy incline.

'He was trying to be careful,' MacRae tells Mahler. 'I don't doubt that, though there might have been a few swear words flying around when I saw what he'd done. But it's slippery as hell up here, and . . . well, you can see for yourself.'

Mahler steps up carefully to look over the barrier tape. The scene tells its own story: a large body sliding down the slope, coming to rest in a heap at the foot. A muddy confusion of tracks at the bottom where the man had scrambled to get back up and, beyond the tape, so many footmarks round the perimeter that it looks as though the entire team had joined in the rescue effort.

Fergie sucks in a breath. 'Bet the CSI guys loved this. They still here?'

MacRae indicates a pair of white-suited figures working near what looks like an alternative access road. 'Signs of recent use by a vehicle over there, unlikely to have been any of the site traffic.'

Mahler nods. If they're able to recover something useful from the vehicle tracks, it might just make up for the preservation of evidence disaster he's looking at right now. 'Good. Where's our heavy-footed doctor friend?'

MacRae takes them over to the evidence collection area and introduces them to Dr Grey, a tall, slump-shouldered man in an ill-fitting Teletubby suit. He's staring into the depths of a takeaway coffee, and Mahler's first thought is that whatever MacRae might have said in the heat of the moment, Grey's been saying that and more to himself.

'I thought it was just more rubbish at first,' he tells Mahler. His voice is calm, almost detached, but his hands are gripping the cup as though to keep it steady, and the knowledge of what he's found is stamped across every line of his weary, good-natured face. 'But something made me take another look. I saw it was the sort of thing a little girl might wear – pink and glittery, you know? I moved a couple of overhanging branches out of the way, and that . . . that was when I saw the blood.'

Mahler nods. The T-shirt and child-sized rucksack are already on their way to the forensics lab, but the images MacRae had shown him and Fergie as they walked up the approach path told their own story. The upper part of the child's top had been covered in a dull, maroon-brown stain and the unicorn pattern on its front matches what Erin MacKenzie had been wearing on the afternoon of the party.

'Did it look as though the items had been deliberately hidden, would you say? Or dropped by accident?'

Grey gives a weary shrug. 'Who can say? When I slipped, I caught the branch to steady myself and the whole damn lot tumbled after me. I . . . I'm sorry. I just wanted a better look.'

'Aye, well, you got that.' Fergie's voice is tight with frustration. 'Christ, didn't you—'

Mahler holds up his hand. 'You said the T-shirt was bloodstained. So you noticed that right away?'

'I . . .' Grey swallows. 'It was hard not to. But, of course, the top was covered in mud, so I suppose I jumped to that conclusion, yes. Believe me, I hope I'm wrong—'

'God's sake,' Fergie snaps. 'You're a doctor, man. Did it look like blood to you?'

Grey puts the cup down, the tremble in his hand more pronounced. And gives an exhausted nod. 'Yes, Sergeant. It looked like blood to me.'

Erin

When she wakes up, she doesn't open her eyes. Doesn't even move her head, though her hair, sticky-damp and smelly where she's been sick over herself, is lying across her mouth.

She doesn't do any of those things because she's not awake, not really. She's dreaming, one of those sneaky, scary dreams that used to make her yell out loud, even though Mam says she's a big girl now and should know better than to wake the whole house with her noise. She's dreaming, that's all.

Because none of this is real – not the cold, hard floor she's lying on, not the thin blanket she's wrapped herself in to try and keep warm. Not the darkness, thick and stinking of petrol. Not the sore place on the back of her neck or the scratches on her arms that she can't remember getting, but doesn't want to look at in case . . . in case she does remember. So yes, she's having a bad dream. A horrible, scary one, but it isn't real. Nothing here is real. Nothing.

If she squeezes her eyes shut and keeps her head buried in the blanket, she can tell herself that. Make herself believe she's in her own bed, Tess snoring at her feet and making smelly dog-farts in her sleep. Make herself believe she's clean and warm and safe.

And if she keeps on believing that, maybe when she opens her eyes again it'll be true.

IO

Haven Cottage, by Muir of Ord

'Woman's got a sense of humour, I'll give her that.' Andy Black squints at the ceramic plaque on the gatepost outside the house Max Bradley's mother had moved into less than two months earlier.

'Haven Cottage' is a squat box of a building with walls the colour of three-day-old porridge, mottled with rust stains from the ancient drainpipes and decrepit guttering. Some haven, this – down a rutted single-track road outside bloody Muir of Ord, a town so ugly the rest of the Black Isle tries to pretend it simply doesn't exist.

'If you had an ex-con son you needed to stash away somewhere, this would fit the bill all right, wouldn't it?'

'It's secluded enough,' Nazreen agrees. 'But Bradley must know we'll come here. Why risk it?'

'Nowhere else for him to bloody go, is there?' Andy shakes his head. He hadn't meant to raise his voice, but, Jesus Christ, the lassie's supposed to have brains as well as looks. 'Naz, listen.' He gives her a smile to show he isn't pissed at her. 'Your first major investigation, right? Keen to learn as much as you can, get yourself noticed?'

'Of course, sir.'

'Right. So this is where you learn that most folk are as thick as bloody pig shit – and they make the mistake of thinking we are too. Look, Bradley's got no one else to turn to, has he? No one except his mammy, who's changed her name and hidden herself away up here, at the arse end of bloody nowhere, hoping we wouldn't notice. More fool her, eh?'

They leave the car at the gate and walk up the short, rutted driveway. Andy checks out the smart little Mercedes runa-round sitting in front of a ramshackle wooden garage. The car's showroom-neat, splashes of mud on the wheels the only sign it's ever been anywhere more rural than the M25 in its life.

Andy grins at Nazreen, a curl of excitement building in his gut. The woman's a neat freak, one look at her car's enough to see that – unless she's discovered a sudden passion for doing up wrecks like Haven Cottage, she'd never up sticks and move hundreds of miles to a place like this. Not unless the move was for a completely different reason.

'Lesson two, Naz. Observation.' He points at the half-open M&S carrier sitting on the front seat. 'Fair bit of food there for a wifey living on her own, eh? No meals for one and—'

'I'm sorry, you can't leave your car there.'

Black turns to look at the woman standing in the doorway. Anthea Bradley is somewhere in her late fifties – model-thin and tall, with startling plum-coloured hair. Attractive enough for her age, Black supposes, though he's never been keen on the half-starved look himself.

'DI Black, DC Khan.' He flashes his ID, nods at Nazreen to do the same. 'It's about your son, Mrs Bradley. Mind if we come in?'

'My name's Newman, inspector. I don't use Bradley any more. And yes, I do mind, actually – the place is a tip, and I have things to do.' She looks them up and down, then sighs. 'At least let me collect my shopping first.'

She squeezes past Andy, gets the carrier from the car and nods at them to follow.

Inside, the house is half building site, half slum. The hallway is stacked with cardboard boxes, and he trips over a pile of old newspapers at the entrance to the kitchen, scattering them across the floor. Naz bends to pat them into a rough stack, and he takes a moment to enjoy the sight before turning to Anthea Bradley, or whatever the hell she's calling herself these days.

'Bit isolated out here, isn't it? Must be a bit of a change for you, after Kingston-on-Thames.'

'Why do you think I bought it?' She nods a thank you at Naz and sweeps past him into the kitchen, dumping her shopping on the table. 'After what happened, I wanted to get as far away as possible. Surely you can understand that.'

Aye, right. He ignores the stony-faced look she's giving him and whips out the most recent mugshot they have of her wee pervert of a son. Not looking quite as pretty as he'd done at his trial, but child molesters usually don't after a spell behind bars.

'Your boy's not at his notified address, Mrs Bradley. Hasn't been there for a week or two, it seems.' He shoves the mugshot under her nose, follows up with one of Erin MacKenzie. 'See this wee girl? She went missing in Inverness around the same time as your Maxie dropped off the radar. Just a few weeks after you bought your little Highland hideaway here.'

The attitude she's been giving him vanishes, just like that. She drops into a chair, grey-faced, trembling. 'No. You can't think—'

'That there's a connection? Yes, I bloody can.' He pushes Erin's photo at her again. 'Where's your son, Mrs Bradley?'

'I don't know.'

'Try again.' He raises his voice, just enough to show her he isn't falling for her crap. 'The truth this time. Where's he hiding?'

66

'I don't . . .' Her voice changes, falters. 'I . . . I need . . .' Bradley gropes for her bag, her other hand pressing against her chest.

Andy feels a bubble of panic rise behind his ribs. What the fuck's going on? She's—

Naz shoves him aside. She riffles through the bag, pulls out some sort of inhaler and puts it into the woman's hand. 'This one, yes? Don't try to talk, just nod.' She guides the woman's shaking hand to her mouth, watches her use the spray and gives her a reassuring smile. 'That's good. Sit quietly for a minute, now, and let it take effect. DI Black will make you a cup of tea.'

Andy's on the point of refusing when he catches the look on Naz's face. Fuck's sake, how was he supposed to know there was something wrong with the woman?

Rattled, his own hand not completely steady, Andy fills the kettle. He gets a mug from the shelf and starts rooting around to see where Bradley keeps the tea, but she holds up her hand to stop him.

'Leave that, please. And listen to me.' Her voice is still shaky, but there's a dark bitterness there too that takes Andy by surprise. 'I haven't seen my son since the day he was convicted. I think . . . I think he's a thoroughly despicable human being, frankly. I doubt he even knows where I am – and, believe me, I have every intention of keeping it that way.'

'You'll be happy to put that in a statement, then? And for us to take a look around while we're here?'

Her mouth sets in a grim line. 'Do what you have to, Inspector. Then kindly get the hell out of my house.'

No hesitation, no attempt to put them off. Which is when Andy knows for sure they're wasting their time. Oh, they go through the motions, but it's obvious there's nothing to find – a quick search of the house and grounds shows no sign of anyone but Anthea Bradley living there. She's likely lying through her teeth about having no contact with paedo boy, but Andy's willing to bet they're smart enough to have used cheap, untraceable pay-as-you-go phones to set up any arrangements.

Her statement, when she gives it, is total bollocks. With a nod at Nazreen, Andy chucks his card on the table, says a few polite words he doesn't mean and stamps off to the car. When she follows, a few minutes later, she's got an envelope in her hand.

'Her spray's almost out,' Naz tells him as she gets in. 'I said we'd drop this into the surgery for her on our way past. That's all right, isn't it?'

Andy opens his mouth to tell her, no, it bloody isn't – they're not running a delivery service for the families of perverts like Max Bradley. But Naz's seat belt is twisted and her top stretches interestingly across her chest as she tries to untangle it, so he takes a moment to appreciate the view. When she looks up, he decides to give her a break. This time.

'You thought she was on the level?'

'I thought she was becoming unwell, sir. And I thought you'd want us to balance the needs of our investigation with her well-being – we can do an ANPR check on her vehicle location following Bradley's release, check prison visit records to verify her story, before deciding if we need to talk to her again, surely?'

Andy stares at her. 'Are you telling a superior officer how to run an investigation here, Naz? Because that would not be a smart move on your part. Not at all.'

Jesus Christ, who does she think she is? Not that long ago, she'd have been playing cops and robbers at Tulliallan College. The shine hardly off her new boots, and she's giving him advice? He thinks about what they used to do to some of the young female PCs in his Strathclyde days as part of their initiation into the job. Thinks about that for a long time and watches the blood rise in her face. Good. A little respect for a senior rank is well overdue, in his opinion.

'Of course not. I just meant there are other avenues we can explore—'

'We?' He shakes his head. 'No, DC Khan, you'll be doing that when we get back to Burnett Road. I will be . . . following up some leads in connection with an ongoing case. Is that clear?'

'Absolutely.' She clicks her seat belt into place and gives him an earnest I'll-try-harder kind of smile. 'No disrespect intended, sir.'

'Fine. We'll leave it there, then.'

'But seeing we're talking about respect . . . if I catch you staring at my tits again, you'll get my knee where it hurts most. And then I'll hit you with a harassment charge. Sir.'

Six-thirty in the evening, and the sun's beginning to fade. It's cooler than it has been, but still warm enough to sit at one of the pub's outside tables and look out across the water. Enjoy a meal and a bottle of a local craft beer, maybe, suck in a few lungfuls of lochside air and tell yourself life's pretty good. If that's the sort of crap that floats your boat.

Andy Black glances at the couples sitting outside – tourists, most of them, judging by their optimistic shorts and T-shirts – and leaves them to deal with the gathering clouds of midges. Inside, apart from a guy slumped on a stool and a trio of hill-walker types sprawling at one of the tables, the bar is deserted. As Andy orders his pint and whisky chaser, the guy slides off his stool and weaves an unsteady path to the door, mobile in hand. Bird or a taxi, Andy's guessing. Maybe both, eh? A taxi-driving bird. Lucky bastard.

Andy picks up his drinks and heads for the window table in the far corner. Wedged in by the bogs, its top ringed with the ghosts of long-emptied glasses, it looks like somewhere a man can sit and get on with the business of getting hammered in peace. And tonight, that's exactly what he plans to do.

This isn't his sort of place, truth be told – when he goes out drinking, he goes out drinking, not to stare out the windows of some poncey lochside pub peddling tartan and shortbread-tin pish to wide-eyed tourists too daft to know they're being conned. But unless he wants to run into half of Inverness's pimple-chinned, hoodie-wearing lowlifes, The Keg isn't an option, and even The Fluke's gone a wee bit too upmarket for his liking recently. There's 'Spoons, of course, and the Heathmount, but they're always hoaching with cops, and to-night he's had more than enough of the job to be going on with.

It's not the knock-back from wee Naz that's bugging him – Christ, plenty more fish where that had come from. Tastier ones, too. But when Anthea Bradley had started struggling for breath, he'd had a nasty moment or two. If Naz hadn't worked out what the matter was . . . Something cold brushes the back of his neck at the thought of what might have happened then.

Andy raises his pint glass to the mournful-looking Highland cow in the painting over the fireplace, knocks half of it back in one and follows it with the chaser. At least there's one cop he can be sure he won't run into, no matter which pub he chooses.

Mahler doesn't drink at all, as far as he knows. A glass of posh vino with his pal the pathologist, probably, or a wee after-dinner brandy – nothing more than that. If there hadn't been that thing with Karen Gilchrist, Andy would have put Mahler down as a gay himself – fancy suits, fancy way of speaking, groomed to within an inch of his life.

In a way, that would have been easier to deal with. Would have given him a handle on the guy. As it is . . . as it is, Mahler's not someone he can get the measure of. And that bothers him. But there's a lot that Mahler doesn't know, for all his fancy

70

ways. And there's a lot Andy hopes to Christ he never finds out. Not him, not anyone at Burnett Road.

When the Chief had called him out of the briefing earlier, Andy's gut had cramped in anticipation of what was coming, but Hunt had just spouted his usual pish about teamwork and challenging environments – if he meant having to work with Lukas Mahler, then, aye, Andy supposes that's pretty fucking challenging all right.

He reaches for his pint and sees he's looking at an empty glass. Need to sort that, pronto. He pushes his chair back, gets up to go for a refill. And the guy he'd clocked when he came in, the guy who'd been hunched over a pint at the bar, is standing in the doorway – standing upright, sober as a fucking judge and staring right at him.

'Something I can help you with, pal?'

The guy turns and heads outside, but Andy's not letting it go, not tonight. He starts to make for the door . . . and trips over a backpack one of the hairy-kneed morons in walking boots has dumped on the floor by their table.

Andy untangles himself and sticks two fingers up at the moron. He barges past the drinkers at the bar and out the door, but thanks to hiker-boy, his watcher's got too much of a head start. By the time Andy gets outside, the man has gone.

I I

Day 10

Monday, 30 May

He's fourteen years old, and he's running for his life. Running for both their lives, though he doesn't know that at the time.

Lukas is flying down the stairs, bare feet slip-sliding on the treads, the smell of blood and fear everywhere. His mother's screams have ended, but there's no safety in that silence, and his heart is thumping, his breath coming in frantic, despairing gasps—

Mahler jerks awake, sweat-drenched despite the breeze coming through his open window. All the things he's seen, all the horrors his work has shown him, and this nightmare is the one he can't escape from. Two and a half decades later, it's still stalking him, etching its fear on the back of his throat. If memories had colours, Mahler thinks, his would be scarlet burned on black. And livid, like the fading of old bruises.

He sits up, unclenches his fists. Forces his breathing back to something approaching normal. Out of habit, he reaches for his phone, but for once there are no messages, not even from his mother; with her medication stable and her new interest in photography, the last few months have been good ones. It won't last, he knows that, and he suspects she does too, but he's grateful nonetheless.

5.40 a.m. On any other day, he'd go for a run. He can't face that, not today, but he needs to clear his head before going in to Burnett Road. He gets up, throws on some clothes and walks down to the Ness Islands.

This early in the morning, Inverness is barely awake; minimal traffic on the bridge, only the odd jogger or dog-walker making their way along the silver-dusted river. In a couple of hours, the city will come to life. Shop and office workers will appear, optimistic riverside bar and café owners will glance at the sky and put out tables. And the tourist season pipers will arrive, setting up by the Town House or the Market Steps to inflict 'Scotland the Brave' on as many eardrums as possible. There aren't many reasons Mahler's grateful for working in an anonymous sandstone building by a stretch of waste ground at the other end of town, but lack of proximity to the bagpipers from hell is definitely one of them.

He's reached the large clearing close to the play area before he's sure he's being followed. A first-time jogger struggling with the unaccustomed exercise, that's what he'd thought at first, but there's a clumsy attempt at stealth in the heavy-footed tread behind him. And when he bends to retie a lace, Mahler senses movement on the edges of his vision, as someone ducks back quickly towards the shelter of the trees.

Mahler looks round, casually, as though he's simply stopped for a breather. And spots the man almost immediately, lurking in ineffectual cover by a clump of alders. An attempt at intimidation – or is he simply no good at his job? Either way, Mahler's not inclined to cut him any slack. He turns and heads for the smaller of the bridges, making his way back towards the main road. If his tail is going to try anything, Mahler knows it has to be soon.

It happens as he reaches the path leading to the steps – the sound of lumbering footsteps, a burst of laboured breathing and a hand clamping down on his shoulder.

Mahler pivots, fast, and gets his attacker on the floor. Before he can react, Mahler drops with him, planting a knee in the small of his back to keep him there. With one hand on the man's neck and the other restraining his arm, Mahler takes a closer look at his assailant's beefy forearms and pudgy, tattooed neck as the man thrashes beneath him. And realises exactly where he's seen them before.

'Wullie.' Mahler stares down at the sweating, purple-faced shape of Cazza MacKay's favourite henchman, Wullie Grant. 'Out for an early-morning jog, were we?'

Grant gets one finger free, uses it to give a predictable gesture and bucks his hips in an attempt to dislodge Mahler. 'Get off – you're fucking suffocating me, man!'

'I'd be more concerned about your kidneys, if I were you.' Mahler presses his knee a little more firmly into Wullie's back, and the movement stops. 'Better. Now, you have a choice – stay there and inhale some more foliage while I call for backup, or tell me what's going on. Frankly, I don't mind which. Are we clear?'

Wullie growls something into the pile of leaves he's lying in.

Mahler decides it's probably an affirmative, and eases his pressure on the man's back. Slightly. 'Wise choice. So, talk.'

'Give me a fucking minute here!' Wullie spits out a leaf, glares at Mahler with the eye that isn't currently pressed earthwards. 'I've to give you a message – Mr MacKay has concerns he wants to discuss with you about the fire at his new gaff down the Longman. As a local businessman, he feels—'

'Cazza's feelings are not my problem. And, as he's no doubt been informed, the enquiry is being handled by CID, not the MIT. If he wants to discuss it with anyone there—'

'Mr MacKay wants to discuss it with you, pal. No one else. You've to come with me, and – Jesus, you're breaking my bloody back!'

The anger rushes in from nowhere, a dark engulfing tide. Pressing his knee into the man's back, pushing his nose and mouth further into the soil and leaves, Mahler looks down at his hands, curled into eager, damaging fists, and feels the burn of shame and memory. Not from nowhere, he concedes. The anger never comes from nowhere.

He slackens his grip on Wullie's neck, keeps his knee where it is but releases most of the pressure as he leans forward. 'Tell Cazza I'm a bit busy right now trying to find a missing child – as soon as a CID officer is available, I'll send them over to take a further statement. Say "yes" if you think you can manage that.'

He listens to Wullie's growl, opts to take it as an affirmative and nods.

'Right. I'm going to stand up now, and walk away. And so are you – in the opposite direction. Got it?'

An attempt at a nod. Good enough. Mahler releases his hold, moves quickly out of range.

Wullie scrambles up, shaking off random bits of greenery, and takes a step towards him, hands arranging themselves into damage-delivering mode.

Mahler shakes his head. 'Bad idea, Wullie. Very bad idea.' He stands his ground. Waits.

After a moment, Wullie gives a sullen shrug. 'Wouldn't dirty my hands with you, anyway. Not until Mr MacKay tells me to.'

'Very wise.' Mahler starts to walk away, turns back. 'By the way, you might want to have a word with your tattoo artist. Maybe buy him a dictionary, if you're planning any further work.'

Wullie plucks a final twig from his hair, drops it on the ground. 'Why the fuck would I want to do that?'

'Up to you, of course,' Mahler tells him. 'But it's supposed to be, "Living the Dream," Wullie. As in D-R-E-A-M. Not D-R-A-M.'

6.30 a.m. The MIT room at Burnett Road is empty apart from Nazreen, who's at her desk already, half hidden behind a pile of printouts and a giant coffee mug. Deep in concentration, she barely lifts her head to acknowledge his greeting, so Mahler carries on to his office to look through what Fergie's sent him on the arson attack. They're still waiting for the official Fire and Rescue Service report, but the initial off-the-record comments from the attending officers are pretty clear: Cazza MacKay's new venture had been comprehensively, deliberately torched.

'Picked just the right moment, too,' Fergie tells Mahler when he gets in. 'Whoever it was waited until the place was all fitted out and ready to open. Someone wanted to hit him where it would hurt most, boss. In the wallet.'

'That explains my encounter earlier this morning.' Mahler updates Fergie on his run-in with Wullie Grant. 'From which I gather our friend MacKay is well and truly rattled.'

Fergie nods. 'Pissed off someone he shouldn't have, sounds like. And the Fire and Rescue guys are saying it looks a bit more professional than some wee chancer with a can of petrol and a grudge. All the same, there's something about the feel of it . . .' Fergie shrugs. 'Sure you want me to pass it onto CID?'

Mahler looks across at the whiteboard with Erin MacKenzie's school photo. And back at his sergeant. 'We've got our hands full right now, wouldn't you say? Let them have it, Fergie.'

He watches the rest of the MIT as they file in for the morning briefing. And sees the same angry frustration on every weary face. After all the hours they've put in, after the appeals and the days of searching, finding Erin's bloodstained T-shirt has moved the forensic investigation forward. And hit the team's morale like a medicine ball in the guts.

They'll carry on pushing themselves, of course they will; it's what they do. But they need to feel they're getting somewhere. He needs to hold that promise out to them.

'Everyone here?'

A quick check round the room reveals a large, leather-clad exception; Andy Black's absence is irritating, but hardly unusual. And, frankly, not that much of a negative.

'Right, progress so far. Donna, where are we with tracking down Liam Buchan?'

'Hasn't been at his place in Burghead for a few weeks, boss. He did mention the weekend away with his girlfriend to a neighbour, though. The guy said Buchan asked him to sign for a delivery he was expecting. Apparently Buchan said he'd be back Tuesday morning to collect it.'

'Right.' He glances at his watch. 'Amanda McIver's cleaner said they were due back from Edinburgh this morning – head round there in a while and have a word. If Buchan's not there and she can't give us a straight answer as to his whereabouts, we'll organise a little reception committee for him when he collects his delivery in Burghead tomorrow morning.'

Mahler takes the briefing round the sub-teams. Faster than normal; keeping them on their toes and the questions to a minimum. Noting positives like the footage from the riverside CCTV and the high level of calls from the public after Fergie's media appearance. Because there's no way he can make his next update feel like any sort of positive.

'So, the items found yesterday by the final search team.'

Silence as they look at him; bracing themselves, he knows, for what's coming.

'I spoke to the MacKenzies last evening with Dawn. They've confirmed Erin went to the party wearing an identical T-shirt.'

Murmurs from the back of the room. He holds up his hand for silence.

'We don't have the forensics through yet, so for now that

information stays within this room. What we will be releasing shortly is a statement on one Maxwell Edward Bradley – yes, *that* Bradley. Out on licence less than a month ago and strongly suspected of taking a road trip to visit his mother who now lives in scenic Muir of Ord. Nazreen, you and DI Black spoke to Mrs Bradley yesterday?'

'Sir.' She darts a glance at the half-open door, frowns, and starts to read from her notes.

It shouldn't be down to her, of course; Andy Black should be here updating the team. But after that momentary flustered look, the report Nazreen gives is thorough and professional. So why is Mahler picking up a faint but growing unease from her as she delivers it?

As Fergie starts giving out the day's actions, Mahler takes Nazreen to one side and asks if she's heard from Andy Black.

'I think . . .' she glances at her notebook. 'DI Black may have said something about a meeting today. First thing.'

'First thing.' Aye, right. Fergie's favourite utterance floats into the air between them and takes up residence. 'Yesterday's visit to Mrs Bradley – is there anything else we should be aware of? Something that occurred to you afterwards, perhaps. We don't always pick up on these things immediately.'

'I reported all our progress, sir.' She looks across at Fergie, who's giving out the daily assignments. 'I think DS Ferguson has some actions for me, if that's everything?'

It isn't. Human interaction has never been Mahler's forte. But there's something going on here, something that goes beyond the usual mild distaste Andy evokes in female officers. He makes a mental note to have Fergie speak to her and heads to his office to make a start on the email and paperwork mountain that the daily admin demons delight in sending to his door.

He's barely got through the first half-dozen when a waft of expensive cologne from the doorway makes him look up.

'A useful briefing, this morning.' Chae Hunt closes the door, moves the overflow filing from its temporary home on the spare office chair and sits down. 'I caught the last few minutes on my way past. I assume we'll be chasing the forensics today? And following up on Bradley's last-known movements?'

So the lurker at the door hadn't been Andy Black, after all. 'Of course, sir.'

He gives Hunt a rundown of the team's planned actions. Watches Hunt nod in all the right places, ask all the right questions. And tries to shake the feeling he's watching an Oscar-worthy acting performance. Hunt's there for a reason, that's obvious. But it's not to get a rehash of the morning's briefing notes.

'Good, good.' When Mahler's finished, Hunt flashes his expensive bridgework in a faintly impatient smile. 'DCI Wallace assured me you were on top of things. I just wanted to impress on you the need to keep me – keep both of us – abreast of any developments as soon as they occur. The longer this case continues—'

'The more uncertainty Erin's parents have to endure. I'm aware of that, sir.'

'Of course. You'll also be aware that we need to look at managing our resources for maximum effectiveness.' A pause. 'The remains found at the Farr View development, for example – where are we with those?'

Mahler stares at Hunt. Tries to tell himself he must have misunderstood what the Chief's just asked him. 'Sir, it's barely been five days since CAHID took charge of the remains. Given that they almost certainly date from some seventy years ago, I wouldn't have thought—'

'That it's a priority? Of course not. But our "Slackbuie Man" is still a murder victim, Inspector. Someone's missing family member.'

Slackbuie Man. The phrase had appeared in the local press

soon after the discovery of the remains. Then the national media had picked it up by chance. Picked it up and run with it, stretching a minor story into days of increasingly bizarre speculation about the victim's identity. And Mahler begins to get a hint of where this is going.

'I heard the radio interview with Mr Thane this morning, sir. Quite a bit of disruption over at the building site, I understand – treasure-hunters and a couple of druids, wasn't it? Plus a paranormal investigator or two. But I'm not clear what you expect the MIT to do—'

'Then let me be clearer, DI Mahler. Get onto Dundee and get our victim identified. Speak to any surviving family, then pull something together for our friends in the media to put an end to all this woo-woo nonsense.'

'Now, sir? In the middle of the hunt for a missing child?'

Hunt's expression darkens. 'Watch your tone, Inspector. No one's suggesting you divert resources from the Erin MacKenzie enquiry—'

'That's exactly what you're doing – for something that's going to die down in a week or so anyway. And getting Fraser Thane off your back isn't—'

'That's enough!' Hunt gets up, takes a step towards him. Stops and shakes his head. 'You're under pressure, so I'll overlook that. This time. But here are two pieces of advice for you – learn to manage your resources more efficiently before bleating about additional workloads. And don't ever, ever make those kinds of insinuations again.' He crosses to the door, looks back at Mahler. 'Keep me informed, DI Mahler.'

Mahler makes himself stay seated as Hunt leaves. Keeps his hands on the desk in front of him, until the shuddering, urgent need to grab his laptop and introduce it to Hunt's head has passed. He closes his eyes, concentrates on the rhythm of his breathing.

The smell of blood and fear. His mother's screams—

No. Not now.

Mahler opens his eyes, makes his hands unclench. Makes the bright flow of anger through his veins cool and dissipate, until he can almost contemplate a morning at his desk, doing the sort of admin he suspects will ultimately turn him into someone like Hunt. Almost.

He opens his emails, finds the address for Dr Li at CAHID, sends her a quick query. And looks up to see Donna standing in the doorway, her hand poised to knock.

'Boss, you free? I saw you were with the Chief Super—'

'He's gone. But if this is any more bad news—'

A shake of her head. And a big enough grin to convince him that, for once, it's nothing of the sort. 'I rang Mandy McIver's mobile, just to check if they were back, and Buchan answered. And he's very keen to talk to us. Before we say a word to Mandy.'

12

Forty-five minutes later, a sweating, grey-faced Liam Buchan is sitting in an interview room in Burnett Road, glumly confessing the sordid details of a complicated lifestyle involving two 'serious' girlfriends, both of whom he's apparently engaged to. He signs his statement willingly and provides enough evidence to make it obvious he's telling the truth. To Mahler and Donna, at least.

'Cheating little bastard!' Donna watches Buchan make his way back to his car. 'No wonder he looks so shifty. How the hell has he managed to lead a double life for four bloody years?'

Mahler shrugs. 'His job, probably. Though he doesn't seem bright enough to keep it up forever. Let's head over to the McIvers' as planned – their initial statements need clarification on a couple of points, and I want to see the house's layout for myself.'

He's chosen to take his BMW rather than a pool car. But the look of distaste on Mandy McIver's face as she opens the door to him and Donna makes Mahler contemplate turning up in Fergie's repulsive Audi if he needs to make a second visit.

'I really don't know what else we can tell you.' A faint frown appears on her chemically enhanced forehead as she ushers them in. She takes them through to the open-plan family room, waves them over to a long leather sofa and perches on the edge of a seat opposite them. 'I mean, you talked to everyone at the time, didn't you? The house was full of police, and the girls were so upset—'

'Of course they were.' Donna gives a sympathetic smile. 'It must have been awful for them. And for you. But when something like this happens, folk often need a bit of time to get over the shock. That's why we like to talk to them again after a while, see if there's anything they maybe forgot to mention at the time. And you and Olivia are our most important witnesses, of course, so anything you can think of would be really helpful.'

'I don't see how we're witnesses.' A flicker of irritation in the wide, carefully made-up eyes. 'We didn't even know Erin had gone until the pizza was delivered.'

'Even so, we need you to take us through the day once more,' Mahler tells her. 'Unless you'd prefer to call in at Burnett Road to speak to us, of course—'

'God, no!' She pushes her chair back a little, gives him a horrified look. 'There's no need for that, surely? Livvy's got her dance class at eleven-thirty, though, so I'll need to be out of here by ten past at the latest.'

'We'll be done ages before then,' Donna assures her. 'So, you said in your statement the girls arrived between twelve and twelve-thirty.'

'More or less, yes. There were a couple of latecomers, but they were definitely all here by one. I'd set up a cute wee finger buffet for them in here, with lovely organic treats from this gorgeous little café my friend runs. And Livvy's birthday cake, of course. She wanted chocolate, but then we saw this darling unicorn one at the Courtyard in Dingwall—'

Mahler senses a detailed description of the cake is imminent and cuts in swiftly. 'So, lunch and cake around one. And afterwards?'

'The Beauty Box girls turned up for Livvy's pamper party. Eventually.' Her face tightens, a momentary tracery of lines appearing round her eyes and mouth. 'I'd told them no later than two, and I swear it was nearer half-past before they got started on the manicures. And they got glitter all over the bloody floor. They did knock a wee bit off the bill, mind you.'

Donna smiles her encouragement. 'I bet the girls loved it, though, didn't they?'

'Absolutely! They had their pampering sessions, then I put on Livvy's new Ariana Grande DVD. I was ready for a wee bit of peace by then, I can tell you.'

Mahler nods. 'Understandable. And you were with the girls all afternoon?'

'Of course I was! Do you think I'd go out and leave them on their own or something?'

Mahler glances at Donna. Yes, she's seen it too. A momentary sliding away of the eyes, a tightening of the mouth. Not an outright lie, perhaps, but it's not the whole truth, either. And they haven't got time for anything but the truth right now.

He glances at Donna's notes, making sure Amanda McIver sees him doing it, and leans forward.

'This is important, Mrs McIver. I need you to be very clear about this, so I'll ask you again – did you leave the girls alone at any point during the afternoon?'

'I told you, no! At least . . . I mean, I went to the bathroom. And once they'd settled down, I went and had a wee Prosecco in the lounge. What?'

'How long were you away for?'

A flush of colour creeping up her cheeks. 'I wasn't . . . Look, I was only in the other room, for God's sake! You make it sound like I'd abandoned them. I poured my Prosecco and had a wee sit-down— Christ, after three hours of ten-year-olds screaming their heads off, you'd have done the same. I was gone for maybe fifteen minutes. Twenty, tops.'

'Amanda, it's OK,' Donna produces a reassuring smile. 'No one's saying you did anything wrong. But you didn't tell us this at the time, and it could be important. Those sliding doors to the garden – did you have them open all afternoon?'

'Well, yes. It was a nice day, and they could always have a go on the trampoline if they wanted to let off steam. But if anyone had come in that way, I'd definitely have heard them.'

Over the noise of a dozen rampaging ten-year-olds, high on unicorn cake? Mahler doubts she'd have heard anything short of a marching band tramping through the flower beds that afternoon. And a quick glance at the garden tells him it slopes away from the house, towards the burn. If Erin's abductor had come from that direction, there's no way Amanda McIver could have seen him from the other room.

Mahler nods, thanks her for her help. He resists the urge to tell her it's probably ten days too late and asks if they could have a word with her daughter. 'Livvy might remember something too, you see. Something she forgot to tell us earlier.'

'I suppose so. She's still very upset, though. Traumatised, really.'

Amanda McIver goes to call her daughter.

Donna looks across at Mahler. 'Twenty minutes?'

'Long enough.' And based on what they've heard, he's not inclined to take that particular estimate as gospel.

Another shout from the hallway, followed by the sound of a slamming door and footsteps on the stairs. Moments later, Livvy comes in and sits across from Donna, tucking her legs up beneath her. She's a tiny, blue-eyed version of her mother, down to the glossy lips and off-the-shoulder top. Mahler can't detect any outward signs of the trauma Mandy had warned them about, but when Donna opens her pocket book, there's a flicker of wariness in the girl's eyes.

'Your mam told us about your lovely unicorn cake,' Donna tells her. 'And then the Beauty Box ladies came – how cool was that! Did everyone get a makeover? It must have taken a wee while.'

A shrug. 'I told the other police lady all about it when she was here. I had mine done first, because I was the birthday girl. I got a strawberry facial and a manicure.' She casts a critical eye at Donna's hands. 'You should get Shellac on those. Nice colour, though.'

'Thank you. What colour did you have on your nails?'

'Peacock Shimmer. Morgan had Fuchsia Flower, Jasmine didn't want her nails done but went for Tangerine Dream on her toes—'

'And Erin? Can you remember what she chose?'

'I . . .' A look of confusion crosses her face. 'I think maybe Erin didn't want anything done.'

'No facial, no nails? Nothing?' Donna looks up at the mother and back at Livvy. 'So, while the Beauty Box ladies were doing everyone's nails, what was Erin doing?'

An odd, sideways glance at her mother. 'I . . . I don't know. I don't remember.'

Donna gives her an encouraging smile. 'Okay. I know you talked to the other officer about this too, but I need you to think really hard for me now. When was the very last time you remember seeing Erin?'

'I told you, before the pizza came.'

Donna flicks back a couple of pages in her pocket book, glances at the section she's marked. 'Yes, that's right, you did say that. What was Erin doing when you saw her?'

'I . . . I don't know what you mean. She was just there.'

Another glance at her mother. 'We need to go to my class now. Miss Carter doesn't like us being late.'

Donna shakes her head. 'You won't be. I just wondered why you remember seeing her then. Was she talking to someone, or—'

'Morgan and Jasmine.' Livvy gives a triumphant grin. 'I remember now. Then she went to the loo.'

'No.' Mandy frowns. 'No, that . . . that's not right,' she tells Mahler. 'I heard Morgan talking to someone in the hall, then Erin came upstairs and went to the loo. But that was at about three-fifteen. I remember because I was watching an eBay auction that finished at ten past.'

Donna glances at Mahler, gives a slight shake of her head. As he'd thought, that definitely hadn't been part of the original statement.

He nods, turns back to Mandy. 'You're sure about the timing? And that it was definitely Erin who came upstairs at that point?'

'Yes, and yes.' Her voice is whisper-thin with shock. 'My bedroom door was open, and I caught a glimpse of her in the mirror. Look, I had no idea—'

'No. Unfortunately, neither did we. So just to be clear, the last time you saw Erin at the party would have been around three-fifteen?'

A horrified nod. Donna takes her through a revised statement as Livvy sits next to her mother, picking at the chipped polish on her thumbnail. No, Livvy shrugs when Donna tries to clarify what she'd said the last time. No, she wasn't sure if she'd seen Erin after three o'clock. Maybe it was a girl who looked a bit like Erin? She must have got mixed up, that's all. No, there's nothing else she wants to tell them about the party. Nothing at all.

Donna closes her pocket book, glances at Mahler, who nods. Livvy's not telling them everything that happened at the party, that much is obvious, but they're not going to get anything more from her today. He thanks Mandy for her time. And leaves, before he's tempted to say anything else.

'We'll speak to the other girls again, boss.' Donna catches up with him as he reaches the car. 'Find out what they were talking to Erin about, whether they can remember seeing her later than Livvy did. At least we're closer to a real timeline now.'

'We're closer, all right. We now know we can forget about that twenty-minute timeframe we've been working on – and all the checks we've done on our friends on the register? They're going to have to be done again, every single one of them. Because Erin MacKenzie could have gone missing any time from three-fifteen to bloody six o'clock.'

Tam Bell shared Police Scotland, Highlands & Islands Police Division's post:
35 mins

Highlands & Islands Police Division today released details of a man they are keen to talk to in connection with the disappearance of Erin MacKenzie on Friday, 20 May.

Maxwell Edward Bradley, aged 38, was released from Leyhill Open Prison in Gloucestershire on 18 April but failed to comply with the conditions of his licence. His licence has therefore been revoked.

Bradley is described as being 180 cms tall, of average build, with mid-brown hair and brown eyes. He has an English accent and may have grown a beard since his release. He is believed to have connections to the Highland area.

Police Scotland is appealing to the public for any information which could help to trace him. Anyone with information about Bradley's whereabouts should call police on 101 or Crimestoppers on 0800 555 111.

---

416 Shares

Dylan Main 2hrs:
Is this the guy that took Erin? What's the pedo bastard doing up here?

Ewan Polson replied:
That's him.

89

Tam Bell:
It's him all right. Can't share the link for some reason, but google him. Guy's a fucking monster, got put away for 6 years and he's out already. Needs finding and stringing up pronto.

Dylan Main replied:
Your joking. Too quick. Needs to be locked in a room with a couple of hungry Rottweilers, see how long he'll fucking last then. Or the parents of those poor bairns. They'd soon sort him out.

Izzy MacLeod:
Oh my God. They think he's up here? ANIMAL! How come he's out of prison anyway?? Makes me sick.

Tam Bell:
Makes us all bloody sick. Supposing the cops get him, what then? Back into a comfy wee single room at another open prison. What are scum like that even doing in an open prison? None of this rehabilitation bollocks. Once a pedo, always a pedo.

Dylan Main:
See if I ever got my hands on him, he wouldn't last 5 minutes.

Ewan Polson:
Aye, right . . .

Dylan Main:
Aye, it is fucking right! You got a problem with that?

Izzy MacLeod:
Dylan, Ewan This is meant to be a support group for Erin's family. We ask you not to swear and not to make threats or say things that might lead to violence or people taking the law into their own hands. Could I ask you to read the pinned post at the top of this page and please moderate your language. Thank you.

Facebook Messenger:

Message Requests
You have added **Ewan** to Messenger.
Dylan has added you to the secret group, **Justice for Erin.**

Ewan:
What's this secret group bollocks?

Dylan:
Thought we could have a better talk here than in the other group.
Tam's in too. That Izzy woman was getting on my tits. No swear-
ing, no action, just a lot of oh dear isnt it awful.

Tam:
Hes right. While were fannying about in Facebook groups that
pedo's out there right now, doing god knows what to that wee
lassie. Makes me sick to think about it.

Ewan:
Me too. Were not the cops, though. What can we do about it?

Dylan:
Depends if your all talk or if you want to do something about him.
I mean, really do something.

Tam:
Like what? You don't even know where he is.

Ewan:
Maybe hes psychic. Got a couple of crystal balls.

Dylan:
Ha fucking ha. If your serious about getting off your arses and
doing something about him, theres ways and means, but we can't
go into them on here. Send me your mobile numbers and we'll
talk.

13

Day 11

Tuesday, 31 May

6.30 a.m. Fergie coaxes the Audi into its usual space by the recycling bins at Burnett Road. All in all, he thinks, the car's running well enough considering that wee bump he had a week ago – clutch is a bit sticky, but the burning-rubber smell the boss is always complaining about seems to have disappeared. Well, more or less. He shoulders the door open and climbs out, looking round to see what sort of a day it's going to be.

No rain, not yet, but Ben Wyvis is swathed in cloud and there's a heaviness in the air which usually means it'll be throwing it down by lunchtime. It's the sort of grey, cheerless morning that makes Fergie wonder if Andy Black hadn't had the right idea about upping sticks and heading across the pond for a life of pulling pints in the Florida sun.

No one's quite sure what went wrong for him over there. Fergie's heard rumours, of course, about some sort of financial falling-out with his brother, but he reckons it's much simpler than that. There are a few jobs he can imagine Andy doing if he finally leaves the force, but they mainly involve leather jackets and glowering. No surprise if he couldn't cut it as a smiley, how're-you-doing-there pub landlord type.

There's no sign of Andy's Honda in the car park, which is

absolutely fine by Fergie. What he's been doing these past few mornings . . . well, he's pretty sure the boss wouldn't object. It's on his own time, after all, and it's connected with a case they're working on. All the same, it's not what you'd call officially sanctioned, and he probably doesn't need to bother the boss about it. Yet.

Fergie looks round again, locks the Audi and walks across to the entrance.

'I didn't speak to Erin at all at Livvy's party. I don't know why Livvy would say I did. I'm not friends with Erin and I don't think Livvy is either. I asked her why she'd invited Erin, but Livvy just said it would be fun. I didn't see Jasmine speaking to her either. I don't know why Livvy said she did, but maybe she thought it was someone else.'

Donna closes her notebook, gives Mahler a weary look. 'We got the same crap from Jasmine, except she turned on the waterworks when Naz asked her if she was absolutely sure. Sorry, boss – it's like they've learned a bloody script or something. I'm damn sure they're lying their heads off, but I don't think we'll get anything else from them. We've still got a couple of girls to speak to again, though . . . and I got the feeling they're not all fans of Livvy McIver and her pals.'

'So why would she invite them?' Mahler shakes his head. 'Never mind. Talk to the other girls and then give Livvy another go – if anything happened at that party which might have caused Erin to leave under her own steam, we need to know about it.'

'Will do.' At the door to his office, Donna turns back. 'Boss, the forensics that came back . . . it's been eleven days, now. If Erin was hurt when that bastard took her, if she was bleeding that much—'

'I know. But we'll find her, Donna. We will.'

He watches the door close behind her. Hopes his words hadn't sounded as hollow to her they did to him. But after this morning's briefing, when he'd broken the news that the blood on the T-shirt was a match for Erin, he'd seen the team's reaction.

They'd expected it, of course they had. Nodded, squared their shoulders and filed out to get on with the day; Pete had retreated to his stuffy viewing room to pull in more CCTV footage based on the revised timeline. Fergie had gone back to checking out Anthea Bradley's movements over the last few weeks and co-ordinating the other lines of enquiry. Andy Black, never one to look a gift opportunity in the mouth, had gone to do what he does best, banging on doors and shouting as he seized the chance to revisit the area's small, repellent cache of registered sex offenders. And every one of them had done it carrying a little less hope with them.

Mahler finishes emailing his update to June and pulls up Maxwell Bradley's file again. He looks at the calm, unremarkable face that Bradley's patients had put their trust in only a few years ago.

By the time he'd been released, that face had changed. Scarred by a knife attack during his first year inside, the image staring up at Mahler from the final page of Bradley's file is a face a child would shrink from. A face, surely, that would stay in the memory of anyone who'd glimpsed it? And yet, with a beard to hide the scars, perhaps a thick pair of glasses—

His mobile buzzes on his desk. He doesn't recognise the number, but the voice belongs to Craig Falconer, one of the forensic anthropologists who'd been sent by CAHID to look at the remains found at Slackbuie.

'Inspector?' Falconer sounds simultaneously excited and embarrassed as he apologises for not responding sooner to Mahler's email. 'Lauren only forwarded your email late yesterday or I'd have got in touch earlier. I've just sent you and Sergeant Ferguson the cleaned-up images I mentioned the other day – you know, the ones from my mate, the World War Two specialist?'

It's news to Mahler. So Fergie's been following this up on his own? 'Perhaps you could refresh my memory about your discussion.'

'Oh. Okay. Well, as I told Sergeant Ferguson, we were right about the first set of dog tags – British Army, World War Two issue. Reasonably well preserved given their age, so—'

A knock at the door. Fergie's face peering through the blind. Mahler sighs, asks Falconer to wait a moment. He beckons Fergie in and puts the scientist on speaker. 'I'm sorry, go on.'

'Right. Well, we should be able to decipher the wording on those quite quickly for you – that should give you a surname and rank to work with, at least. But the second set of tags are the really interesting ones. Quite poorly preserved, sadly, so I'm not sure how much information we'll be able to recover from them. But Sergeant Ferguson was spot on. As you'll see from the images I've sent you, the second set of tags were standard Wehrmacht issue – sorry, that means they were German army tags, and—'

Mahler resists the urge to eye-roll. 'I'm aware of what that means. Please, continue.'

'Right. Well, that brings me to the most fascinating part of the whole story – the gun found with the remains.'

In spite of himself, Mahler's intrigued. 'Are you telling me it wasn't the weapon used in the victim's murder?'

'Oh, it's the murder weapon all right,' Falconer assures him. 'No question about that. But it's not a British sidearm. It's a P08 Pistole Parabellum – better known as a German Luger.'

'So the murder victim was buried with a set of German army dog tags and shot with a German army-issue pistol?'

'Intriguing, isn't it? Quite a story there, I'm guessing, even if it is a cold case.' Falconer gives a low chuckle. 'Times like these, I wish I could borrow the Tardis for a couple of hours, don't you?'

'Indeed.' Mahler thanks Falconer for his input, ends the call and turns to Fergie, whose crack-of-dawn, extra-early starts over the past week are suddenly starting to make sense. Along with the ongoing mystery of Donna's disappearing biscuit stash.

'It's still an ongoing investigation, boss. I wasn't taking any time away from the Erin MacKenzie case—'

Mahler holds up his hand. 'Perhaps not. But you worked unauthorised overtime on this case, on top of the extra we've all been putting in on Erin MacKenzie, flouted God knows how many health and safety regulations . . . and you kept me completely in the dark about the whole thing, making me look like a prize pillock in the process. God Almighty, Fergie, when were you going to tell me what you were up to – five minutes before you keeled over at your desk?'

'Sorry, boss.' Fergie attempts to look contrite. 'But that's what I was coming to tell you. I've traced the family who lived at the farm during the war, and one of the daughters is still alive. Not only that, but she's still in this area. She's over eighty, but she sounds sharp as a tack, and—'

'You've already spoken to her?'

'Sort of, aye. Obviously I didn't go into detail – didn't want to upset the poor wifie by talking about dead bodies over the phone – but I was thinking I could maybe take a wee turn over there to see her. Just to tie things up, like.'

'And how long's that going to take?'

'Ach, not long, boss. Fifteen minutes there, wee chat, fifteen back? Less, if we take your car.'

'Don't push your luck.'

Fergie doesn't need a DI along for the ride; he's more than capable of following this up on his own, and they both know it. Mahler's got enough admin on his desk to keep him occupied for the rest of the week, and June Wallace is going to be screaming for it long before that. Anyway, taking a personal interest in the case would feel a little too much like dancing to Chae Hunt's tune for Mahler's taste.

And yet . . . a Luger, and a set of German dog tags, buried with a wartime murder victim. Mahler has to admit, it's intriguing . . . and, he suspects, nothing like the tick-box, media-friendly story the Chief is hoping for.

'Fine.' He picks up his keys, closes the laptop. 'Fill me in on the way. But no more covert ops like this one, understood? I'll cover your arse this time if anyone queries what you've been up to, but don't count on it again.'

It takes the full fifteen minutes to get to Ella Kirkpatrick's house on the outskirts of Culloden, even in Mahler's BMW. The local schools won't break up for another month, but the Highland tourist season has already started. The cruise ships have returned to Invergordon, and Mahler's forced to crawl behind one of the vast tour buses chartered by the cruise lines until it lumbers off towards the battlefield.

'Culloden, then the Clava Cairns,' Fergie tells him. 'That's where they'll be off to. It's all that *Outlander* stuff – you know, the bit where Claire goes through the stones and ends up getting chased by a bastard redcoat? The Yanks are just daft for it. Mind you, some of the things I've heard of folks getting up to out there—'

'Spare me. Please.'

Mahler turns off the main road, follows the satnav for a mile or so past dense Forestry Commission woodland until they come to what looks like an old farm track.

The building at the end of the track would have been the original farmhouse, Mahler assumes, although someone's added a modern glass extension to the traditional stone building. There's what looks like a semi-derelict byre to the side of the farmhouse and a further track looping back towards the main road. Halfway down this second track, backing onto a cluster of trees, stands a modern, white-harled bungalow with a disabled-access ramp outside.

'Odd kind of place to end up, at her age,' Fergie comments as Mahler pulls up. 'You'd think she'd want folk round about her, in case . . . well, just in case.'

'Perhaps Mrs Kirkpatrick prefers her own company.' A not unreasonable standpoint, in Mahler's view. 'Let's see what she can tell us about our mystery man, shall we?'

Before they get halfway up the path, the bungalow's front door opens. An elderly woman with a cloud of thick, silver hair takes a couple of careful steps to meet them, holding out a hand in greeting. Ella Kirkpatrick is leaning heavily on a stick and one side of her mouth is pulled slightly awry, but there's a sharp, measuring quality in the look she gives them.

'Inspector Mahler . . .' her eyes switch from Mahler to Fergie, and back again. 'Yes, that's you, isn't it?' She frowns, puts her head on one side, as though she's trying to work something out. 'Not quite home yet, not in the ways that matter. You will be, though, in time.'

'I'm sorry?'

She shakes her head. 'No, I'm sorry. I get wee . . . wee flashes about folk sometimes, that's all. Just ignore me.' She turns to smile at Fergie. 'We spoke on the phone, didn't we? So you must be Sergeant Ferguson . . . well, come in, come in. I'm afraid you've had a wasted journey, though.'

She takes them through to a small, neat lounge with French doors opening out onto a paved sitting area, with a substantial cottage-style garden beyond.

'You said you wanted to talk to me about the old farm.'

'About the remains that were found there, yes. You said you saw an article about it in the *Courier*?'

Ella nods. She waves them over to a pair of surprisingly contemporary-looking armchairs and eases herself down onto the remaining chair, an old-fashioned leather wing-back, with a hiss of pain. 'You can't imagine . . . I just couldn't believe what I was reading.'

'It must have been quite a shock. But you'll understand we're keen to find out anything which might help us identify the victim.'

'Goodness me, yes.' The hint of a shudder in her voice. 'Of course, you'll have all your procedures to go through, won't you? Even though it was so long ago.'

'He'll have had a family, though,' Fergie tells her. 'Maybe they're all gone now, but we've still got to do our best for him.' He explains about the two sets of dog tags found with the body. 'That's all we've got, Ella. So if there's anything you can tell us – anything at all – it would be really helpful.'

'I . . . yes, of course. I see.' She glances uncertainly at Mahler. 'But I was only a little girl during the war, Inspector. I don't think there's anything . . . Oh my goodness, I completely forgot to offer you a cup of tea. Would you like some? I've got a tray ready in the kitchen—'

Before she can struggle to her feet, Mahler shakes his head. 'But thank you. We were hoping you could give us a little background about the farm at that time. You lived there with your parents, and . . .' he glances at Fergie, 'your sister May. But there was no one else working on the farm?'

A shake of her head. 'It was just us. Oh, before the war you'd get a few poor souls needing a day's work, but then all the men were called up, weren't they? May moved away in 1949, and we . . . we lost touch, I'm afraid. She died in 1960.'

'I'm sorry. It's a long time ago, I know, but can you remember any unusual happenings during the war? Any unexpected visitors, maybe? Even if it mightn't have seemed that odd at the time.'

'During the war?' She gives him a gently incredulous look. 'With petrol rationing and rail travel reduced to the absolute minimum? The Highlands were practically closed off, Inspector. And there was nothing out of the ordinary about our lives, nothing at all.' She closes her eyes, leans her head back for a moment. 'They were good years, you know, mostly. It surprises a lot of folk to hear that, but it's true. Farming was a reserved occupation, so my dad wasn't called up. It was hard work, though, even when the POWs started coming—'

Fergie leans forward. 'There were German prisoners of war working at the farm? Are you sure?'

'Oh, yes. Italians first, then Germans later on. There was a camp somewhere out Torbreck way, I think.' She gives a faint smile. 'I remember the first time we saw them, May and me. Staring at them as though we expected them to have two heads and a tail or something. They didn't, though. They were just . . . men. Tired, sad men, far from their homes.' Her eyes widen. 'Oh my goodness, you don't think – I mean, there were rumours afterwards that some of them were SS, but they didn't seem that dangerous, not to me. You don't think maybe one of them had something to do with this?'

'I think it's unlikely. But thank you, you've been very helpful,' Mahler tells her. 'We won't take up more of your time, but . . . no, please, you don't need to—' He holds up his hand to forestall her, but she's getting to her feet, leaning on her stick and the arm of her chair to push herself laboriously upright.

'Nonsense. It's only manners to show your visitors out.' She sets off slowly for her front door, Fergie and Mahler following. 'Sorry I'm a little slow – not too good on my legs since I had that stroke a while back.' She glances at Fergie, shakes her head.

'Don't look at me like that, Sergeant, I'm fine here on my own. My neighbour's a doctor, and I get a Tesco delivery each week – so I'm not ready for the old folks' home just yet.'

'It would be nice to have a bit of company, though, wouldn't it? Must get lonely out here by yourself sometimes.'

She smiles at Fergie. 'You're not a man who does well on his own, are you? But I couldn't be doing with people around me all the time. It would have you running for the hills too, wouldn't it, Inspector?'

The sudden humour in the sharp old eyes takes Mahler by surprise. 'It certainly would. Enjoy your independence as long as you can, Mrs Kirkpatrick. There's nothing further we need to talk to you about right now, but if you think of anything else that could help us. . .' he holds out his card to her. 'Please?'

For a moment, he doesn't think she's going to take it. Then she nods slowly. 'I'll get in touch, of course. But it was all so long ago . . . whoever killed that man, they must be dead themselves by now. And there's a wee girl still missing from the town, isn't there? Missing for nearly two weeks, the *Courier* said.' She gives him a gently reproachful look. 'I don't mean to tell you your job, Inspector. But surely it's her you should be looking for? Not another dead man.'

14

Back at Burnett Road, Mahler heads for his office. And runs into Pete Noble, taking the stairs two at a time on his way from his third-floor viewing cupboard, a laptop under his arm and looking more like an excitable ginger Labrador than ever.

'Boss, I think we've got something. A vehicle. I was running through the Archive Centre footage again, and—'

Mahler's mobile buzzes in his pocket. He pulls it out, half glances at the text, but it's only a standard meeting reminder from his mother's support worker. He sets the phone to mute, nods at Pete. 'The MIT room. Show me.'

With Andy Black out thumping on doors in Merkinch and the rest of the team on follow-ups, only Donna and Nazreen are at their desks, pulling a report together. Mahler beckons them over as Pete sets up the laptop.

'I'd been working back from the report of Celeste's attempted abduction,' Pete tells them. 'Gave it a decent tolerance either way, in case it was the guy those walkers had reported seeing at the river. And this is what I turned up.' He hits play, and the image of a light-coloured van parked by the Archive Centre fills the screen. 'It's not great quality, and the angle means I can't get a clear view of the number plate. But it's clearly a scruffy old van, right?'

Naz starts to say something, but Pete holds up his hand. 'Aye, I know. It could just be a couple of workies parked up, having their lunch. But it just . . . it didn't sit right with me, somehow. So then I took another look at the traffic footage from the junction at Columba Gardens on the day Erin disappeared – wound it right back to the morning this time. And look what turns up just after 11 a.m.'

Donna comes closer, peers at the footage of a grimy white van turning into the site of the new housing development that's taking shape close to the McIvers' house. And shakes her head. 'Pete, it's just a contractor's van. We watched half a dozen like that going in and out of the site when we were down there that first day – and we checked with the site office. Every single van that came in there got logged in and out.'

'You didn't check this one. I'll bet my Eleven Doctors anniversary T-shirt you didn't, because I don't think it was there. Take a good look at the van, then I've got one more clip to show you.'

The number plates are too grimy to decipher, but Mahler spots a dent on the nearside wing. And the thing that sits between his shoulder blades, the instinctive something he's learning not to dismiss too easily these days, gives a faint, anticipatory twitch.

'Okay, here it is.' Pete runs the final clip. Time-stamped at 5.45 pm, it shows a line of vehicles leaving the site and turning onto the main road. Mahler counts three light-coloured vans, a couple of beaten-up cars, two dark 4x4s. And, at the tail end of the line, a grimy white van with mud-covered number plates and a dent on the nearside wing.

Donna folds her arms, frowns at Pete. 'I don't get it. Yes, it's the same van both times, there's a dent on the wing – I get that. But what do you mean, it wasn't there?'

'It wasn't at the site.' Nazreen looks at the frozen image of the van and back at Pete. 'I mean, it wasn't part of the traffic leaving the site, was it?'

'What better way to hide?' Mahler stares at the screen. And calls himself several kinds of half-wit for not working it out sooner. 'There was a track running along by the burn, wasn't there?' He wouldn't have said it was wide enough for something van-sized, but with care and determination . . . 'Erin's abductor waited there, screened by the trees. And then he joined the line of genuine site traffic leaving in the evening.'

'No one would have noticed one more van, would they? And there's no CCTV until you come to the junction,' Pete points out. 'So, yes, I think that's what he did. He took Erin, he put her in the van . . . and then he drove her out under everyone's noses. And she wasn't even reported missing until after he'd gone.'

Silence; thick, appalled. Sickened. A look of rising horror on their faces as they start to process what that might mean.

Donna reaches out, slams the laptop shut. 'Christ, I can't look at that any longer. That bastard—'

'Okay, enough.' Mahler clears his throat. Shuts down the slideshow that's started playing in his head of Maxwell Bradley's uncounted, unnamed victims. 'We can stand around being horrified, or we can use what we've learned to get out there and find her.'

His muted mobile vibrates in his jacket; another reminder, probably. He ignores it, turns to Pete.

'We can try for a partial plate, can't we? I know the quality's bad, but do the best you can with the images we've got. Donna, grab Big Gary and go out to the site – I don't believe no one noticed the van the entire time it was parked there. Did no one get out to stretch their legs, answer a call of nature? For heaven's sake, someone must have seen something!'

There's no 'must' about it, of course. Another unwelcome image flashes into his mind, of Erin's abductor, rank and sweating in the darkness of his van as he waited to carry out the final stage of his plan. Because it was planned, Mahler's convinced of that. But why there? Why then? Why Erin?

'Nazreen, I need you to—'

'Sir, the van.' There's a look of sudden realisation stamped across her face. 'I didn't think anything of it at the time . . . but when DI Black and I visited Anthea Bradley, there was a light-coloured van parked by the foot of her drive.'

15

Day 12
Wednesday, 1 June

There's no sign of a van as Mahler and Nazreen pull up outside the cottage at 9 a.m.; not the grimy white one from the CCTV footage Pete had found, at least. A battered green pickup truck with a dandelion logo is parked by a crumbling summer house and, further up the drive, two men in overalls are unloading a local glazier's van. But Anthea Bradley's car is missing. The mobile number she'd supplied goes straight to voicemail, and when Nazreen tries the landline again, they hear it ringing out unanswered in the cottage.

'She's no' here, pal.' The older of the two men puts down a toolbox by the front porch and walks over, squinting at them in the sun. 'But if you've come to measure up for the kitchen . . .' he spots the warrant card Mahler's holding up, and a look of relief crosses his face. 'She called you, then. Good.'

'I'm sorry?'

'That's why you're here, isn't it?' He turns, points at three window frames propped by the door. 'Bloody vandals! She's only just moved in, too.'

Mahler bends to examine the frames. They're the old-fashioned, multi-paned style, and he'd assumed they were being replaced with something more modern. But when he looks more closely, he can see that every one of the panes has been smashed.

'Do you know when it happened?'

'Last night – got the call from her this morning. Normally we wouldn't have managed to get out here so quickly, but we'd a job booked down in the Muir, and . . .' he shrugs. 'She said it wasn't urgent, said it was just kids, but I could tell the poor wifie was really shaken up. Will you be dusting for fingerprints or something?'

'Not at this stage.' Mahler silently curses the report that had come in the previous afternoon of another abduction attempt at one of the local schools. It had turned out to be a false alarm, but it had tied up the team for hours, meaning he'd needed to reschedule the planned visit to Anthea Bradley until this morning. 'Did Mrs . . . did Anthea say when she'd be back?'

The man shakes his head. 'Just said she's got a couple of appointments in Inverness. Do you want me to get her to ring you?'

Mahler hands him a card. 'As soon as possible, please. In the meantime, we'll have a look round.'

Nazreen gives him an anxious look as she follows him inside. 'Should we be doing this, sir? I mean, we don't have a warrant, and—'

'And we have good reason to suspect a crime has been committed.' He glances round the kitchen and living room and heads for the stairs. 'Though I'll lay odds Mrs Bradley's got no intention of reporting it.'

Upstairs, there's a narrow landing with two small bedrooms but no bathroom. The slightly larger of the two is obviously Anthea Bradley's. The other looks as though it would struggle to house anything bigger than a child's bed, and is in the process of being converted into an en suite. Mahler looks in briefly and heads for the other room.

'You really think her son's been hiding here?'

Mahler crosses to the window. And finds what he's been looking for. 'I'd guess someone certainly thinks so.' He beckons to Nazreen. 'Look at this.' He holds back the curtain so she can see the shattered glass for herself. 'Every single pane, just like downstairs. Just like the other room. This isn't some bored teenage vandal, Nazreen – this was a deliberate, sustained attack. And I guarantee Anthea Bradley wasn't targeted at random. I'm guessing whoever did this knows exactly who she is. And who her son is.'

'How? She's changed her name, she's never used social media – someone would have had to have been watching every move she's made for years. Either that, or. . .'

Or there's been a leak. Mahler doesn't spell it out; the look on Nazreen's face tells him he doesn't need to.

She shakes her head. 'It has to be someone at the Met. I can't believe anyone in our team—'

'Where it's come from doesn't matter right now. If there *has* been a leak, Anthea Bradley's lucky to have escaped with a few broken windows. Let's take a look outside, shall we? Those gardeners seem very busy by that old summer house.'

'It's a wreck, sir. DI Black inspected it when we were here and he almost fell through the floor.'

'It's also an excellent vantage point to observe the cottage from,' Mahler points out. 'That makes it worth a second look.' Though he suspects there won't be anything to find; if Maxwell Bradley had been discovered hiding here, it's likely they'd be looking at more than some minor vandalism right now. Which doesn't mean that the stone-throwers have given up. Or that Bradley's mother might not be in danger. He tells Nazreen to check out the rear of the cottage, and continues up to the summerhouse.

The *Bizzy Lizzies* gardeners, two young women in sturdy

boots and overalls, are clearing what looks like decades of weed growth from a patch of ground close to the summerhouse.

'Vegetable garden,' the dark-haired one tells Mahler. 'Anthea's very keen on being self-sufficient out here. Knowledgeable, too.'

'Indeed.' Mahler pushes open the summerhouse door, releasing a mushroom cloud of dust, and looks inside. The wooden floor has completely fallen away in places, and the remaining boards look as though no one's trodden them for years. 'Quite a job you've taken on, isn't it? Have you been here all week?'

It is a big job, dark-haired Kerry agrees. Yes, they did start on Monday. They don't recall seeing a white van parked by the house, but they've made a couple of trips to the tip with the stuff they've cleared from the garden, so they haven't been here all the time. And Anthea's had folk calling at the house every day about all the improvements she's got planned for the cottage.

'She's on her own, then? No partner, anything like that?'

'Not that I've seen,' Kerry tells him. 'I might be wrong, but I got the feeling she'd had a bad time with someone. Needed to make a fresh start, get right away from things. And if you're from down south . . . well, this must seem about as far from anywhere as you can get, don't you think?'

Mahler looks back down at the cottage. It's not that far from the village, but the track leading up there is easy to miss. And after years of neglect, the cottage's garden has almost vanished, surrendered to the creep of bramble and dog-rose bushes. He can see why, if Kerry's right, Haven Cottage might have looked like the perfect hideaway to Anthea Bradley. But did she genuinely want to escape her past, or had she always planned to create a bolthole for her evil son on his release from prison? Surely Max Bradley wouldn't have been content to hide here for very long?

He thanks Kerry and heads back to the car as Nazreen appears from the path leading to the rear of the cottage.

'Nothing?'

She pulls half a dozen burrs off her jacket and shakes her head. 'No sign of anyone living rough either. Sir, for what it's worth, I think Mrs Bradley was being straight with us. I know I've not been on the team long, but—'

'But nothing,' Mahler tells her. 'You're smart, you're hard-working, and your judgement's as valid as anyone else's. And I happen to agree with you – I don't think we'll find Max Bradley here either.'

Someone does, though. Someone knows exactly who Anthea Newman is. And who her son is. The question is, how?

'We still need to talk to Anthea, though. Come on, time to get back to the shop.'

16

At Burnett Road, Mahler goes to find June Wallace and bring her up to date. It's not a task he's looking forward to; once he tells the DCI someone's leaking sensitive information on a high-profile case like this, she'll have to call in Professional Standards. And once the suits have been summoned, they'll descend on the MIT like a pack of ravening, sharp-suited dementors. Mahler's had experience of trying to run a big enquiry with PS breathing down his neck, and it's not something he's keen to repeat.

As he knocks on June's door, his mobile buzzes; three angry bursts, like a trapped wasp. He's reaching for the phone with his other hand when the door is wrenched open, and his raised fist stops inches short of hitting Chae Hunt in the face.

'Inspector.' The Chief looks him up and down. 'Glad you could make it . . . eventually. Come in.'

Make what? Mahler glances at his mobile as he follows Hunt inside. And watches the screen fill with messages he hasn't had time to look at. Including one from June telling him to get back to Burnett Road for an urgent two o'clock with Hunt and Andy Black.

'Sorry, ma'am.' A glower from Black as June waves Mahler

to a seat. 'I'm afraid your message was delayed. Have there been any developments?'

'Developments.' June swivels her iPad towards him. 'You could say that, aye. Christ, Lukas! I thought Dawn was watching out for crap like this?'

With a slow build of anger curling in his gut, Mahler skim-reads the article on the tabloid's website.

As a hatchet job on his team's performance to date, it's a pretty good one, he'll give the writer that much. The MacKenzies' exhausted faces stare up at him beneath a banner headline asking 'Why Can't Police Find Our Erin?' The article goes on to give a day-by-day account of the case so far, with quotes from 'a source close to the investigation'. And ends with an image of him and Fergie walking away from the site where Erin's T-shirt had been found. Thanks to the photographer, Fergie's acquired an extra chin and a village-idiot expression. And the angle Mahler's been snapped at makes him look as though he's auditioning for the lead in a straight-to-Netflix vampire movie.

'Ma'am, this isn't Dawn's fault. The MacKenzies are close to breaking, and—'

'I don't care whose fault it is! That wee girl's been missing for two weeks and her parents are up the bloody wall!' June shakes her head. 'Two fucking weeks, Lukas. And this "sources close to the investigation" shite . . . this is them just pissing in the wind, right? Because if it isn't—'

'I'm not sure, ma'am.' Mahler updates her and Hunt on his visit to the cottage. 'I think we've been looking in the wrong place,' he finishes. 'If Max Bradley wants to disappear, he'll do it properly – and he's got to know his mother is the first person we'd talk to. I can't see him being that predictable. Plus, if he's using the van we caught on CCTV, all he has to do is keep on the move.'

'Skivey Pete's trying to get a partial plate,' Black puts in. 'If we can get that—'

'It'll help, yes. And CSI have taken tyre impressions from the track by the building site.' Mahler doesn't point out the impressions will only be useful if they get their hands on the van; even Andy Black should be able to fill in the blanks on that one. 'But what I saw at the cottage looked like a deliberate attempt to intimidate, ma'am.'

'You're sure it wasn't just vandals?'

Mahler shakes his head. 'She'd been targeted. By someone who knows exactly who she is. And who her son is. Which means—'

'We're making sod all progress and leaking like a bloody sieve,' Chae Hunt snaps. 'Yes, thank you, DI Mahler. I'd worked that out for myself.' He turns to June Wallace as his mobile bleeps an alert. 'I'm supposed to be on my way to Gartcosh by now. Get to the bottom of this, June, and do it quickly. The last thing we need is Professional Standards crawling all over us.'

Silence as the door closes behind Hunt. June sighs, rubs the muscles at the base of her neck. 'You heard the Chief. Any bright ideas before we call in the suits? Because they're like sodding vampires, that lot. Invite them in once, and—'

'We don't need them.' A dull red tide creeps up Andy Black's neck as June and Mahler turn to look at him. 'I mean, I think I might have said something.' He swallows. 'Been overheard saying something. Sorry, ma'am.'

'Tell me you didn't say what I thought you just said. Tell me you couldn't possibly have been that stupid.'

Black flushes again. 'I was talking to one of the DCs after the last appeal. I thought the press guys had all packed up, but there must have been one still hanging around. Bastard.'

'Jesus Christ, Andy.' June gives him a look that would blister paint. 'Are you sure?'

'Can't see how else it could have happened, boss. Unless . . .' he looks suddenly uncomfortable. 'Ach no, Naz wouldn't have spoken out of turn. Surely not.'

'DC Khan?' Mahler shakes his head. 'She left to do follow-ups with Donna, if you remember, Andy. You're probably right about the press stragglers, though – but then most officers could put their hands up to being caught out once or twice like that, Ma'am. In fact, didn't the Chief once—'

'Enough!' June glares at them both. 'Just a stupid fuck-up, eh, Andy? Well, God knows that's not hard to believe, given your recent track record! No, don't waste my time trying to make excuses – go and get that bloody van traced. Lukas, you stay there. We're not finished yet.'

She waits until Black has left, turns to Mahler. 'Right, then – so why the hell didn't you send Fergie out to see Anthea Bradley instead of going yourself? Fancied a wee trip to the Black Isle, did you? And did it really take both of you to talk to one wee old wifie about the Slackbuie victim?'

'The Chief made it clear he wanted senior officers to be more visible, ma'am.'

'He meant at briefings and media appeals, not haring round the countryside with Fergie like bloody Wallace and Gromit! From now on, your team does the running around and you handle the back-room stuff. We clear?'

'Ma'am.'

'Bloody better be. What about that Buchan guy, the two-timing boyfriend – no chance he did snatch Erin and try to grab the other lassie, I take it?'

'His story all checks out, ma'am. He's a cheat, not a child abductor.'

'Bugger.' June straightens her back, rolls her shoulders. 'Andy's convinced Bradley's our man with the van. But you don't seem so sure.'

He shakes his head. 'Bradley abducting children himself would be a significant departure from his previous MO. I think we need to avoid developing tunnel vision here.' On the other hand, impossible to know how six years inside might have shaped him, Mahler supposes. 'We do need to speak to Anthea, though.'

'Leave that to Fergie or Naz. You need to talk to the Mac-Kenzies again, see if they're up for doing another appeal. Show them we're doing everything we can to find Erin.'

'Just to be clear, ma'am – you want me to address their concerns by telling them exactly what we said last time?'

'Aye, Lukas, exactly that. Unless you think ignoring them sounds a better plan.' She waves a weary hand at him. 'Now bugger off – and if I see your face again today, it had better be bringing me some good news.'

There's nothing Mahler can say in response to that; nothing he trusts himself to say, at least. He heads for the MIT room to check in with Fergie . . . and runs into Andy Black, scratching at an inflamed pimple on his face as he lurks on the half-landing.

'Something I can help you with, Andy?'

'What are you now, a fucking boy scout?' Black wipes his hand on his jacket, takes a step towards Mahler. 'All for one, one for all, that kind of crap? Didn't need my arse saving in there, pal. Not by you. Got it?'

'Your arse can burn in hell for all I care – and if you try to shift blame for your own shortcomings onto one of the DCs again, I will drop you in it without a moment's thought. But if Professional Standards get their claws into us, we can forget about finding Erin MacKenzie. Maybe bear that in mind next time your mouth gets ahead of your brain.'

Mahler starts to walk on, but Black moves to straddle the stairwell, blocking him. 'You don't get it, do you? There are folk here who've got kids – folk putting in all the hours God sends to find that bastard Bradley. You think his mother just moved up here through some amazing fucking coincidence? Because I don't.'

'And if it isn't him? If some bizarre coincidence is exactly what it is, and Anthea Bradley suffers because we're all obsessed with her son?'

Black gives him a disgusted look. 'Christ, and you used to be one of the Met's finest?' He steps aside, makes an ironic 'after you' gesture to let Mahler pass. 'Bet they were glad to see the back of you, eh? Listen, pal, it's not rocket science – we find Bradley, we find Erin. End of story.'

Several possible responses Mahler could make to that; before he can select one, his mobile bleeps with another alert. He takes it out, glances at the screen. Two missed calls. A text from Dawn, the FLO. And a voicemail from a number he'd never expected to hear from again.

17

Late afternoon. The day's warmth fading but not entirely gone as Mahler walks down to the river to meet Anna Murray. She's sitting outside Eden Court Theatre, quick, nervous fingers flying over the keys of her laptop, the fading sun touching her hair with copper.

At the sound of his footsteps, she looks up. Smiles. And that alone is enough to make him wish he'd hadn't had to keep her waiting. But his visit to Erin MacKenzie's parents had been a tortuous experience for everyone concerned. He's not sure what had been worse, in the end: the dawning contempt on Grant MacKenzie's face as he realised all Mahler had to offer was the possibility of another TV appeal, or seeing the slow death of hope in her mother's eyes.

'I'm late, I know. I'm sorry,' he tells her. 'Work's pretty fraught right now, and—'

'The little girl who's missing? Yes, of course. I should have gone into Burnett Road, asked to see you there, but I just . . . I couldn't make myself walk through the door. Pathetic, huh?' She puts the laptop into her rucksack and stands up. 'Do you have time for a coffee?'

Lines of strain around her eyes, a telltale tightness in her jawline. Whatever this is about, Mahler can see it's already taken its toll on her.

'Of course.'

The café in the theatre complex is quiet, caught in the lull between the afternoon and evening performances. She looks round while he places their order. And picks the same booth he would have chosen himself, he realises, away from the counter and the few other customers.

Mahler walks over with the coffees, puts them down on the table. He watches her fingers tremble as she reaches for her cup. And, not for the first time, he wishes for some of Fergie's laid-back warmth, his knack of putting people at their ease. But when had any of his encounters with Anna Murray been remotely easy? Neither of them, he suspects, do easy very well.

'This isn't fair on you, is it?' She empties a sugar sachet into her espresso, swirls her spoon through the crema. 'I'm sorry. That day at Tomnahurich . . . I'd gone to Morven's grave to get my head straight about a few things, and when you arrived, I . . . I overreacted.'

'No apology needed. Being back in Inverness after so long is bound to feel strange. Your mother will be glad to have you here, of course, but for the first few weeks you'll feel as though you're between worlds, caught in a kind of limbo.'

A faint smile at that. 'Of course, you would understand – that's exactly how it feels. Though I've moved out of my mother's now.'

'You're still in Inverness, though?'

She shakes her head. 'Renting in Dornoch at the moment while I look around for something permanent. It's more convenient for the History Centre. And Mam and I . . . we work better with a little distance between us.'

From what he remembers of Yvonne Murray, his preference would be a couple of continents. Though viewed from the outside, he supposes his own situation doesn't look much different. 'You're enjoying the move to Highland academia, then?'

'Early days, but yes, I think I am.' Her smile dies. 'Lukas, I need to show you these. And ask if there's any way you can make them stop.' She unzips the rucksack, takes out a handful of letters and puts them on the table.

No need to ask what they are or who they're from; the thin prison paper is unmistakeable. Mahler picks one up at random, opens it, and feels the slow pulse of anger start to build, deep in his gut. Page after page, filled with Jamie Gordon's dense black handwriting. How in God's name had her sister's killer been able to bombard her with filth like this? 'How long has this been going on?'

'The first one came while I was still in San Diego. It was . . .' She gives a quick, shuddering breath. 'It was a bit of a shock, to say the least. They started coming regularly after that, then there was a gap of a few weeks. I never responded, so I suppose I thought he'd given up. Then I came back here, and they started again.'

'He knew you'd moved back to Scotland?' How the hell had Gordon managed that?

She nods. 'I thought I could ignore them and he'd stop eventually. But the latest one was addressed to my mother. I managed to get to it before she did, but if it happens again . . .' She shakes her head. 'Mam can't deal with this, Lukas. It would destroy her. If there's any way you can stop him—'

'I can, and I will. There are safeguards in place to prevent this happening, and I've no idea how he managed to get round them. But he won't do it again, I promise you.' And if that involves paying Gordon a personal visit at HMP Perth to clarify the consequences of trying to contact Anna again, Mahler's got no problem with that. None at all. 'Are you going back to Dornoch now? If not, perhaps—'

Bleeping from his mobile. He looks down to see a missed call from Fergie and another from Pete Noble.

'Sorry, I need to get back to Burnett Road. May I keep these?'

'Of course.' She reaches for the letters at the same time as he does; it's a second's contact, a momentary brush of fingers, nothing more. Nothing of substance. Nothing that should send sensations shivering up his arm, each individual hair standing on end after she's pulled her hand away.

'Anna, I . . .' Clearing his throat. Looking away until he's sure his voice and his face are under control. 'I'll probably need to talk to you again about this.'

'Yes.' Colour climbing in her cheeks. 'Yes, of course. Ring me whenever.' She takes out a card, scribbles something on the back and passes it to him. 'My work contact details . . . and my new address. In case you need it.'

The early-evening theatregoers are starting to arrive as they leave Eden Court and walk back towards the river. A vast tour bus is manoeuvring into the cathedral car park, the driver inching the huge vehicle past a dark 4x4 that's apparently in no hurry to go anywhere.

'So many visitors this summer.' Anna winces as the tour bus squeezes through the gap. 'I don't remember the tourist season being this busy when I was growing up.'

Mahler nods. 'But we always seem to accommodate them, somehow. Without the town feeling overcrowded.'

A genuine amusement this time in the look she gives him. 'We? So you're a born-again Highlander now too?'

'So it would seem.' They've reached the junction with Ness Walk. Mahler turns to her. 'I'm glad you told me about the letters. Don't worry about James Gordon − I'll make sure he doesn't bother you or your mother again. And . . . and take care, Anna. I'll be in touch.'

He watches her walk back down the riverside towards the Archive Centre. Waits until she's out of sight, and the sensation of her fingers against his begins to fade, before he heads back towards Eden Court to pick up the BMW.

He's almost at the Bishop's Palace when the man sunning himself on the grass by the entrance rolls onto his back and gets to his feet.

'Grand day, eh?' Cazza MacKay dusts down his jeans, nods at Mahler. 'The tourists will be loving it. They'll be sick of all those bloody pipers before long, though — can't your lot do something about them? Fucking public nuisance, that.'

'You followed me from Burnett Road?' The rage, primed since Anna had shown him those bloody letters, arrives fully formed and ready to go. 'How long have you been lurking there?'

'Just called into Eden Court for a wee latte, that's all.' A humourless grin appears and disappears on Cazza's face. 'Sent you a message the other day, son. Wullie said—'

'Wullie's a thug who's lucky he didn't get lifted. And my answer hasn't changed — CID are looking into the fire at your premises, and they'll continue to do so. Following our time-scale, not yours.'

'Your timescale can go fuck itself, son. Want to know why?' Cazza pulls out his mobile, touches the display and holds it in front of Mahler. 'Take a look at this. Last night, some bastard set fire to a bundle of rags outside Gemma's place and stuffed them through her letter box. Nice, eh?'

Mahler stares at the blackened remains of what had been Gemma Fraser's front door. So that's what Fergie had been calling him about. 'Is she all right? And the children?' He reaches for his mobile. 'Let me check in with Burnett Road—'

Cazza shakes his head. 'Put your wee Bat-phone away. She heard the racket at the door and put the fire out in time. She's okay – scared out of her fucking mind, but okay. I've sent her and the bairns to stay with her mam while your lot tramp all over her place. Point is, son . . .' he jabs an angry finger at Mahler, 'the point is, I'm being targeted. And so's my fucking niece. That place those bastards torched? It was going to be a beauty salon – a wee surprise to cheer her up a bit. And they took it away from her.'

They're starting to attract attention from a group of curious theatregoers. Mahler moves away from the entrance, waits until the group has passed by. 'Why would anyone do that? Unless you've got her mixed up in something—'

A motorbike roars past, then another. Cazza follows them with his eyes. When he turns back to Mahler, there's a tension about him that hadn't been there a moment ago. 'Are you fucking stupid? Wee Kevin, that's why. I told you, her man heard something he shouldn't have and he ended up dead. I gave you a name, Mahler. Told you who to look for, and you did nothing.'

So that's where this is going. The man called Hollander – the Mr Big of a multinational crime empire with his fingers into everything from drugs to people trafficking, according to Cazza. The man who'd sounded like a lead worth pursuing during the hunt for Kevin Ramsay's killer. The man Mahler's team had tried everything to trace. Tried, and failed.

Mahler shakes his head. 'Thing is, Carl, I took you at your word. Threw resources into finding Hollander, talked to people who knew people . . . and no one had heard of him. No- one. Now I'm supposed to believe he's coming after you and Gemma, nearly two years later?'

'I never said it would be easy, did I?' Cazza breaks off, looks round as though he's heard something. 'Look, I stuck my neck out at the time. Asked a few too many questions myself. And I got . . . hints . . . to leave it alone.' His face darkens. 'Fucking big ones, towards the end. But Gemma's not been coping since it happened. Took some pills just after Christmas, and . . .' he shrugs. 'I started poking around again, stirred things up a bit. Maybe.'

Believable? Perhaps. Mahler still isn't buying the invisible man scenario, but something's certainly got Cazza rattled. 'So, tell me what you've got, and we'll take it from there.'

Cazza shakes his head. 'I've got nothing yet. Just whispers – and don't get any ideas about pulling me in, I'll deny every fucking word of this.'

Of course he will. Mahler's sorely tempted to do it anyway, but his officers are stretched to the limit as it is without spending fruitless hours on a 'no comment' interview with Cazza. 'Then you're wasting my time. Call into Burnett Road when you're ready to talk.'

Mahler's turned away, heading for the car park when Cazza moves to block him.

'Did I say we were done? We're talking here and now, son—'

'No, we're not. Come in and make a statement, Carl. That's how it works.'

Walking away again. Stopping. Listening to the traffic noise behind him, trying to assess what's changed. Because there's a twist of unease at the back of Mahler's neck, a half-instinctive prickle of foreboding that makes him turn and walk back to Cazza. Before he's halfway there, the engine of the 4x4 he'd noticed earlier bursts into sudden, snarling life.

And Mahler's running now, launching himself on Cazza and shoving him sideways into the hedge, as behind them someone screams and the roar of the engine grows to fill the world.

A blow to his side, as though he's been punched by a giant fist. Pain ripping through him. Then nothing.

123

18

Brightness, and a hum of voices. A slumped, vaguely human-shaped outline drifting in and out of focus beside him. And pain – a concentrated mass of it, starting somewhere above his right knee and ending just below his collarbone. No plaster that Mahler can see when he pushes down the sheet, so nothing's broken, but the whole of his right side is a battered landscape of red and purple bruising beneath the shredded remnants of his shirt. Mahler turns his head and something pulls along his cheekbone. Stitches?

'Nurse said not to touch that, boss.' The blurred outline shifts, settles into Fergie sitting on a plastic chair next to the trolley Mahler's lying on. He comes closer, peers at Mahler's face. Winces. 'Man, you took a fair crack under your eye there. Let me get someone—'

'In a minute.' Fighting the unsteadiness he can hear in his voice, the thump-thump of his heart as he realises where he is . . .

Blood on the stairs. Running for his life. And his mother . . .

He grips the sides of the trolley and pulls himself up, looks round at the curtained-off A&E cubicle. 'How long have I been here?'

'I was on my way back to the shop when the call came in,'

Fergie tells him. 'Ambulance was still on the scene when I arrived, so I got the uniforms to round up any witnesses and take statements. That would have been . . .' Fergie looks at his watch, 'a couple of hours ago. You were drifting in and out so they took you for a scan, patched you up and parked you here. Boss, no offence, but you look dog-rough. I'm getting the nurse—'

A couple of hours? Mahler holds up a hand. 'Wait. What about MacKay – do we have an update on him?'

'The man you came in with?' A head of bright pink hair pokes through the curtain, looks him up and down. 'He's just gone up to ICU. So, how are you feeling, now you're back with us?'

'Never better.' Mahler pushes the cover the rest of the way down and swings his legs onto the floor. Rests for a moment to take stock; breathing is painful and the room's not completely in focus, but things are manageable. At the moment. 'Could you organise a discharge form for me, please?'

The curtain swishes fully open. The pink-haired nurse treats him to an eye-roll as she consults the chart at the foot of his bed, shakes her head and starts to list all the reasons he shouldn't even think about leaving hospital for twenty-four hours. When it's obvious Mahler's not going to change his mind, she stalks out, muttering about finding a doctor to make him see sense.

'Boss, don't you think she's got a point? You look—'

'Dog-rough. You said.' Mahler reaches for his phone and his wallet containing his warrant card, looks round for his jacket.

Fergie shakes his head, picks up a carrier bag by his chair and passes it to Mahler. 'Sorry, boss, your jacket's had it. But while you were having your scan, I nipped home and picked these up for you. Zofia's nephew is staying with us, and he's about your size.'

Mahler opens the carrier bag, takes out a pair of tracksuit bottoms and a hooded, zip-up top. Unless he's planning to ask

Fergie to help him get them on, the tracksuit bottoms are a non-starter, but the hoodie should just about fit . . . He catches sight of the logo on the back. Takes a closer look. And raises an eyebrow at Fergie.

'Sorry, boss. Just grabbed the first thing I saw.'

Mahler sighs, tries to tell himself no one will notice he's apparently a member of the Night's Watch and struggles into the hoodie.

When the doctor arrives, she looks him up and down. Checks his chart. And shakes her head. 'Feeling fine, are we? Enjoying that funky "ribs kicked by an elephant" sensation? No, don't answer that.' She hands him a clipboard and a pen. 'X marks the spot.'

Mahler starts to thank her, but she cuts him off.

'Seriously, don't. There's an RTC due in from Moy and I'm two nurses down – if you're determined to play macho man and stagger out of here with two cracked ribs and a suspected concussion, I'm not going to waste my time trying to talk you out of it.'

She reels off a string of warning signs he needs to look out for, tells him to pick up a prescription for painkillers at the hospital pharmacy and hurries off towards the sound of approaching sirens.

Macho man. Mahler shakes his head. He'd laugh, if he thought his ribs would stand it.

He gets to his feet, ignores the look Fergie's giving him and makes his way slowly along the corridor. By the time he reaches the exit, his hands are sticky-damp with sweat.

Blood on the stairs. Running for his life . . .

He wipes his forehead. Makes himself turn and walk away from the exit, back to the lifts, earning another concerned look from Fergie. 'You okay, boss?'

'The nurse said Cazza was in ICU, didn't she? We need an update on his condition.'

But when they get to the intensive care unit, there's little information to be had. No, the staff nurse informs them, Mr MacKay hasn't regained consciousness. No, she couldn't say how long it might take. And no, there is no possibility of seeing him, however briefly. None at all.

In the end, Mahler gives up. Cazza isn't talking. Isn't likely to be talking for hours. And hanging around the hospital until he wakes up isn't an option.

Riding the lift back to the ground floor, Mahler catches sight of his reflection in the mirrors: slumped, grey-faced, he could pass for an extra in a bad zombie movie. Even without the appalling hoodie.

Out of the lift, back along the corridor. Stopping halfway to steady himself as the walls blur briefly.

'Boss?'

'I'm fine.'

And finally, they're outside. Fergie goes to collect the car while Mahler waits by the entrance. He's sweating as though he's run a marathon, but the frantic thumping of his heart is slowing and the cold sickness in the pit of his stomach is starting to recede. When the Audi pulls up, he manages to ease himself into the passenger seat and get the seat belt fastened.

'Right, then, let's get you home.' Fergie thumps the gear-stick until it finds something approximating first, and the Audi lurches towards the exit.

'Not yet. I need to write this up, and—'

Fergie stamps on the brake. Cuts the engine. And stares at him as though he's lost his mind. 'Have you bloody seen your-self? You nearly passed out in the lift.'

'It won't take long. Let's go.'

'Boss—'

'Christ, Sergeant, will you just get on with it!' And now he's shouting at Fergie. Perfect. Mahler sighs. 'That wasn't . . . Look,

I have a thing about hospitals.' Not all hospitals, as it happens. Just this one. Just that particular department. But Fergie doesn't need to know that. 'It comes on me unexpectedly sometimes.'

'Ach, no worries.' Fergie starts up the engine, heads up to the Inshes roundabout and onto the dual carriageway. 'You still look like crap, though. And if June Wallace wants to know what eejit let you discharge yourself, I'm planning to lie through my teeth. Just so's you know.'

'Very wise. In fact . . .' Mahler pauses. Recalls some of June's more spectacular explosions. 'In fact, consider that an order.'

Messenger Group: Justice for Erin (secret)

Dylan:
What the fuck happened tonight! **Ewan**, **Tam**, thought youse were all up for it? Did ur mams all send you to bed without ur tea or something?

Ewan:
Cow reported what we did on Tuesday night, that's what fucking happened. Two cops nosing round first thing this morning, asking questions and giving me evils. Fucking two of them! Some Asian bint in a headscarf and a flash-looking posho looking down his nose at me. I was fucking bricking it, man.

Tam:
So your just giving up?

Ewan:
Didnt say that. But we've got to be a bit clever next time. My boss would skin me alive if he knew what we did.

Tam:
What's his problem? Got a bit of business out of it, didn't he? 😄 😂

Dylan:
Ewan's right. Do this wrong and we're all in trouble. We're trying to catch a pedo not land ourselves in fucking Porterfield.

Tam:
Jesus Christ. Over a few broken windows?

Ewan:
You didn't see the look on that big cop's face. He knows fine it wasn't just kids. What if they're staking out the place?

Tam:
Fanny.

Ewan:
U calling me a fanny?

Dylan:
Fucks sake. Cops are chasing their tails right now looking for that wee lassie. And we all know its to late for her. Going to turn up dead somewhere and that pervert will get away with it if we don't flush him out. That what u want to happen?

Ewan:
How? There's no way hes hiding out at his mam's place. The boss and I were in every room in the house and I had a good look round just like you said. Shes on her own.

Dylan:
She's helping him. Got him hidden somewhere, bringing him food, stuff like that. All we have to do is find out where he's hiding out.

Tam:
We're not the fucking cops.

Dylan:
That's right, we're not. We're better than them. Because I know how to make her tell us where he is.

19

Day 13
Thursday, 2 June

8.00 a.m. A slow stream of bodies making their way into the MIT room, trailing coffee and sausage-in-a-roll aromas . . . or, in the case of Andy Black, less fragrant odours. They stop short when they catch sight of Mahler waiting by the whiteboards. He's managed to struggle into the spare shirt and jacket he keeps on the back of his door, but his ribs feel as though they've been wrapped in barbed wire and the bruising under his eye is a lunar landscape of purple and blue.

'Jeez-oh.' Black saunters to the front, makes a show of looking him up and down. 'Heard you'd had a wee run-in with someone last night, but fuck me, that's one hell of a doing you took there. Put you in Raigmore, so I heard.'

'Just a few knocks and scrapes.'

'Tell that to your face.' Black peers at the bruising below his eye. 'Not looking so pretty now, eh? Got to hurt, that.'

'Aye, but his face'll get better. You're stuck with the one you've got.'

A voice from the back of the room; Pete, Mahler's guessing. And a quickly suppressed snort of laughter that sounds suspiciously like Nazreen. He gives them a warning glance.

'Settle down, children. Andy, if you're planning to stay for the briefing—'

Black shakes his head. 'Places to be, lowlifes to lift. Perverts to put the fear of God into. Don't worry, I'll be back for our two o'clock with June. If you last that long.'

Worth responding to? Only if he wants to end up explaining to June why Andy's head had collided with the whiteboard in a freak accident. Repeatedly.

'Right, then.' He waits until Andy's left, nods at Donna to close the door. 'Updates. Pete, where are we with the partial plate you were working on?'

For once, the news is promising. Pete's managed to enhance some of the CCTV footage to indicate an 'E' as the first letter, and 'K' as the final one. And there's progress with the forensics too; a set of surprisingly clear tyre tracks have been lifted.

'We've got a possible sighting at the Inshes roundabout,' Pete tells him. 'Heads up towards Cradlehall and Smithton . . . and that's where we lose him.'

'So, he turned off. Or parked up somewhere out of sight – at least we've got an area to focus on now. Remember his penchant for building sites? Plenty of construction work happening around there. Farm tracks, too – anywhere our man could be lying low. Well done, Pete.' Mahler turns to Donna and Nazreen. 'What about the girls from the party – any progress there?'

There is, it turns out. One of the Beauty Box women from Livvy McIver's party has just got back from holiday. And she remembers seeing two girls arguing with Erin around three o'clock.

'She's sure it was Erin?'

'One hundred per cent,' Donna tells him. 'She called us as soon as she landed in Aberdeen and saw the papers. And she's pretty sure Erin went out into the garden afterwards. By herself.'

Which isn't that far from the burn. And the track where

it's looking more and more likely Erin's abductor had lain in wait.

Mahler nods. 'Okay. Gary, any joy at the building site?'

'Nothing definite. Place was full of vans coming and going all the time we were there. But . . .' he checks his notes, 'couple of boys I spoke to said they saw one parked along the track around lunchtime. Didn't think anything of it at the time, but they can't remember ever seeing the guy around the site.'

'So, no description then?'

'One of them skived off for a quick fag break, thinks he might have glimpsed a beard and glasses. Maybe. Sorry, boss.'

Mahler shakes his head. 'No need for apologies. Media Liaison can put out a press release with the new information we've got, and we'll revisit everything we have on the attempted abduction of Celeste Taylor.'

'What about Bradley's ma? She's got to be involved, right? Guy can't just disappear without someone helping him.'

'Which is why we're keeping an eye on her,' he tells Gary. 'If either of them makes contact, we'll know about it. But right now, let's focus on what we do have. Because we're making progress here – it might not feel like much, but I promise you, we're going to get this man. And we will find Erin . . . we'll find her, and we'll bring her home safely to her parents. Because of the work you're doing.'

Enough to buoy them up? He hopes so. He needs them not to count the days since Erin disappeared and draw the inevitable conclusion. He needs them to focus. To believe. Because he's about to push his already overstretched team to their limits.

'Right, then. I'm sure the rumour mill has been working overtime about the . . . incident . . . I was involved in yesterday.'

A beep from Fergie's mobile. Then one from his. Surely June Wallace can't have read his email already?

He holds up his hand to quiet the murmuring at the back of

the room. 'Much as I hate to spoil anyone's fun, this is what actually happened.'

He keeps it as short and factual as possible, but there's no way of sugar-coating the next part.

'This was an attempt on Cazza MacKay's life, pure and simple. DI Black and I will meet with the DCI this afternoon to discuss resourcing, but the fact is, we now have another major investigation on our hands. So yes, I know, the timing stinks – and no, it won't be easy. But we will deal with it.'

Silence as they process that. Fergie hands out the daily allocations and Mahler watches the team file out. At the door, Pete turns.

'Boss, I've been keeping an eye on some of the social media stuff about Erin. There's the usual mix of folk weighing in – hand-wringers and headbangers, basically – but there's one of the groups I'm not sure about.'

'Meaning?'

Pete shrugs. 'Just a feeling at the moment. Couple of really vocal folk dropped out suddenly, and I'm wondering why. I'll keep monitoring for a while, if that's okay?'

'Of course.' Mahler's learned to trust Pete's instincts about these things. 'But keep me informed, yes?'

'Cheers, boss.' Pete grins, nods at the table behind Mahler. 'Cool hoodie, by the way.'

Fergie closes the door behind Pete. Looks at the hoodie, crumpled on the desk where Mahler had used it as a pillow. 'You stayed here all bloody night? For God's sake, boss—'

'I needed to be here. Look, I'm on borrowed time – as soon as the DCI reads the report I sent her, she'll want a full debrief. I can't lead this investigation, so it'll be down to Andy Black. And you.' And if June Wallace or the Chief find out he discharged himself last night . . . 'So, let's move things on as far as we can before then. Where are we with the remains found at Slackbuie? Any update on a possible identification so we can draw a line under that one?'

In answer, Fergie takes out his mobile, passes it to Mahler. 'Email came in from that pal of Dr Falconer's, the World War Two military expert guy. He's managed to trace the owner of the British dog tags. Not sure about drawing a line under things, though . . . turns out the lad buried in the midden pit was Ella Kirkpatrick's uncle.'

20

Ella Kirkpatrick takes longer to answer her door to them this time. She looks frailer, too, her cheekbones sharper and the hollows of her collarbones more pronounced. But Mahler still gets the same odd sensation of being assessed as her grey-blue eyes sweep over Fergie and back to him.

'Are you sure you should be here, Inspector? Forgive me, but you look as though you've been in the wars.'

'It tends to come with the job. May we come in? We need to talk to you about the remains found at Slackbuie.'

'Ah.' She looks at Fergie, and back at him. 'And it's something I'll need to sit down for, isn't it? I can see by your faces. Fine, then, in you come.'

She leads them through to the neat sitting room again, sits and listens as Fergie takes her through what Dr Falconer's colleague had discovered.

'My uncle Aeneas?' She shakes her head. 'No, he never came home from the war. He was listed as missing in action . . . after El Alamein, I think. And you said there were German dog tags found with . . .with the body. Surely you've got the wrong person?'

Mahler shakes his head. 'I'm afraid not. The tags belonged

to a young German army officer who was killed at Tobruk. It seems that many servicemen were in the habit of collecting German or Italian dog tags as souvenirs, and we're assuming that's what Aeneas— Mrs Kirkpatrick, are you all right?'

Her eyes are closed, the pulse in her throat jumping as she grips the arms of her chair. Mahler gets up to go over to her and a bright burst of fire from his injured ribs makes him hiss with pain.

Ella's eyes fly open. 'Shouldn't be here, son. I told you. Sit down now, I'll be fine.' She relaxes her hands, takes a slow, careful breath. 'So, Aeneas has been there all this time and no one ever knew?'

'I'm afraid so.' He doesn't spell it out, but one person had known, of course. Aeneas's killer.

Mahler glances at Fergie, who picks up his cue.

'Ella, I can see this has come as a terrible shock to you. Are you okay to answer a few wee questions for us, just to help us piece together what might have happened? If you're not feeling up to it, we could always come back—'

A shake of her head. 'You're here now. And I . . . I don't always keep well. What do you want to know?'

'You said Aeneas was reported missing in action.'

'My granny got a telegram, yes.' She gives him a bewildered look. 'So how can it be him? I'm sorry, I . . . I don't understand.'

'Neither do we,' Fergie tells her. 'That's why we need your help, Ella. You definitely never heard anyone say he'd come home – even if only for a short time?'

'I told you, no one ever saw him again. People just . . . they knew what that telegram meant, you see. It meant he was never coming home.' She looks down at her hands. 'There were so many folk like that, back then. So many . . .'

Mahler nods. 'This is difficult for you, I can see that. I'm sorry. Do you remember much about your uncle, Ella? Is there

anything you can tell us about him, maybe, to help us understand what happened to him?'

She looks confused. 'I don't really know what you want me
to say. He was just Uncle Aeneas to me.'

'Was he well liked, do you think? Easy to get on with . . .
or did he have a bit of a temper? Get into the odd argument,
maybe? Because I'm wondering if he may have fallen out with
someone who bore him a grudge. And when he came home
unexpectedly, after so long . . . If there's anything you can think
of, anything at all—'

'After all this time? Inspector, I can barely remember what
he looked like. It was nearly seventy years ago, and I was just a
little girl. And my memory's not what it should be, sometimes.'

Mahler starts to say something, but she shakes her head.

'I'm sorry, I think I need to be on my own for a while now.
This is a terrible, terrible story you've come to me with, and I
. . . I need a bit of time to try and come to terms with it.'

The news has clearly taken its toll; there's a tremor in her
right hand which hadn't been there earlier, and she doesn't get
up to see them out this time.

'Poor old wifie.' Fergie looks round, gives a half-wave in the
direction of Ella's sitting-room window as they walk back to
the car. 'Not the sort of news you want to get at her age, eh?
Though it's closure of a sort, I suppose.'

'Perhaps.'

It's certainly sufficient for the Chief's purposes; sufficient
to finally lay to rest the stories of ghosts and ancient treasure
hoards that had disrupted Fraser Thane's construction empire,
however briefly. But all they've done for Ella is exchange one
uncertainty for another. And Aeneas's murder is the coldest of
cold cases, Mahler knows that. With no living witnesses and no
leads to follow, it's one they're unlikely to solve. 'We'll get a
report in to the Fiscal, and—'

Buzzing from Mahler's mobile as they reach the car; a series of angry whines, like wasps trapped in a jam jar as the phone signal kicks in again. It's patchy around here, as in so many places outside the city. A huge irritation. Sometimes. At others? Not so much.

The painkillers are wearing off. He gets into the Audi slowly, dry-swallows a couple more tablets before easing the seat belt round his burning ribs.

'You okay?' Fergie glances over at him. 'Because you don't—' he breaks off, stares at the line of scowling red emojis on Mahler's phone. 'Christ, is that from Braveheart? I'm guessing she's read your report about Cazza, huh?'

Either that, or Andy Black's decided to update June about it himself. 'It looks like the DCI's now up to speed with events, yes.' He winces as Fergie thumps the gearstick into first and the Audi lurches forward. 'Back to the shop, then. And if you can manage not to hit every single pothole on the way, so much the better.'

By the time they get back to Burnett Road, his chest feels as though there's an ever-tightening vice clamped against his ribs. When Fergie stops before the speed bump at the barrier to let him out, Mahler rips off his seat belt and exits the Audi with all the agility of a ninety-year-old.

Inside, he stops to catch his breath before calling the lift up to June's floor; unless he wants to pass out on the half landing, taking the stairs isn't an option today. And he's under no illusions about the thinness of the ice he's currently skating on. If June's got the slightest concern about his fitness for duty, she'll order him to take sick leave . . . and that means Andy Black running the MIT on his own. The team deserve better than that, and Mahler's got no intention of letting them down.

The lift reaches the ground floor and the doors slide open. Nazreen is standing there, talking into her phone. She looks up.

Sees him. Ends the call. And before she says a word, he knows whatever she's come to tell him, it's going to be bad.

'Sir, Control's just had a call from Culduthel Primary. They think . . . It looks like another girl's been taken.'

Her name is Lena McNally. Ten years old, like Erin. Blaze-red hair and a defiant, arms-crossed pose in the photo Mahler pins to the whiteboard in the incident room. Vanished in broad daylight, like Erin; this time, from the playground at her school.

'How?' Andy Black's standing in the middle of the room, feet planted wide, hands bunched into fists as though he's readying himself for a fight. 'How can a wee girl just walk out of school on her own and not be missed for forty fucking minutes?'

'A stupid bloody mistake, that's why.' A moment's inattention by a harassed school secretary juggling phone calls – one about a missing delivery and the other from Lena's mother – is all it had taken. Michelle McNally had rung to say Lena had a GP appointment, and the secretary had duly passed on the message to Lena's teacher, who assumed Lena had already been picked up by her mother when she didn't return to class at the end of break time. Only the secretary had written down the wrong time; when Michelle had arrived to collect her daughter, Lena had been gone for almost forty minutes.

Black shakes his head. 'Stupid cow. Hope she's proud of herself.'

'Not helpful, Andy.' Mahler nods at Fergie to close the door; June Wallace was supposed to be joining them, but he suspects the DCI is juggling several balls right now, particularly if she's been called in for an update by the Chief. Which at least means his scheduled bollocking will have been postponed for the moment, Mahler supposes. 'Let's focus on what we have, shall we? Firstly, there's a verifiable timeline. We've got a last reported sighting of her walking towards the trees at the far end of the school grounds during morning break. And I think we've got something else too.'

He brings up a map of the immediate area on the screen behind him. 'This is the location. The school grounds back onto the park, and there's a footpath running beside them leading to the main road. Look familiar?'

Donna nods. 'It's the same pattern as Erin. But there's nowhere to hide a van around there—'

'Yes, there is.' Big Gary walks up to the map, points. 'I walk my girlfriend's dog there sometimes. You can't really see it on here, but there's a clearing just beyond the entrance. It's not great cover, but if it was in the middle of the day when folk are at work . . .' He shrugs. 'Not going to notice it, are they? Most folk are glued to their phones half the time anyway.'

Mahler nods. 'Good. We'll get CSI out to check for tracks. Pete, can we look at—'

'Not buying it.' Andy Black scrapes at a raw spot on his chin, licks the residue from his finger. 'He knows we're looking for a guy in a van, it's been all over the TV and the papers. But he still lurks near a school – a fucking school! – on the off-chance he can get a wee girl on her own and grab her. And just like that, he gets lucky? Don't bloody think so.'

It's a good point, and it's been bothering Mahler too. 'And the attempt on Celeste Taylor only failed because her brother appeared unexpectedly. So, what's happening? How did our man know exactly when he'd find them on their own?'

'He knows them,' Nazreen offers. 'Or knows their families, somehow.'

'Max Bradley?' Andy Black gives her a disgusted look. 'Who the hell would let him anywhere near their children?'

Mahler holds up his hand. 'Let's stick with "the abductor" for now – until we've got actual evidence, anything pointing to Bradley is purely circumstantial. So, whoever it is, somehow he's able to access information about the girls he goes after. How? And why these girls? Is it the information he obtains that makes the difference, or is there something else going on?'

'You're not seeing it.' Donna walks over to the whiteboard, points at the photos pinned there. 'None of you are seeing it. He didn't want just any girls. He wanted those girls. Look at them – one blonde, one dark, one red. It's like he's collecting them. Adding them to a set, or something.'

A twist of ice, deep in Mahler's gut. And a memory surfacing that stops him in his tracks and puts Maxwell Bradley right back in the frame again. Because Donna's right. *Almost* right, he amends. And he should have known what was happening, should have seen the shape of it coming together long before now. As the murmuring starts, he holds up his hand for silence.

'Donna's picked up on something there,' he tells the room. 'Something we need to take very seriously, given the possibility of Maxwell Bradley's involvement in this enquiry. I wasn't on the Met team involved in the original investigation, but I know how bloody hard they worked to put a case together on him that the CPS would accept.'

Andy Black stares at him. 'Why hard? Christ, what the guy did—'

'Was a hell of a lot more than what he was sent down for. Yes, they got him on various making and sharing counts. But Bradley was more than just the group co-ordinator. Bradley was the . . . the CEO of the entire vile undertaking. Oh, he was careful to keep his own hands clean – there was no evidence of his being involved in any paedophile activity himself. But he was the procurer-in-chief, the man who catered to his group's repulsive tastes.' Mahler runs his tongue over his suddenly dry lips. 'He basically supplied anything he was asked for . . . so if Bradley is the man we're looking for, the girls won't be for him. He'll be stealing them to order.'

Silence. Anger and disgust settling on every face as they process what he's telling them. Not shock, not disbelief, because they're in the Job and the Job has shown them all horrors enough, even in Inverness. But something like this . . .

'Jesus Christ, it's a paedophile ring.' Andy Black stamps up to the whiteboards, jabs at Maxwell Bradley's face staring out at them. 'He's out, and now he's back in fucking business. Aye, he's gone to ground somewhere, but he's still got the contacts, hasn't he? Still taking requests from whatever bunch of perverts he's hooked up with now. And his mother . . . she's the fucking negotiator.'

21

The team who'd brought down Maxwell Bradley and his vile organisation has been disbanded. Leo Whitford, the DCI who'd overseen the operation, has retired, and it takes Mahler half a dozen misdirected phone calls before he finally traces Bea Colgan, Leo's DI. She's no longer a DI, which is hardly a surprise, given her ability and drive. But her move to a high-profile role within the Special Operations Directorate is one Mahler definitely hadn't bargained for.

'Saw the way the wind was blowing, Lukas,' Bea tells him. 'Restructuring on the cards, people jockeying for position, you know how it goes. Though you got out yourself, didn't you? Over the border and back to bonnie Scotland, yeah? And, och, I never even knew you were Scottish! So, what can I do for you, laddie? Not got any wayward diplomats up there doing naughty stuff amongst the heather, have you?'

Mahler does his best not to wince at her version of a Scots accent. 'Not exactly. What we might have is Max Bradley setting himself up in business again.'

'And I thought I was done with thinking about bastards like that.' Her voice is flat, resigned. 'Okay, let me have it.'

Mahler takes her through the events surrounding Erin's

disappearance and the attempt to grab Celeste, ending with Lena's presumed abduction. 'The Bradley connection might not hold up,' he finishes. 'But the paedophile ring theory—'

'Yes, it's possible.' Bea gives him a brief, disturbing account of some of the set-ups she'd come across in her previous role. 'The dark web's one route they use to avoid detection through standard internet channels,' she finishes. 'And, of course, remote areas like yours are perfect hiding places for scum like that. But if it is Bradley, he's unlikely to go hi-tech this time round. It's how we found him in the end, so I'll lay odds he'll set things up locally at first before getting the word out to a wider area. Don't forget, he hasn't got the funds or the position he used to have, and he broke his conditions of licence. He'll have to keep his head down and start small. *If* it's him.'

'You don't sound convinced.'

A faint sigh from the other end of the line. 'Two things that bother me about that scenario. Think about it – snatching the girls locally doesn't make sense in your neck of the woods. Too damn risky, for one thing. If you need a couple of pre-teens to fulfil an order, you don't grab them from somewhere they're bound to be missed. Mind you, he could be operating from somewhere else entirely and using his mother's location as a smokescreen.'

Fulfilling an order. Mahler swallows down the sourness at the back of his throat. 'You said there were two things.'

Bea's sigh is louder this time. 'The attempted abduction? It's messy, and Bradley doesn't do messy. But whoever it is, if your man is stealing them to order, he's still one girl down . . . and that means he's going to need a replacement. Soon.'

'A replacement. Of course.' The sourness is back in his throat. Mahler thanks Bea for her help and ends the call. He's standing up to head for the MIT room when Andy Black's number flashes up on his mobile.

'She's gone.' The phone signal near the Muir is notoriously bad, but the contempt in Black's voice cuts through the random bursts of static. 'You hearing me, Mahler? Anthea Bradley's done a fucking runner – left her car outside Muir of Ord bloody Co-op and vanished. I knew we should have lifted her the first time I fucking saw her!'

'Arrest a woman suffering from a serious heart condition, without reasonable grounds? Can't think of any way that could come back to bite us on the arse, can you?'

Mahler puts the phone down on the desk, lets Black rant on while he tries to work out where the hell they go from here. When the decibel level drops, he tells Black to check with the gardening service Anthea had been using.

'They were in the middle of a big landscaping job for her, and they worked there on a daily basis – find out if she said anything that could help us track her down. Same with the glazing firm she employed. Her neighbours, too. I know her cottage is quite isolated, but they might have seen something.'

Grasping at straws, maybe, but they can't afford to waste time. In spite of Bea's misgivings, it looks as though Black's been right all along. Anthea Bradley's renovation plans for her cottage were simply a smokescreen for her real purpose in coming to the Highlands: to find an isolated location from which she and her vile son could put his repulsive hobby on a commercial footing.

Mahler drafts a holding statement for Media Liaison to give out. At some point, either June Wallace or the Chief will have to get in front of the cameras, but this will buy the team some time. Anthea Bradley's car will need to be recovered and thoroughly examined, too. He puts in an urgent request to authorise recovery and forensics and adds a note to have the CCTV footage from outside the Co-op called in.

Next, he checks team allocations, wincing at the number

of overtime hours the MIT has already burned through. Naz is at Lena's school, talking to the distraught staff, and Donna's staying with the parents until Mahler can locate more Family Liaison hours from somewhere. Fergie's organising the house-to-house and Pete's collating the ANPR intel from the main road by the school.

At least this time they know what they're looking for: a white van with the partial plate Pete identified from the abduction of Erin MacKenzie. For the first time since her disappearance, it feels as though they've got a decent lead. Mahler looks up at her photo on the whiteboard and tries to tell himself it hasn't come too late to save her.

He emails June an update and a warrant request to search Anthea Bradley's cottage. Remembers he needs to talk to Offender Management to see if there's anyone on their current radar who would make a good initial contact for Bradley. Mahler reaches for his phone to make the call, and remembers it's still in his jacket. Without thinking, he twists round in his chair to get it. The movement sends a jolt of pain arcing across his chest that makes him gasp.

He closes his eyes, makes himself take a breath that feels as though it's a knife slicing between his injured ribs. When his breathing steadies and he opens his eyes, June's standing in the doorway.

'Ma'am.' He pushes his chair back, starts to rise, but she shakes her head.

'Sit down.' She walks over to the desk, sits down. 'We need to have a conversation, Lukas. Not just you and me this time – the Chief's read your report about last night, and he is not a happy bunny. Seeing Cazza MacKay's name mentioned in the same breath as one of his serving officers pushes all his bloody buttons.'

'Ma'am, I've explained what happened—'

'Aye, I know that. But Cazza bloody MacKay, Lukas! Have you any idea how close to the edge you're dancing there? You're lucky the Chief didn't insist on getting the suits involved.'

Mahler's pretty sure luck had nothing to do with it; if Hunt had given way on that, it was purely down to June's efforts. 'Ma'am, I'm grateful. We both know Cazza's dodgy as they come, and he pushes everyone's buttons. Mine included. But someone tried to kill him yesterday, and that makes him a victim in my book. Like Gemma Fraser. Like Kevin Ramsay.'

The look June gives him is a millimetre away from an eye-roll. 'Why do you think I've got a uniform clocking up overtime I can't afford, guzzling tea and biscuits outside ICU right now? I can join the dots as well as you can, son – and you're right, something stinks here. But until Cazza regains consciousness, we've got nothing but a few seconds' CCTV of a 4x4 with fake plates. And one chancer of a DI who thought I'd not check whether Raigmore actually said he was fine to be discharged.'

'I'm . . . in some pain. But I can move and I can function. And you need me—'

'I need you fit. Right now, you're a danger to yourself and your colleagues. So get your arse out of here and don't come back until Monday morning, in time to have it well and truly kicked by the Chief. Are we clear?'

He starts to say something, but June shakes her head.

'Home, Lukas. Now.'

Lena

By the time the movement stops, Lena's awake. Not properly awake, not really, because she can't open her eyes and everything still feels fuzzy, as though some part of her's still dreaming. But awake enough to feel the rough cloth covering her face, the sharpness of whatever's been used to tie her hands digging into her wrists. Awake enough to know that something bad has happened to her. *Is happening. Will happen—*

The sounds of car doors opening and closing. Voices. Footsteps coming closer. Another door, and then a burst of sudden brightness.

Lena tries to wriggle away from the glare, but her legs won't work properly. And there are hands, too, clamping round her waist and others gripping her ankles. Hauling her towards the light. Taking her somewhere, like they did that other girl. The one her mother says is likely dead already.

She screams again and again, as loud as she can, but the thing wrapped round her head swallows the sound and she knows no one's going to hear her. So she kicks out, hard and fast, and her foot connects with a soft, fleshy something that jerks away from her quickly. Men's bits, maybe, Lena thinks. *Good.* That's what tough girls do when they're in trouble, she's seen it on the telly. They kick men right in the bits and then they get away.

A grunt of pain. A man's voice, swearing at her, calling her an evil little bitch. Letting go of her ankles so that her legs drop to the ground.

Lena twists her body, whips her head from left to right. If she can get the rest of her free, maybe she can . . .

A growl of anger from the cursing man. An explosion of pain, thunder-loud against her right ear. Then nothing.

When Lena opens her eyes again, she still can't see. The rough cloth that had been over her face is gone, but there's only darkness everywhere she looks. The left side of her face feels hot and strange, like when she had a bad tooth and her cheek all swelled up, and there's a nasty taste in her mouth, but her hands are still tied behind her back so she can't feel her face to see what's wrong. And there's a smell – an awful smell coming from somewhere that makes her stomach want to turn itself inside out.

She's cold, too. Really cold, and there's a lump in her throat that could be tears. Could be, if she lets them. But she won't. Tough girls don't cry, they . . . they think. They find out stuff and they make plans. And that's what she needs to do.

Her eyes are getting used to the darkness, enough that she can see greyish shapes, outlined against the gloom. What looks like an old wardrobe. Boxes, all piled up on top of each other, a heap of old clothes over in one corner. She's lying on some hard metal thing, like an old-fashioned bed with a thin sort of blanket thrown over it. Maybe if she can get off the bed, she can find something to cut whatever's round her wrists?

Lena wriggles on her side and inches her way forward until her knees bang into something hard and slimy-damp, something that has to be a wall. It hurts, and the lump in her throat gets bigger. But she swallows hard. *Tough girls don't do that. They just don't.*

She turns round, wriggles back the way she'd come and her feet catch in the blanket, pitching her forward onto a rough earth floor.

Her sore face hits the ground, filling her mouth with blood and puke from the smell, the awful smell that's so much closer now. And the lump in her throat is so big, if she doesn't let it out she's going to choke on it . . . Because she's not a tough girl after all, she knows that now. She's just Lena, alone in the dark. Alone, and scared.

She starts to cry. Big, gasping sobs that hurt her chest and make her whole body shake . . . Then stops, the tears sticking in her throat, as something moves in the darkness by the piled-up boxes.

It's slow and sneaky, that movement, as though it belongs to something that likes to hide in the dark. Something with too many legs and eyes. Too many teeth. And Lena doesn't want to have seen it – she wants never to have seen it or heard the odd, rustling sound it made.

But she has to know what it is. Has to. Because anything's better than imagining all those eyes and teeth . . .

'Who . . . who's there?'

No answer.

She calls out again. She stares at the piled-up boxes until her eyes start to go funny. She hears another rustle, fainter this time. And a horrible, horrible groaning sound, like nothing she's ever heard before.

Lena scrabbles backwards, using her bum, her hands, her heels, anything to gain purchase on the evil-smelling floor. Anything to get away from whatever's making that sound.

Which is when the pale white hand comes out of the darkness. And reaches for her.

22

Day 15
Saturday, 15 June

'Boss, I'm not sure about this.' Fergie turns in to Raigmore Hospital, joins the queue of vehicles waiting for the car park. 'I'm supposed to be picking Zofia up in an hour, and I still need to get that squeaking sound looked at.'

'We could hardly take a pool car, could we? I'm on sick leave, and you're off duty. And there's no way I was going to let you loose in mine. Not after last time.'

Fergie sniffs. Bit uncalled for, that, he reckons. That wee dent he'd put in the boss's Beamer was months ago. It was a shame about the hub-caps, mind you. But that was the price you paid for leaving a flash motor like that unattended down the Ferry. 'Aye, well. That wasn't exactly what I meant.'

After a couple of wee false starts, he manages to squeeze the Audi into the parking space he's had his eye on. It's as close to the hospital entrance as he can manage, because, frankly, Mahler doesn't look like he'd cope with the walk from the far end of the car park.

'This okay for you?'

'Fine.' Mahler undoes his seat belt, eases it over his chest. And sits back with a hiss of relief that tells Fergie he's far from pain-free, in spite of the pills. 'Look, you don't have to come any further. I'll tell June Wallace I took a taxi, went in to see Cazza on my own—'

'Aye, and she'd believe that.'

When the news had come in that Cazza had regained consciousness and been moved out of intensive care, Mahler was already on sick leave. Technically. But when the boss had rung him up to ask for a lift into town, Fergie had a feeling it might involve a wee side-trip to the hospital.

He shakes his head. 'Let's face it, boss, Braveheart's going to skin us both alive when she finds out. This way, at least you've got me as a witness to whatever guff Cazza tries to tell you. Just don't expect me to wish him a speedy recovery, eh?'

A nod. 'Thank you. I . . . I appreciate that. Come on, then, let's see what he's got to say for himself.'

The big, ginger-stubbled uniform stationed outside Cazza's room looks as though he's been making himself comfortable; when Fergie and Mahler come round the corner, he's clutching a mug of tea and a mini-pack of Jaffa Cakes. Judging by the biscuit wrappers on the chair next to him, it's not his first wee break of the day.

'Sir!' He catches sight of Mahler and jumps to his feet, setting off a tea tsunami in his mug. 'Sir, I was just—'

'Checking our ID and noting down our names,' Mahler tells him. 'Then cleaning up your uniform, returning your mug to the nurses' station and coming back here to act like a police officer on duty and not some sort of human dustbin. Yes?'

PC Jaffa Cake gulps, scribbles something in his pocketbook and takes off down the corridor as though his arse is on fire.

Fergie watches him vanish round the corner and follows Mahler inside. For a moment, he thinks PC Jaffa Cake has screwed up and they're in the wrong room. The man lying in the bed is a scrawny-looking specimen with grey stubble and a fading suntan beneath a mosaic of purple and red bruises. Then his eyes snap open.

'Oh, aye. I was wondering when you two would show up. Get permission from my doc to come and hassle me, did you?' He squints at Fergie, grunts, looks Mahler up and down. 'Christ, you look as shite as I feel. What are you doing here, checking to see if I'm still breathing?'

'Something like that.' Mahler pulls out the chair by the bed and lowers himself down carefully. 'Time to get real, Carl. We've got things to talk about, and not much time to do it in. The hit-and-run – you think the man called Hollander was behind it, don't you? So, convince me.'

'He's behind fucking all of it, son.' Cazza reaches for the water glass on the nightstand by his bed, takes a tentative sip. 'Folk that work for him, at least. Killing wee Kevin, the fire at the beauty salon, the bastards that put the frighteners on wee Gemma . . . it all goes back to him, in the end. Remember me telling you not to get on his radar?' He puts the glass down, lets his head sink back against the pillows. 'Turns out I should have taken my own fucking advice.'

'So you're just going to let it go now, is that what you're saying?' Mahler shakes his head. 'Because I have to tell you, I'm not buying it. Fergie?'

'Me neither.' Fergie picks up the chart at the foot of Cazza's bed, scans it. 'Man alive, Carl – if it hadn't been for my boss here, Gemma and her mam would be picking out a plot for you at Tomnahurich about now. You going soft in your old age?'

A wheezing laugh, followed by a grimace. 'Jesus, that hurts. Listen to me, son. Go in all guns blazing, and you'll never get near Hollander. Never. You're like . . . like tiny wee fish food and he's a damn great shark.'

Mahler shrugs. This isn't anything he hasn't heard before. 'So why come to me about him in the first place?'

Cazza raises his head, looks at him. 'You don't start with the shark, do you? You start with the other wee fish food swimming round him. Pick them off, one at a time. And that's your fucking job, not mine.'

'So, we go after your competition and leave the field clear for you?' Mahler shakes his head. 'Not how it works, Carl. You need to tell us—'

'Christ, how many times? You need to go after them, son, and you need to do it soon – because if you don't, they'll go after you. You, and that bonny girl you were with at Eden Court.' He grins at Mahler. 'Morven Murray's sister, isn't she? I remember her from all the trial coverage. And if I remember her, you can bet other folk will too.'

Fergie moves then. Moves to clamp his hand on the boss's arm before he takes another step towards the bed. Because the look on his face isn't one Fergie's seen before. And he's damn sure he doesn't want to see it again.

'I hope that wasn't a threat, Carl. I really do. Because if Wullie Grant or any of your knuckle-dragging minions so much as breathe on her—'

'Aye, I know fine what you'd do. Your face is telling me.' Something feral in the grin Cazza gives Mahler then, something that makes Fergie itch to see him in a cell at Burnett Road, in spite of his battered features and bandaged chest. 'Might even be fun sometime, if you fancy a square go.' The grin fades. 'But right now you're being stupid, I'm tired and my chest is fucking killing me, so I'll spell it out for you. Hollander's boys tried to off me – and thanks to you, they failed. So you're well and truly on their radar now, son. You, and everyone connected to you.' He reaches for the call button on his bed, holds it up to show them. 'Now piss off before I get the nurse to throw you out for harassing me.'

Mahler nods at the door. Fergie follows him outside and back to the lifts.

'So what do you think, boss? About this Hollander guy?'

Mahler gives him a weary look. 'God knows. If Hollander does exist, why has no one heard of him?'

'Aye, I don't get that either.'

Fergie watches the boss as they walk across the car park; there's a little more colour in his face, but he's breathing heavily by the time they get back to the Audi.

'Someone's definitely gunning for Cazza, though. Not seen him that rattled before.'

'Agreed. But nothing he's said takes us much further forward.' Mahler gets in carefully, eases the seat belt round himself. 'Look, I'm sorry to have dragged you out here for nothing. Please give Zofia my apologies for wrecking your weekend.'

Fergie shakes his head. 'Not nothing, boss. And Zofia . . . well, she wasn't in the best tune anyway this morning.' He tells Mahler about the phone call she'd had yesterday evening from her cousin in Leeds. 'Agata's been there for sixteen years, working as a pharmacist. Two bairns in school, married, mortgage, the lot. And some wee bastards graffitied her house and told her to fuck off home to Poland. She's worried sick, boss, and it's got Zo worried too. What the hell am I supposed to say to her – it'll all die down again after the vote? Because right now, I can't see it.'

Mahler shakes his head. 'The vote will be over and done with in a few weeks. Oh, there will always be idiots and xenophobes around, but it's hard to believe the electorate en masse could be quite that stupid.'

Fergie shrugs. He thinks most folk are all too ready to believe any sort of bollocks if they hear it often enough. But he's not really one for politics, so what does he know?

'Let's hope you're right, eh?' He starts the Audi's engine,

waits for it to stop coughing. 'What's the plan about Hollander, then? Assuming Cazza doesn't clype to his lawyer about our wee visit.'

'Officially, I can't be involved in the investigation. Un-officially?' Mahler taps his contact list on his mobile, brings up Karen Gilchrist's details. 'We have a friend in SOCA at Gartcosh, don't we? I think it's time we had a catch-up.'

23

Day 16
Sunday, 16 June

9.15 a.m. The kind of summer morning the tourists probably think is typical of Inverness. Bright sky, shimmering river. Ben Wyvis in the distance, topped with the last of the winter snows. The streets clean and the alkies off their benches outside Poundland. And Flora MacDonald up on her pedestal by the castle, gazing out over the Ness with her dog at her side. Either looking for a last glimpse of her bonnie prince or making sure the feckless Stuart wino's actually gone for good, depending on your view of Highland history. Andy Black's pretty sure which one gets his vote.

He goes over to his bedroom window, opens his blinds. Looks down on the unlovely sight of the wifie from the downstairs flat picking up after her dog in the manky communal back garden. An actual shite start to what'll be a typical shite Sunday, then. Good to know.

He shaves, throws on yesterday's hoodie and jeans and heads across to Aldi for a couple of cans of pick-me-up. Last night's curry is lying in his gut, but it's not a peaceful sort of lying; if he doesn't anaesthetise it with a hair of the dog, Andy's got an idea it might decide to make its presence felt again.

He gets what he needs from the supermarket, throws in a

twin pack of sausage rolls for the protein and sets off for one of the benches along the canal. Quick dose of fresh air, that's what he needs after last night. It had started well enough, he remembers that. Bit of nonsense with the blonde lassie from McCallums, music loud enough to set the eardrums buzzing, just the way he likes it. Afterwards . . . aye, well, afterwards it gets a wee bit hazy.

Andy gets his phone out, checks the messages. None from the blonde lassie, but he'd half expected that. The other one, though . . . He must have deleted it, he thinks. Not there now, anyhow.

He settles down on his favourite bench to watch the joggers puffing past towards Torvean. Fucking stupid way to spend a Sunday morning, that, he always thinks. Keeping yourself fit, watching what you eat, cutting down on the drink to buy yourself a couple more years in a care home. Big fucking deal.

He wolfs down one of the sausage rolls, opens his first can . . . and the twitch at the back of his neck, the cop's instinct that's never played him wrong in all his time in the job, tells him to turn and face the guy walking towards him along the towpath.

At first glance, he looks like Mr Average. Average build, average features, average height. But Andy's pretty sure Mr Average doesn't wear designer watches that cost a couple of thousand for a stroll along the canal.

'DI Black.' The man flashes an amiable grin, takes a seat on the bench. His voice is a mix of smoothed-out central belt and something more exotic, something Andy can't place. 'Lovely morning, isn't it? Perfect for a little chat here by the water. Don't you think?'

'Don't think I know you, pal.' Andy puts his can down, folds his arms. 'Want to tell me where we've met and how you know my fucking name?'

The grin fades fractionally. 'We met recently over a drink . . . though we weren't on speaking terms then, of course. But now the people I work for are keen to get a conversation started.'

Andy looks him up and down. Switches the chinos and Barbour outfit for jeans and a dark top, the canal for a lochside pub. 'The Dores Inn, aye? Suppose you tell me who you work for. And why the fuck I should care.'

'Why don't we call it a . . . multinational undertaking? Which happens to be recruiting at the moment for your particular skill set.'

'My skill set's spoken for.'

'What we had in mind was a bit of freelancing. Suitably remunerated, naturally.'

'Meaning?'

The guy sits back, watches a couple of cyclists ride past. 'Warren Jackson. A friend of yours from way back, yes? He had an . . . arrangement with us. A partnership, if you want to call it that. And now we're in the business for a new partner.'

Aye, right. Andy's got a good idea what sort of business they're in. The kind that involves brown envelopes and bundles of used twenties. 'Warren Jackson was a good cop. He put guys like you away all the time.'

'And how do you think he did it? He wasn't that good a cop, DI Black. Not without a bit of help . . . and from what I hear, your career could use some assistance after your little hiccup over in the States recently. Or have I got that wrong?'

The twitch at the back of Andy's neck is jumping now. How the hell does this guy know about that?

He shakes his head. 'Whatever you're selling, I'm not buying, pal. Now piss—'

The man's hand shoots out and closes round Andy's wrist as he's about to get up. 'Not a good idea. Pal. Not a good idea at all.' He smiles at a passing dog-walker, watches until she's out of sight. 'Look, you weren't expecting this, I get that. So why don't you take a little time to think things over? In the meantime, here's a little something to be going on with.'

He lets go of Andy's wrist, reaches into his jacket to take out a padded envelope and lays it on the bench between them. The flap is open, facing Andy, and the contents are bulky enough to make the envelope bulge in the middle.

And all Andy has to do is shake his head. Tell the guy to get lost, and mean it this time. Stand up, and walk away.

But the envelope . . . He can't help measuring that puffed-up centre and running crazy mental estimates of how many little somethings might make it bulge like that.

He takes out his keys, uses the one from his lock-up to lift the flap. And isn't quick enough to hide the wash of disappointment that fills him when he sees the contents.

The guy's smug, mock-sympathetic smile makes Andy want to take the keys and push them right into his face.

'What's this?'

'Intelligence, Andy. Intelligence. Let's call it a little insurance policy for you, shall we? And a way of getting in touch, once you've thought things over.'

'And if I say no? What then, a couple of big bampots waiting for me outside The Fluke one night to break a few bones, that it?'

The man shakes his head. 'Not how we operate. If you're not interested in doing business with us, that's your choice . . . Trust me, we've got plenty of other options to explore. But let's just say you come highly recommended.'

His gut gives a sick little twist. That bastard Jackson. Three years since the guy he'd thought of as his friend had been sent down; and Andy had sweated through a few bad nights back then, when it had all blown up. A few fucking awful days too, come to that, when he'd expected Professional Standards to come knocking on his door on an hourly basis.

And he hadn't even done anything, had he? Not anything he'd left his prints on, anyway. Not anything traceable – unlike Jackson. After the dust from Mahler's investigation had settled, Andy had been so bloody grateful he'd survived that he hadn't stopped to wonder why his old pal hadn't handed him over to save his own neck. But Andy's working it out now, all right; when push came to shove, Jackson *had* handed him over. Just not to the suits.

He shakes his head. 'Not happening, pal. Going to chuck this in the nearest bin . . . if I don't take it in to forensics, that is.'

The smirk on the guy's face tells him exactly how much luck CSI would have if he did pass it to them. 'Your choice, Andy. Your choice. But a word of advice – don't take too long to think things over. This is what you might call a limited-time offer.' He gets to his feet, looks up at the brightening blue of the sky. 'Going to be a fine day now the sun's properly out, don't you think? Good to meet you, Andy. Take care.'

24

Day 17

Monday, 6 June

'Lukas.' Karen Gilchrist sounds less than delighted to hear from him, though that could be down to her location; he can hear seabirds crying and the steady chug-chug of an engine over the kind of howling wind he associates with the wilder stretches of Scottish coastline. 'Let me guess, you've been leaving me messages for the last two days because you're desperate for a wee catch-up.'

Almost a year since Karen Gilchrist's transfer to the Serious Organised Crime Taskforce at the Gartcosh crime campus, and Mahler can hear the new confidence in her voice. Her promotion to DI had been no more than she deserved, and he'd fully supported her application to the taskforce, even though Gartcosh's gain had been Inverness MIT's loss.

'No need, Fergie keeps me up to date with all your achievements – of which you should be very proud, by the way. But I'm actually calling about a mutual friend of ours.'

A sigh from the other end of the line. 'Not going to like this, am I? Okay, then, go for it. But I can't do anything until I get back to the shop. I'm on a bit of a fishing trip today.'

Which may make two of them, Mahler suspects. He gives Karen a rundown of his encounter with Cazza at Eden Court and what had happened at the hospital. When he finishes, there's silence on the other end of the line, punctuated with the random cries of what sound like herring gulls.

'Christ, Lukas. You know we looked into all this Hollander stuff in connection with Kevin Ramsay's murder and came up with a big fat zero. This is Cazza spinning you the same line he fed us back then, that's all.'

'I don't think so,' Mahler tells her. 'Someone tried to take him out, and it looked pretty damn professional to me. Big black 4x4, cloned plates, the works. Remind you of anything?'

'Kevin Ramsay's murder. Aye, I get that. But Cazza—'

'Cazza's shaken, Karen. And *if* Hollander is behind this, I think he's got good reason.'

Her sigh is louder this time. 'And you want me to dig up the invisible man for you, right? What makes you think—'

Shouting at the other end of the phone. Several sets of booted feet, running on what sounds like shingle. Sirens.

'Fuck, that's not supposed to – look, I'll see what I can do, right? Got to go.'

A burst of static and the call disconnects. Mahler pushes back his chair to go and find Fergie, and his mobile flashes up a reminder for his scheduled bollocking by June Wallace and the Chief. Ah well, at least it spares him the overtime spreadsheets for a while.

He stands too quickly and the pain in his ribs rips through him.

Andy Black leans back in his chair, looks him up and down. 'Easy does it, eh? Wouldn't want you to do any more damage to yourself.'

'Your concern is truly touching. Where are we with Anthea Bradley – did Pete chase up that CCTV footage from the bus station?'

They'd drawn a blank with her neighbours, none of whom

could pinpoint the last time they'd seen her. But Black's search of the cottage had turned up Tuesday's *Inverness Courier* and the Inverness bus timetable lying on the dresser in the kitchen. Conclusive? Hardly. But at least it gives them a starting point.

'Going through it now. Just got her call logs, too – what's the betting we find a list of calls to a burner phone we trace right back to her paedo son? Told you all that "fresh start" nonsense was a load of shite.'

'Perhaps.' Though something about Black's summary of the search he'd supervised at Anthea Bradley's cottage is nagging at Mahler. 'We're checking with all the contractors she had working there too, yes? The gardeners seemed to think—'

His mobile bleeps with a text alert; June Wallace, no doubt, reminding him of the impending kicking the Chief will be champing at the bit to inflict on him. Mahler sorts out a debrief session with Black after his meeting and goes upstairs to June's office, to be confronted with a locked door and a text telling him she's halfway down the A9 with the Chief, heading for a hastily rescheduled strategy meeting at Tulliallan.

Don't think you're off the hook, mind, it reads. *Keep your head down, get on with those overtime projections and stay out of trouble until I get back. That last bit goes double for Andy Black.*

Overtime projections. Evaluations. Quarterly assessments. Admin tasks begetting admin tasks; and they're part of his job, of course they are. A soul-destroying, endlessly self-perpetuating part. But still, part of what he signed up for as a DI. He's supposed to manage and direct investigating teams, not muck in with them on the day-to-day stuff. There are plenty of good coppers on the ground right now, doing what needs to be done: tracking down witnesses, taking statements. Putting in the legwork. No reason for him to get out there and do any of it himself.

No reason, except it's been seventeen days since Erin

MacKenzie's abduction, four days since Lena McNally's. And each and every minute of those days is pressing down on him, urging him to move, to act, to *do*. They're running out of time; he knows it, everyone in the MIT knows it, and he suspects June Wallace knows it too.

Mahler runs through the day's allocations in his head. Fergie and Gary are following up reports of a burnt-out van near an abandoned lock-up in Smithton. Donna's talking to the staff and children at Lena's school and Nazreen's ploughing through the CCTV footage and call logs with Pete. It's a thankless, eyestrain-inducing task, but right now it's potentially one of the best chances they've got of picking up Anthea Bradley's trail. Which feels like a good enough reason to give up on the overtime projections and get a progress update.

He heads up to the cramped, airless cupboard Pete's currently having to use as a makeshift viewing room while the existing one gets upgraded. Mahler isn't expecting Anthea Bradley's call logs to lead him directly to her son. But if she did travel to Inverness, they should be able to triangulate her calls from there and pick up any anomalies.

'You must be psychic, boss.' Pete looks round as Mahler enters. There are blue-black rings under his eyes and a pile of empty KitKat wrappers by his console, testimony to the hours he's spent trawling through the footage. 'I was just going to text you.'

'You've got something?'

Pete rubs the ginger bristles on his chin. 'Something, yes. Not exactly sure what, though. Naz?'

Nazreen nods. She puts down her 'Staggies since 1929' mug, pulls up a file on her monitor. 'These are the calls to and from Anthea's mobile for the last month. A couple to her GP, one to cardiology outpatients at Raigmore, gardeners, kitchen fitters, glaziers . . . all perfectly normal, standard stuff. And then, there's these two.' She taps the screen with her pen, ignoring Pete's tut of annoyance. 'The first number rings her for the first time on Wednesday evening – ten calls, roughly twenty minutes apart, all lasting less than a minute.'

'Nuisance calls?'

'Looks like it, doesn't it? Most likely a burn phone, not on any sort of contract. But then there's these.' Nazreen points out the list of calls from a second number. 'Only three calls from this one, all on the Thursday morning. First call under a minute at 8.03, the next ten minutes later – this was much longer, nearly twenty minutes. Final one at 9.20, again for less than a minute. If I had to guess, I'd say she was making arrangements with someone.'

And there it is, at last. Not excitement as they stare at Naz's screen – at this stage, it's a possibility they're looking at, no more than that – but if the second phone belongs to Maxwell Bradley, and they can trace Anthea's movements after she left Muir of Ord . . .

'What about the bus station CCTV? If we can work out which bus she took from Muir of Ord to Farraline Park—'

Pete pulls a face. 'That's where it gets complicated. We've scanned all the footage from the Wednesday morning until DI Black and Gary visited on Thursday, and Naz has checked with the driver on that route last week. No one matching Anthea Bradley's description came into Inverness by bus on either day.'

'What about the other direction? Could she have gone to Dingwall, taken a train or bus from there?'

'We're still waiting to hear back on that,' Nazreen tells Mahler. 'And if she did, tracing her movements from there is going to be almost impossible. But we don't think she did. Because there's something else too.' She points to another of the entries. 'This call here, the one to Raigmore? Turns out she was ringing to check the time of her appointment on Friday.'

'And we know this how?'

'Ah.' A sudden flush of colour in her cheeks. 'It seems her daughter was supposed to be giving her a lift home, but got the arrangements mixed up. The receptionist she spoke to was quite worried about Anthea, because she'd been so careful to check her appointment time and then didn't attend.'

'Her daughter, I see. This would be a daughter we weren't previously aware of, I assume? One that happens to work for Police Scotland, North Division? In the MIT?'

'Sorry, sir.'

Mahler watches the flush deepen. Sighs. 'I assume her daughter's aware of the consequences of trying to obtain confidential patient information by deception?' Before she can say anything, he holds up his hand. 'No, don't answer that. Please. So, as late as – when did she call the hospital, Thursday? – as late as Thursday morning, she fully intended to keep her appointment.'

Nazreen nods. 'She's got unstable angina, boss. My grandad had it too, and it's not something you mess about with. I think if she'd been able to keep that appointment, she'd have done it.'

The knife-twist of a migraine, slicing at his optic nerve. Mahler stares at the screen. Too many anomalies, here; too many pieces of a pattern refusing to come together. And through them all, a curling thread of unease.

'Right. Pete, chase up the bus driver on the Dingwall route. I agree it's unlikely, but we can't rule it out yet.' He starts to say something else, glances at the email that's just hit the inbox on his mobile and smiles. 'And, for once, we have some good news – Nazreen, go downstairs and scare up some transport for us. The warrant's just come through for us to search Anthea's property.'

25

The gardeners haven't been told to stop their work at the cottage, it turns out; as Mahler and Nazreen are driving out to Muir of Ord, Kerry from *Bizzy Lizzies* rings Nazreen back to say they'd been called away to another job but were planning to resume work at the cottage in a couple of days.

'Anthea's all right, isn't she?' On speaker, Kerry sounds genuinely concerned. 'We thought she looked a bit under the weather on Wednesday, but she just said she'd had a bad night.'

Nazreen thanks her for getting in touch, ends the call. 'The kitchen fitters weren't due back until tomorrow anyway,' she tells Mahler. 'So, if she did need to organise a getaway, it makes sense for her to do it when she knew no one would notice she'd gone for a day or so.'

'You don't think that's what happened, though, do you?'

'She seemed on the level to me, boss . . . I know, I know, we need to stay objective. But she seemed like she'd genuinely been through a nightmare and was desperate to start again.' She gives an embarrassed shrug. 'Maybe she just managed to pull the wool over my eyes, that's all.'

It's possible, of course. But in a choice between Nazreen's assessment of Anthea Bradley's character and Andy Black's,

Mahler knows whose judgement he'd favour. And there's a twist of unease working its way between his shoulders as they head out over the Kessock Bridge and up to Tore; the sort of twist he might have dismissed, back in his Met days. 'We'll know more once we've taken a look round. Let's reserve judgement until then.'

By the time they turn up the rutted single-track road to the cottage, the weather has turned. Sullen grey clouds are gathering, veiling the tops of the hills, and the first drops of rain are starting to fall as Nazreen pulls up outside the cottage.

Even in the space of a few days, the building's begun to revert to its previously abandoned appearance. The bright new UPVC windows look brash and out of place, like Hollywood-white veneers on an ageing rock star.

As they walk up the path to the front door, Mahler looks up at the two upstairs rooms with their twin dormers. And pushes aside thoughts of Shirley Jackson's Hill House and things that walked alone there. 'There's a key under the pot of geraniums, Gary said.'

At the sound of his voice, Nazreen jumps. 'Sorry. It's just . . . it's a bit weird, isn't it? Empty houses always give me the creeps.' She finds the key, goes to fit it in the lock. And the door swings open.

Mahler and Nazreen exchange glances. The lock and wooden door are undamaged, so Andy's search team had located the key and been able to enter without causing any damage to the property. And not even Andy would have left a property lying open after a search if the means to secure it were so easily to hand.

Wordlessly, Mahler digs in his pocket, retrieves two sets of nitrile gloves and passes one to Nazreen. He calls out to identify himself, waits for a response, then pushes the door open.

Motioning to Nazreen to follow, he checks the kitchen and

the living room. No sign of anyone in either of the downstairs rooms, but the pull between his shoulder blades is getting more insistent. He heads towards the stairs. And stops short at the first bright splash of scarlet on the wall above the bannister.

'Sir, what's—'

Mahler holds up his hand for silence. Listens, then tries another call out, though by now he's certain he won't get a response; the house carries the chill of somewhere that's been uninhabited for several days. Careful not to touch the bannister, and walking to the side of where most people would instinctively tread, he follows the line of red upstairs.

He peers into the smaller bedroom, still in the process of being converted to an en suite. Nothing but a pile of plumbing components and a few shattered tiles that have spilled out of a box, perhaps casualties of the search Andy Black's team had carried out. A spatter of red on the door frame, as though someone had brushed against it on their way past.

He turns towards the main bedroom, and almost collides with Nazreen. She's standing stock-still, her eyes wide as she stares through the open door to the scarlet and black devastation in front of her. Sticky-bright pools of red coagulate across the floor and up the walls, a brutal patchwork that makes the breath slow in Mahler's throat. Until he takes a closer look at the texture of what's smeared across the wood-panelled door.

The chill on the back of his neck subsides. A little. He touches a cautious nitrile-gloved finger to one of the thicker smears, takes a confirmatory sniff and turns to Nazreen. 'Not what it looks like. Smell this.'

She leans forward. Inhales. And lets her shoulders slump in relief. 'Paint. Bloody bastarding . . .' she shakes her head. 'Sorry, sir. For a moment, I thought . . .'

'Me too. But I think we can take that . . .' he gestures at the trio of paint tins abandoned on the floor, 'as fairly substantial evidence to the contrary, don't you?'

'Just vandalism, then?' She gives him a dubious look. 'Feels more personal than that.'

'Oh, it's very personal.' He points at the paint-soaked ruins of what had been an antique lace bedspread and white pin-tucked pillowcases. 'You don't do that to someone's private space unless you've really got it in for them. This is very deliberate, very targeted harassment – and I'll lay odds, whoever smashed her windows is responsible for this too.'

'An escalation?' Nazreen nods. 'They must have been watching her. Then when she went out . . . How did they know where the spare key was, though?'

'It's where everyone hides it, that's how. There, or under the mat. And if they'd just kicked the door in, she'd have known something was up – this way, she's got a nice little surprise waiting when she goes upstairs.' Mahler takes a final look round, nods at Nazreen. 'Come on. We'll take a look round outside, then call it in. We need a proper forensics team in to go through this.'

The rain is coming down in earnest as they retrace their steps. While Nazreen takes the back garden, Mahler makes his way up to the patch of rough ground the gardeners had been clearing by the summerhouse, taking care to walk on the remains of a gravel path rather than the soft soil. The summerhouse's position on the slight rise makes it a perfect vantage point for anyone wanting to keep watch on the house below, and if the perpetrators have left any forensic evidence nearby which might be recoverable—

He can hardly hear the noise at first. It's a distant buzzing, almost inaudible above the increasingly heavy rain, so barely-there that for a moment Mahler doesn't connect it to the prickling at the base of his neck.

Footsteps on the gravel behind him. He turns to see Nazreen coming up the path towards him. And his slight shift in position lets him pick up on something else, something he's missed until now: a faint but unmistakeable odour seeping from the gaps in the sagging door frame.

'Sir—'

He raises a hand. 'Wait.' He walks up to the summerhouse door. The glass panes look smoky, opaque, as though someone's been spray-painting them from the inside. But the paint isn't solid; as he gets closer, he can see it shifting. Moving.

Mahler reaches out and taps one of the panes with his gloved finger. Disturbed, the smoke-shape moves again. And reveals the source of the smell the sacks of manure the gardeners left behind hadn't quite been able to mask.

He steps back from the door. Composes his face. Turns. 'Call this in please, Nazreen. It looks like we've found Anthea Bradley.'

The rain is starting to ease by the time Mahler gets back to Burnett Road. He'd left Marco McVinish, the pathologist, at the scene with the CSI team, complaining about the precarious condition of the summerhouse floor.

'If you're thinking about asking me to pinpoint time of death, don't bother,' Marco had growled through his face mask at him and Nazreen. 'The best I can offer you at the moment is that the blowflies have been having a party in this poor wifie, which occurs approximately forty-eight hours after death. Assuming I survive crawling around in this bloody deathtrap with nothing more deadly than a splinter or two in my arse, you'll get the rest when I'm back at Raigmore.'

Marco hadn't been any more forthcoming on the likely cause of death, though Mahler had expected as much; Anthea Bradley's body had been lying just a few feet from the entrance to the summerhouse, her head thrown back and her hands curled into fists. Dark fluids had soaked from her into the rotting floor, and her face . . .

Mahler knows there's nothing to be read from the expressions on the faces of the dead; muscles contort post-mortem through simple physiological processes, nothing more. But seated at his laptop after everyone else has left, typing up the report June Wallace will want the minute she gets back from Tulliallan, the memory of the look on Anthea Bradley's face refuses to leave him. And it's telling him there had been nothing peaceful about her final moments.

'Thought you'd still be here.' June Wallace pushes open Mahler's office door, looks round. 'Any coffee on the go? I'm fit to drop. And if there's any of those Harry Gow dream rings left from Donna's birthday . . .' she catches sight of his expression, sighs. 'Aye, well, I suppose that was too much to hope for. One of her KitKats, then.'

She drags out the only spare chair in his office, the one wedged against the filing cabinet, and slumps down onto it. The hollows under her eyes are so dark, Mahler suspects the throwaway comment about being close to collapse isn't far off the mark; on the other hand, he's pretty sure spending an entire day in Chae Hunt's company would produce a similar effect in ninety-five per cent of the population.

'Coffee,' June reminds him. 'Strong and sweet enough to stand the spoon up in . . . and then you can tell me everything about this monumental fuck-up I've just come back to.'

'Ma'am.' There are other responses he could make, but his sense of self-preservation kicks in just in time. Mahler has no idea how she's heard about the discovery of Anthea Bradley's body so quickly; he's only halfway through the report he'd been writing and June's been driving back up the A9 for the last three hours. But knowing how eerily attuned she is to everything that happens at Burnett Road, he isn't ruling out some sort of telepathic Bluetooth connection with the building.

He sets up his coffee machine, borrows milk from Pete's supply and retrieves two of Donna's KitKats before returning to the office. When he sets them down in front of her, June raises an eyebrow.

'Double rations, eh? Christ, now I know it's bad.' She takes a long drink from the coffee mug he hands her, rips the paper off one of the KitKats. 'Right, then. Spill.'

'Ma'am, my report—'

'Will be the first thing I read tomorrow morning, trust me.' She takes another gulp of coffee. 'But it's been a long day, Lukas. For both of us. Right now, the edited highlights will do just fine.'

26

Day 18

Tuesday, 7 June

Livvy McIver wakes up to the sound of her mobile buzzing under her pillow. She keeps her eyes closed for as long as she can and turns her face away from the noise, but it's no good. The sound feels as though it's coming from inside her brain, as though there's something in there making it happen. Making them do it. She doesn't think that's true, not really. But she knows it isn't going to stop until she looks at what they've sent her this time.

She sits up in bed, pulls the duvet up to her neck in spite of the sun glinting through the gap in her bedroom curtains and reaches for her phone. The screen fills up immediately, but Livvy doesn't think there are as many messages as last night – maybe it's like Mummy says, and they're starting to get bored of tormenting her?

She opens the first message. Looks at the photo she's been sent and the words someone's written underneath it. And that's all it takes to make her start crying again, like last night. Like yesterday teatime. Like all the other times Mummy doesn't know about.

She scrubs at her eyes. It isn't fair. Jazzy and Morgan were just as mean to Erin as she was; more, really. Whose idea had it been to invite Erin to her birthday in the first place? Not hers. Why would she invite Erin with her wonky smile and her cheap New Look trainers? They'd never gone around with Erin, never, and suddenly she thought they were all besties?

Oh, she thought she was so clever – always showing off in class, answering Miss Christie's questions before anyone else had a chance – but she was too stupid to work out that no one liked her, no one wanted to be her friend. That takes a special kind of stupid.

Livvy can't even remember now why Morgan and Jazzy had wanted her to invite Erin, or what it was they'd planned to do. But they hadn't had time, anyway; Erin's goofy smile had faded when she'd seen that no one wanted her there, and she'd wandered off into the garden.

Stupid, stupid Erin. Why hadn't she just gone home? Her dad could have picked her up in that ratty old van of his, and then she wouldn't have . . . the thing wouldn't have happened to her that none of the grown-ups want to talk about. And Livvy's friends – girls she *thought* were her friends – wouldn't be sending her these mean texts. Wouldn't be telling *their* families, their big brothers and sisters, that it was her fault the thing had happened. Wouldn't be making her wish school had broken up already and she was on her Florida holiday with Mummy and Liam.

She pushes back her duvet, opens her curtains to see if it's as nice and hot as the warm breeze coming through her open window suggests. If it gets really hot, maybe she can get Mummy to let her stay off school today. She can pretend her tummy's hurting again, put her fingers down her throat to make herself throw up like Morgan's sister does. Then maybe—

There's something moving underneath the big sycamore at the bottom of the garden. No, not moving, Livvy decides after a moment. It's just the wind catching the slumped dark shape, making it look like it's alive. It reminds her of when they'd been sorting out old clothes to send to the charity shop and the bin bag had toppled over because she'd got bored and stuffed it too full. It's sort of like that . . . but not quite.

She thinks about getting Mummy to go and look with her, but Mummy had another fight with Liam last night and she's always the bitch from hell the morning after, Livvy's heard her say so on the phone to Granny. Maybe she'd thrown Liam out again and that was why the house was so quiet? It'd be funny if that was a bag of Liam's favourite designer shirts getting filthy out there.

Livvy pulls on her sweatshirt over her pyjamas, slips her feet into her trainers and goes downstairs. She slides the patio doors open and sets off towards the tree, wondering if Mummy's chucked out that manky blue shirt he's got with the little pineapples on it. And his big smelly loafers? That would be so—

She's not far from the tree when her foot catches in the leg of her pyjama trousers. She trips and pitches forwards, into the patch of muddy shade beneath the sycamore's dense branches. And lands next to the thing she'd taken for a bag of discarded clothing.

A voice calling out to her, sounding like her mummy. Footsteps running across the grass towards her. Arms scooping her up, carrying her back to the house, the voice that sounds like her mummy telling her to hush, that everything's okay. But Livvy knows that isn't true. The noise inside her head has changed, and there's nothing okay about it. Nothing.

She clamps her hands over her ears, trying to block it out. Because she knows what the thing is now. *Who* it is now.

And why she's screaming.

It's the call that part of him had always known would come. The call everyone at Burnett Road had braced themselves for, as the days had passed and hope's slow erosion had begun. But no shell of professional detachment can withstand the sudden sharp reality of a child's unnatural death. Mahler pulls up outside the McIvers' house with the knowledge of his failure playing inside his head on a bitter, endless loop.

He talks to the first responder officers, checks the McIvers are being made comfortable while the inevitable tests and elimination procedures take place. The procedures are necessary, but Livvy's traumatised enough for him to insist the McIvers' GP is called as well as the girl's grandmother. The press are already starting to arrive, and the McIvers aren't in any state to deal with them. Mahler positions one of the first responders on the front door and the other by the side gate to discourage any scoop-hungry journalists before he heads for the McIvers' back garden.

The scene examiner and forensic teams have only been there for a short time, but they've clearly been working flat out to secure the locus. Two-thirds of the garden, from the edge of the decking down to the cluster of trees at its perimeter, have been cordoned off with incident tape. Dull metal plates mark out the approach path to the CSI tent where white-suited figures swelter in the heat of a bright June morning.

The bearlike figure of Marco McVinish is standing in the doorway of the tent, stripping off his nitrile gloves and pulling down his mask. Looking as though what he's just seen is going to stay with him for a long, long time. The pathologist looks up at Mahler's approach. And gives a nod of confirmation before he can ask his first question.

'Erin,' McVinish tells him. 'You'll want the parents to make a formal ID, but there's no doubt. The face is . . . it's not pretty. But it is recognisable.' He swallows, looks away. 'Just about.'

Mahler nods. He'd guessed it was bad as soon as the news had come through. There are ways to hear beyond the professionalism of police call-handlers' reports, ways he's learned through hard experience during his time in the Met. And Marco is no stranger to the landscapes of unnatural death; if what he's seen inside that tent has unsettled him this much . . . Mahler calms his breathing, glances at the pathologist.

'Fiscal's been, I take it?' At Marco's nod, he pushes back the tent flap. Looks inside. Takes a deep breath that makes the pain in his ribs sing and turns back to Marco. 'The thing on her neck? The . . . the sore?'

'At a guess? Some sort of bite. But, as you saw, there are multiple injuries, so . . .' he shakes his head. 'I won't know more until I can get her back to Raigmore.'

'Of course.' Mahler lifts the tent flap again, calls the scene examiner over. 'Any idea how much longer?'

She frowns, looks back at one of her colleagues who's placing a small plastic marker by a greyish object close to the body. 'We're working down by the burn as well, so it'll be a while yet.'

'That's where she was brought here from?'

'Looks like it – there are some interesting tyre tracks we'll be lifting. Soil's a bit churned up, though, so it's not that straightforward.'

Mahler nods. It never is, in his experience. 'Let me know when she's ready to go, can you? If we time it right, I can keep our media friends busy, and—'

'I'll do that.' Andy Black appears by the entrance, his white Teletubby suit straining at the seams. He'd been down for a half-day stint at court with a drugs-related assault case, so Mahler hadn't expected him to attend this call-out; but apparently bad news isn't the only thing that travels fast.

Black pushes back the flap, takes in the scene inside the tent. 'Jesus, what a mess. We need to talk to the parents pronto, before some fucking journo does it for us.' He gives Mahler a thin, malice-edged smile. 'You're the one they know best, aren't you? And I doubt the Chief wants you showing your face on camera right now. Doesn't inspire confidence, does it, battered-looking cops showing up on the evening news?'

He has a point, Mahler supposes. Though whether Black's growling bouncer persona will do much better is debatable. But he's right about Erin's parents; they need to know the brutal way their ordeal has ended. And they deserve to hear that kind of news from someone who isn't Andy Black.

'Fine.' He turns to Marco McVinish. 'Anthea Bradley. Any update there?'

'Preliminary findings should be with you and DI Black here tonight,' the pathologist tells him. 'But, basically, her heart was a ticking time bomb. She was taking betablocker and angina medication—'

'Natural causes, then? Like a heart attack?'

The pathologist nods at Black. 'Exactly like that. I understand she was on a waiting list for bypass surgery, but looks like she ran out of time. So, no need to keep your case file open on her. Welcome news, I expect.'

'Aye. Good.' Black pulls out his mobile, grunts in satisfaction at the text that's just arrived. 'I'm off back inside – GP's here to see the mother and the wee girl. Hope he can give her something to calm her down, eh? That bloody crying goes right through you after a while.'

Marco McVinish shakes his head as Black returns to the house. 'Back of the queue when they were handing out the empathy gene, your Andy. I've always suspected as much. He's right about one thing, though, your face is a bloody mess.'

'Occupational hazard.' Mahler winces as the pain in his ribs bites again. 'Anthea Bradley . . . given the substantial insect presence on the body, how accurately could an approximate time of death be determined, would you say?'

Marco frowns. 'The blowfly–maggot–blowfly life cycle fol-lows quite a standard pattern, so that will be in my report. If you wanted to be more precise, you'd need a forensic entomol-ogist, of course – they can take into account factors like seasonal variations, local weather conditions and so on.' He glances at Mahler. 'Something bothering you about her, Lukas? The mas-sive coronary infarction she suffered—'

'Was undoubtedly what killed her. Yes, I know.'

Death by natural causes. And that should be the end of it. Should be. But as Mahler walks back to his car, he can't forget the expression he'd glimpsed on Andy Black's face as he looked down at his mobile. It had been a momentary oddness, no more than that, and it had been gone in a fraction of a second.

But it had looked a lot like relief.

Messenger Group: Justice for Erin (secret)
TUES 18.06

Ewan:
Dylan, Tam can u get back to me? Need to talk to youse.
19.20

Ewan:
Not joking here guys, we need to talk.
19.57

Ewan:
Jesus Christ. Left youse both messages on ur mobiles and ur still not answering – what the fucks going on? Not gonna stop so youse need to talk to me. No joke. **Dylan** will you answer your fucking messages man? I need to fucking talk to u. You too **Tam** fucking Bell.

Tam:
Christ man stop it. Are u off ur fuckin head? My wife thinks I'm cheating on her now with all ur bloody calls. Whats wrong with u?

Ewan:
Don't u watch anything but the bloody fitba? She's dead!

Tam:
Who?

Ewan:
Who'd you fucking think? THEY FOUND HER DEAD AT HER FUCKING HOUSE.

Ewan:
They're talking to my boss, **Tam**. Crawling over the wifie's house like a swarm of fucking midgies! What the fuck do we do now?

Ewan:

Tam u better speak to me. U too **Dylan**. If u don't talk to me theres others I can speak to. U know who I mean.

Dylan:

STFU **Ewan**. No joke. STFU and stop talking shite.

Ewan:

Acting the big man now eh? U think Im just letting this go?

Dylan:

Last chance to STFU you wee numpty. Call me or **Tam** again and we'll fucking do you.

Dylan has left the group Justice for Erin (secret).
Tam has left the group Justice for Erin (secret).

27

On his way back to Burnett Road, June texts Mahler to tell him their meeting has been moved to the Chief's office. Clearly, by saving Cazza MacKay's hide outside of one of Inverness's most scenic locations in the height of the tourist season, Mahler's so offended Chae Hunt that the Chief plans to deliver the scheduled arse-kicking in a suitably formal environment.

Chae Hunt looks Mahler up and down as he comes in, nods, motions him to a seat. So he isn't in for a nuclear-level bollocking, Mahler realises; at least, not without having the chance to defend himself.

'DI Mahler. Your punctuality's improving, I see. Only ten minutes late today.'

'I apologise for my lateness, sir. I've just come from the Mac-Kenzies'. Their daughter's body was dumped in a friend's back garden in the early hours of this morning, and they're on their way to Raigmore to identify her formally right now – so you'll excuse me if my time management slipped a little under the circumstances. Sir.'

A puce-tinged flush creeps over Chae Hunt's tanned features. 'DCI Wallace has updated me fully on Erin MacKenzie, Inspector. Not that there's much to update, is there? So far, the only progress your team can point to is a partial number plate, some abysmal CCTV footage and a person of interest who seems to be running bloody rings round you!'

'Sir, that's not—'

June raises a hand to stop him, turns to Hunt. 'DI Mahler's aware I'll be instigating an urgent review of both the Erin Mac-Kenzie and Lena McNally cases, sir.' It's the first Mahler's heard of it, but the look she gives him is enough to warn him into silence. 'In the meantime, Cazza MacKay—'

Hunt nods. 'MacKay. Yes.' He flips open a folder on his desk, turns it round so that the contents are facing Mahler. 'These arrived in the post room yesterday morning. Any comments?'

Mahler looks down at the photographs in front of him. There are three in total, all showing him talking to Cazza. All skilfully shot to make a conversation that had lasted a few minutes look like a meeting of colleagues. Or co-conspirators.

'Sir, as I stated in my report, I had arranged to meet Anna Murray. We discussed the letters she'd been receiving from James Gordon, her sister's killer. I assured her we'd take action to stop this harassment, and—'

'And Cazza MacKay popped up from nowhere, like a genie out of a bottle?' Chae Hunt's botoxed forehead makes an attempt at a frown. 'Fortunately, Dr Murray confirms your account, and the emergency call logs and witness statements support your version of events. No, DI Mahler, do not inter-rupt – I say "your version", because, frankly, you're damn lucky corroborative evidence exists. Otherwise, you'd be having a discussion with Professional Standards about your relationship with MacKay . . . and in all likelihood, DCI Wallace and I would be dealing with Erin MacKenzie's murder and Lena McNally's abduction with you on bloody gardening leave!'

'My relationship?' He swallows the first comment he's tempted to make. 'Sir, that's ridiculous. Cazza MacKay's a fading wannabe crime lord with just enough smarts to stay out of prison. If he ever slips up and I get a chance to put him there, I'll give it my best shot. But, right now, he's genuinely scared because he thinks someone's out to get him – and, if anything, these photos bear that out. What better way to stop an investigation in its tracks than attempting to frame one of the officers involved?'

The Chief glances at June, who nods. 'It makes sense, sir. MacKay's premises have been targeted over the past few months. This could be an escalation.'

'Cazza's convinced it's linked to his renewed efforts to look into Kevin Ramsay's murder,' Mahler tells them. 'We can't afford to ignore the possibility that he's right.'

Silence, then Hunt sighs. He returns the photographs to the folder, closes it. 'Fine, I'll go along with it for now. DI Black will head the investigation under DCI Wallace – DS Ferguson will assist, but you'll take no part in it. Is that clear?'

'Sir, Fergie's already stretched across two live enquiries—'

The puce-tinged flush returns. Hunt shakes his head. 'No more. Not one bloody word. You've got a dead wee girl, and another who's running out of time unless you pull your finger out and find her. I'd suggest that's more than enough to be going on with.' He glances down at his mobile as a message flashes up on the screen. 'I have another appointment in fifteen minutes. June, we'll meet later. DI Mahler, see to it that you and I don't.'

A nod is the only response Mahler trusts himself to give. He rises awkwardly, his ribs on fire, and follows June out.

'Ma'am, I—'

'My turn.' She marches down the corridor, unlocks her own office. 'Inside. You and I need to have a wee discussion. If you think *that* was a bollocking, I promise . . .' she glances at him, shakes her head. 'Ach, sit down, man . . . or stand, whatever's easier for your ribs. It was tough going at the MacKenzies today, wasn't it?'

'It goes with the job, Ma'am. But yes, it was . . . it was difficult.'

His job, today, to bring the death message to Krysia and Grant MacKenzie. His job to explain to them their long wait for news of their daughter had ended in the worst possible way. His job to bear witness to the way Krysia had begun to moan like a wounded animal, grasping for her husband's hand, while Grant MacKenzie had sat, unmoving, his eyes fixed on Mahler. Not understanding anything but the finality of *dead*. And in the end, what else had they needed to understand?

June nods. 'Aye, no wonder. Not a reason to commit career suicide in Chae Hunt's office, though, was it? You do not piss off a superior officer, Lukas. Not when he's holding photos of you looking cosy with Cazza bloody MacKay in his hand.'

'About which he'd made up his mind in advance.'

She gives him a weary look. 'Ach, give the attitude a rest, man. It doesn't suit you. Remember, you've only got me and the Chief on your back – he's got folk coming at him from all sides. So, a wee bit of slack-cutting required, eh? Because last time I heard, we're supposed to be on the same team. And, right now, that means finding the bastard responsible for Erin's murder.' Her expression hardens. 'Before he does the same to Lena.'

No banter in the incident room, not today. When Mahler gets back from his meeting with June, his team are waiting for his briefing in near-silence. Even Andy Black is hunched over his laptop, working through his emails, an event so rare Mahler suspects it ought to be recorded for posterity in the annals of Burnett Road.

He can sense the build up of frustrated anger in the room; in spite of all the hours they've put in, in spite of every lead they've followed, they've failed Erin MacKenzie. Failed her in the worst way possible and, right now, the knowledge of that failure is etched across every single person's face. Including the battered, exhausted one that had stared back at him from his mirror as he'd shaved that morning.

'Right, then.' Straightening his shoulders. Pushing down the pain in his ribs as he crosses to the whiteboards to begin the briefing. 'Andy, if you're happy to start with—'

'Need to head out.' Black closes his laptop, slings his jacket over his shoulder. 'Got a message about one of our pals on the register that might be worth a follow-up. Fill me in later, aye?'

'Of course.' If Andy does have a potential lead, he's kept it to himself, judging by the look on Fergie's face. Mahler's guessing neither of them have been told yet about working together on the Cazza MacKay enquiry, but he can't see that collaboration going well, in spite of Chae Hunt's orders.

But right now, Mahler's got more to worry about than Andy Black's lone-wolf cop impression. The impetus that had driven the team on is faltering; they're losing heart, and he can't let that happen.

As the door closes behind Andy, he peels Erin MacKenzie's photo from the board. Holds it up, making sure it's in every-one's eyeline. And drops it in the bin.

Gasps from around the room. Silence, as they process what they've just seen. And then a slow ripple of anger. Good. That's the reaction Mahler wanted.

'Our killer thinks this is what he's done to Erin,' he tells them. 'He thinks he's destroyed her, turned her into someone who no longer matters. A non-person. But we don't think that.'

He retrieves the photograph, puts it back on the whiteboard in its original position.

'We think Erin matters, and Lena matters. We think every-one touched by what's happened matters – and that's why we keep going. Why we keep knocking on doors, why we spend hours looking at grainy CCTV footage and wading through the crank calls that come through after our appeals. Because we know somewhere in there, we'll find the link we're looking for. The clue that makes it all start to come together.'

Silence once he stops talking. He catches a few nods, the odd doubtful look in his direction. Understandable, Mahler supposes; he'd meant to bolster their morale, not give them a bloody lecture. He glances at Fergie, who picks up his cue.

'Erin's post-mortem is scheduled for tomorrow morning,' Fergie tells them. 'Forensics are being pushed through as fast as possible, including a set of fresh tyre marks near where we think the van was parked when Erin was abducted. If the two sets match, we'll know we're on the right track.'

Mahler nods. 'And Pete has identified a further digit on the van's licence plate, so the updated info will feature on STV and BBC news tonight, as well as Moray Firth Radio and our social media accounts. But that's only half the story.' He points at the third photograph on the whiteboard. 'Lena McNally's been missing for five days. We don't know why Erin was killed, but we have to assume Lena's in even greater danger now.'

'Why now, though?' Nazreen points out. 'Why keep Erin for nearly three weeks, and then kill her? And to dump her back at Livvy McIver's house like that . . . he was taking a hell of a risk.'

Gary shakes his head. 'He doesn't see it like that. He's laughing at us, telling us he can do what he likes and we can't stop him.'

'Then he's due for a shock, isn't he?' Mahler snaps. 'But Nazreen's right to ask the question. He *did* dump Erin. The question is, why? And why there, of all places?'

'Something went wrong,' Fergie offers. 'The killing might have been an accident, or maybe whatever deal he'd got in hand was cancelled? Either way, he wanted to get rid. So he wrapped her up like a piece of rubbish. And he left her there to show us what he thought of her. And us.'

Donna nods. 'It's like returning something you bought online because it wasn't quite what you wanted. Hassle-free, no return postage. Bastard.'

'It's quite an escalation, though,' Mahler points out. 'High-risk, too, just to stick two fingers up at us – there's no way he didn't leave any trace evidence this time. And if he's taking risks, he's making mistakes. Which we'll use to find him and bring him in.'

After the briefing, Fergie hands out the allocations. Mahler watches the team leave; Erin's murder has left its mark on every one of them, but their anger feels more focused. More purposeful. For now.

'They're calling him the Child Snatcher.' Fergie takes out his mobile, passes it to Mahler so he can see the digital edition of the local weekly paper. 'Front page here, top billing on STV news. Makes him sound like something out of a bloody Disney film.'

Mahler shakes his head. 'Nothing cartoonish about this character.' He glances at Fergie. 'Will you attend Erin's p-m? There's something I need to take care of.'

Something he shouldn't even be thinking about. Something that goes against the Chief's direct order to keep away from the Cazza MacKay investigation and will probably earn him a disciplinary if Hunt ever finds out. At the bare minimum.

'Aye, I thought there might be.' Fergie puts his mobile away, picks up his jacket. 'You know Cazza's probably lying about this Hollander guy, right? Giving us a made-up monster to hide the truth about whatever he's mixed up in?'

'Of course. But if he's telling the truth, and something happens—'

Fergie sighs. 'Aye, I get that. Just . . . watch your step, boss. If Cazza's telling the truth about Hollander, the bastard's got you in his sights already.'

28

A screaming, wild-eyed woman, dressed in filthy rags, is dragged bruised and bleeding to the doors of Dornoch Cathedral as a jeering crowd looks on. She holds out a pleading hand to one of the onlookers as she passes, but the man shakes his head and turns away.

'She had been a lady's maid, once upon a time.' The cameras following her, Anna Murray walks slowly through the churchyard. 'Janet Horne had travelled abroad, had seen more of the world than many of the people who came forward to accuse her – and maybe in the end that counted against her as much as her daughter's deformed hand or her own increasing confusion. Certainly, the sheriff who condemned her, Captain David Ross, had no hesitation in pronouncing both Janet and her daughter guilty of witchcraft and sentencing both to death.'

Anna turns, points at the castle. 'The women were imprisoned in Dornoch tolbooth – it's gone now, but we think this is where it would have stood. Somehow, Janet's daughter managed to escape before the sentence could be carried out. But for Janet, there was to be no way out.'

'Okay, that's a good one.' As Mahler watches, a grinning, ponytailed man in painfully bright trainers and a logoed hoodie unhooks something from Anna's peacock-coloured scarf. 'Tea and comfort break, everyone. Back here in twenty minutes for the burning.'

'Thanks, Geoff.' She rummages in the pocket of her coat, pulls out her mobile and holds it up, moving it around in a side-to-side motion. Mahler's time in the Highlands has taught him to recognise it instantly.

'Signal's not too bad in The Courthouse,' Mahler tells her as he walks down the path towards her. 'I've heard their coffee's worth a try too.'

Enough warmth in the smile she gives him for Mahler to hope it might survive the news he's come to deliver. 'Hey, if it's good enough for the History Centre staff . . . how did you know I'd be here?'

'Your colleague, Dr McCormack, told me where to find you.'

They walk over to the café in what until recently had been the town's former courthouse. Mahler had visited it once, briefly, before it closed in 2013, but he has to admit the building's transformation into a bright, high-ceilinged café/restaurant has been sympathetically carried out. They place their order and find a quiet table near the back.

'I didn't realise witch trials were a feature of the Highlands,' he tells her as they wait. 'That was what you were filming, wasn't it?'

'This section, yes. I'd written a paper on women's experiences in Highland culture last year, when the production company I'd worked with on the Clearances documentary got in touch. Which is how I ended up freezing in the grounds of Dornoch Cathedral, telling poor Janet's story in part one of "Wise Women, Witches and Warriors" – and before you ask, the title wasn't my idea.'

'It sounds very . . . intriguing.'

'Stop smirking, then.' A smile to soften the look she gives

him. 'Yes, it's a bit cringeworthy. But I'm not doing this for graduate students – I want people who've never stopped to think about their history to be pulled into these sorts of stories. And moved to find out more about them, I suppose. I'm not going to apologise for that.'

'Of course not.' But he'd come to warn her about Hollander, hoping to persuade her to keep a low profile; filming a documentary about one of the grimmest periods in Scotland's history pretty much guarantees the opposite. 'Why Janet Horne – purely the Dornoch connection?'

A shake of her head. 'Janet was a victim of the times she lived in – poor, with a disabled daughter, likely suffering from dementia when she was accused and condemned. My next segment is about the land reform activist and poet, Mary MacDonald from Skye. Màiri Mhòr nan Òran was loud, she was fierce, and she wasn't anybody's victim.'

'She sounds like quite a character.'

'She was. Màiri didn't . . .' she glances at him, and her smile fades. 'You're not here to talk about my work, though, are you? Your face is full of bruises, and you look like you're in pain when you walk. Do I take it we're having a semi-official, chargeable-to-expenses coffee, Lukas?'

'Not exactly.' He nods a thank you to the waitress as their drinks arrive. 'Though this . . .' he indicates the bruising over his swollen cheekbone, 'is part of why I'm here.'

He gives her a heavily edited version of his encounter with Cazza MacKay and its aftermath. By the time he's finished, she's drunk her coffee and has ordered another to go.

'And you think I should be worried, is that it?'

'I hope there's no need,' Mahler tells her. 'I hope the . . . individual . . . I mentioned is spinning me a line and hoping I'll bite. But I can't – won't – take that risk. And no, this isn't an official discussion.'

194

It's almost the exact opposite. By revealing details of an on-going investigation to a civilian, he's crossed a line, and Mahler has no illusions about what June would do if she found out. But if Cazza's right and Hollander does exist, Mahler's now squarely in his line of fire – and, by extension, so is Anna.

'I need you to be aware that the possibility exists. And I'm asking you to be vigilant, until I get more of a handle on what I might be dealing with.'

'You *are* worried, aren't you? You wouldn't be here, otherwise.'

'I witnessed a hit-and-run that looked like a hell of a lot like attempted murder – and would almost certainly have succeeded if I hadn't happened to be there. So yes, Anna, I'm bloody worried!'

Mahler has to admire the former courtroom's acoustics. The fractional rise in his voice is enough to make the staff behind the counter turn to look at him, and a harried-looking woman with a sleeping infant on her knee gives him the sort of glare June Wallace would be proud of.

'I'm sorry. Look, I didn't mean to alarm you—'

'I'm not alarmed.' A hint of steel in her smile. 'Alarmed isn't something I do these days, not after Jamie Gordon.' She picks up her takeaway coffee, glances at her phone. 'I ought to get back, Geoff will be wondering where I am. Walk with me?'

'Of course.'

Downstairs to find the weather has changed again; swollen graphite clouds are scudding across a gunmetal sky, and the warmth has entirely gone from the air.

Anna wraps the peacock scarf around her throat, gives a mock-shiver as they cross over to the cathedral gates. 'High summer in Dornoch. Yay. Still, at least it should be atmospheric enough for Geoff now.'

'Yay indeed. There's been nothing more from Gordon, I take it?'

Anna shakes her head. 'He wanted a response from me. When I didn't give him one . . .' She shrugs. 'Maybe he's realised it's never going to happen, and moved on.'

'Maybe.' Though Mahler doesn't believe it, and the sudden tight set of her jawline tells him Anna doesn't either. James Gordon had killed three people, including Anna's sister; and if it hadn't been for Anna putting herself in danger in order to trap him, he might never have been caught. 'The harassment charges I threatened him with should certainly have concentrated his mind, but if there's any recurrence—'

'I'll let you know, I promise.'

They're almost at the entrance to the cathedral. Ponytail Geoff is fussing with Janet Horne's rags and casting anxious glances at the sky as the small group of extras dressed as towns-people shelter under the trees.

'Is this where Janet was killed?' Mahler asks. 'Outside the cathedral?'

Anna shakes her head. 'There's a memorial stone marking the spot in a back garden, not too far from here. It's got the wrong date on it, but then her name probably wasn't Janet, so . . .' she shrugs. 'At least her daughter escaped the fire. Though no one quite knows how.'

'Perhaps she was the real witch.'

'Perhaps she was.' The rising wind catches her hair, whips it across her face, so he can't tell if she's smiling or not. 'Lukas, I think they're waiting for me—'

'Of course.' He can see Ponytail Geoff hovering by the cathedral's Victorian Gothic entrance, waiting for him to stop holding up their filming schedule. 'I should get back to Burnett Road too.' Fergie is attending Erin's post-mortem, and June will expect a briefing later that afternoon. But there's a pull between Mahler's shoulder blades, an indefinable something that makes him hesitant to turn and walk away. 'Anna, take care. Please. After the filming's over—'

'I'm not going to hide myself away, Lukas.' A flash of impatience in the look she gives him. 'It's taken me a while, but I'm starting to enjoy my life all over again – so don't ask me to give up on that, because I won't. And this could all be nonsense, couldn't it? You said yourself, this guy could just be spinning you a line.'

'It's not out of the question.' Though it's hard to see what Cazza would have to gain from lying about it. 'Believe me, on this occasion I'd be delighted to be proved wrong.'

Anna raises a hand in farewell, heads over to Ponytail Geoff to prepare for the afternoon's filming.

Mahler's on his way across the churchyard to pick up his car when a thought occurs to him. He turns to call after Anna. 'So, if the title of your documentary is, "Wise Women, Witches and Warriors" . . . which one represents a warrior?'

'You're the detective, Lukas. Let me know when you work it out.'

29

Fergie loves being a cop. It's pretty much all he's ever wanted to be once he realised no football club was ever going to come knocking and Starfleet Academy wasn't going to be recruiting any time soon.

He moans about the job, of course he does; he's seen more changes in the three short years since Police Scotland was formed than in the previous ten, and not all of them have been to the good. Closing Inverness's control room and moving its functions to Dundee is the latest daft notion to come out of the bigwig's conference at Tulliallan; and if they can't see that's an almighty fuck-up waiting to happen, Fergie's got an email he can send them from a Nigerian prince who's looking for a bank account to rest his millions in.

But still, the job is in his blood. He'll deal with the changes, deal with the paperwork, the new initiatives that turn out to be a lot like the old ones under a fancy new name. Deal with it all, every last bit of it, because the reason he does the job is that dead wee girl in front of him, lying on a steel table in the mortuary suite at Raigmore Hospital.

Fergie watches from the viewing gallery as Marco McVinish and the assisting pathologist go about their work. A big, cheerful bear of a man, McVinish is a different person here, his voice measured and professional as he records each detail of the death Erin MacKenzie had endured. Too many details, in the end, for Fergie to take in; his mind slides away from the dry precision of that narrative, closing him off from having to hear it spoken aloud. He can just about cope with the written report McVinish will send on, but the words are burning into his brain, leaving images there he doesn't want to see.

He hates this part of the job, hates having to be a mute witness to a ten-year-old girl's final indignities. But though the boss had asked him to attend, Andy Black was going to send Nazreen instead, and Fergie's damn sure it wasn't to broaden her experience of the MIT's workload. He zones out, lets his head fill with nothing until McVinish's voice cuts in to say he's finished.

'Give me five minutes, then come round to the office,' the pathologist tells him. 'I'm sure you've got some questions, and I'm guessing you'd prefer me to answer them in more neutral surroundings.'

Right on both counts. Fergie nods, turns his back on the sight of that small, pale body lying on the stark metal table. McVinish isn't the only one who needs a wee minute right now. Not for the first time, Fergie wonders how the man can stand to do the job he does, day after day. Though McVinish could just as well say that about him, Fergie supposes.

He straightens his tie, stretches his back to ease the stiffness he can feel gathering there, and adds another query to the list he's made before heading to the pathologist's office. As usual, the aroma of freshly made coffee greets him before he's halfway there.

McVinish looks up as he enters, waves him over to a chair and hands him a mug. 'Here, you look like you could do with this. Milk's in the fridge behind you, if you need it.'

'Black's fine, thanks.' Fergie's got no intention of putting anything in his stomach that's been near a pathologist's fridge. Or anywhere near a mortuary suite, frankly. When McVinish rips open a pack of chocolate digestives and holds it out to him, Fergie's gut gives a queasy little roll.

'No? Well, I suppose I should be watching my sugar intake anyway.' McVinish gives the pack a regretful glance and puts it back in a drawer. 'So, Erin.' A look of pain crosses his face. 'The bairns . . . they're the worst, you know. After twenty-five years, they're still the bloody worst.'

'No argument there.' Fergie checks the notes he's made. 'Can I confirm you said there was no evidence of sexual assault?'

The pathologist nods. 'Which is one mercy for the poor child – and for her parents, of course. But she was filthy, dehydrated, and the condition of the organs I examined . . .' he shakes his head. 'I'll send an initial report over tomorrow morning, but the full version will have to wait for the blood and toxicology results to come back.'

'Toxicology? You think she was drugged?'

'I located what looks like an injection site, which might explain how she was abducted without a struggle in the first place. What I didn't find was evidence of violent death.'

'She wasn't murdered, then?'

McVinish gives him a withering look. 'Define murdered. Oh, there's no evidence of violent assault – no bruising round the neck, no petechiae to indicate strangulation, no broken bones – but there's massive damage to her internal organs. Together with the specific pattern of skin discolouration on the neck and chest, my initial conclusion would have to be that she died of complications arising from sepsis, most likely septic shock.'

'Blood poisoning? How the hell did that happen?'

McVinish shakes his head. 'Again, we need to wait for the test results. But my guess would be the infected wound on her neck. Once the infection had entered her bloodstream, without proper treatment it would have spread rapidly to other parts of her body. Make no mistake about it, Erin died a miserable, lonely death, in considerable pain . . . So, no, she wasn't stabbed or strangled or battered to death. But was she murdered? As far as I'm concerned, absolutely.' McVinish finishes the rest of his coffee, stands up. 'Enough for now?'

'Christ, aye. More than enough.' Fergie puts the mug down, gets up to go. 'What stage are you at with Anthea Bradley – waiting for test results there too?'

The pathologist gives him an irritated look. 'You as well? I've had Andy Black bending my ear about her this morning already. Look, I'll get the report over to you as soon as I can, but—'

'Andy Black's already chased it up?' It's news to Fergie. What the hell is Andy Black doing bothering McVinish when he's supposed to be looking at the Cazza MacKay hit-and-run?

'He certainly has. And I've already told him, there's no question in my mind that her death was down to anything other than natural causes. There was extensive scarring to her heart, she had a history of cardiac problems, so . . .' McVinish shrugs. 'I didn't find anything that would make me question that finding. Hopefully that's clear enough for you *and* Andy Black.'

And why does Fergie feel the pulse in his neck give a wee, interested twitch at that? 'Thanks, doc. He'd likely just have been dotting i's, crossing t's, that sort of thing.'

A snort from the pathologist. Aye, well, Andy Black isn't exactly famed for his i-dotting and t-crossing, and Fergie's betting McVinish knows that as well as he does. But there's a whisper in Fergie's head now, one he wishes would shut the fuck up and give him peace. He takes his pocketbook out again and glances at it, puts on his just-need-to-check-something expression.

'You said the only way to be sure about the time of death

would be to send the beasties to a bug man for analysis, is that right?'

'It's very unlikely he could be that exact,' McVinish corrects him. 'Though he could potentially establish a more accurate time of death. But if you're not treating this as suspicious, I'm not sure—'

Fergie nods, puts his pocketbook away. 'Aye, neither am I, doc. Neither am I. But could you do it for me anyway? Let's call it dotting a few more i's.'

30

Dornoch is only forty miles from Inverness. Forty fast miles, usually, for Mahler's BMW, flying down the A9 and over the bright blue Dornoch and Cromarty firths. But a tailback at the Tore roundabout means by the time he gets back to Burnett Road, he's running nearly fifteen minutes late for the afternoon briefing and Andy Black has started without him.

'You made it, then.' Black folds his arms, looks Mahler up and down. 'Not looking great, though. If you're not fit to be here—'

'I'm fine. Apologies, everyone, for my lateness. The curse of the Tore roundabout strikes again.' Groans of fellow feeling from the Black Isle commuters in the team. Mahler ignores the pain in his ribs from running up the stairs, attempts a smile. 'I'm afraid the force was not with me this morning.'

'Aye, well.' Black gives him a sour look. 'You've not missed that much, I suppose.' He gives Mahler a quick update on the media appeal Lena McNally's parents had taken part in the previous evening. Clearly devastated, tormented by thoughts of what might have happened to their daughter, they'd sparked a massive public response and the phone lines had been overwhelmed with calls offering information.

'Ninety per cent of them'll turn out to be headbangers, as per usual,' Black points out. 'But all we need is one decent sighting of that bloody van and we'll have the bastard. It'd help if we'd more than two bloody digits from the number plate, mind. What about it, Pete?'

Pete looks up from his iPad, shakes his head. 'This isn't *CSI* off the telly, and I'm not a bloody magician – I've enhanced the footage as far as I can. But Naz and I have got a list of possibles together, and we're working through it. So far, we've got it down to about 500. Including half a dozen in Swansea, and three in bloody Leeds. We're doing our best, but—'

Andy Black gives him a disgusted look. 'And how long's *that* going to bloody take?'

'It's sounding hopeful, Pete.' Mahler shares Black's impatience, but he also knows how hard Pete's been working on the footage; disparaging what he's achieved so far won't solve anything. 'Keep on it. What about Anthea Bradley – any updates on her last-known movements?'

Pete grins. 'As it happens, yes. Only came in this morning, but her debit card was used on Friday lunchtime at Tesco Inshes. And yes, there is footage, which . . .' he taps the screen on his iPad, drums his fingers on the desk. And gives a shout of triumph. 'Ya beauty! Here you go.'

He angles the screen so they can all see the footage. It had been raining heavily, so the figure at the hole-in-the-wall cash machine is wearing a jacket with the hood pulled up, but it's obviously a woman. She keys in the pin number with no hesitation, withdraws what looks like a substantial amount of cash and stuffs it in her pocket.

'Took out the maximum,' Pete confirms. 'She heads round the side of the building where the garage CCTV picks her up briefly, and walks off towards Drakies. Or Raigmore, I suppose – she had an appointment there, didn't she?'

Nazreen frowns. 'Yes, but it was in the morning. That clip's timestamped 16.27.' She peers at the screen. 'Can you play it again, please? And freeze as she types in the numbers?'

When Pete runs the footage, she asks him to pause it again as the woman turns away, and shakes her head.

'Sir, I'm sorry, but . . .' she peers at the screen again and looks up at Mahler. 'I don't think that's Anthea Bradley.'

'Of course it's her.' Andy Black's staring at the frozen image in front of him. 'Look at the way she's got her hood over her face – she's taking cash out to give to her paedo son until they can collect on their next deal, and she doesn't want to be identified.'

It's certainly a plausible explanation. But there's something about the figure on the screen that makes Mahler think Nazreen could be onto something. 'Why don't you think it's her?'

'The hands, sir.' She points at the image again. 'See, when she stuffs the cash in her bag? Flash jewellery and cheap acrylic nails. Her build's all wrong, too – Anthea was tall, but really skinny. This woman's about the same height, but she's much rounder.'

Mahler nods. He'd only seen Anthea Bradley once, but she'd been rail-thin then. And he's betting Nazreen's called it right about the hands. 'So, someone else has Anthea's card and PIN. Who? And how did she come by them – did Anthea give them to her? If so, why?'

'Max Bradley's got a girlfriend,' Black offers. 'Has to be. She's in on their scheme too, goes to get cash for him using Anthea's card, all going sweet as a nut. Then something happens, they fall out and do away with Anthea.'

Fergie shakes his head. 'Not unless they killed her by giving her a massive heart attack, they didn't.' He gives the team a brief run-through of Marco McVinish's post-mortem findings. 'Need to wait for the full report, but there's no doubt she died of natural causes. There's a wee question mark over the time of death, but the doc's following that up, so we'll know more about it in due course.'

'Where's that going to get us?' Black demands. 'Fuck's sake, if the wifie died a natural death, that's it for us, end of – it's Erin MacKenzie's bloody unnatural one we need to focus on. And that means catching Anthea Bradley's pervert of a son. And whoever he's been doing business with.'

'The child-trafficking angle needs to be followed up,' Mahler agrees. 'Which means we step up our liaison with Offender Management and also PPU – we need to know if any of this rings any bells with them.' The Public Protection Unit is as stretched as the MIT, but if the girls are being stolen to order, the MIT's going to need the other agencies' expertise. 'But until we've got something concrete linking Bradley to Erin and the other girls, we keep investigating all aspects of her abduction and murder. So, we keep chasing that van, we keep asking why and we keep asking how. How did Erin's abductor know where to find her on that specific day? How did he know when Lena would be alone and vulnerable?'

'He was stalking the girls,' Donna puts in. 'Watching them for weeks. When he saw they were on their own, he grabbed them.'

Mahler shakes his head. 'It's more than that. He knows these girls – knows their families, their routines – and we need to find out how. In the meantime, Andy's got a point about a possible girlfriend – in which case, we can't rule out her being involved in the actual abductions. Pete, keep tracking all Anthea's cards. Her bank will have frozen that one, but the credit cards might take a little longer. And if our mystery woman's used one and got away with it once, she might try again.'

Silence. A few nods, but no comments, no suggestions. Mahler looks round at the team. Sees the weariness, the confusion stamped across their faces; too many strands to this enquiry, too many leads that end up going nowhere. Too many patterns refusing to form.

He crosses to the whiteboards, moves Erin's photograph to the remaining unused board. 'Erin MacKenzie. Murdered by person or persons so far unknown. So far.' He lets that register, lets them absorb her image as a living child once more. And turns to Fergie. 'You attended the post-mortem this morning. Can you take us through the initial findings while we wait for the full report?'

Fergie nods. His report isn't long, and it isn't detailed. It doesn't have to be; by the time Fergie's finished, they look sickened by what they've heard. Sickened, but determined.

Mahler leaves Andy Black and Fergie to hand out further allocations and checks his messages; nothing from Karen Gilchrist yet about Hollander, but if the man's as elusive as Cazza MacKay seems to think, Mahler suspects she'll have her work cut out. He decides to give her another day before chasing it up, turns to head for his office. And realises he's missed the red voicemail icon on his phone.

Mahler plays the message, then listens again; the words are hushed, a little breathless, but their meaning is perfectly clear. And the twitch between his shoulder blades is telling him they might turn out to be the break his team so desperately needs.

He looks round for Fergie, waves him over. 'Ella Kirkpatrick watched the McNallys' appeal yesterday evening,' Mahler tells him. 'Watched it twice, in fact. And she thinks she's seen the van we're looking for.'

31

Ella Kirkpatrick is standing in the doorway of her bungalow when Mahler and Fergie pull up. She's leaning heavily on her stick, and although there's a strong wind rising, she's only got a thin cardigan draped over the light summer dress she's wearing. But it's her expression that bothers Mahler most: there are blue-black shadows under her eyes, and the strong lines of her face are tight with agitation.

Fergie gives Mahler an uneasy glance. 'Boss, she doesn't look—'

'I know.'

Mahler gets out, hurries up the path as fast as his ribs will allow.

Up close, Ella's appearance is even more concerning: there's a vagueness in her eyes as though she's not entirely sure of her surroundings, and she's unsteady on her feet in spite of the stick.

'Ella, shall we go inside? It's a little chilly out here.'

'Inspector?' A frown, then the vagueness disappears. 'And Sergeant Ferguson, too . . . My goodness, you're right. It's freezing, isn't it? Come in, both of you.'

She leads them through to her small, neat living room, waves them to the chairs.

'There's a tea tray set in the kitchen, if you can bring it through for me, Sergeant. Rock buns too, if you fancy.'

Fergie pats his stomach, grins. 'Need to keep an eye on this, but thank you.' He takes out his pocketbook, flips it open. 'Ella, you said you'd seen a van similar to the one we're looking for in connection with the abduction and murder of Erin MacKenzie. Can you tell us about that?'

'Yes, that's right. I saw it turning into the end of the drive two nights ago.'

Mahler leans forward. 'What time of day was that?'

'It wasn't day at all, it was two o'clock in the morning. The first time, I thought someone had maybe just got lost and turned in by mistake. But I remember thinking it was a funny time of night for folk to be driving around down here. Then, two nights ago, it happened again.'

'Two o'clock? Are you sure?'

'Yes, Inspector, I'm sure.' Sharp grey eyes meet his. 'I'm old, Mr Mahler, I'm not daft. And I don't sleep well enough to have been dreaming, if that's your next question. Not at that time of night.'

'I understand. I suppose it was too far away for you to make out any of the registration number?'

'Much too far. There was something odd about the sound, though. Something . . .' she makes an irritated noise, shakes her head. 'It's gone, I'm afraid.'

Fergie glances at Mahler. 'Not to worry, eh? Let's just see if I've got the rest of it right, now.'

He takes her through what she'd told the control-room call-handler, going over the other sightings she'd mentioned. Her recollection of some details is perfectly precise, but she's hazy on others, including the vehicle's size and approximate colour.

Mahler shifts in his chair; his ribs are still painful and there's a gathering tightness at the base of his skull as he realises they're wasting their time. Ella Kirkpatrick is sharp, but she's in her eighties and she's said herself, she doesn't sleep well. How easy would it have been for her to mistake or simply misremember what she'd seen? Easy, and completely understandable. But in the meantime, any chance they have of saving Lena McNally is slipping further and further away . . .

'Inspector?'

He realises he's entirely missed the last part of Ella's sentence. He starts to say something, but she shakes her head.

'Ach, never mind.' She unhooks her stick from the arm of her chair, struggles to her feet. 'Will you come into the kitchen with me? There's something I want you to have. No, Sergeant, you just wait there. We won't be a moment.'

Mahler glances at Fergie, shrugs and follows Ella to the kitchen. She goes to the dresser, takes out a small glass bottle and pours some of its contents into a cup, which she holds out to him. 'Here. I made it up the other day, so it should still be fresh enough.'

Mahler takes the cup, inspects the yellowish liquid. 'What is it?'

'It's a tisane for your head.' She looks up at him. 'Bad today, isn't it? Oh, don't worry – it's just a herbal tea, that's all. Fever-few and valerian, picked by moonlight and sweetened with a bit of honey. But it'll stop you feeling like your brain's going to burst out through your ears.'

He looks at the cup, and back at Ella. And takes a cautious sip. The tea tastes vaguely of grass clippings, but it's not actively unpleasant. 'How did you know?'

'My sister was the same. I recognised the look.' She opens a drawer in the dresser and takes out an envelope. 'Here's a wee packet I made up for you. Take a cup as soon as you feel a headache starting and it'll help to ease things.'

'That's . . . very kind. Thank you.'

'No thanks needed. I've seen too many folk suffering to stand by and watch if there's something I can do to help . . . it isn't a cure, though.' An odd compassion in the sharp grey eyes. 'Not for what ails you.'

Right now, he'll settle for something that deals with the symptoms. But when he starts to tell her that, she shakes her head.

'Not the headaches. The thing that lies behind them.'

'I don't understand—'

'You do. You're carrying something that's too big for you, son. And you don't need to.'

The smell of blood and fear. His feet, slip-sliding on the stairs . . . And out of nowhere, an image of Anna Murray's dark hair and slate-grey eyes.

Mahler pushes back the thought, starts to tell Ella she's mistaken. And turns at the sound of footsteps approaching the back door.

'Ella, is everything okay?'

The door opens, and a slim, forty-something woman with bright chestnut hair appears.

'I was on my way out, and I saw—' She stops short at the sight of Mahler, shakes her head. 'Bloody hell, not again. You lot never give up, do you?'

She has a faint non-local accent, one Mahler can't quite place, and she's glaring at him with undisguised hostility.

When Fergie appears in the kitchen doorway, she whips out her mobile and holds it up so they can see she's about to film them. 'Listen, Ella doesn't need any double glazing, so you two can sling your hook. And she doesn't care about solar panels—'

'Quite right, too. That's not what we're here about, though.' Fergie gets out his warrant card, introduces himself and Mahler. 'You'll be . . . Kat, is that right?'

The woman nods. 'That's me. May I look at that?'

She studies the warrant card carefully before handing it back with an apologetic smile.

'Sorry. But we have to be careful.' She turns to the older woman, raises her voice slightly. 'Ella, love, do you have that shopping list you were going to do for me? It's Tuesday, remember. The day we put your Tesco order in.'

'Is it?' Ella looks confused. 'I thought you did that on a Thursday.'

'No, love, Tuesdays.' Kat pats her arm. 'Don't worry, we can do one now – it won't take long. I'll just see your visitors out for you, shall I?'

'My visitors? Yes, I. . .I suppose so.' Ella glances at Mahler, gives an uncertain nod. 'Well, goodbye, then. It was good of you to come.' Before he can say anything, she goes over to the sideboard and takes out a pen and notepad. 'I'll just make a start on my list for you, Kat.'

Mahler glances at Fergie, shrugs. They leave Ella sitting at her kitchen table, and walk with Kat to the end of the path. She glances back at Ella's bungalow, and turns to Mahler.

'Look, I'm sorry I gave you a hard time in there. It's just Ella's a trusting soul, and when I saw that old car outside her place . . .' she gives him a puzzled look. 'Are you, like, undercover, or something?'

An understandable reaction on encountering the Audi, Mahler supposes. 'We're following up reports that a vehicle similar to one we're looking for may have been seen in this area. It's a light-coloured—'

'Oh my God.' Kat's eyes widen. 'It's about those poor kids, isn't it? The ones some sicko abducted. But why would you think . . .' She breaks off to glance at Ella's bungalow again, where one of the living-room windows has been opened and the curtain pushed to one side. 'Ah. Okay, I get it. Look, I think maybe we'd better talk over at mine.'

Kat takes them across to the farmhouse and leads the way into the kitchen. A conservatory's been added on at some point and Mahler doubts the burgundy-coloured Aga is original to the property, but there's a welcoming, comfortable feel to the room in spite of its size.

She offers them coffee, puts a pot on the Aga. And apologises again for being overprotective of Ella. 'She's great for her age. She really is,' Kat tells them. 'But lately, she . . . well, she's started to get a little forgetful.'

Mahler looks down at the envelope in his hand. 'Are you talking about a medical condition?'

Kat shakes her head. 'My husband's a doctor, and he doesn't think there's anything to worry about yet. But she can get . . . well, a little mixed up, sometimes. Oh, nothing major,' she assures him. 'On her good days, she'll still be out there, hanging up her washing or splitting kindling for that open fire of hers. But the good days are getting fewer now. I do worry about leaving her on her own sometimes, but I only do part-time at the leisure centre, so I'm usually here to keep an eye on her.'

'That's very good of you,' Fergie tells her. 'Many folk wouldn't bother these days, Mrs . . .?'

'Kat, please. Kat Evans.' She pours the coffees, puts them on a tray with a plate of shortbread and carries it over to the table. 'Ella was very good to us when we moved up here. Helped us settle in, get used to living out in the country . . . not that we don't love it now,' she assures them. 'It's a great place to finally put down roots.'

Fergie nods. 'It is that. Quiet, though, if you're not used to it. So, if you'd seen the sort of vehicle we're looking for, I'm guessing you'd remember it? Can't be many cars come down this way.'

Kat thinks for a moment, then shakes her head. 'Sorry, there's

been nothing like that around here – and you're right, I'd definitely have noticed. I mean, there's an old cottage further down
the road that's been empty for ages – estate sale, I think – that
someone must have bought as a fixer-upper. The "for sale"
board's gone, and we've seen vans going up and down the road
there a few times. Maybe that's what Ella saw?'

At two in the morning? Mahler glances at Fergie. 'It's a fair
distance from her bungalow to the actual road. Quite hard to
see a vehicle so far away, I'd have thought.'

'Well, yes.' Kat gives him an apologetic look. 'But sometimes
Ella goes for a bit of a wander. Oh, nothing dangerous, but I've
found her at the top of the road a couple of times. And I've
noticed her days and nights can get a bit muddled.' She glances
at her watch. 'If there's nothing else, I ought to go and help her
with her shopping list.'

No, Kat tells them apologetically, she's never met the new
owners of the cottage further down the road. And there had
been nothing unusual about the vans she'd seen going down
there, nothing at all. Mahler passes her his details, asks her to
get in touch if anything occurs to her, but it's clear Kat's got
nothing more to tell them.

Kat walks back towards the road with them as far as Ella's
bungalow. She looks up at the living-room window, waves at
the figure standing there.

'Waiting for me, bless her. She likes me to check her cup-
boards, make sure she doesn't run out of anything.'

'So what's the future for Ella?' Fergie asks. 'If things get
worse, I mean. It'll be a lot for you and your man to cope with.'

Kat gives him a quick, unhappy nod. 'I know. But neither
of us have much of a family . . . no kids yet, either, though we
keep hoping. So I suppose we've adopted Ella, in a way. And if
things do get worse . . .' She swallows and looks away. 'If that
happens, she won't be on her own.'

Back at the car, Fergie turns to Mahler. 'Poor Ella, eh? Still, good to know she's got someone looking out for her.' He frowns. 'You don't think . . . I mean, we gave her a hell of a shock, didn't we, raking up all that stuff about her uncle? I hope to Christ we didn't set anything off.'

'I'd say that's unlikely.' Though there *had* been a marked change in Ella since their first meeting. This time, she'd seemed muted, somehow; diminished. Though perhaps on their previous visits, they'd simply caught her on her good days.

'We'll take a look at the cottage Kat Evans mentioned,' he tells Fergie. 'Ella might have got her timings mixed up, but that doesn't mean she imagined the whole thing. And a semi-derelict cottage sounds like just the sort of place our man might choose to go to ground in.'

32

When Andy gets back to his place, it's just after ten, and the wifie from the downstairs flat is on her way out with her wee rat of a dog. He holds the door open for her – minding his manners, just to show he can, sometimes – but instead of a nod or a smile of thanks, the sour-faced old bitch gives him a look that would turn the milk, picks up the dog and scuttles past as though he's got something disgusting wrong with him and she's worried it might be catching.

Andy turns to watch her make her way down the street. Fine, then. The next time rat-dog's out taking a dump in the communal garden, it might find some careless person's left the gate to the street standing open. Wee taste of freedom, eh? It's not like ratty-boy would come to any harm, is it? Not unless it happens to be the day for the bin lorries to come round. And as Andy happens to know, survival of the fittest is what it's all about.

Inside his flat, he dumps his carrier of takeaway on the kitchen table, crosses to the fridge and gets out a beer; not the good stuff, this, just some cheap rubbish he picked up from Aldi, but it's good and strong and there's a shelf full of it in the fridge. More than enough to get completely out of his skull, if he has a mind to . . . and with the knowledge of what he's about to do burning a hole in his brain, getting completely out of his skull sounds like a fucking great idea.

Andy chugs the beer, tosses the can in the recycling and gets out another. Thinks about opening it, sending it the way of the first, but the sight of his reflection in the window pulls him up short. Christ, he looks like his old man, slump-shouldered, sweating like a pig. Scared. Aye, well, no fucking wonder.

He puts the beer down, straightens his shoulders and goes into the bathroom. Kneels down and works the bath panel free, so he can reach in for what's hidden there. And touches only empty space.

His gut lurches, sending the sour taste of the beer he's swallowed back into his throat. When his fingers eventually find a corner of the padded envelope, they're shaking so badly it takes him two attempts to work the fucking thing loose from the corner it's become lodged in. At last, he manages to get it free.

Andy opens the envelope, takes out the phone. Stares at the dark screen while the light fades and the shadows grow around him.

Even now, with the mobile in his hand, what happens next is up to him, he knows that. He can put it back into the envelope, stuff it inside his jacket. Take a walk down by the canal and drop it in. And walk away . . . walk away and don't look back.

Only that's not really an option any longer, is it? Anthea fucking Bradley had seen to that.

He might still be in the clear, that's the worst of it. He and Gary *had* done a decent search at her place, no-one can say they hadn't. He'd gone up as far as the summerhouse, looked in the window . . . Okay, he hadn't walked right up to the door, hadn't tried the handle. But the floor was fucking rotten, he'd seen that the first time he'd looked round with Naz. No way he was going in there to fall through the floor and break his fucking neck. He's a good cop, not a bloody suicidal one.

There was no reason to do any more than he'd done. No reason to think Anthea Bradley's body could already have been lying there . . . and no reason – no fucking reason at all – to think she'd been dying of the massive heart attack that killed her as he'd glanced in the window and then walked away.

And that's not all he has to worry about, is it? There are other things he's seen, things he's walked away from . . . and he's got a sudden, sick certainty that the guy he'd met at the canal knows about every fucking one of them. Him, or the people he works for.

A line of sweat trickles down Andy's back as he thinks about what he's about to do. But what choice has he got? He'd thought his number was up three years ago, when Lukas Mahler had transferred from the Met. Sharp-suited pretty boy, with his posh accent and his bloody mental mother, Mahler had been June Wallace's wee pet poodle from day one.

He'd gone after Warren Jackson like a fucking guided missile, and Andy had spent a few sleepless nights back then expecting posh boy to tap him on the shoulder too. But turns out Mahler isn't half the cop Andy is, when the chips are down. Doesn't have the killer instincts, you might say.

Oh, the smug bastard's riding high right now, but Andy knows better than anyone how careers can be made and unmade on the turn of a single case. He just hasn't had Mahler's luck, that's all. But that can change. *He* can change it, if he has the guts to follow through on the lifeline he's been offered.

There's going to be a price to pay, he knows that. Signing up with the kind of folk who run canal guy means crossing a line . . . and yes, he's come close to that particular line a couple of times before, peered over the edge once or twice, maybe. And told himself he'd never step across.

But things change, right? The note that had been pushed

through his letter box late last night had offered him the kind of intel on the MacKenzie girl's murder that Lukas fucking Mahler would sell his mental mother for. If it's on the level, if the location Andy's been promised checks out, it's time up for Bradley and his paedo gang, and Andy will get a wee bit of the recognition he deserves. While posh boy's career vanishes down the fucking toilet.

And even if somewhere down the line it all goes bad, even if all the bridges Andy's going to cross go up in flames behind him . . . if he can take Lukas Mahler down with him and trample his career into the dust, it will all have been worth it.

As the last of the light dies, he touches the screen and makes the call.

33

Day 20

Thursday, 9 June

It's the rain that wakes Mahler in the end; not the start of it, but its ceasing.

He'd driven as far as Glasgow in the muted, not full-dark of a Scottish summer evening, but the clouds had started to gather just before Gretna. By the time he'd left the M6 at Shap, the sky was a murky, end-of-days black, driving near-horizontal rain against the BMW's windscreen for the final fifteen miles.

When he'd pulled into the car park opposite the police station in Kendal, it was just after two in the morning; too early for his nine a.m. meeting with the man he'd come to see, too late to book into a guest house or B&B. So he'd reclined his car seat, stuffed his padded jacket between the headrest and the door and slept until – he checks the time on his phone – just after seven. Good enough.

He peels his face from the jacket, finger-combs his hair and stretches his back carefully to ease his bruised ribs, before getting out of the car and heading across the road to the police station. He's just finished signing in when a tall man with close-cropped greying hair puts his head round the door leading from the front desk to the rest of the station.

'DI Mahler? Bloody hell, you're keen. When did you leave

Inverness, the middle of the bloody night?'

Jake Enderby, the DI from Cumbria CID Mahler had spoken to on the phone, is a big, cheerful Yorkshireman with the bull neck and slightly offset nose of a former rugby player – prop, Mahler's guessing, something that relies on a decent mix of brawn and brain.

'Around ten, actually.' Mahler picks up his visitors' pass and follows Enderby through the reception area and into the station itself. 'I need to get back up to Inverness as soon as possible. It's definitely Maxwell Bradley you have in custody?'

Enderby's call had come out of the blue at seven the previous evening, when Bradley's details had been red-flagged with Police Scotland's interest. As soon as Mahler had got the call, he'd got authorisation from June Wallace to go down to Kendal and talk to Bradley. He's not entirely sure how Chae Hunt had managed to circumvent the inter-force formalities, but for once he's grateful for Hunt's networking expertise.

Enderby nods. 'Paedophile ex-doctor, skipped off from his notified address, on his way back to jail and good bloody riddance? That's the one. If you've got something better than that to hit him with, go for it. His lawyer's on the way, though, so I'm not sure you'll get much out of him.' He looks at his watch. 'Got time for coffee and a bacon buttie before Harriet the Hatchet gets here, if you like? You'll not want to face her on an empty stomach, trust me. Nor Bradley, come to that.'

Harriet the Hatchet? Mahler nods, follows Enderby through to the canteen. Between bites of bacon roll, he fills him in on why he's driven through the night to talk to Bradley.

When he's finished, Enderby shakes his head. 'And the second one's been missing for, what, a week?' At Mahler's nod, he sighs. 'Ah, Christ.' He stands up, puts his plate and mug on a tray stand by the door and cracks his knuckles. 'Right, then. If you're done, let's see if Mr Bradley and the Hatchet are ready for us. I've reserved interview room 3 for them, so the buggers should be nice and chilly by now.'

Mahler returns his crockery and follows Enderby to an interview room on the ground floor, where Bradley's waiting with his solicitor. Mahler doesn't necessarily share his colleagues' view that defence briefs are devil-spawn with yawning abysses where their souls should be, but he detects a distinct tang of sulphur in the air as the thin-faced, sharp-suited young woman breaks off her conversation to glare at Enderby.

'Heating not working again, Inspector? Funny how it always happens when I'm sitting in with a client.'

Enderby gives her an affable grin, makes a show of loosening his shirt collar. 'Don't know what you mean, Harriet. Feels quite snug to me. Right then, shall we get on?'

He's barely finished the introductions before she turns to Mahler, holds up her hand.

'Before we start, I want it clearly understood that my client has agreed to this interview against my advice. He stresses that his only wish is to clear his name of any involvement in the tragic death of this little girl and to assist Police Scotland in any way he can. If at any point he indicates he wishes to terminate the interview, that is what will happen. Is that clear, Inspector Mahler?'

'How very noble of your client. Yes, that's perfectly clear.'

Mahler turns to look at the man he's come to see. In the flesh, Bradley looks better than his prison mugshot had suggested. His complexion still carries a hint of prison grey, and there's nothing pleasant or innocuous now about his face with its tracery of scars. But in the short time he's been at liberty, he's gained weight and lost the hollow-eyed look that had stared out at Mahler from the prison images he'd seen.

Mahler gives his details and a brief explanation of the purpose of his visit.

'I'd like to start by asking Mr Bradley about his movements on the following dates, if I may.'

Mahler lists the dates Erin was taken, the attempt to snatch Celeste Taylor, and finally Lena McNally's abduction.

Bradley listens impassively, his arms folded over his chest, before shaking his head.

'You've lost three little girls in as many weeks? Dear, dear.' He gives Mahler a mock-sympathetic grin. 'A little careless, don't you think? And, before you ask, of course I've heard about what happened. I do watch the news, you know – what I don't understand is why you're asking me about them.'

'If you need me to refresh your memory about your recent custodial sentence, I'd be delighted. Otherwise, I think we can take your interest in little girls as read, don't you?'

A flush on Bradley's cheeks. His solicitor turns to growl at Mahler, but Bradley smiles and pats her arm. 'Down, Harriet. The inspector is under a bit of pressure, that's all. He's got a crime he can't solve – two crimes, in fact, and one near miss – and he's itching to put my name to them.'

The smile dies as he turns to Mahler. 'Only you're just pissing in the wind, aren't you, Inspector? I've been living with my girlfriend near Grasmere since I left London. And believe me, if it hadn't been for a bloody speeding ticket outside Windermere, I'd still be there.'

'Your girlfriend.' Mahler tries and fails to keep the incredulity out of his voice. 'A recent relationship, I take it. And I assume the question of why you were supposed to comply with the conditions of your release never came up?'

A burst of anger flares across Bradley's face. 'As it happens, we corresponded while I was in prison. Fell in love, and planned a life together.' He produces a vague, soft-focus smile for the benefit of the wall-mounted recording camera. 'After everything I'd been through, getting to know Caro was like . . . well, like

223

being reborn, I suppose. I knew I'd found my soulmate, and as soon as I was released, I couldn't wait to be with her. I know I should have notified my change of address, but what can I say? *Amor omnia vincit*, after all.' The smile switches off as he turns to look at Mahler. 'Caro will vouch for my whereabouts on every one of those dates, and so will her sister and brother-in-law . . . so I'm afraid it looks like you've had a wasted journey. Now, if that's everything—'

'Not quite. I'm afraid I'm also the bearer of bad news about your mother.'

'My mother?' Bradley frowns. 'I don't understand – Anthea lives in Kingston. What's she got to do with a cop from darkest Jockland?'

The first genuine reaction of any kind Mahler's had from Bradley. Unfortunately, it's not the one he'd been hoping for.

Mahler informs him about Anthea's move to the Highlands and her subsequent death. Bradley listens with perfect composure, then breathes out slowly.

'Thank you for telling me. So, Anthea's gone at last? Well, good bloody riddance to her.' He raises an eyebrow at Mahler. 'Oh, please. You're shocked? My mother abandoned me, Inspector – during the worst period of my life, she didn't write, didn't visit and she made it clear she never wanted to see me again. Do you seriously expect me to mourn for that?'

Mahler shakes his head. 'You'd have to be able to pass yourself off as human, and I'm pretty sure that's beyond you. Please pass my deepest sympathies to your girlfriend – and enjoy meeting up with your old friends on your return to prison.'

Bradley's solicitor starts to protest, but Mahler's heard enough. He leaves the interview room, heads back along the corridor to wait for Enderby by the front desk. When the Cumbrian officer appears a few minutes later, he's accompanied by Bradley's solicitor, who gives Mahler the kind of frostbite-inducing glare he suspects even June Wallace might find it difficult to match.

'Just so that you're aware, Inspector, my client is most un-likely to be returned to prison,' she tells Mahler as she's signing out. 'And, rest assured, a complaint about your behaviour today will be going to your superior as soon as I get back to my office.'

Before he can reply, she sweeps past him and out into the car park.

'I'd watch your back if I were you,' Enderby tells him. 'Don't think you've made a friend there. Come on, I'll see you safely to your car – after that, you're on your own.'

Before they're halfway across the car park, the clouds disap-pear and the sky turns black.

'Why they call it the Lake District, I suppose,' Enderby com-ments, as the heavens open. 'You still planning to drive back to Inverness today?'

Mahler nods. He isn't going to get anything else from Brad-ley, and Fergie's just messaged him to say there's been another attempt to use Anthea's debit card at a cash machine in town. He thanks Enderby for his co-operation, but the Yorkshireman shakes his head.

'Sorry you didn't get what you came for. Cocky bastard, isn't he? And as for the girlfriend . . . Christ knows why any woman would take up with someone like him. We'll check out the alibis he's provided, but I have to say, I don't think he's your guy. Do you?'

Mahler shakes his head. He'd watched Bradley throughout the interview, and there had been no 'tells', nothing at all in his body language to suggest the man was lying.

'I suspect Caro and her family have only encountered the charming side of his personality . . . and, given a receptive audi-ence, he's quite capable of painting himself as a victim of a cruel miscarriage of justice,' he admits. 'But no, Bradley isn't the man I'm looking for.'

Hard to say it out loud. Hard to acknowledge the taste of his failure, bitter as ashes in his mouth. The team's best lead – their *only* real lead – has turned out to be a dead end.

'And you bloody needed him to be.' There's genuine sympathy in the look Enderby gives Mahler. 'Real punch in the guts, isn't it? Know how that feels, as it happens. Just before I transferred from Leeds, we had two little lasses abducted, one after the other. Five years ago, that was.'

'What happened?'

'Don't know to this day . . . never found them, never found who took them. No leads, no sodding forensics, nowt. Parents went through hell. Father of one of the girls topped himself, and the other marriage broke up.' He shakes his head. 'Christ, it were a bad time. Some cases stay with you forever, don't they?'

They've reached Mahler's car. Enderby shakes Mahler's hand, wishes him a safe journey back.

'Best of luck, right? When you get the bastard, I'll be cheering you on.'

34

11.20 a.m. Andy walks into the MIT room and looks round. With Mahler gone and Gary down at the court, it's quieter than he'd like, but he knows that won't last for long once the rumours start to spread. Well, this time he doesn't have a problem with that; as far as Andy's concerned, the sooner the whole fucking station finds out who he's got waiting for him in the custody suite, the better. And that includes Chae Hunt and June Wallace.

Skivey Pete looks like he's actually working, for once. He's got two laptops in front of him, his wee ferrety face screwed up in concentration as he scribbles something on a notepad. Andy leaves him to get on with whatever the hell he's doing and looks round for someone who's actually on the same fucking planet.

He glances at Donna, then Nazreen. Well, why not? Let her see what real police work looks like. Show her he's not the type to bear grudges.

'Right, then.' He crosses to the whiteboards, draws a circle round the details of the van Mahler's stuck up there. And scores a big fat line through it. 'Piece of good news to put smiles on all your faces. We've got what looks a hell of a lot like the van used to abduct Erin and Lena – and we've got the lad it belongs to waiting downstairs for us to have a wee word with him right now.'

And that's all it takes. Folk sitting straighter, turning to look at him as that wee crackle of excitement hits the room. Andy grins, nods. Fills them in on Aaron Keenan . . . and Christ, there's enough to fill in there, all right.

Once he's taken them through the interview strategy, he nods at Nazreen.

'Right, you're with me today. We'll head downstairs in—'

'Sir?' She looks up from the file she's been studying, frowns. 'DI Mahler asked me to—'

'DI Mahler's not here.'

June Wallace's blue-eyed boy has finally slipped up, as Andy always knew he would. Hared off down to Cumbria to inter- view Maxwell Bradley, and for what? Andy's got the van, he's got the wee pervert who's more than likely responsible for killing Erin MacKenzie . . . and in a few hours, he'll have him charged and banged up. Case fucking closed. And Naz is more worried about pushing bits of paper around for Lukas fucking Mahler?

He walks over to Nazreen's desk, stares down at her. 'I'll be interviewing Keenan in about five minutes, and you'll be going in there with me. Or did you want to have a wee discussion about that, Nazreen? Because—'

'Tell you what, I'm free right now.' Fergie appears in the doorway, carrying a box of files. He dumps it on a vacant desk, gives Andy a grin. 'Paperwork can wait a wee while, eh? And we're due a bit of luck, aren't we? Between the two of us, we'll soon have the guy sussed.'

Andy weighs it up. Nazreen's been getting a bit too big for her boots recently, and she needs to understand that when a su- perior officer tells her to jump, she fucking jumps. But Fergie's a good DS; a bit too far up Mahler's arse, maybe, but he'll be a damn sight more use in an interview room than Nazreen wet-behind-the-ears Khan.

Andy looks at his watch, nods at Fergie.

'You and me, then. Come on.'

When they get downstairs, Keenan's waiting for them in Interview 2 with one of the uniforms. Use of a duty solicitor offered and turned down, all by the book, all properly recorded.

Andy can feel the adrenaline coursing round his nervous system as he looks Keenan up and down; going to be quick and easy, this one, he can feel it. Keenan's a skinny guy, scrawny pink neck poking out of a filthy Spiderman T-shirt. Shoulders slumped, right leg juddering as his eyes dart round the room like he's looking for an escape route. Not today, Spidey-boy, not today.

Andy lets Fergie take him through the humdrum stuff, the 'confirm this is your address' 'how long have you lived there' foreplay. Keenan answers eagerly, head bobbing on his skinny wee neck as Fergie softens him up. Nicely done, Andy has to admit.

Fergie wraps up his intro, and Andy leans forward.

'So, you drive a blue Fiesta.' Andy opens his folder, takes out a photo but keeps it face down. 'No other vehicles kept at your place?'

'No, nothing.'

'Uh-huh. And you're the only one who parks there? No neighbour using your space occasionally, that sort of thing? Visitors, friends, anything like that?'

'I don't . . . I don't have a lot of visitors. It's how I like it.'

Andy turns over the photo, slides it across the desk. 'Showing Mr Keenan the image of a white van with a dented nearside wing. We found this van parked by the side of your house,

Aaron. Any idea where it might have come from? Take your time, now.'

'Christ, it's about that wee girl that vanished, isn't it?' His eyes dart from Andy to Fergie and back again. 'Look, I don't know why it was there – I've never seen that van before! And I don't . . . I don't like wee girls like that.'

Sweat beading on Keenan's forehead. Andy leans forward, lets the guy see he's got him sussed.

'Sure about that, are you? Because liking wee girls like that's what got your cousin on the register. How's Kyle doing these days, by the way?'

And there it is, the look Andy's been waiting for. The look that tells him Keenan feels as though a giant hand's gripping his nuts and twisting them. Slowly.

'Kyle's . . . I haven't seen Kyle in months. We don't keep in touch. What he did was disgusting!' His voice is high, panic-stricken.

Oh, but Andy can feel he's close to telling them everything. So fucking close . . .

'I need a bathroom break. Please, I can have a break. Can't I?'

'Fine.' Andy closes the folder, leans forward, and the guy flinches. 'You have your wee break, Aaron. But just so's you know, there's a forensics team going over every inch of that van right now. After they've done that, they'll start on your house – and once they've done that, we'll be having another wee talk. So if you've got anything to get off your chest, you go and have a think about what you're going to say to us next time we see you. Have a good, long think.'

Andy watches Keenan being led back to the holding cell.

'Rattled,' he tells Fergie. 'We'll let him stew for a bit while the CSI boys do their stuff. What's the betting we'll get DNA from Erin and Lena in the house as well as his van?'

Fergie shrugs. 'The van, definitely. The house . . .' He shakes his head. 'I don't know. He's not on the register, he doesn't have a record apart from a caution for shoplifting four years ago, and he's bloody terrified. I reckon someone's pushed him into letting them keep the van on his drive.'

'Kyle, you mean?' Andy nods. 'Aye, maybe. Could even be working with that bastard Bradley, I suppose. All the more reason to get the truth out of him, then, isn't there? There's one more wee girl out there we need to recover, and we need to stop him taking any more.' He glances at his watch. 'Grab a coffee if you want, then back here in ten. I want him and his paedo pals in our cells before our twelve hours are up.'

Andy watches Fergie wander off outside, mobile in hand. No prizes for guessing who he'll be reporting in to – right up Mahler's arse, just as he'd thought. But Mahler's three hundred miles away, and Andy's just fine with that. By the time Mahler gets back to Inverness, all that will be left for him to do with this enquiry will be a wee bit of form-filling.

And Andy's just fine with that too.

35

4.40 pm. When Mahler gets back to Inverness, he's been driving for over six hours without a break. His ribs had been uncomfortable but bearable when he'd left Kendal, by the time he turns into Burnett Road, they feel as though they've been wrapped in barbed wire and roasted over an open fire.

He parks and makes his way slowly across the car park to the entrance, skirting the side overlooked by June Wallace's office. If the DCI happens to look out and see him, Mahler doubts she'd be impressed, and he doesn't blame her. With Maxwell Bradley effectively ruled out of any involvement in the so-called 'Child Snatcher' abductions, all he has to offer the team is another dead lead. And the black cloud of failure, dogging every move he makes like a gaunt, malignant shadow.

He heads upstairs to the MIT room to give the team his report. And finds the room deserted. Where the hell is everyone? He reaches for his mobile and remembers too late he'd dropped it under his seat as he'd eased himself carefully out of the BMW.

He curses, starts to go back downstairs and realises the white-board displays have been altered. Maxwell Bradley's name has been crossed off the 'persons of interest' board and a new name added.

'Aaron Keenan.' Andy Black appears in the doorway, followed by Fergie. He pats the folder he's carrying. 'Downstairs having a wee rest in our single accommodation before I have another chat with him about the van I clocked sitting on his driveway.'

'*The* van? The one we've been looking for?'

A grin from Andy Black, and a more cautious nod from Fergie. 'Looks like a good fit to me, boss. The guy swears blind he's never seen it before, though.'

'Aye, well, he would say that, wouldn't he? Seeing that his cousin's Kyle "Kiddie-fiddler" Keenan.' Black gives Mahler a dismissive glance. 'Before your time. But, trust me, that's quite a family.'

He walks up to the whiteboard, takes a photograph from his folder and pins it to the board. 'White transit van, grubby, dent in the nearside wing. Number plate starts with an "E", ends with a "K". Sound familiar? CSI are taking it apart this very minute – and, believe me, Aaron Keenan is shaking in his fucking shoes right now.'

Black steps back from the board so Mahler can take a closer look. 'You know what this means, don't you?' A wide, exultant grin spreads across Black's face. 'It means we've fucking got him. By tomorrow morning, he'll be charged with Erin's murder. And—'

'What about Lena McNally? He's got to have her hidden somewhere. If there's a chance she's still alive—'

Black shakes his head. 'Bugger all chance of that, and you know it. Best we can do for that wee girl's parents is to find out where he's put her body and make sure we get him and the rest of his paedo friends banged up for what they've done.' He glances at his watch, gives a satisfied nod. 'Right, he's had enough of a break, and we're on the clock. Fergie, downstairs with me in five, aye?'

Black heads for the door, turns to look at Mahler. 'No offence, but you look like you're dead on your fucking feet. Time to knock off for the day, eh? I'll tidy this one up for the team and get an email off to June.'

As soon as Black's gone, Fergie gives Mahler an apologetic look. 'Boss, I tried to text you—'

'Doesn't matter.' Mahler hadn't checked his messages since Perth, and after that the Slochd and Drumochter mountain passes would have prevented any of Fergie's messages from getting through. 'What's your assessment of Keenan – does this feel like the right call to you?'

'Not sure, boss. His cousin *is* on the register . . . and if there's an innocent explanation for that van being on his driveway, I can't bloody think of one.'

'But?'

Fergie shrugs. 'But you didn't see the state of him downstairs. I swear he looked like the sky had fallen in on him or something, and he'd got no idea why. My best guess? If that is the van and Erin's and Lena's DNA is all over it, it'll be Kyle who's involved, not Aaron.'

'Sounds reasonable. So, how did we trace the van back to Keenan?'

'Pure bloody luck,' Fergie tells him. 'Andy and Gary were just coming back from a follow-up with Cazza MacKay, when Andy spotted the van on Keenan's driveway.'

'Parked in plain sight?'

'Seems so, aye. What are the chances, eh? If Andy hadn't insisted on following it up . . .' Fergie looks at his phone as a text alert bleeps. 'Christ, I'd better get downstairs. We picked him up this morning, so we're on the clock for detaining him with charges. And, boss . . . I'm sorry, but Andy's right. You do look like absolute shite. Maybe clocking off for the day isn't such a bad idea?'

After Fergie's gone, Mahler goes over to the whiteboards. Looks at Erin, then at Lena, and mouths a silent apology to them both. He'd failed Erin; failed to save her from her killer and failed to track him down. But he has to believe there's still a chance to save Lena.

Donna had been onto something when she'd said the Child Snatcher was collecting girls who fit certain physical characteristics; Erin had been blonde, Celeste dark and Lena is a brilliant redhead. But something had gone wrong after he'd taken Erin, and he'd thrown her away like a rejected toy. So, while his set is two girls short, Lena might still be alive; traumatised, terribly hurt, perhaps, but still alive. Unless . . .

Mahler looks at Lena's photograph again, takes in the set of her jaw, the defiant half-scowl.

Unless she'd done something to annoy him.

Lena

Cold.

Lena can't remember the last time she's ever been this cold. Her whole body is shaking, and she can't seem to make it stop. She's thirsty, too, but the water the man in the mask had left her tastes funny. And the last time she'd drunk the whole bottle, she'd felt weird, as though she was floating.

It had lasted for ages, the funny, floaty feeling. And at first, it had felt nice – she didn't feel the cold any more, and the horrible, smelly room hadn't seemed so dark. But then the noises she keeps hearing seemed to get louder and more scary. And the thing that had been in the corner had come out again and crawled towards her, holding its hand out and speaking in that raspy, croaky voice that made her think of all the scary stories she's ever read, of ghosts and monsters and . . .

Lena shakes her head. She'll have to drink the water in a little while, she knows that. The last time she didn't drink it, the man in the mask had taken her jacket away. To teach her a lesson, he'd said. Teach her to be a good little girl. So, next time, she'd tried to pour some of it away and pretend she'd drunk it. But he'd knelt down and stared into her eyes and he'd known she hadn't drunk it. And he'd slapped her so hard, again and again, that she'd wet herself. Did it in her pants, just like a baby. And then he'd laughed.

He'd given her another bottle, told her he'd be back to check on her in a little while to see if she'd learned her lesson. Then he'd reached out and patted her hair, like he was petting a puppy or a kitten. And the whole of her skin had wanted to slide off her body and run away from him.

She looks across at the bottle and the bag of crisps he's left her. Her throat is so dry, she thinks the crisps would choke her, but she knows what she's got to do now. She'll drink the water and eat some of the crisps. And she'll try not to look at the corner where the monster-thing had hidden.

Because the scariest thing of all had been when the man in the mask had come back and Lena had pretended to be asleep. She'd covered her face with her arm and peeped out through her fingers as he'd gone over to the corner and picked up the monster-thing. He'd walked past her, carrying the thing, and taken it outside like it was a piece of rubbish.

But Lena had seen its long blonde hair, the way its skinny grey fingers made patterns in the dust when he'd tripped on something and almost let it go.

That's when Lena had known it wasn't a piece of rubbish. And it hadn't always been a monster-thing. Before it had come here – before the man in the mask had caught it – it had been a girl like her.

A girl called Erin.

36

Day 21

Friday, 10 June

Bad omens, like coincidences, are not a concept Mahler places much faith in. But a gaggle of journalists camped outside a police station in the middle of an enquiry is a sight no serving officer wants to see. Particularly when it's accompanied moments later by a text from their superior officer inviting them to get their arse up to the MIT room ASAP.

He looks round the car park, takes a quick inventory as he walks to the entrance; June Wallace and Chae Hunt, both in before 8.00 a.m. Journalists at the gates, senior officers in the building . . . Mahler makes his way upstairs, praying this doesn't mean the thing he's dreaded since Lena was abducted has finally happened.

June is with Andy Black in the MIT room. As Mahler walks in, they turn to look at him and June shakes her head.

'Jesus Christ, the state of you – Andy, you'll have to do it. He looks like he's gone ten rounds with the Incredible bloody Hulk.'

'I don't see—'

'Enough.' June holds up her hand, cuts Black off. 'The media liaison lassie's waiting for you downstairs. Go out there with her and read the statement, give them the usual "thank you for your attention" guff, and disappear – no questions, no hanging around. Got it? And for God's sake, give your hair a comb.'

Black growls an acknowledgement, slings his jacket over his shoulder and leaves.

June watches him go, turns to Mahler. 'Andy's raging that we let Keenan go last night. Thinks he's the front man for a paedophile ring that had links with Bradley and his ma.'

Mahler shakes his head. 'Nothing from my Kendal trip to bear that out, ma'am.' He'd already emailed her in the early hours, but he gives her a quick verbal report of his meeting with Bradley. 'If there is a ring operating here, it's a home-grown one. But why leave the van out in plain sight?'

'If it is the van. So far, forensics haven't found a damn thing – why do you think I had to let him go? I'm not having this messed up, Lukas. The next time we bring someone in, I want charges lined up and ready to go. And I want Lena McNally safe home with her folks . . . What?'

The ice between his shoulder blades eases. A little. 'Ma'am, I saw the Chief was in, and I thought—'

'You thought we'd found a body.' June shakes her head. 'Aye, that's the first thing that runs through my mind these days whenever I get a bloody text. No, the Chief's just here to discuss some . . . forward-planning issues, that's all.' She gives him an odd, sideways look. Sniffs. 'What the hell have you got in that travel mug? It smells like something you'd put down drains.'

He looks down, realises she must mean Ella's tisane. 'Herbal tea, ma'am.' He hasn't noticed any strong smell or taste from the bright yellow liquid, but his headaches have definitely eased since he's started using it. 'Very invigorating.'

Another sniff. 'I'll stick to my coffee, thanks.' She glances at her watch as the team start to file in. 'Right, then. I want a joint briefing with you and Andy this afternoon – and I'll expect an

239

update to give the Chief this evening with clear actions we're taking to move things forward.'

She heads for the door, turns.

'And Lukas? I don't want to get that message about Lena. Ever. Understood?'

No answer he can give her, apart from a nod as the MIT room fills up. Donna first, then Gary, the odour of freshly inhaled nicotine clinging to their clothes and hair. Fergie's next, talking into his mobile, looking weary and grim-faced.

They'll have seen the clutch of journalists as they arrived, just as Mahler had; and he knows they'll have the same thoughts running through their heads as he had. He's got little enough good news to bring them this morning, but at least he can take their greatest fear away. For now.

Once Pete and Nazreen arrive, Mahler brings them up to date with his Kendal trip, then the decision to let Aaron Keenan go. 'I know, it's frustrating. But finding the van takes us a step closer to finding whoever killed Erin and abducted Lena.'

'Forensics?' Gary puts up his hand. 'If that's the van, surely they've got something by now?'

Mahler looks down at his iPad. He'd have thought so too, but he hasn't seen any of the emails he'd expect from them in a case like this. And Fergie's shaking his head.

'Nothing yet, apparently,' Mahler tells the room. 'But we're building a wall of evidence here, and we can't risk proceeding further without proper foundations.'

A frown on Fergie's face, telling Mahler he'd come perilously close to channelling Chae Hunt. He winces, abandons any further construction metaphors and crosses to the whiteboards.

'The forensics will have a huge part to play in this enquiry. But until our CSI friends come through for us, it's back to traditional detective work.'

He picks up a marker and red-lines the photograph of Maxwell Bradley.

'Clean slate time. Put Bradley to one side in your heads, because we've nothing linking him to any of this. What else do we have – about the van, about the girls, their parents, their friends – anything?'

'Sir, the van.' Nazreen nudges Pete. 'We think . . . Pete's sure it's been cloned. Aren't you?'

Pete flushes, nods. 'Just a hunch I had,' he tells Mahler. 'I got a pal in Forensics to send me the VIN from the engine, did some checking, and guess what? They don't match. The plates are from a white transit, all right, but it was last owned by a retired plumber from the north of England called Alfred Miller – who died in a rest home in Harrogate in 2011.'

'What about tax and insurance?'

Nazreen grins. 'All fully paid up . . . and listed as at Mr Miller's address, so someone's determined to keep that vehicle on the road. All we need to do is find out who.'

And there it is. The whisper-faint touch at the back of Mahler's neck, telling him that here, finally, is the path they need to follow.

'Well done.' He looks round the room, sees the rising excitement on all their faces. 'In fact, bloody well done, you two! Keep on it.'

He adds the new information to the whiteboard, turns to Donna.

'What about the girls – any luck with finding any common ground between them?'

She looks doubtful. 'Yes and no. Turns out Celeste Taylor and Lena were both keen gymnasts. Celeste gave up earlier this year, but Lena still went to classes regularly. If there is a paedophile ring operating here, staking out wee girls' exercise classes would be one way to pick their targets, wouldn't it? Couldn't find a link to Erin, though.'

'Two out of three's sounding pretty damn good to me at this stage,' Fergie puts in. 'Boss?'

Mahler nods. 'Definitely. Well done, Donna – scare up a spare uniform and talk to the class organiser. Any incidents with peeping Toms, dodgy-looking lurkers, anything a bit off she didn't report at the time but might do now. Check out the parents too – perhaps there's a different link with Erin, one we haven't uncovered yet.'

He looks back at the whiteboard, runs through it all in his mind. Frowns as a thought strikes him. 'Kyle Keenan's on the register, yes? So why haven't we picked him up at his notified address? I want all his family spoken to, all his contacts looked at . . . and I particularly want to know if he has any friends or acquaintances in the north of England.'

He lets Fergie give out the remaining allocations, watches the team disperse at the end of the briefing. They're still dog-tired, but the news from Pete and Nazreen has lifted them; there's a crackle of energy in the room that they'd all sorely needed after the news of Aaron Keenan's release.

'Good briefing, boss.'

Mahler turns to look at Fergie. He'd been quieter than usual during the meeting, but Mahler had put that down to weariness following the Keenan interviews. There had been something off in his voice just then, though. Something flatter, more dispirited-sounding than simple fatigue could account for.

'Want to tell me what's wrong? Because there's clearly something.'

Silence, then Fergie nods. 'Maybe, aye. I hope not, but . . . have you had the post-mortem report through on Anthea Bradley yet?'

'I'm not sure. I had a quick look through my emails this

morning, but I don't remember seeing anything from Marco. But he's signed it off as natural causes, hasn't he? Are you telling me there's a problem with that?'

Fergie gives him a troubled look. 'Not with that, no. But . . . ach, I'm probably barking up the wrong tree entirely. The doc told me himself, time of death is never an exact science.'

And that un-Fergie-like evasiveness is enough to tell Mahler something's definitely amiss.

He's about to tell Fergie – *order* Fergie, if necessary – to explain what the hell he's talking about, when Pete reappears. He's out of breath, clutching his iPad . . . and looking very, very pleased with himself.

'Got her,' he tells Mahler and Fergie. 'The woman with Anthea Bradley's cash card? She tried to use it again yesterday evening – the machine by Markies in the Eastgate Centre, this time.'

'CCTV?'

'Oh yes.' Pete beams at Mahler. 'Full face this time. Not only that, but we know exactly who she is!'

37

'That's a rubbish name for a hairdresser's. I mean, *really* rubbish.' Fergie stares up at the black and pink sign above the door of what he's willing to swear had started life as a Portakabin. 'Who's going to get their hair done at "Khloe's Klever Kuts", for God's sake? Sounds like a bloody dog-groomer. And who the hell's "Khloe", anyway?'

Donna shrugs. 'Meant to make her sound like one of those Kardashians, I suppose. You know, a bit exclusive, like.'

A chorus of sniggers from the pair of uniforms behind them.

Donna turns, gives them the kind of bone-freezing stare Fergie's glad he's not on the receiving end of. 'Want to go in first, guys? See if Maire's in the mood for company? No, I thought not.'

Instant poker faces on the two uniforms; aye, well, Fergie can't blame them. Maire Jamieson, who co-owns the hairdressing salon, had been instantly recognisable as the woman who'd used Anthea Bradley's bank card. Only twenty-six, Maire Jamieson's already a legend to the uniformed ranks based at Burnett Road. A wee bit like the Loch Ness Monster, he supposes. If Nessie spent her weekends tanked up on cheap booze, roaming the city centre and picking fights with anyone whose face she took a dislike to, that is.

The uniforms' latest interaction with Maire had been following a fracas in Hootananny, a popular pub specialising in live traditional folk music. With several drinks inside her, Maire had recognised a former love rival and had promptly devised a new accompaniment to the fiddlers' set, by grabbing the bodhrán-player's hand drum and bashing her rival repeatedly over the head with it.

When the police had been called to the ensuing stramash, it had taken four officers to remove her. And Fergie happens to know two of them are still bruised in places they prefer not to talk about.

Still, this is Maire's place of work, it's almost lunchtime and she won't want to make a scene in front of her clients. Maybe they can keep this low-key.

Fergie looks across at Donna. 'You and me first, aye? Keep it nice and calm?'

'Sounds like a plan.'

Donna goes in first, introduces herself to the quiet-looking, silver-haired woman at the reception desk. So far, so good . . . until the woman turns her head and screeches 'Polis!' at whoever's behind the bead curtain at the back. Next moment, the curtain is abruptly shoved aside and two faces peer out. Donna calls out a warning, ducks as a coffee mug flies towards her. And mayhem promptly ensues.

One of the uniforms is the first to go down, felled with a barrage of shampoo bottles that spill out their contents mid-air, turning the floor into a rainbow-coloured skating rink. As Maire's clients bolt for the door in a flurry of black capes and highlighting foils, Fergie's slammed against the reception desk.

He gets to his feet just in time to avoid being thumped with the cash box by the silver-haired woman, and spots a pair of overall-clad legs in work boots lumbering towards the door, looking strangely out of place in a hairdressing salon. When Fergie identifies himself, the legs turn to chuck a chair at him and then speed up. Fergie shakes his head. Sod this for a game of soldiers.

He sets off in pursuit, calls out again and launches himself at the chair-thrower's knees, bringing them down on the strip of grass by the bins. Their skinny, red-haired owner looks as though he's going to throw up, so Fergie hauls him to his feet and takes him through the arrest procedure. He clams up when Fergie asks him for his details, but Fergie tells him not to worry, there'll be plenty of time for a chat back at Burnett Road.

By the time Fergie's finished, a spitting, cursing Maire's being led out of the salon, sandwiched between the uniforms; to their credit, they're a lot scruffier than when they went in, but they look more or less in one piece. And they've got Maire, which means there's a drink on Fergie's tab at the Heathmount tonight for them both. There's no sign of Donna, though.

Fergie's about to hand Legs over to the uniforms when she appears. She's dabbing at a cut on her cheek and her white blonde hair is dripping with what Fergie sincerely hopes is only Irn-Bru, but she seems pretty cheerful for someone who looks like they've just been spray-painted with hair dye.

She goes over to join him, grins. 'That was fun, eh? Got my cardio in today, for sure. Who's your friend?'

Fergie shakes his head. 'Mr Nobody as yet. I've a feeling he'll be a bit more talkative once he's back at Burnett Road, though. Because there's a nice wee splash of red paint on one of his work boots . . . and I've got a pretty good idea how it got there.'

'Fergie's chair-thrower is called Ewan Polson,' Mahler tells June and Andy Black at the afternoon briefing. 'Maire's significant other. He was one of the glaziers working at Anthea Bradley's house. He was also a member of a Facebook group called "Vigil for Erin", which discussed all aspects of Erin's abduction. Pete's been monitoring the group, and the most vocal members – including Ewan – all left around the same time. We're calling in his mobile records, but it seems likely that Ewan and the others were in contact outside of Facebook.'

'And turned into a band of bloody vigilantes.' June aims a glare at Black. 'Which we nudged in the right direction with our statement about Bradley.'

Mahler shakes his head. 'Not necessarily. We assumed there must have been a leak, but it's looking more like a combination of sheer bad luck and carelessness on Anthea's part – she'd changed her name, yes, but not on all her documents. Ewan could easily have seen some paperwork while he was working at her place and put two and two together.'

Black nods. 'Makes more sense. So, was Mad Maire in on it too?'

'Fergie's still interviewing,' Mahler tells him. 'Ewan seems overwhelmed by being in custody, so Maire or the other group members may have been pulling his strings.'

June nods. 'Keep me updated. And I want—' she breaks off as her mobile buzzes on the desk. She picks it up, glances at the screen. And shakes her head, as though she's finding it hard to interpret what she's seeing.

She stands up, stuffs the phone in her pocket. 'Need to make a call, so we'll have to finish now. Stay in the building, though, both of you. We'll pick this up later.'

Andy Black gets up, leaves, and Mahler starts to follow suit. He's almost at the door when June calls him back.

'Lukas, wait a moment. You didn't attend Anthea Bradley's post-mortem, did you?'

'That was Fergie, ma'am. I'm afraid I haven't seen the report yet, but I can chase it up with Dr McVinish if you—'

'No need. Thanks.' An odd, tight look on her face. 'Go on, then, back downstairs. I'll call you both up when I'm free.'

And it's that look, the exact counterpart of what he'd seen in Fergie's expression, that gives him the final push along the road to something he's managed not to see until this moment. An unbelievable something, something even now he's struggling to imagine.

He goes downstairs to find Fergie. If he's finished interviewing Ewan and Maire, Mahler has a few urgent questions of his own he needs to ask him. But before he even reaches the MIT room, Donna comes rushing out to meet him. And the look on her face tells him that whatever she's going to say, it won't be any kind of good news.

But when it comes, it's the last thing he'd been expecting.

'Boss, a call just came through from the Control Room. It's Aaron Keenan. Someone's beaten him half to death, and he's been taken to Raigmore. They . . . they aren't sure if he's going to make it.'

38

'Paramedics said it's a miracle he was still alive.'

Back from Raigmore Hospital's ICU, Gary looks shaken by the time he's finished giving his report to the team. Mahler can hardly blame him; the list of injuries Keenan had sustained included a ruptured spleen, internal bleeding and multiple fractures.

'And the prognosis? Is he expected to recover?'

'Touch-and-go, they said. Caught a glimpse of him as they wheeled him in, and his face looked like a burst football. If there's bleeding on his brain . . .'

'Jesus Christ.' Andy Black's face is paper-white. 'How did it happen, in broad daylight? Didn't anyone—'

Footsteps. Fast, angry, coming along the corridor to the MIT room. Mahler heads for the door, but he's too late; June Wallace is there, standing in the doorway. Looking as though she's ready to tear someone apart, and enjoy doing it.

She looks round the room, and her eyes fasten on Andy Black. 'Gang's all here, I see. Perfect.' She turns to look at Mahler. And gives him one of the few truly terrifying smiles he's ever seen her produce. 'Fergie, can you take over, please. Lukas, Andy, a word. My office.'

Major bollocking time, then; June wouldn't interrupt a briefing for anything less. As he follows June and Andy Black, Mahler tries to work out what they could both have done to warrant it.

Upstairs, June ushers them into her office, closes the door. And waves them to the chairs by her desk. 'Sit. I've got a video clip to show you, from this morning's STV news – it's not very long, but I think you'll find it interesting.'

She taps a couple of keys on her laptop, turns it round so they can see the external shot of Burnett Road, before it cuts to Andy standing next to the press liaison officer. Mahler listens to Andy read out the prepared statement, watches for anything to explain the gathering fury on June's face, and draws a blank. Until, after Andy's told the waiting journalists he won't be answering any questions, a voice asks if the name of the man they've just released without charge is Aaron Keenan.

Mahler can see the moment it registers with Andy, see him frozen in shock, before he turns away and walks slowly back to the entrance.

June reaches over, pauses the clip, and gives Andy that dangerous smile again. 'Comments, Andy? That must have given you a bad moment, coming out of nowhere like that.'

A dull flush creeps up Andy's neck. 'Of course it bloody did! But I didn't confirm anything, ma'am. No way did I do anything wrong.'

'Aye, that's what I thought. Until I saw this.' June rewinds the clip. And pauses it at the moment when Andy's almost turned his back on the cameras. Almost, but not quite. Not enough for them to miss the unmistakeable hint of a smirk as he turns away. 'Do I need to run it again, or do we understand one another?'

'I . . .' Andy's face has gone beyond white, turned a hue so colourless Mahler doesn't even have a name for it. 'Ma'am, no. I don't need to see it again.'

June's eyes are blue ice as she stares at him. 'Tell me I'm imagining that look on your face, Andy. Tell me you are not fucking smirking about releasing the name of a man we hadn't even called a person of interest yet!'

'I never meant . . .' He shakes his head. 'Christ, I never said a word, it was just . . . I couldn't help my bloody face, could I? Anyway, the van was at his house! What's the innocent explanation for that? God's sake, what else do we fucking need? As soon as the CSI guys have finished—'

'They have finished, Andy. I'm looking at the damn report right now, and the van's so fucking clean you could take out someone's appendix in it.' June snaps the laptop shut, slides it out of the way and leans forward so that her eyes are inches from Black's. 'And to make matters worse – to put the absolute sodding tin lid on it – I've just got a note through from Dingwall Traffic. When Erin was being abducted, Aaron Keenan was being given a speeding ticket. In sodding Keiss, nearly a hundred miles away. Tell me how he could have been in two places at once, Andy – is he Dr sodding Who or something? Christ!'

'Why the fuck didn't he tell us that in the first place, then?'

'I don't know! And right now, I don't care.'

'He's involved. He has to be—'

'He is not fucking involved. He's in bloody ICU in Raigmore because you made his name public, and some knuckle-dragging vigilantes put two and two together and came to the same conclusion you did. The same *wrong* conclusion. And that's not what we do, Andy. Is it?'

'Ma'am, I—'

'No, it sodding isn't! We look at the sodding evidence and we sodding well follow it. We get rattled by the press, of course we do, but we don't let it show. And we don't ever throw someone to the sodding vigilante wolves because of it. Have you got that?'

'Ma'am—'

'Have you sodding got that?'

'Yes, ma'am.'

'Yes, ma'am.' June shakes her head. 'For the love of God, Andy. Just . . . just go home, man. The Chief and I need to work out what the hell to do with you.'

'Ma'am—'

'Out! Now!'

Silence after Black's gone. The fury slowly fading from June's face, leaving her paler than Black had been.

'Ma'am.' Mahler clears his throat. 'With respect, I'm not entirely sure—'

'Why you needed to see that? Two reasons.' She opens her desk drawer, removes a bottled water and takes a sip. 'One, I know how rumours start, and I know fine well there'll be rumours flying round within the hour about where Andy's gone, and why. You'll be taking on all his workload while he's off, so it's only fair you understand why.'

Andy's entire workload. Mahler feels the twist of tension knot itself at the base of his skull. Well, it won't be the first time he's taken over Andy's cases; and Andy hasn't exactly been a constructive presence in the MIT room recently. 'You said there were two reasons?'

June nods, takes another sip of her water before answering. 'Anthea Bradley's post-mortem. Fergie told you he'd asked for additional information about an approximate time of death, didn't he?'

'He said there were a couple of things to be clarified, yes. But her death was due to natural causes, so I don't see . . .' He *had* seen it, though, Mahler realises. Seen the relief on Andy's face when he'd heard the post-mortem results, but told himself he'd misread it. 'How accurate is it possible to be?'

There's no humour at all in the grim smile she gives him.

'Probably not accurate enough. At least, I hope not. Because if there was a way to prove that Anthea Bradley could have been lying dead in that summerhouse when Andy searched her place, I swear I . . .' she shakes her head. 'Never mind. Go back to your team and light a sodding fire under them. If we ever needed some good news, it's now.'

'Ma'am.' He turns to go. And stops as he realises what's been bothering him since June had told him and Andy Black about the forensic team's findings. 'You said forensics had drawn a blank with the van because of its condition. So it has to have been deep-cleaned, yes? And we know Aaron's got nothing to do with it. So someone tried to set him up, Ma'am. Someone who knew he'd be an easy target because of his brother. And knew how to go about it.'

'Christ.' June reaches for her water bottle, takes another drink. Grimaces. 'It could still be an organised gang. If they knew about Aaron through his brother—'

'They'd have to have ready access to the equipment needed. They'd need to know enough about our processes to make sure there was nothing in that van we could use. And they'd need to know how to maximise the chances that we'd come across it in his driveway.'

'Ach, Lukas.' June lets out her breath in a long, weary sigh. 'You know what you're saying here?'

He does. But it's not something either of them want to say out loud. Yet. 'It doesn't have to be someone in the job. Not directly. All they'd need is enough insider knowledge to know what we'd be looking for.'

'Aye?' She takes off her glasses, pinches the bridge of her nose. 'You'd better find them then, hadn't you? Find them bloody fast.'

39

Back to the MIT room, to break the news that the team is now one member down; not the news Mahler wants to deliver in the middle of this investigation, even if that member is Andy Black.

They don't look particularly convinced by his explanation that Black's had to take some time off unexpectedly, but it's all the information he can give them. It won't stop the rumours spreading, but he suspects June knows that perfectly well; this is about damage limitation and keeping them focused.

He tells them that Fergie will be running the Cazza MacKay hit-and-run enquiry and reporting directly to June Wallace and schedules another briefing for the following morning.

'Pete, keep digging into the history of that van – any recent camera pick-ups, and if so, where? What about tax and insurance?'

'On it, boss.'

'Good. Nazreen, we shouldn't be able to mislay someone who's on the register indefinitely. I want Kyle Keenan found, and I want to know how he's linked to that van. Is Fergie still with Polson?'

'Just missed him, sir. Polson requested another break, and Fergie thinks he's going to ask for the duty solicitor. Oh, and Fergie said he's put your mobile in your office.'

Mahler frowns, pats his pocket and realises he must have left it on the desk by the whiteboards when June had hauled him and Andy Black upstairs.

He nods his thanks and tells her to send Fergie through to him as soon as he's finished with Polson. He goes back to his office, and finds three missed calls on his mobile, one from his mother and two from numbers he doesn't recognise.

He's about to call them back when there's a knock on his door. Donna's there with Nazreen, and there's no mistaking the excitement on their faces.

'Boss, I think we've found a link between the girls. Erin and Lena were both registered with the same doctors' surgery – not only that, but Lena had an appointment on the day she disappeared, and Erin hadn't long finished a course of antibiotics for an ear infection.'

'With the same doctor?'

Donna shakes her head. 'It's still a link, though, so I'm checking out all the practice staff.'

'Good. Start with anyone who's joined them relatively recently, and work back. Anything else?'

Nazreen nods. 'There's a definite Aquadome connection, sir. Celeste Taylor's mother works there part-time, and—'

'Aquadome?' Something there, he's sure of it. Something he's heard recently, in connection with another case . . . 'I need to check something on the whiteboards.'

He follows them through to the MIT room, runs his eye down the crossed-off bullet points until he finds what he's looking for.

'Kat Evans,' he tells them. 'Ella's neighbour, dropped in on her while Fergie and I were talking to her about the van she'd reported seeing. She works at the Aquadome. And her husband's a doctor.'

Donna frowns. 'Not aware of a Doctor Evans in any of the local surgeries, boss.' She opens her laptop, hits a couple of keys. 'Calling up the NHS lists now. Could be a locum, I suppose—'

'We need to find him.' Mahler looks round the room, sees the same gathering excitement on everyone's face. 'Cross-check everyone connected with this case, see if his name comes up. The girl's parents, the McIvers—' he breaks off as Pete looks up from his laptop and gives a whoop of triumph. 'What have you got?'

'The van, boss. Been searching for images on the off-chance, and I think I've got it being left at Polson's house on some YouTube drone footage. It's still coming up as registered at our late plumber's address in Leeds, but—'

'Leeds? I thought he was in Harrogate?'

Pete shakes his head. 'He retired to Harrogate, went into a home there not long before he died. But his business was in Leeds. Is that important?'

Another connection, slotting into place. The memory of a conversation in a Lake District police station that had stuck in his mind without his really knowing why. Until now.

'The DI I met in Kendal had transferred in from Leeds and the last case he'd worked on there – an investigation into two missing girls – is still unsolved. Donna, look for a GP who's moved here from the Leeds/Yorkshire area in the last three years. Cross-check with the date Kat Evans started at the Aquadome.' There's something else, too, something that happened on the final day of the search for Erin MacKenzie—

An incoming call on his mobile. A new number, one he doesn't recognise. But when he answers, the voice on the other end belongs to Ella Kirkpatrick.

'Inspector, I need your help.' She's speaking quickly, as

though she's worried about being interrupted, but her voice is steady, with none of the vagueness he'd noticed previously. 'The little girl you're looking for? She's here. And Kat—'

A cry of pain or fear, he can't tell which, and then a groan. Then silence.

'Hell!' He looks round the room, sees the eagerness on Nazreen's face, nods. 'Right, Naz, you're with me.' He's still talking, issuing instructions over his shoulder as he heads out of the MIT room and down the stairs. 'Donna, get Fergie out of Polson's interview, tell him to grab a couple of uniforms and follow on. Pete, we'll need an ambulance out there too.'

'It's Doctor Grey, boss.' As he reaches the half-landing, Donna calls after him. 'The man you're looking for? His name's Patrick Grey.'

The warmth has gone from the day entirely now, heavy grey rain-clouds filling a gunmetal sky as he and Nazreen head for Ella's. No lights, no noise, nothing to announce their arrival; Ella and Lena may well be injured, and they're definitely in danger. Mahler's got no intention of putting them at any further risk until he knows what he and Nazreen might be walking into.

Nazreen's phone rings as they're turning off the main road. 'Fergie's on his way, sir,' she tells him. 'And Pete's just got confirmation – Dr Grey and his wife moved up from Yorkshire three years ago. They move around quite a bit, apparently.' She looks across at him. 'Do you think . . . does his wife know about the little girls?'

Mahler thinks about the woman he and Fergie had met at Ella's. Thinks about the way she'd introduced herself as Kat Evans, obscuring the link between herself and Patrick Grey. The way she'd painted Ella as a confused elderly woman, possibly in the early stages of dementia.

'She knows, all right.'

When they reach the turn-off to the track leading to Ella's cottage, Mahler pulls in off the road. It's raining in earnest as they get out of the car, heavy, relentless torrents pouring from a near-black sky, which means they should be able to get close to Ella's cottage without being seen. He glances at Nazreen.

'Still no answer from Ella?'

'Sorry, sir. I'll keep trying—'

Mahler shakes his head; either Ella's not there or she's incapable of responding. 'When Fergie arrives, we'll—'

A sharp crack, like the sound of a car backfiring. And a shatter of falling glass. Mahler grabs Nazreen's arm, pulls her to the ground. And puts a restraining hand on her shoulder when she starts to raise her head.

'Sir, that was—'

'A firearm. Yes. Shotgun, at a guess.'

'Bloody hell.' She's reaching for her Airwave, but Mahler shakes his head. He looks round, spots the outline of what looks like a firewood store; it's not perfect, but it's the only cover available and there's a path running alongside it.

He gives Nazreen a push towards it. 'Go. Keep your head down, and take the lower track back to the road. Call for backup as soon as you're out of range. When Fergie arrives, keep him up there until the ARU arrives.'

Nazreen stares at him. 'You can't—'

He can. More than that, he *has* to. Ella Kirkpatrick had been right all along about seeing the van. But when he and Fergie had talked to her, she'd seemed different: on edge, preoccupied. And that was all Kat Grey had needed. No wonder she'd been shaken to find him and Fergie with Ella. But all it had taken to cast doubt on Ella's story was a manufactured mix-up over dates and a not-so-subtle hint about dementia.

And Mahler had fallen for it. He'd alerted Kat and Patrick

Grey, placed Ella in appalling personal danger, and then he'd walked away. This whole mess is of his making, and it's down to him to set things right . . . and if it goes wrong, no one else's neck is going to be on the line because of his stupidity.

'Go.'

Nazreen starts to say something, then shakes her head. She makes for the wood store at a crouching half-run, and drops down onto the path leading back to the road.

He watches Nazreen's progress until she disappears from sight, then circles round the back of the log store. The farmhouse's windowless gable end is facing the firewood store, so he can't be seen until he reaches the set of paving stones leading to the front porch. But once he's there, if anyone looks out of the living-room window, even in this rain . . .

He rounds the corner. And looks up just in time to see the motion sensor light above the porch. He ducks back quickly, tries to process what he's seen. Both the porch door and the door leading into the hallway are open. No sign of movement inside, but there's a pale strip of light bleeding from the door at the end of the hall. And in the instant before he'd ducked out of sight, he'd heard a murmur of voices.

No point trying the front door; as soon as he moves, the sensor will give him away. And the voices were coming from the kitchen, he's sure of it. His only option is to try and enter through the conservatory at the rear. And hope Patrick Grey isn't waiting there, shotgun in hand, to greet him.

The path leading to the back door has been gravelled, so Mahler sticks to the grass, keeping his head down as he works his way round. The conservatory is in darkness, but the door to the kitchen is three-quarters open, enough for him to make out what looks like a bound figure, slumped on one of the chairs.

Ella. He can't see her clearly, but she's moving slightly, enough to reassure him she's not dead. Mahler releases the breath he's been holding, and inches closer to the conservatory doors. He tries one of the handles, and the door swings smoothly open. If he can get closer to the kitchen without being seen . . .

He takes a step inside, and the motion sensor on the outside wall, the one he'd been too intent on keeping his head down to notice, snaps into life, flooding the area with light. Half blinded, Mahler has nowhere to hide as a woman appears in the kitchen doorway.

The shotgun she's holding is levelled at him. And the words he's been about to say die in his throat as she takes a step towards him.

40

'Inspector.' Ella Kirkpatrick nods. 'I thought it might be you.' She lowers the shotgun barrel a fraction, but keeps it trained on him. 'Come in, then. Slowly. And please keep your hands where I can see them.'

She takes a couple of steps back into the kitchen, waits for him to follow. Her face is set in tight, exhausted lines, but there's an air of calmness about her, and she's holding the shotgun with the kind of ease that tells Mahler she knows exactly what to do with it.

His mobile's buzzing in his pocket – Nazreen? Fergie? – but he abandons any thought of reaching for it.

A crunch of what sounds like broken glass beneath his feet. Mahler looks round the room, takes in the shards of ruined crockery strewn across the dresser, a scatter of shotgun pellets embedded in its wood. And tied to the chair beside it, his wrists bound behind him, the slumped and bloodstained figure of Patrick Grey. As Ella waves Mahler over to the chair in the other corner, Grey lifts his head.

'You took your bloody time.' Grey's voice is tight with a mix of anger and fear. He's bleeding from a scalp wound, trails of red journeying down his face to mingle with the vomit on his ruined shirt front. 'Bitch tried to poison me, and kill Kat. You need—'

'Be quiet.' Grey's vocal enough to not be seriously hurt. But if he angers Ella again, that could change. Mahler's mobile buzzes again. He ignores it, and turns to her.

'Ella, where's Kat? Did you . . . has she been injured?'

Her face tightens. 'She's got a sore head, but it's no more than she deserved. She's in the old byre. And I didn't poison your mannie here. I put a wee something in his tea to make him sleep, that's all. I needed him to behave himself before I rang you.'

'You used Kat's mobile, didn't you?' It must have been a pay-as-you-go Kat and Grey used when carrying out the abductions. 'That's why we weren't able to trace it.'

She nods. 'You weren't going to listen to me, were you? Kat told you I was a poor old wifie, away with the fairies. And you believed her.'

'I'm sorry.' A twist of shame as he realises that's exactly what he'd thought. *Copper's gut.* If he'd followed his instincts, how much of this could have been avoided? 'Ella, the little girl you found? Her name's Lena. She's the little girl who—'

'I know who she is. You'll find her in the back of the old byre. I had to leave her there while I dealt with this one, but I made her as comfortable as I could.' A sheen of sweat on her forehead. 'Safe from him.' The shotgun barrel swings towards Grey, who starts to whimper. 'Do you know what he is, Inspector? What he deserves?'

'For God's sake, man!' Grey's crying, tears tracking through the blood and sweat. 'Bloody do something, can't you, she's lost her fucking mind—'

'Shut up.'

As Ella turns towards him, Mahler holds up the phone he's taken from his pocket so they can all hear it buzzing. 'Ella, that's my sergeant. He's on his way here with an armed response unit – that's a group of trained firearms officers – because of the shot I heard. But I know you don't want anyone to get hurt, Ella. Will you let me talk to him? If you put the gun down, I promise—'

'Don't worry about that, Inspector. We'll be done before he gets here.' She draws a ragged breath, leans against the line of kitchen units to steady herself. 'Go on, ask me what you want to know. But put your phone on the table, and don't touch it again.'

Sirens. In the distance, but coming closer. Mahler can't risk going for the shotgun, but if Ella's still got it when the ARU arrives . . .

He touches the green icon on his screen, nods. 'I'm putting the phone down now, Ella.' He places it carefully on the table, turns to her. 'How could you be sure about Grey?'

'You didn't believe me about the van,' she tells him. 'So I needed proof. I knew Kat always goes to the gym on Fridays, so I waited until she'd gone and I went down to the byre. I couldn't get in, but I . . . I heard crying. And then I knew. The front was padlocked, but round the back half the wood is rotten. I got my wee kindling axe and made enough of a hole to squeeze through. And the crying . . . it was coming from *underneath* where the floor should have been.'

She swallows, and the shotgun barrel dips briefly. 'Do you understand what I'm saying? He'd built something, some sort of false floor. And he'd put the bairn in a damn hole in the ground. As though . . . as though she was nothing. Then Kat came in as I was trying to help the wee one stand up. She couldn't believe what she was seeing at first, just stood there with her mouth open. But then she came at me, tried to knock me over. So I clouted her with my stick and down she went.'

'And then you went after Grey here?'

Ella nods. 'I got her phone, sent him a text saying she'd found me in the byre. And then I got my father's gun and I waited for him to come home. Made him drink his tea and waited until I knew I could tie him up without him causing trouble.' She's weeping now, the shotgun shaking in her hands. 'He's got to be stopped, Mr Mahler. I can't let him hurt any more wee girls.'

'He won't! Ella, you *have* stopped him. He's going to prison—'

She shakes her head. 'Not enough.' She half turns, trains the gun on Grey. And slips the safety catch. 'I know what men like him are like. The mess they leave behind them.'

'No!' He takes a step towards her. 'Ella, this isn't what you want. It can't be.' The words dry and sterile on his tongue. Another step. And another. Praying the line's still open, praying none of the response team decide they've waited long enough. 'Put the gun down. Please. I know this isn't who you are. You're not a murderer. So why don't we—'

Something in her eyes, then. Some old, uncharted darkness that makes the words dry in his throat. He stares at her as the pattern forms at last, the final pieces dropping into place.

'Aeneas Grant. The body at the farm. You killed him, didn't you?'

'Christ!' A howl of terror from Grey. He's rocking back and forth on the chair, his head thumping against the dresser as urine darkens the front of his trousers. 'Get her away! Keep that mad old bitch away from me—'

Ella looks at Mahler. Mouths an apology as she raises the gun.

And the door to the hallway bursts inwards. Shouts of 'Police – down, down!' A confusion of dark figures filling the room. Patrick Grey screaming.

Ella starts to turn towards the noise . . . and Mahler lunges for the shotgun, pulling it from her unresisting fingers and forcing her to the ground. He has a fraction of a second to thank his deity, before something that feels as though it's made from cast iron lands on the back of his neck.

His world explodes into pain. And then darkness.

'Saucepan,' June Wallace tells him, as the doctor at Raigmore Hospital's A&E prods the base of Mahler's skull. 'One of those posh French jobs, the ones that weigh a ton. It was on the stand you knocked over as you hit the ground – just as well it was only a wee one, eh? Or I'd be giving you a posthumous bollocking by your graveside, you stupid bloody eejit. Do you think those boys in the ARU got their badges free with a comic book or something? Next time, stand back and let them do their job. Understood?'

'Ma'am.' Mahler grits his teeth as the prodding continues. He'd managed to throw up twice on his way to Raigmore, once over Fergie and once over Nazreen. If the doctor doesn't finish her examination soon, he can't rule out the possibility of an encore. 'Personally, I always thought they came in a job lot from Amazon.'

'Very funny.' June shakes her head at the doctor, who's preparing for another incursion. 'Don't bother – if he's giving me cheek, he's fine. Just give him a couple of those ice packs and we'll get out of your hair. Mind you . . .' She looks Mahler up and down, sighs. 'Ach, you're a funny colour, right enough. Maybe you'd better hang on here for a while.'

'I'm fine, Ma'am. Good to go.' He isn't. But June's been up at the scene while he's been stuck in A&E, and he needs to hear what's been happening. Mahler lurches to his feet, takes the ice packs and the after-care leaflet the doctor forces on him and follows June outside.

As they walk across the car park, the rain starts again. Just a fine rain, this time, barely even a drizzle by Inverness standards.

But after the hospital's stuffy antiseptic warmth, the freshness of the cool night air is exactly what he needs.

June nods at the gleaming white Range Rover at the far end of the car park. 'You okay to make it? Fergie wanted to pick you up, but I thought his bloody Audi might be enough to finish you off – don't even think about throwing up in my car, though, I'm warning you.'

Mahler assures her he's trying extremely hard *not* to think about that. By the time they reach the Range Rover, his stomach's calmer, but his head feels as though someone's attempted to puree the contents, which, he supposes, isn't too far from the truth.

He clamps another ice pack to his neck and climbs in. Carefully. 'Lena, Ma'am – how is she?'

'Recovering.' June manoeuvres out of the car park and round to the dual carriageway. 'Physically, at least. But after what she's been through . . .' Her breath hisses between her teeth. 'Forensics are up at the scene, but we'll get nothing out of that bastard Grey. He's lawyered up already and no commenting all over the place, same with the wife. Fergie and Nazreen are waiting to talk to Ella Kirkpatrick once the doc gives her the all-clear, and—'

'No!' Mahler shakes his head. And nearly rethinks the throwing-up scenario. 'Ma'am, Ella's got a lot to tell us. And I want . . . I need to be there when she does.'

They're only five minutes away from Burnett Road, but a lorry has broken down at the Raigmore roundabout and there's a tailback building all the way towards the city centre.

Waiting at the lights, June glances over at him. Sighs. 'Aye, fair enough. But Fergie will be keeping an eye on you – if you look like you're ready to keel over, he'll be under orders to haul your arse out of there immediately. Got it?'

'Ma'am.'

266

'And Lukas . . . that was a good result. The Chief's got his happy face on, and so have I. Tell your team, aye? Drinks at the Heathmount on me tomorrow night.'

41

It's the stairs at Burnett Road that nearly prove his downfall, in the end. Mahler had coped with the short drive in June's Range Rover and managed to cross the car park without falling over his feet or passing out. But by the time he reaches the half-landing on the stairs to the MIT room, the treads are blurring in front of his eyes and there's a familiar twist of pain settling behind his optic nerve.

No. Not here, not now.

Mahler grits his teeth against the lurch in his gut, hauls himself up the last flight of stairs and across to the washroom. Splashes water on his face and straightens his tie in the mirror, ignoring the bruised and bloody stranger staring back at him.

He makes his way along the corridor to his office, where he changes into the spare jacket and shirt he always keeps there, before heading for interview room 2.

Mahler's got no intention of taking over from Fergie and Nazreen; he's not in any fit state, for one thing. Fergie's perfectly capable of running Ella's interview, and Nazreen deserves this chance to show what she can do after the way she'd handled the situation at the Greys' farmhouse. But he knows he can't go home without talking to Ella again.

At the farmhouse, Mahler had asked her if she'd killed Aeneas Grant. And in the instant before the ARU appeared and chaos began, he'd read the answer in her eyes. He needs to know what happened, all those years ago, needs to know what had driven her thirteen-year-old self to put a bullet through her uncle's skull. And he needs to hear it from her.

When he opens the interview room door, Fergie and Nazreen turn round. The disbelief on both their faces tells him exactly what he looks like, despite the fresh shirt and jacket.

As Fergie tells the recording he's entered the room, Nazreen starts to get up, but he motions to her to remain seated.

'You shouldn't be here, Mr Mahler.' Ella looks exhausted, but she's sitting straight-backed in her chair and her face is oddly calm. 'I'll tell your sergeant what he needs to know. But you've been hurt, and there's more to come for you still. This is your time to heal, if you can.'

Sharp grey eyes holding his. The silence growing. Thickening.

The smell of blood and fear. Feet slipping on the stairs . . .

'I'm sorry, I'm not sure I understand. I haven't . . .' He breaks off as he notices the empty chair beside her. 'Ella, you know you're entitled to have a solicitor here with you, if you wish?'

'I know that. But I don't want one.' She takes a sip from the paper cup beside her, gives him a weary look. 'I've been carrying my uncle's death around for almost seventy years, Mr Mahler. Can you imagine what that feels like? Now there's no one left to be hurt by it but me. And it's time I told the truth about what happened.' She leans closer to the box on the table, clears her throat. 'This is where I talk into, isn't it? Am I close enough to it like this?'

'That's just fine,' Fergie tells her. 'You say whatever you want to, Ella.'

She nods, takes a deep breath. 'Good. Well, then. My name is

Ella Christine Grant Kirkpatrick, and I killed my uncle, Aeneas Grant, in the winter of 1947.'

Fergie starts to caution her, but she shakes her head and carries on talking.

'I shot him with a gun he'd taken from a German during the war as a souvenir. My sister and I buried him in the old midden pit at the back of our farm and covered him with household rubbish and bits and pieces from our barn.' She sits back, looks at Mahler. 'There. That'll be recorded now, won't it?'

'We're recording the whole interview. But now you've told us this—'

'I'll be charged with murder.' She nods, attempts a smile. 'I know. And that . . . that's fine. Is that it all done now? Because that's all I have to say.'

Fergie shakes his head, runs through the caution again and secures her verbal understanding for the recording. 'You said you killed your uncle, back in 1947. But you need to tell us a wee bit more, Ella. About how it happened. Who else was there, why you did—'

'*No.*' Ella's hands are shaking. She reaches for the paper cup, uses both hands to guide it to her mouth. 'I told you what I've done. The rest . . . the rest belongs to me. Can I go back to my . . . my cell now, please? I'm very tired.'

No. Mahler looks at Fergie, sees his own frustration mirrored there. She'd been going to tell them more, he's sure of it. But she can't be denied a break, and—

'He did things to you, didn't he?' Nazreen's voice. Gentle, understanding. Relentless. 'To your sister too, perhaps, or at least he tried to. That's why you killed him.'

Shuddering. Ella's whole body is shuddering, her hands shaking so badly the contents of the paper cup splash over her hands until she puts it down. She meets Nazreen's eyes. And after a long, long moment, she nods.

'Aeneas . . . he was a big man, cheerful man. Always laughing and joking with folk he'd meet, always ready to lend a hand if a sheep got into trouble or you needed help to get a harvest in.' Her voice hardens. 'And he was a filthy, filthy pervert . . . paedophile, you'd call it these days, but it wasn't just bairns he preyed on. He was a brute to his wife, and to any poor female that crossed his path.'

Silence; thick, appalled. Mahler breaks it first. 'No one did anything?'

Ella gives him a pitying look. 'Seventy years ago? You'd still get told off for hanging out your washing on a Sunday. Oh, there would have been whispers, but mostly folk just looked the other way. And when he caught me alone one day . . .' Her voice thickens, breaks. 'The things he did to me. Dear God, I thought I'd die of shame.'

'You didn't tell anyone?'

'How?' She's weeping now, silent, angry tears seventy years in the making. 'How could I ever have done that? I didn't even have the words to tell my mother what he'd done to me when he was home on leave. Then when he came back . . .' Ella draws a ragged breath. 'It was nearly two years after the war had ended. Two whole years without any word from him. Everyone thought he'd been killed – and I was glad he was gone. Glad he was out of our lives for good.' Her mouth twists in a bitter smile. 'Only he wasn't. I was coming back from feeding the hens and he . . . he was just there, standing in the middle of our yard.'

'He went straight to your parents' place? What about his wife?'

Ella gives Mahler a weary look. 'Who knows? All I could think was, he'd come back from the dead to torment me all over again. And then I saw him looking at May. She was the same age I'd been when he . . . he attacked me, and I knew from the look on his face what he was thinking. So I put some crushed seeds in a bottle of Lagavulin and left it out where I knew he'd find it. When he was drunk and snoring, I took the gun and I . . . I shot him.'

'What about your parents?' Nazreen asks. 'Where were they?'

'My father had gone to the cattle mart in Dingwall. Mam was at a neighbour's, helping out the wifie there. She'd gone into labour early, and . . .' Ella shakes her head. 'The poor bairn died, I think. But we knew we were on our own that night, May and I. After I . . . after he died, we dragged him outside and rolled him into the midden. And we cleaned that kitchen – every inch of it – scrubbed it over and over. I knew I'd be caught, mind. Prison and the hangman's rope, that's what was waiting for me.' She looks across at Mahler. 'But then it didn't happen. No one knew he'd been back, you see. The war had been over for two years, and anyone who hadn't come home, well, they weren't coming home. Folk just accepted it.'

'And afterwards?' Nazreen asks. 'You just carried on, with his body so close to where you lived?'

'What choice did I have? Yes, I carried on,' she tells Nazreen. 'It wasn't easy, never think that. I thought about what I'd done every single day, and I tried to feel guilty about it – I'd taken a life, and I knew that was wrong, of course I did. But I knew May was safe, too. And as the years passed, and the land settled, I thought about it less.'

Her mouth thins to a bitter line. 'And that was my sin, you know. Not the killing of one evil man, but the letting go of it. The forgetting. So when another evil man came along, I didn't recognise what he was until it was too late.' She dries her eyes, sits up straighter. 'But I'm very tired, now, and I don't think I can talk about this any more. May I go back to my cell, please?'

It's Fergie's interview, but Ella's looking straight at Mahler. Looking to him for acknowledgement, he thinks, of the story he'd asked her to tell. The thing he'd asked her to relive. After a moment, he nods. 'Very shortly, yes. And thank you, Ella.'

Fergie and Nazreen's job now, to take her to the custody desk and guide her through the formalities of charging and incarceration. Mahler can feel himself sweating in spite of the room's coolness, and he suspects he might not make it as far as the custody desk without throwing up. And Ella's given him the answers he needed to hear. Nothing else for him to do here, surely.

As Nazreen leads her out of the room, Ella turns to look at him. 'Ask someone to make up more tea for you, Mr Mahler. You shouldn't be without it.'

'I'll try. Though I'm not sure who—'

'You'll find someone.' A faint smile for him through the layers of weariness in her face. 'There are still wise women about, if you know where to look for them.'

After they've left, Fergie shakes his head. 'Sometimes you think there's no surprises left in the job. And then, something like this . . .' He looks at Mahler, sighs. 'Boss, we can handle this. The Greys are banged up, Lena's safe, and Ella . . . Ella's where she needs to be for a while. And it's half past bloody midnight. For God's sake, go home and get your head down for a bit.'

Mahler hesitates. His head is throbbing and the strip lights are haloed, blurring. But he's strangely reluctant to leave. Copper's gut? Maybe. There's a restless, gnawing something in the pit of his stomach, urging him not to walk away. But Fergie's right, he realises. The adrenaline that's seen him through the events of the past few hours has gone, and he's running on empty. If their situations were reversed, he'd have bounced Fergie out of the building by now.

He looks at his watch, nods. 'Put the morning briefing back an hour – I'll be in at eight to pull together something for June to give the press.' Though he suspects Chae Hunt is going to want to get his hands on this one. It's got national coverage all over it, maybe even an extended interview on *Reporting Scotland*, and the Chief won't be able to resist. 'And call me if anything crops up. Anything.'

By the time the taxi drops Mahler at his flat on Island Bank Road, it's after one. No point in going to bed, despite his weariness; as soon as he closes his eyes, he knows his mind will start replaying the events of the last few hours. And the restless, unsatisfied thing that hadn't wanted him to leave Burnett Road is still pushing at him, determined not to give him any peace.

He takes another dose of painkillers, folds his jacket under his head on the couch and puts Julie Fowlis on the music system. And exactly forty minutes later, when Julie's haunting voice is taking him to a place where sleep might be a possibility after all, Fergie's name flashes up on his mobile.

'Boss, I'm sorry – I wasn't going to disturb you, but there's been a development with Kat Evans. She's sent her lawyer away, says she's changed her mind and wants to tell us about . . . about what we're going to find up at the farmhouse. But she'll only do it if we're both there.'

2.20 am. Another interview room. Another woman sitting at a table, watching Mahler walk across the room towards her. Another look of concern as he eases himself onto the chair next to Fergie and identifies himself for the recording, sweat breaking out on his forehead at the mild exertion. From anyone else, he might have taken that look at face value.

'Inspector Mahler . . . Lukas, isn't it?' Kat's forehead is bruised and there's a line of stitches across a laceration in her scalp where Ella's stick had hit her, but she seems perfectly relaxed, her hands held loosely in her lap as she looks him up and down. 'Really been in the wars, haven't you?' She shakes her head, gives him a reasonable imitation of a sympathetic smile. 'Hope this won't be too difficult for you.'

'Not in the slightest. But thank you for your concern.' He makes a show of sitting back in apparent comfort, and nods at Fergie to take her through the preliminary set of questions they've prepared. But before Fergie's got to the end of his first sentence, Kat holds up her hand.

'No. This isn't how it's going to be.' She reaches for her paper cup of water, drains it. 'It's very late, and I'm tired.' She gives an unconvincing yawn and settles back in her chair. 'And none of what you're going to ask me matters anyway.'

'I'm not sure I understand, Kat. If you feel you want a break—'

'I'll tell you what I want. And when I want it.' Ice frosting her voice as she glances at the manila folder Fergie's holding. 'So you can chuck that. This isn't your show, boys. Never was.'

Something different in the room now, some darker, heavier thing Mahler can't put a name to. This interview will take them where they need to be, he's sure of that. But it means allowing Kat to feel she's the one in charge. He exchanges a glance with Fergie, nods. And spreads his hands in a gesture of surrender.

'Let's start again, then. What do you want to tell us, Kat? Is it about the girls?'

'Oh, yes.' A slow, anticipatory smile spreads across her face. She sits up straighter, looks across to the camera mounted on the wall. 'I want to tell you about all the dead girls.'

The change in temperature as Kat tells her story exists only in Mahler's head, he knows that. The chill he experiences as she talks about the children she and Grey had preyed on comes from his own exhaustion and the horror of her words, nothing more. But he can't shake the feeling that she's aware of his discomfort. And relishing every moment of it.

She and Grey had met at university – and felt an instant attraction, according to Kat. 'As though we were soul mates. And then we found out we were both huge Lucky fans.' Something sly in the smile she gives him. 'You know Johnny, don't you? He was such an artist, don't you think? A real performer. '

Lucky. The nickname given to John Felix, Natalie Harper's grinning, unrepentant killer. Mahler swallows down the sourness at the back of his throat. In the early days of Erin's disappearance, the media had been blasted for calling up the memory of his crimes; turns out they'd been closer to the truth than anyone had suspected.

'We'll agree to disagree there, I think,' Mahler tells Kat. 'Please, carry on.'

Within a few days of meeting, Kat and Grey had bonded in a dark, obsessive partnership that allowed them to explore their sadistic fantasies. After graduating, Grey had worked as a locum doctor, enabling them to move around the UK and continue their killing career.

'We were planning to move on soon,' she admits. 'We never stayed anywhere longer than three years, usually. But Ella . . . she was a nice old thing, you know? Really kind to us when we moved in.' Her face darkens. 'She changed, though. Looked at us funny, after a while, as though she was working something out.'

Mahler nods. 'The van. She'd started to wonder about it, hadn't she? So that's when you decided to move it. But why did you leave it near Aaron Keenan's house?'

'Oh, come on, Lukas. That's not hard to work out, surely – he was one of Paddy's patients. I mean, we could have chosen anyone, I suppose, but his family connections were just perfect.' A flicker of annoyance crosses her face. 'Paddy was going to add some of Keenan's blood to the rucksack he planted, but somehow he stuffed that up. We shouldn't have cleaned the van so thoroughly, though. A few token spots of blood for your forensics team to find would have been the icing on the cake.'

'Aye.' Fergie's voice is tight, controlled. 'A wee mistake there, eh? Still, we all make them.'

The smile freezes on her face. 'You lot certainly did. Oh, you'll spin it for the media, make yourselves sound like proper little heroes. But we know the truth, don't we? The truth is, you just got lucky.'

'And you got careless. Using one of Patrick's elderly patients' details to keep your van taxed and legal?' Mahler shakes his head. 'Not very bright of you, was it?'

He watches her face change then, watches something leave it; the last faint traces of whatever had allowed her to pass as Ella's warm-hearted, caring neighbour, perhaps. What comes in its place isn't anything he wants to give a name to.

Kat puts her head on one side, looks at him. 'Is that enough to make you feel better, Lukas? One tiny flash of cleverness, to set against all those dead girls? Somehow, I doubt it.' Her smile is bright with malice. 'But that's enough for the moment. Given you a lot to think about, haven't I?'

'You've been very open. I'm curious, though – what made you change your mind about talking to us?'

A shrug. 'Call it adapting to change, if you like. But I'm tired now, and I need to rest. I should probably see the duty doctor, too, if they're still around.'

'Are you feeling unwell?'

'Never better.' Kat gets to her feet. Gives an exaggerated stretch, and rubs the small of her back. 'But it's important I take care of myself at the moment. In the early weeks.'

She glances at Fergie, then back at Mahler, a dark, unfettered glee dancing in her eyes. 'Oh, come on. Surely you've worked it out by now? I've just found out I'm going to be a mummy.'

42

There are six in the end. Six sets of bones in mouldering cardboard boxes, saved from the depredations of small animals only
through the protection of the green garden waste sacks they'd
been stored in. As each one is carried out, the team stops work
and turns to stand in silence.

'Christ, I can't watch that.' Fergie curses under his breath,
turns his head away as the last of the victims are taken to the
waiting hearse. 'Why the fuck wouldn't she tell us who they
are? She told us everything else.'

Mahler shakes his head. In death, the girls had been anonymous, not even a scrawled name or a fading photograph interred
with them to tell anyone whose child they'd been. 'We'll need
to get a forensic pathologist. Nazreen's liaising with the English
forces and we should get DNA matches for them.'

Fergie swallows hard. 'The Greys moved around a lot, boss.
There could be addresses Kat didn't tell us about – temporary
ones, I mean, ones that got missed off the records. So these wee
girls . . . there could be more of them, all over the country.
Couldn't there?'

He wants to tell Fergie it's unlikely. The Greys' crimes hadn't
gone undetected for so long through sheer chance. They had

been that perfect storm of evil, the unholy trinity of intelligence, risk-averse natures and coolness under pressure. They would have known their chances of discovery increased with every crime they committed, every scarred and brutalised body a repository of evidence which could lead to their arrest. And yet with all the victims they'd disposed of, they'd chosen to keep these few pathetic children with them. Had they been special, somehow? Significant?

'I don't know.' Mahler looks for a way to soften that. And finds none. 'I ought to update June and the Chief. I'll see you back at the shop.'

4.30 pm. The MIT room is finally empty. Everyone's exhausted, numbed by the magnitude of what the search has uncovered, and Mahler's sent them all home with instructions not to come in before nine the following morning.

There will be work enough for them to do in the days ahead, but tonight they need to leave the job behind and reconnect with the normality of their lives. If that had ever been a feature of his life, he might have done the same. But anything resembling normality had ended for him when he was fourteen years old; and he had no intention of inflicting what he might construct in its place on anyone.

He's done initial reports for June and the Chief, setting out his thoughts on the amount of liaison likely to be needed with the local forces in England, and requested urgent forensics on the remains. Produced strategies for the next day's interviewing: Patrick Grey, of course, and a follow-up with Kat, but also Ewan Polson's now ex-friends from Facebook, following the recovery of several incriminating texts about the vandalism at Anthea Bradley's cottage.

Thanks to Fergie, at least they now know how Maire had got her hands on Anthea's bank card: Ewan had seen the card lying on the kitchen table, together with its new PIN. In a breathtakingly stupid move, he'd pocketed both. And pushed his stupidity score to even greater levels by giving them to Maire, with entirely predictable results.

There are still loose ends to be followed up, though: how did Anthea get back to the cottage if she'd left her car in Muir of Ord? And what had made her go up to the summerhouse, that final morning? Had it simply been an accident, or had something more sinister been involved?

Even without the spectre of Andy Black's potential negligence hanging over the investigation, Mahler suspects some of the questions will have to remain unanswered. But he's determined to see the group of would-be vigilantes answer for their part in what had happened to Anthea, and to Aaron Keenan, if they turn out to have been responsible for his injuries.

With everything written up, and only a couple of emails remaining to deal with, Mahler's even signed off the overtime records and the last of the outstanding admin; anything to steer his mind away from the image of those mouldering cardboard boxes and what they'd contained.

Six dead girls. Six pitiful, forgotten children.

Mahler shakes his head, drags his attention back to the email he's compiling.

Six. *Six.*

He reaches for his now lukewarm coffee, drains it and goes to put the mug down. But his hand-eye co-ordination has deserted him, hidden under layers of exhaustion and the insistent horror of that repeated number, lodged within his brain.

Six. Six.

The mug hits the edge of his desk, toppling off and shattering as it hits the floor.

Sighing, he starts picking up the debris and dumping it in the bin. But the smaller, near-invisible pieces are like tiny, lethal knives; when he's picked up everything he can see, his fingers are bleeding and there's a thin border of red on both shirt-cuffs.

Blood on his hands, in his hair . . .

'Sodding hell, Lukas.' When he looks up, June Wallace is peering over the desk at him, shaking her head. 'What the . . . no, never mind.' She fishes in her pocket for a tissue, hands it to him. 'Here. Stop bleeding all over Police Scotland property for a minute and close down your emails. I need to talk to you.'

She pulls out the spare chair he keeps in the corner, eases herself into it. June's always been thin, but there's a new gauntness in her face now, as though the events of the last forty-eight hours are beginning to catch up with her. If so, she's not alone; half of the MIT are struggling to deal with what the excavations at the Greys' farmhouse had uncovered. But watching the way she's holding herself, the tension in her neck and jaw, Mahler's convinced that's only half the story. And once she starts to speak, he knows he's called it right.

'Going to be big, this one,' June tells him. 'Big media coverage, a lot of co-operative working with our friends down south . . . including your man in Kendal, of course. Needs to be overseen at DCI level.'

'Naturally, ma'am.' If she's trying to break it to him that his role will be more strictly supervised once the wider investigation gets underway, it's no more than he'd expected. And he's got no problem with that, none at all.

He doesn't envy June the task that's facing her; Chae Hunt will be unable to resist micromanaging, manoeuvring to get his face in front of as many people as possible. Not to mention as many cameras as possible. Though at least that should keep the Chief out of her hair some of the time, Mahler supposes.

June nods. 'Good. I thought you'd agree.' She gets to her feet, goes over to his coffee machine. 'Mugs? Aha, got them. Oh, and here.' She rummages in her pocket, produces a small, squashed cream and chocolate hemisphere, loosely wrapped in a paper napkin. 'Got the last two snowballs from Harry Gow this afternoon. Saved this one for you.'

'Very kind of you.' He lifts a corner of the napkin. And wishes he hadn't. 'Perhaps I'll have it later.'

'Aye, well. Can't have you wasting away. Get some good Harry Gow calories down you – then get your arse out of here and home to bed.'

She has to know that's impossible. 'Ma'am, I can't—'

'You can, and you will.' She makes the coffees, passes him one. And slides the napkin-shrouded confectionery along the desk towards him. 'I'll bring the team up to speed, start things rolling. And then you . . . you'll take over from me next week.'

For a moment, he thinks she's making some bizarre joke; either that, or he's misheard. But the look on her face is enough to tell him it's nothing so mundane. Nothing so harmless.

'And you'll be where, ma'am?'

June picks up her mug, drains half of it. Looks up and meets his eyes. 'I'll be in Raigmore Hospital, Lukas, because I've got a lump. Been hoping the bastard was benign, but . . .' She shakes her head, tries for a smile that doesn't quite come off. 'Always thought it would be the ciggies that got me, but . . . Come on, son, don't look so bloody tragic. It happens.'

'June, I'm sorry.'

'Aye, well.' She clears her throat, makes a show of picking something off her trousers. 'So am I, but there we are. I'm going in first thing tomorrow, and I'm not going to be back to full fitness for a wee while. And I need someone I can trust not to fuck this up.'

'Ma'am, I can't—'

She looks straight at him. 'You bloody can. And don't tell me you don't want it, because I know you do.'

'Not like this! Christ!' He can't sit here, can't listen to this.

He stands up, starts to go towards the door, but June holds up her hand to stop him.

'Get back over here and sit down. Come on, son, we need to sort this now, the two of us . . . and if I can deal with it, so can you.'

'And Andy Black? How do you think he's going to deal with my . . . my promotion?'

'Temporary promotion,' she corrects him. 'You're acting up, that's all, until I'm fit again. Fergie gets acting DI – and Andy will have to deal with it, the same as you would if things had gone the other way.' The grin she gives him is vintage June. 'Which means he'll be watching every move you make, hoping you stuff it up massively. So don't give him the satisfaction, right?'

'Ma'am.' That, at least, he can promise. Though he suspects Andy Black's way of dealing with the situation is going to make life interesting for the entire MIT in June's absence.

She glances at him, sighs. 'Listen to me. I know what you think of him, and I'm not saying you haven't got a point. But Andy . . . when he came to us from Strathclyde, Andy was a good cop. This is his chance to prove he still is.' She finishes her coffee, gets to her feet. 'Right then, I'll leave you to finish what you're doing. Then do what I told you and get out of here.'

'Ma'am, I'm fine to carry on. There are things I still need to do here, and—'

'You're not even close to fine, so don't give me any more crap about it. You're a bloody good officer, Lukas. But there's something eating away at you, something I should have chased you down to Welfare about long before now.'

'Counselling?' As though reliving what he's spent over twenty years trying to bury would do anything other than destroy the self he's rebuilt, piece by painful piece, since then. He shakes his head. 'I don't believe that would be productive, Ma'am. And I'm damn sure you don't either.'

After a moment, she sighs. 'Fine. Then you find your own way to deal with it before it starts holding you back. In the meantime, you've got half an hour to get your arse out of here.'

'June—'

'Half an hour, Lukas. I'm timing you.'

After she's gone, he makes a final attempt to finish his email. Stares at the draft he'd started, scrubs it and closes down his laptop. There's more to be done, of course there is: authorisations, sign-offs, a self-perpetuating mountain of paperwork before the interviews are concluded and prosecution files are put together for forwarding to the procurator fiscal.

But none of it needs to be done this evening, not by him. He looks down at his hands, feels the familiar sense of shame creeping over him as he watches them start shaking. June's right, he needs to leave here, and he needs to do it soon.

It's been years since the flashbacks have been this vivid and this frequent; no reason, on the face of it, that this case should have been the one to trigger a reaction. In his time at the Met, he'd worked investigations just as appalling, absorbed the things he'd seen and locked them away in the corner of his mind where the darkness lived. No rational reason, perhaps. But when had darkness ever needed a reason to break free?

Mahler glances at his mobile as a message arrives from June. He glances at the GIF of a ticking clock she's sent him, closes the message. And looks at the date. Looks, and sees, this time, instead of letting his eyes slide over it as usual.

He picks up his phone again, calls his mother's number. Listens dry-mouthed as it rings out, over and over, and a chill breaks across his shoulders. He grabs his keys and heads for the door, ready to—

'Lukas, I'm so sorry.' When his mother answers, her voice

is quiet but steady, enough to halt the rising tide of his unease. 'I've been watching the news. What a terrible, terrible thing you've had to deal with – I'd never have rung this morning, if I'd known. Was it very bad?'

'It's . . . it's how the job is sometimes. But yes, it was bad. I wanted to call earlier, to see how you are, but—'

'I'm okay.' An old, old pain in her voice, but for the first time, she sounds as though it's one she's managing to handle. 'I'm actually okay, and that's a pretty good thing for today, don't you think? I just wanted to tell you that, to stop you worrying.'

'Are you sure?'

'I'm sure. Are you still at work? Because if you are, I think it's probably time for you to go home, don't you? And let today be over.'

'Funnily enough, that's exactly what my boss said.'

Mahler tells her to take care, ends the call. Looks at the laptop on his desk, the files still waiting in his in tray.

Let today be over. It has a certain ring to it, after all.

He stuffs his mobile and keys in his pocket and heads downstairs, reaching the exit just in time to see the ambulance pull away.

'Trouble?'

Archie, the custody sergeant, gives him a long, appraising look. 'Poor old wifie was never trouble from the moment she came in,' he tells Mahler. 'We kept checking on her, more than we needed to, really, because I . . . I just had a feeling, you know? You do, sometimes. Even had the doc take a look at her, just to be sure. Then ten minutes or so later, I went down to look in on her, and she . . . she'd gone.'

43

Another filthy evening. Wet and miserable, as though even the bloody weather has had enough of pissing around pretending to be summer, given up on autumn and headed straight for winter.

Andy zips up his jacket and walks a little bit further along the canal, pretending to be the sort of nutter who likes nothing better than a stroll beside some water while more water falls on him from the sky and soaks him to the bloody skin.

His own fault, he knows that. He could have told the guy to meet him somewhere else – like somewhere with a roof and a fucking bar, for example. But the more people around, the more people are likely to remember them, particularly when things start kicking off between the two of them. And boy, are they going to kick off. If the bastard ever turns up, that is.

Andy checks the time on his phone. Quarter past, and he'd told the guy to be here by ten. What the hell is he playing at?

Andy reaches the cluster of trees by the bend in the path and turns back. He'll give the bastard another five minutes, and then . . . *Aye, and then what? You planning to complain to someone, big man?*

Aye, well, maybe. Maybe that night when he'd taken out the mobile he'd been given and stared at it for ages before making the call, he'd have been better walking down here and chucking it in the canal right away. But it isn't like he'd had much of a choice, is it? And anyway—

There's a figure waiting by the bench. All in black, only semi-visible against the dark bushes, like a fucking vampire or something. Andy's heart does a weird double beat, and his mouth dries. Christ, no wonder he hadn't seen him . . . well, the guy's here now. And he's got some explaining to do.

As Andy reaches the bench, the man steps out of the shadows.

'DI Black, here you are again. What was it—'

Andy shakes his head. 'Don't you "DI Black" me. You fucking set me up!' As soon as the words are out, he realises it's true. 'You knew the van was parked up by Keenan's house, you knew I'd find it if you told me to keep my eyes open around there.'

'And you did find it, didn't you?'

'Yes, I bloody found it! But it had nothing to do with either of the Keenans, did it? Aaron was telling the truth, he hadn't seen his cousin for years – and Kyle's got fucking diabetes. He's on the waiting list to get his bloody leg amputated. Oh aye, and Maxwell Bradley? When Erin went missing, Bradley was three hundred fucking miles away. So give me one good reason why I shouldn't take you in to Burnett Road right now.'

The man looks him up and down, and shakes his head. 'That really wouldn't be a good idea, now would it? Face it, your investigation was going nowhere. We gave you a lead in good faith, and you cocked it up. You, DI Black. No one else . . . and, frankly, you're lucky to still be in a job.'

'I'm bloody suspended pending an investigation!'

'You'll survive. Oh, your personnel file will make interesting reading, but that's nothing new, is it? Whereas DI Mahler . . . he's come out of this looking pretty good, hasn't he?'

'He got lucky.'

And luck can run out, even for a cocky bastard like Mahler. Andy thinks about telling the guy that Mahler needs to watch his step, that not everyone at Burnett Road thinks the sun shines out of his backside. But something in the guy's face makes him keep that thought to himself. For now.

Andy gets to his feet. 'We're done here. You've got five minutes to disappear, or you're heading for Burnett Road—'

'I don't think so.' The man touches an app on his mobile, holds it up so Andy can see the video filling the screen. 'Not unless you want this landing in the Chief Inspector's inbox. Maybe STV and a couple of the nationals too. Just for fun.'

Andy runs his tongue over suddenly dry lips. Two men sitting outside on a bench by the canal, deep in conversation. The video shot at just the right angle to show hardly anything of the man taking an envelope from his jacket and putting it on the table between them. But the man reaching out and taking the envelope . . .

Andy shakes his head. 'I'm being given information in connection with an ongoing investigation. It's not—'

'Cash? Of course not.' The man kills the video, puts the phone away. 'But as of this morning, there's ten grand sitting in your current account that'll give your credit rating a little boost. And keep the wolf from the door a little longer . . . though explaining where it came from might get slightly tricky. If anyone started asking, that is.'

'You're lying.' Andy's sweating now, the enormity of what he's done a massive, boulder-like weight in the centre of his chest. 'This is finished, you get me? Over.'

'Sorry, Andy. You made that choice the minute you didn't walk away.' A smile stretches the man's thin mouth. 'Didn't your mother warn you about doing deals with the devil? As far as you're concerned, that's exactly who your new employers are . . . and, trust me, they always collect on what they're due. Always.'

Silence. The weight expanding inside Andy's chest as he tries to think of a way out of . . . of whatever this is. Tries, and fails.

'What do you want me to do?'

'Right now?' The man shakes his head. 'Nothing. You've signed up, and for now, that's enough. Keep your head down and behave yourself when you get back to work – when there's something you can help us with, we'll be in touch.'

44

'Acting DCI? Jeez-oh. And you've got DI?'

There's disbelief, amazement and maybe, Fergie thinks, just maybe, a wee dash of envy in Karen Gilchrist's voice when he tells her about their promotions. Though he wouldn't have minded a touch less amazement when it came to his own little nudge up the ranks.

'Aye, well, it's just temporary. Just while June Wallace is off sick,' he reminds her. 'I doubt the boss would have wanted it like this.' Health reasons is the only explanation he'd been given for June Wallace stepping down, but Burnett Road's rumour-mongers are going full pelt already . . . and though he hasn't said so to anyone, not even to Zofia, he thinks this time they might be on the right track. 'Fingers crossed for a full recovery, eh?'

'Christ, yes. Let me know if there's, like, flowers or some-thing I can put in for.' A pause. 'So, is Lukas taking time off at the moment too? His mobile keeps going to voicemail, and he asked me to check up on something for him.'

So it's not just his calls the boss is avoiding, then. 'Just a couple of days,' Fergie tells her. 'Probably swotting up on DCI stuff at home, knowing him. But if it's connected with an on-going case—'

'It is . . . well, sort of.' Another pause. 'You're dealing with the Cazza MacKay stuff now, aren't you? It's about that.'

A wee prickle on the back of Fergie's neck. He'd a good idea Karen hadn't just rung to catch up on the craic. And now he thinks about it, he can make a good guess at what Mahler had asked her to find out. 'So, did you manage to get anything for us on this Hollander guy?'

A longer pause, this time. And something oddly stilted in her voice when she answers. 'Just what I warned Lukas I was likely to get. Everything I tried came back with the same response – we don't hold any records for anyone by that name.'

'Right. And that would be the official response, aye?'

'Fuck's sake. It's the only response I can give you, Fergie – no official records are held for that name. None at all. Do you understand what I'm telling you?'

Oh, yes, he understands all right. Message received, loud and clear. 'I got that, yes. Thanks, Karen.'

'No bother.' Relief in her voice as she realises he's taken everything on board. 'Right, I have to go. Speak soon, eh? Take care.'

Somehow, Fergie doubts that.

He ends the call, thinks about letting the boss know what Karen's told him. What she *hasn't* told him, Mahler would probably point out; which is true enough, strictly speaking. But Karen's careful wording had told its own story.

Fergie doesn't have any time for the tinfoil-hat brigade with their conspiracy theories, but the more he thinks about the conversation he's just had with Karen, the weirder it becomes. If there *is* anything to this Hollander stuff, it'll have to keep for another day. If Karen with her Gartcosh clearance can't access anything about Hollander, Fergie doubts he or the boss will do much better going through official channels. And that's just fine by Fergie; the red flags in the road just mean they'll have to hunt around for an alternative route, that's all.

But not yet. Uncovering the truth about Hollander is going to be a long-fought battle, he can see that. And the boss needs to be in better shape than he is right now to deal with it. What the media are calling the 'Child Snatcher' case has taken its toll on everyone in the MIT; everyone in Burnett Road, come to that. But it's torn lumps out of the boss at every twist and turn, and Fergie doesn't know how much Mahler's got left in him to deal with anything this big.

Fergie's never been much of a fan of this counselling malarkey; the thought of sitting in a wee room with a box of tissues on the table and whale music coming through the speakers while he spills his guts to a shrink gives him the dry heave, truth be told. But he's got Zofia to listen to him, pass him a beer . . . give his hand a wee squeeze, maybe, if the darkness he's been dealing with at work won't let him go when he gets home. The boss has no-one.

Fergie looks down at his phone. Weighs up the chances of Mahler coming into work next week to tear him a new one if what he's planning to do right now goes wrong. And decides he'll probably do that anyway, no matter how things turn out.

He looks up the number. And makes the call.

Full dark is hard to find in the height of a Highland summer, even by late evening. Mahler has closed the blinds, drawn the curtain across the doors leading to his balcony, but even then the light hasn't been banished entirely. Stray patches of sunlight are seeping through the gaps, glinting off mirrors and painting random patterns on the ceiling.

There is silence, though. He's closed all but the small ventilation windows, so the sounds filtering in from outside are muted, and the children who'd been playing in the Islands have all gone now. Soon, the silence—

Doorbell.

Doorbell.

Thump.

Thump.

Doorbell.

Fergie? Marco McVinish, perhaps, on a Fergie-sponsored mission of mercy?

Mahler thinks about staying where he is. Sticking on his noise-cancelling headphones and continuing to watch the flickering images on the screen in front of him, until whoever it is admits defeat. But the thumping and ringing don't seem to be diminishing, in volume or in frequency, and there will be enough for him to deal with on Monday without having to explain why a patrol car was called out to investigate a disturbance at Acting DCI Mahler's riverside apartment block.

He gets to his feet, pulls on his trainers. Goes to the door and yanks it open.

'Fergie, for Christ's sake—'

'He called me.' Anna Murray's standing in the hallway with a holdall and a bag of groceries. 'Said you were a bit under the weather.'

'And this is what, tea and sympathy?' He shakes his head. 'I'm sorry, he shouldn't have done that. I'm fine. A few difficult days at work, but I'm—'

'Oh, for goodness sake. Here, put these in the kitchen.' She puts the bag of groceries into his hands. 'This is a one-off, by the way. I make coffee, but I don't cook.'

She pushes past him, looks round as though she's getting her bearings, and heads for the living-room. Opens the blinds, pushes back the curtain. And stares at the news footage on the TV screen in front of her.

'How long have you been watching this?'

'Anna, please. This isn't a good time.'

She turns her head, looks at him. Sighs. 'Why do you think Fergie rang me? Listen, how about this – I'll make coffee, you wash, shave, change out of . . .' she glances at his dark T-shirt and jeans, 'tragic goth mode, and we can talk. Or not. Your choice.'

No. There's no magic release to be found by talking, he learned that long ago. And Anna's only just survived her own demons; he'll never inflict his darkness on her willingly. He starts to tell her he's grateful for her concern, but he needs to be alone. And finds himself taking her through to the kitchen, showing her where he keeps the coffee.

'Good.' She opens the cupboard, reaches for the cafetière. Waves a dismissive hand at him. 'Ten minutes. Go.'

The aroma of fresh coffee reaches him as soon as he's out of the shower. He dresses, shaves the parts of his face that aren't still too painful to touch and goes through to the living room. The TV is dark, and Anna's tidied away the newspapers with Erin MacKenzie's face looking out from every front page, next to images of the Greys' farmhouse. There's music playing quietly in the background, too, Julie Fowlis' crystal-perfect version of 'Blackbird'.

And Anna can't be here. Whatever misguided kindness has brought her to his door, he needs to tell her to leave. While he still can.

'Clean tragic goth.' He gestures at his fresh clothing. 'Best I could do.'

Anna looks up, smiles. 'Acceptable. Here.' She waits for him to sit down, pours a coffee and puts it in front of him. 'Fergie said you'd been promoted. Should I congratulate you?'

'Christ, no. It's not as though I . . . I did anything to merit it.'

'You saved a child's life, Lukas.'

'And let another one die! Missed things I should have seen, didn't make connections I should have picked up on . . . and

294

made a traumatised old woman relive the worst time in her life. Oh, and let's not forget, she died too! She died, and I as good as sentenced her to it.'

His hands are shaking again. He puts down the coffee mug, stands and crosses to the window. Holds up his hand to stop her when she starts to say something.

'Anna, this is a mistake. I'm sorry, but I don't think—'

A hand covering his own. Anna's fingers wrapping round his and leading him back to the sofa as the next album track begins and 'An Eala Bhàn' fills the room.

'One of my favourites, this,' she tells him. 'I'd have said you were a Runrig fan, mind, from the T-shirt. I'll see if you've got any of their older stuff after this.'

No words. None he can make himself say to her, not yet. No apology he can give for the grief that comes in spite of his attempts to hold it back, while Anna puts her arms round him and Julie sings of love and death and hope.

Neither of them had closed the blinds again, and by five the sun is streaming through the window directly above their heads.

Mahler twists his head, glances at his watch. Tries to move his arm out from underneath Anna and slide a cushion there instead to avoid waking her, but the couch isn't designed for anything that complicated and his arm has gone to sleep. The cushion slips off and lands on the coffee table instead.

Anna stirs, sits up. Turns to look at him. 'You stayed there all night?'

'You fell asleep while I was making more coffee. It seemed unkind to leave you on your own . . . though I might have reconsidered, if I'd known about the snoring.'

'You're not funny.' She reaches for his wrist, peers at his watch. Groans. 'Especially not at this time in the morning.' She pushes back the throw he'd used to cover them both, stands up.

'God, my back. Could I grab a glass of orange juice before I head back up the road? There was a carton in with the shopping I brought you yesterday.'

'You're going back to Dornoch?' He glances at the holdall she'd brought with her. Curses himself for the hope he'd briefly entertained. 'I thought—'

'I have a ten o'clock I can't get out of. And if you're making rude comments about my snoring – which, by the way, I absolutely do not do – I think tragic goth boy will manage a little better today, don't you?'

'Of course.' He gets to his feet. Stares down at the faded Runrig T-shirt he'd inflicted on her yesterday evening. Tragic goth boy, indeed. 'And I should apologise for how you found me yesterday. Fergie shouldn't have—'

'Stop that.' A brush of his fingers with hers. Kindness, and an unexpected something in her smile that makes him catch his breath. 'I watch the news, Lukas, and I read the papers. And I can't imagine what you've had to deal with over the past few days. You don't need to apologise for . . . for being human.'

'It's not just that. I'm not . . . Anna, there are things in my past that sometimes. . .' he shakes his head. 'The truth is, I'm not sure you should be anywhere near me. Tragic goth or not.'

'I think we'll probably just need to see how that goes, won't we?' Anna picks up her jacket, heads for the door. 'Don't worry about the orange juice, I probably should get going.'

Mahler picks up her holdall, goes after her. 'Don't you want this?'

Anna turns to smile at him. 'I never said I wasn't coming back, did I? Have a good day, Lukas.'

45

Thursday, 23 June
Tomnahurich Cemetery

He had thought she would have to be buried in the rain. But by the time Mahler gets to the place where Ella's been laid to rest, the sun has come out to burn off the last of the morning mists and touch the ancient trees with light.

As he'd expected, he's the only mourner. Ella had no living relatives, and the events at what the media have dubbed 'The Horror Homestead' have brought out the ghouls and would-be ghost hunters in force, meaning the simple ceremony she'd requested in her will needed to take place in conditions of near-total secrecy. Tomnahurich is a closed cemetery now, but Ella's family plot had still had room for her, and Mahler's glad of it. He suspects the windswept modernity of somewhere like Kilvean wouldn't have been to her taste.

He strips the wrapping from the flowers he's brought, looks round for somewhere to get water to fill the vase at the base of the weathered headstone. And sees a flash of white, coming through the trees towards him.

'It was today, then. I thought that's what you said.' Anna's wearing the peacock scarf again, but her jacket is a pale denim over her summer dress. 'The way you talked about her . . . You were fond of Ella, weren't you? I think she touched something in you.'

'Ella was . . . she was admirable. Perhaps that's an odd thing to say about a murderer. But she saved her sister from her uncle, Aeneas Grant, in 1947 – and seventy years later, she saved Lena McNally from the Greys.' A sudden tightness in his throat. 'I feel genuinely privileged to have known her. I'm just sorry I couldn't save her.'

Anna gives him a curious look. 'How do you know you didn't? Her uncle's death couldn't have been an easy thing for her to live with, Lukas. She was eighty-three years old, with a bad heart. Maybe she'd been waiting for a chance to tell her story.'

'Perhaps.' But not the one he'd given her. Not the one that had ended in her death. He holds up the flowers. 'Do you know where I can get water for these?'

'Give me a minute.' Anna walks off down the path and disappears round the corner, leaving the silence around him a little heavier, a little more encompassing.

Mahler looks round at the ancient cemetery, the graves wound around the high green mound at its centre. The coldness touching the base of his neck has nothing to do with logic. And everything to do with legends of a haunted hill.

He rolls his shoulders, turns to watch for Anna coming back along the path towards him. And, after a while, the feeling fades away.

'Found a bottle by the tap. Here, pass me your flowers.' She adds the water to the vase, strips away some of the leaves and splits the stems slightly before kneeling down to place the roses in the container. 'There, that's better.' She starts to straighten up, and stops abruptly. 'Oh, that's interesting.'

She brushes away some of the moss from the inscription. 'Buried with her mother, it looks like, and . . . who would this be? Her grandmother, from the dates? Not her husband, anyway.'

'I've never heard of that before.' Mahler bends to take a closer look. 'Does it happen often?'

Anna frowns. 'Well, it's not unheard of for women to be buried with their parents, especially in old cemeteries like this with family lairs. But just the female line? Not in my experience.'

She clears a little more moss from the headstone. 'The family seems to have come from near Dornoch originally. I wonder why they didn't have a plot up there? And . . . Oh, now that *is* curious. Very curious. You see this carving?' She traces a small, blurred outline near the base of the stone. 'A little hard to make out, but I'm almost sure it's a hare.'

'And that's curious because . . .?'

'It's a pagan symbol. Associated with the goddess Eostre – witches, moon magic, that sort of thing. Quite subversive to put one in a Christian cemetery, actually. What?'

It's a herbal tea, that's all. Feverfew and valerian, picked by moonlight.

Mahler shakes his head, tells himself not to be ridiculous. But he feels a sudden impulse to walk out of the cemetery gates. And keep walking until he's back out in the noisy, unmuted world again. 'Did you want to visit Morven before we go?'

Anna shakes her head. 'Let's leave the dead in peace for today, shall we?' She holds out her hand to him. 'There's a coffee with my name on it over at the Botanic Gardens, if you fancy a walk.'

Peace. After everything Ella endured, he hopes that's what she's found. Mahler nods, summons a smile from somewhere. And finds himself walking out of Tomnahurich with Anna's fingers wrapped round his, which is a new and wondrous thing that brings him more peace than he deserves.

As they reach the gates, his mobile beeps a text alert. He

apologises, fishes it out. Glances at the message he's been sent. And starts scrolling through the text to find the words that will help him make sense of what he's reading.

'Lukas, what is it? What's wrong? Is Grace—'

He shakes his head. 'It's a message from Fergie. Anna, I'm sorry.' Gripping her hand now, trying to find a way to make what he has to tell her something that won't break her. 'It's James Gordon. He. . . he's appealing his conviction.'

Acknowledgements

Again, so many people to thank who provided help, inspiration and a much-needed breath of sanity throughout the process of bringing this book into being: Francesca, Bethan, and Jade at Orion, the ever-magnificent Alison Bonomi at LBA Books, the Savvies and the Frisbees (you know who you are). Nan Steele and Ella Doonar, two indomitable spirits I'm completely in awe of (sorry I borrowed your name for one of my characters, Ella, but I think you'd have liked her).

Ruth, Roseanne, Thelma and Anne, for your friendship and support. Alison MacDonald, facing adversity with more grace and courage than I could ever muster. Martin, Nicola and Roy for their continuing encouragement (and impressive stealth marketing in various shapes and forms). Anne Nicolson-Craig, for a chance remark about midden pits in country areas that gave me the perfect place to hide a body. And of course the good citizens of the Sneck, who haven't (yet) run me out of town for turning Inverness into a Highland version of Midsomer . . . which leads me on to a more serious note.

As far as possible, I strive for accuracy in my novels. I know I'll never manage it one hundred per cent (one of the reasons Lukas and the MIT are going to have to do a quick flitting from

Burnett Road in book three – aargh!), but generally I keep my locations absolutely authentic. But this time, because of some of the subject matter, I've deliberately fudged some of the geography. It goes without saying that the events and persons portrayed in this book are entirely fictional (saying it anyway, though, just to drive the point home), but there is no way I wanted to set some of the distressing and disturbing events that take place in the book at any easily pin-pointed location in the city. This is fiction, and that's how it's intended to be read.

Anyway, that's all from me for now. Hope you liked my book, and if you're interested in finding out more about the Lukas Mahler series and plans for book three, you can find me on:

🐦 @HighlandWriter

🌐 margaretmortonkirk.wordpress.com

**Don't miss the first gripping
crime thriller from Margaret Kirk . . .**

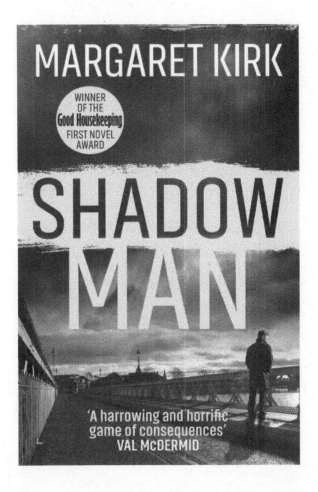

Keep reading for an exclusive preview!

1994

By midnight, there are bodies everywhere. Her tiny flat is crammed to bursting, but people are still stumbling through the door, waving packs of Stella or Strongbow and wrapping her in cheerful beery hugs.

She doesn't remember inviting them all – doesn't recognise half of them, when she stops to think about it – but so what? For the last four years, she's been juggling coursework with her shifts at the all-night garage, slogging away at her degree while it felt like the rest of the world was out getting laid, or legless. Or both.

Doing it her way, she'd told her parents. Standing on her own two feet, and they couldn't argue with that, could they? Even if Mum had thrown a massive wobbly at the thought of her baby girl rejecting St Andrews and choosing to study at Glasgow.

But with her finals out of the way, she's officially an ex-student. So tonight, it's party time – shedloads of booze, the flat decked out with tea lights and a joke seventies glitter-ball, and all her mates from uni, ready to make a night of it.

Not all of them, though, a snide little voice reminds her. *Things didn't exactly go to plan there, did they?* She shakes her head, swallowing the tightness in her throat . . . and suddenly he's there, watching her from the doorway.

The room's too dark, too smoky for her to see more than his outline, but she knows it's him. Who else could it be? She starts to wave him over, and he steps into the light . . . and it isn't him after all, just some boy she vaguely knows from class.

She drags her hand down, but he's already seen her. He breaks into a grin and starts to push his way towards her – Christ, surely he can't think she'd been waiting for *him*? She spots some girls she knows over to his right and heads straight for them, as though that's what she'd been going to do all along. When she looks back over her shoulder, he's gone.

She squeezes past a nest of couples snogging by the kitchen door and grabs a random can from the table. *Gary,* that was his name, she remembers. He'd given her and Morven a lift to uni when the buses were on strike, walked to the library with them a couple of times – God, but he was a twat. Still, she's ashamed of blanking him like that. But seeing him standing there, just for a moment she'd thought . . .

Someone's messing with the music. Morrissey's cut off, dispatched by the Proclaimers, and then everyone's joining in, even the close-to-comatose, doing the whole 500-mile-walking, arm-swinging thing until she feels the floor bouncing under her feet.

She shoulders her way through the sweating, heat-sticky bodies until she reaches the balcony and pulls the curtains closed, muting the sounds from inside.

Movement behind her. The curtains lifted by the breeze, she thinks at first, their extravagant lengths belling out and pooling at her feet. But no, it's more than that . . . the curtains parting and the music blaring briefly as someone slips through to stand behind her, just beyond the edges of her vision. Calling her name, but quietly, so that she has to strain to hear them.

She spins round, and her heel catches in the curtains. Her right foot slips and she stumbles sideways. Her arms flail, reaching out for something to hold on to, but the curtain is wrapping itself around her, covering her eyes and the railing is right behind her, she can feel it cold against her back – Jesus, if she falls, if she goes over . . .

Arms round her waist, peeling away the curtain, scooping her up and out of danger. Holding her gently, as though she's made of glass.

She looks up at her rescuer, and her eyes widen. Of all the people . . . she starts to ask him what the hell he's doing there, but he puts his finger to her lips, smiling as though he knows a really cool joke, one he can't wait to share with her.

He raises her higher, holding her away from his body. She shakes her head and starts to struggle – why's he mucking about like this? Can't he see how dangerous this is, how close they are to the edge . . .

He turns, still holding her, leans over the railing.

And lets her go.

1

TUESDAY, 27 MAY 2014

Gatwick North Terminal

Thump.
Thump.
Thump.

Detective Inspector Lukas Mahler looks down at the object battering his left shin.

A chunky boy with a brutal haircut and the hint of a brow-ridge smirks up at him from astride a yellow and black striped suitcase with stubby feeler-like handles projecting from its front and stuck-on features. Some kids' TV character, Mahler thinks, that's what it's supposed to be. Only the eyes are peeling off and half its mouth is missing, giving the face a lopsided look that's either sad or psychopathic, depending on your point of view. Today, Mahler inclines towards the latter.

The boy is reversing, gearing up for another assault. Before he reaches ramming speed, Mahler swings his cabin bag across and dodges to the right, as far as the taped barrier will allow. He glances at the child's mother, but her eyes are glued to her mobile, pudgy thumbs flying as she carries on a life-or-death discussion by text. Consulting a child-rearing expert, he decides, fielding a further assault. That, or a pest control service.

Boarding for the Inverness flight is only thirty minutes late, but the queue has been funnelled into a narrow, glass-walled walkway and left to swelter in the midday sun like ants under a magnifying glass. Sweating gently in his dark suit, Mahler tries to ignore the twist of pain circling the base of his neck. And wonders why Dante had imagined there were only nine circles of Hell.

By the time boarding finally starts, he's wielded the cabin bag three times and his shirt is sticking to him. As soon as he's seated, he strips off his jacket and loosens his tie. He takes out his book, lets it fall open at one of his favourite passages, but the migraine is settling in now, a steady, white-hot pulse that had stalked him through the service and its aftermath. He dry-swallows a pill and leans back, waiting for the plane door to close.

Only it isn't happening. The buzz of chatter rises and falls, punctuated by the inevitable wailing baby, as the minutes pass. Then, as the flight attendant starts a rambling explanation, a woman appears in the doorway.

Head lowered, she hurries along the aisle. She isn't limping, not exactly, but there's a stiffness to her walk that marks her out as different. Mahler, who knows all about different, watches her progress.

She reaches the row opposite his and slides over to the window. He glimpses pale, sharp features, catches a muttered curse as her hands fumble with the seat belt . . . thin, jittery hands, making a pig's ear of the simple task. A nervous flyer, apparently. Perfect.

Mahler sighs, more audibly than he'd intended, and the woman turns to glare at him. At which point he abandons the book and reaches for another painkiller. He weighs the consequences of taking it now or later. He looks back at the woman and goes with now.

When the engines start up, he glances at her again. Pre-take-off weeper or belligerent, in-flight screamer? After the look she'd given him, Mahler can't quite see her as a weeper. But not a vomiter, please God, he thinks. Not today.

He wills the meds to do their stuff and closes his eyes. When he opens them again, the plane is taxiing down Inverness Airport's one and only runway. Mahler straightens his tie and watches as the passengers begin their restless, end-of-flight manoeuvring. As usual, those in the aisle seats hold all the cards – they're up and in position within seconds of the 'fasten seatbelt' signs going off, building little fortresses of luggage to guard their place in the queue. The window-seat baggers and the mid-rowers are trapped, unable to see over the wall of bodies, but tensed, like runners on starting blocks, ready to surge forward the moment the doors are open. All except the woman.

He'd expected her to scramble to her feet, ready to bolt with the herd, but she hasn't moved. Even when the exodus begins, the woman stays in her seat, pale hands clenched on her thighs, her jawline . . . oh, that jawline has nothing to do with nerves, he's suddenly sure of it. There's something driven in the sharp, travel-weary features and cool grey eyes, something that catches him in spite of himself.

He leans forward to take a closer look, and an expanse of sweatshirt-clad belly rears up in front of him, blocking his vision. By the time the man has wrestled a padded jacket the size of a small duvet from the locker above Mahler's head, the woman's seat is empty.

Mahler hoists his bag onto his shoulder and leaves by the rear steps, joining the crocodile of passengers filing into the tiny terminal. The woman is a little way in front, heading for the airport's only baggage-reclaim carousel. An ordinary woman, he decides, that's all. No reason to keep her in his eyeline. No reason her thin, pale face shouldn't blend into the sea of unmemorable others . . . no reason until the conveyor belt shudders into life, and she darts in to pick up a bag. And backs *away* from the exit that leads to the main concourse.

And there it is. Copper's gut, Raj used to call the odd, half-formed imperative he's following, and Mahler supposes it's as good a name as any. Not a thing that will let itself be named, this raw, unfocused thing, not yet. But a discoverable thing, Mahler thinks. A thing to be probed. To be *known*.

He watches her tie up her hair and stuff it under a sludge-coloured baseball cap. She's deliberately standing to one side, letting the other passengers flow towards their waiting friends and family. And then she's moving, merging with a group of earnest German tourists as they head out into the concourse.

Looking for someone? No, Mahler thinks, she's hiding. Hiding in plain sight. But why? And who from?

He ducks past the queue for the parking machines . . . and collides with Suitcase Boy's mother, who's lumbering across the concourse like a juggernaut in flowered leggings to embrace an older woman. A relative, he assumes, judging by their shared fashion sense.

By the time he's extricated himself, the woman has gone. He body-swerves Suitcase Boy, who looks to be planning another ram raid, and runs to the exit. Just in time to see the airport shuttle disappearing through the car park barrier.

'No need to rush, boss – I've got ten minutes left on the ticket.'

The words are punctuated by a crunching sound. Mahler turns to see Detective Sergeant Iain 'Fergie' Ferguson ambling towards him, clutching a family-sized bag of crisps.

'What are you doing here? I thought you were jetting off to the flesh-pots of Marbella on Tuesday?'

'Me too.' Fergie upends the bag and funnels the last pieces into his mouth. 'But Zofia and me had a wee domestic at the weekend, and there was bugger all point going on my own, so I turned in for a few extra shifts. And got told to go and get you as soon as you'd landed. Didn't you check your phone?'

'Not yet. There was a woman on the flight—'

'Oh, aye?' Fergie manages to wink and grin at the same time, giving him the look of a leering potato. 'Fit, was she?'

Mahler rolls his eyes. 'Could you get your mind out of your boxers for one second? She was . . .'

He glances at Fergie and shakes his head. Trying to avoid someone? Behaving strangely in a public place? Undoubtedly. But half the travelling public could probably put their hands up to that one. And on the spectrum of measurable oddness, Mahler knows perfectly well where most of his colleagues would place him. So he's got nothing he can offer Fergie, no rationale for her continuing presence in the forefront of his brain, unless he holds his hands up to a hunch. And he doesn't do hunches.

Oh, Raj would have gone for it, no doubt about that. Raj had believed in the whole copper's intuition, weird-feeling-in-my-water thing – he'd clung to it like an access-all-areas pass, no matter what. And look where that had got him.

'Forget it.' He switches on his mobile and scrolls through the alerts. No surprise about the first three. But the fourth? 'Any idea why I'm being summoned?'

Fergie shrugs. 'Braveheart wants you in asap, that's all I know. I was at a house-breaking in Ardersier when I got told to play taxi driver. But if you wanted to drop in on your mam first—'

Mahler shakes his head. His mother has only called three times, which means she's basically okay and her support worker has his number if anything changes. And for DCI June Wallace to call him in fresh from the airport . . . well, whatever's up, it can't be good.

'I'll look in on her after I've been to Burnett Road. Better not keep the DCI waiting.'

Fergie's ancient Audi is parked between two sleek black 4Ð4s, looking more like a dustbin on wheels than ever.

'Hold on a minute.' Fergie heaves open the passenger door and slides a slag heap of fast-food debris off the seat and into the footwell. 'There you go. What?'

'Nothing.' Mahler sits down, trying to ignore the sludge-like stickiness under his left thigh. He takes a couple of shallow breaths, inhaling the fags and fish supper fug that constitutes the Audi's atmosphere. And something else, something eye-wateringly ammoniac . . .

'What is making that godawful smell?'

'Weird, isn't it?' Fergie fishes out a Homer Simpson air-freshener and hangs it from the mirror. 'There, that'll sort it till I've time for a wee tidy-up.' A sideways glance at Mahler. 'Boss, I meant to say . . . I'm sorry about your pal. That was an awful thing. Awful.'

'Yes. Thank you.'

'Aye.' Fergie clears his throat. 'Aye, well. Better no' keep herself waiting, eh?' He does something unspeakable to the Audi's gears and the car lurches towards the exit.

Mahler grits his teeth as a series of clunking noises chart their progress over the speed bumps. 'Not a good idea, no. But let's see if we can make it back without being pulled over by our friends in traffic this time, shall we? And for pity's sake keep that window open.'